Decision
and
Destiny

By DeVa Gantt

DECISION AND DESTINY
A SILENT OCEAN AWAY

Decision
and
Destiny
COLETTE'S LEGACY

DeVa Gantt

AVON

An Imprint of HarperCollinsPublishers

DECISION AND DESTINY. Copyright © 2009 by DeVa Gantt. All rights reserved. Printed in the United States of America. No part of this book may be used or reproduced in any manner whatsoever without written permission except in the case of brief quotations embodied in critical articles and reviews. For information address HarperCollins Publishers, 10 East 53rd Street, New York, NY 10022.

HarperCollins books may be purchased for educational, business, or sales promotional use. For information please write: Special Markets Department, HarperCollins Publishers, 10 East 53rd Street, New York, NY 10022.

FIRST AVON PAPERBACK EDITION PUBLISHED 2009.

Designed by Rhea Braunstein

Library of Congress Cataloging-in-Publication Data
Gantt, DeVa.
    Decision and destiny : Colette's legacy / DeVa Gantt.—1st ed.
        p.   cm.
    ISBN 978-0-06-157825-0 (acid-free paper)   1. Young women—Fiction.   2. Rich people—Virginia—Fiction.   3. Domestic fiction.   I. Title.
    PS3607.A59D43   2009
    813'.6—dc22
                                                                                2008043295

09   10   11   12   13   WBC/RRD   10   9   8   7   6   5   4   3   2   1

To Mom,
for her steadfast support
and encouragement in all our endeavors,
especially the Colette Trilogy.

DIRECTORY OF CHARACTERS
for *Decision and Destiny*

ON CHARMANTES:
The Duvoisin Family:

Frederic Duvoisin—Patriarch and master of Charmantes; son of Jean Duvoisin II, founder of Les Charmantes (deceased); brother of Jean III (deceased)

Elizabeth Blackford Duvoisin—Frederic's first wife (deceased 1808)

John Duvoisin—Only son of Frederic and Elizabeth; heir to the Duvoisin fortune (born 1808)

Paul Duvoisin—Frederic's illegitimate son (born 1808)

Colette Duvoisin—Frederic's second wife (born 1810; deceased 1837)

Yvette and Jeannette Duvoisin—Twin daughters of Frederic and Colette (born 1828)

Pierre Duvoisin—Youngest son of Frederic and Colette (born 1834)

Agatha Blackford Ward Duvoisin—Older sister of Frederic's late wife, Elizabeth; John's aunt; Frederic's third wife

People living in the Duvoisin Mansion:

Charmaine Ryan—Heroine of the story (born 1818 in Richmond, Virginia), governess to the Duvoisin children; only child of Marie and John Ryan

Rose Richards—Elderly nursemaid to Yvette, Jeannette, and Pierre; formerly nanny to John and Paul; originally hired by Jean II to care for Frederic as a young boy

Professor Richards—Rose Richards's husband; formerly tutor to John and Paul; initially hired by Jean II as a tutor for Frederic (deceased)

George Richards—Rose and Professor Richards's grandson; close friend of John and Paul; production manager and overall supervisor of island operations (born 1809)

Duvoisin Servants:

Jane Faraday—Head housekeeper
Travis Thornfield—Butler and Frederic's personal valet
Gladys Thornfield—Travis's wife; Agatha's personal maid
Millie and Joseph Thornfield—Travis and Gladys's children
Felicia Flemmings—Housemaid
Anna Smith—Housemaid
Fatima Henderson—Cook
Gerald—Head groom
Bud—Stablehand

Islanders:

Dr. Robert Blackford—Island physician; Agatha's twin brother; older brother to Frederic's first wife, Elizabeth; John's uncle
Harold Browning—Charmantes' overseer
Caroline Browning—Harold's wife; sister of Loretta Harrington
Gwendolyn Browning—Harold and Caroline's only daughter
Stephen Westphal—Charmantes' financier; manager of the town bank
Anne Westphal London—Stephen's widowed daughter; resides in Richmond
Father Benito St. Giovanni—Island priest
Jake Watson—Harbor foreman
Buck Mathers—Dockworker
Madeline Thompson (Maddy)—Mercantile proprietress
Wade Remmen—Lumbermill operator
Rebecca Remmen—Wade's younger sister; friend of Gwendolyn Browning
Martin—Town farrier
Dulcie—Proprietress of the town tavern

In Richmond, Virginia:
Marie Ryan—Charmaine's mother, abandoned as a young child at the St. Jude Refuge (deceased 1835)

John Ryan—Charmaine's fugitive father
Father Michael Andrews—Pastor of St. Jude's Church and Refuge
Sister Elizabeth—Nun and teacher at the St. Jude Refuge
Joshua Harrington—Charmaine's first employer
Loretta Harrington—Joshua's wife; sister of Caroline Browning
Jonah Wilkinson—Captain of the *Raven*, the Duvoisin merchantman
Edward Richecourt—Duvoisin lawyer

In Memory:
Adele Delacroix—Colette's mother (deceased)
Pierre Delacroix—Colette's brother (deceased)
Pascale—Colette's childhood girlfriend

Chapter 1

Tuesday, August 22, 1837

*P*EACE *of mind!* Oh, the oblivion of peace of mind! They were Charmaine's last thoughts as she drifted off to sleep. Like a prayer answered, she succumbed to a deep and restful slumber, the first she'd had in three long nights.

Songbirds in the great oak just outside her window awoke her, and she lay abed enjoying nature's symphony, a harbinger of the brilliant day ahead, one that was perfect for a picnic. She rose and peeked into the children's room. They were fast asleep. She began to dress, determined to get an early start.

The letter she had written to Loretta Harrington sat propped on her chest of drawers. She scanned the pages, resurrecting the turmoil of the past three days.

> *I was pleased to receive your letter . . . I am quite well . . . The children are a constant comfort to me and I enjoy my position on the island . . . I still do not understand Mr. Duvoisin's marriage to so cruel a woman as Agatha Ward . . . I avoid her whenever possible . . . Paul is the consummate gentleman, and aside from Rose and George Richards, I sometimes feel he is the*

only friend I have in the house . . . George returned this past week, but you should not harbor hope of him as a possible suitor . . . my thoughts have been far from such concerns . . . John Duvoisin has ventured home, even though it is whispered his father forbade him to do so. His presence has rekindled my former reservations concerning matrimony. I can understand Frederic Duvoisin's disdain for his own flesh and blood, for John is a rude, ill-bred, detestable cur who spends his days closeted in his apartments drinking from dawn to dusk. I've tried to avoid him at all costs, but he appears at the worst possible times, and I find myself poorly equipped to respond to his sarcasm. He has taken a dislike to me for a number of reasons. He's learned of my father, undoubtedly through his intended bride, the widow Anne Westphal London . . . Do you know her? But I am not the only person he ridicules. He wages war with practically everyone, including his aunt or stepmother, as the case may be . . . Tell Mr. Harrington he was never more correct in his opinion of a person than he was of this man. Please give everyone my love . . .

Sighing, she tucked the letter into its envelope. Then she sat at her dressing table and began brushing out her unruly hair.

The serenity of the morning was shattered by a series of vociferous oaths that brought her straight to her feet and into the corridor. Joseph Thornfield was racing down the stairs, a wooden bucket tumbling after him, ricocheting off the walls and splattering water everywhere.

"Damn it, boy! I love hot baths almost as much as I love music, but I refuse to be scalded into singing soprano in a boys' choir!"

Charmaine turned toward the bellowing voice, and her jaw dropped. There stood John Duvoisin, dripping wet from head to toe, leaning far over the banister, and shouting after the servant boy.

He was naked save for a bath towel clasped around his waist, unperturbed by his indecent state of undress. Charmaine compared him to Paul—the gold standard by which she assessed all men—annoyed to find his toned body rivaled his brother's: wide shoulders, corded arms, and taut stomach, which sported a reddish hue. Belatedly, she realized she was no longer staring at his back. She grimaced as she lifted her gaze and her eyes connected with his. A jeering smile broke across his face, his pain apparently forgotten now that he had the governess for an audience.

"You're as red as a ripe apple, my Charm. I thought my brother had shown you a man's body, or did I interrupt that lesson in anatomy the other night?"

Degraded, Charmaine marched back into her bedchamber and slammed the door as hard as she could. Her gratification was minimal; it was a full minute before his laughter receded from the hallway.

It was still early when she left her room again. Her plans for a quiet breakfast had been dashed. John had effectively roused the entire household, except for Agatha, who ate in her boudoir. Paul, George, and Rose converged on the staircase. Charmaine prayed John would be delayed, but, lately, none of her prayers were being answered. He appeared just as they reached the dining room.

"Good morning, everyone!" he greeted brightly, winking at her.

She glowered in response, but he dismissed her, settling at the table with the children, who were thrilled to see him. She hesitated, debating where to sit. With Paul still talking to George in the archway, she remained indecisive.

John noticed at once. "Do you plan on eating, Mademoiselle, or will you just stand there and watch us? You paint the picture of a wounded dog awaiting table scraps."

The demeaning declaration stung like salt in an open wound,

the promise of a brilliant day rapidly fading. Taking courage, she stepped closer.

"Ah yes," he mused, pretending ignorance of her quandary and coming to his feet, "the lady expects a gentleman to help her with her chair, but since Paul is preoccupied right now, I suppose a *convict* like me will just have to do!"

He rounded the table and pulled the chair out for her. With a great flourish, he whisked a napkin through the air and dusted off the seat cushion, finishing his theatrics with a servile bow and a gesture she be seated. She did so with as much aplomb as she could rally, but as she spread her serviette in her lap, her eyes went to Paul, whose jaw was clenched in monumental self-control.

John returned to his own chair, and chatted with George, Rose, and the children, the meal uneventful until Jeannette produced the letter Charmaine had written to Loretta Harrington.

"Shall I give this to Joseph to post, Mademoiselle?"

Charmaine cringed. "Yes, please," she hastily replied.

Too late! John's interest was piqued, his brow raised. She knew that expression: it meant trouble. Sure enough, he stopped Jeannette as she passed behind him and removed the envelope from her hand. "What have we here?"

"A letter," Paul snapped.

"A letter?" John mimicked. "Thank you for explaining, Paul. I'd almost forgotten what a letter looked like. But Miss Ryan hasn't forgotten, has she?"

Charmaine paled, but John pressed on, tapping the envelope against his lips. "Mrs. Joshua Harrington of Richmond, Virginia. Harrington . . . where have I heard that name before? Ah yes, the merchants' convention last year. Joshua Harrington was leading the protest against import tariffs. I remember him quite well now. A short-tempered man, if my memory doesn't fail me, short and short-tempered."

"I found him quite the contrary," Paul argued.

"Now, Paul," John countered jovially, "he isn't a *tall* man by any measure."

George snickered, but Paul's brow knitted in vexation. "I was speaking of his temperament!"

"Well, I don't know which side of him you saw, but he quickly lost his temper when I spoke with him."

"Were you taunting him, John?"

"Why would I do that? He just doesn't have a sense of humor, that's all. I simply commented that, with a name like Joshua, he had to be a prophet and should consult with God before delivering his next ludicrous speech. After that, he wanted nothing to do with me, which suited me just fine."

Paul closed his eyes and shook his head in exasperation.

"But that is neither here nor there, is it, Mademoiselle?" John continued, serious again. "You have correspondence to post, and Joseph normally sees to such errands. However, he is busy cleaning up the mess in my room. Therefore, I volunteer to deliver it to the mercantile for you."

"That is very noble of you, John," Paul responded before Charmaine could object. "However, Miss Ryan would like to know it was, in fact, delivered."

"Now, Paulie, are you suggesting I would drop this by the wayside?"

"Let us just say I, too, am gallant, John. Since you have no reason to travel into town, while that is my very destination today, let me take it."

"No, I think not, Paul. You see, I do have a reason to ride into town. I have my own letters to post, and since Miss Ryan doesn't trust me, this is the perfect opportunity to prove to her I'm not the scoundrel she imagines me to be—that her letter will be delivered to the mercantile, intact."

"John—"

"Admit it, Paul. You have an ulterior motive for visiting the mercantile. A tête-à-tête with Maddy Thompson perhaps?"

"I'm finished playing games with you, John," Paul snarled. "If you insist on posting the letter, then by all means, go ahead."

"Oh goodie!" John exclaimed, inciting a chorus of giggles from the girls.

For Charmaine, however, the fate of her correspondence was far from settled. "Had I known my letter would cause such a quibble," she laughed artificially, "I would have left it in my room. Best I post it myself." She leaned forward to remove it from John's hand, but he held it out of reach and disagreed glibly.

"The children have lessons, do they not? Surely you won't allow a personal matter to interfere with that? No? I didn't think so. But fear not! I give you my solemn oath as a gentleman; your letter will remain safe in my hands. If there is something else that troubles you, George will vouch for me when I tell you that—unlike a certain individual who shall remain unnamed—I have never bent so low as to read someone else's private mail."

Charmaine reddened.

"Besides, I don't need to read your letter to know what you think of me. You've made that abundantly clear on a number of occasions."

Charmaine remained closeted in the playroom with the children, hoping upon hope John would leave for town and she'd be free to arrange a picnic lunch with Fatima. It was nearly eleven and unlike Paul, who had spent the morning in the study with George, John had dawdled the last three hours away. Where was his ambition to carry out the task for which he had so eagerly begged at breakfast?

Presently, she turned her mind to an arithmetic lesson, trying not to dwell on her two latest predicaments: the postponed picnic and John's delivery of her letter to the mercantile. Would he read it?

He could, and she'd never know! Fool that she was, she had committed her hatred to paper, and now the devil himself possessed it!

John Duvoisin. Yes, she hated him! Hated how he scorned and mocked her. Hated how he singled her out and ridiculed her just for the fun of it. Hated how he presumed to know so much about her character. Hated how he loved to make everyone miserable. Hated him like she hated her father. Hated him, hated him, hated him! Colette's words of long ago haunted her: *Just remember . . . you hate him first.* Hate him first? What came after that? She seemed to remember something about loving him. Ridiculous! She'd hate him first, second, third, and forever. She prayed fervently for the day when he would pack his bags and return to Richmond. It couldn't come soon enough.

Beyond the confining room, doors banged shut and footfalls resounded in the corridor, setting her on edge. She left Jeannette and Yvette to their problems, and stepped onto the veranda. The breeze was invitingly cool for August, rustling the leaves of the tall oak overhead. Looking toward the paddock, she was rewarded with the fine sight of Paul, who stood with arms akimbo, conversing with George and two stablehands. Charmaine admired the authority he projected, lingering on his broad shoulders and lean torso, slim waist and well-defined legs, the muscles in his thighs sculpted against the dark fabric of his trousers. Highly polished ebony riding boots finished the lusty figure he cut. She closed her eyes to the heart-thundering image and remembered that first day on the *Raven*, his shirt doffed, the play of muscle across his broad back and arms, deeply tanned from the island sun. He was the embodiment of the perfect man, like the great Roman statues in the museums of Europe.

She thought of their kiss in the gardens last night, and her heart raced. His embrace had been passionate and longing, and despite her inhibition, she relished the pleasurable memory. His racy invitation simmered in her ears, and she breathed deeply, counseling herself to tread cautiously. She was playing with fire. It would be best to avoid another such encounter. Even now, she realized how difficult that would be, for as he clasped an easy arm around the shoulders of a young stable lad, she fancied herself in those strong arms once again.

The main door banged shut, and the vision was lost. Charmaine gingerly stepped forward and peered down, jumping back when the devil incarnate descended the portico steps. He wore a brown leather cap, white shirt, light brown trousers, and matching boots. His gait was lazy, yet deliberate, a self-assuredness she would love to see crushed. In her brief three-day experience, she knew this would never happen. She had never met anyone who exuded such confidence, not even Paul. Colette's remarks once again echoed in her ears: *He's an enigma . . . a one of a kind.* Thank God, one was quite enough!

He was halfway to the stables when Paul stepped out of the circle of men. Charmaine held her breath when they reached each other and Paul initiated an exchange, a concise remark she couldn't hear. John waved a letter in his brother's face: *one single solitary letter.* He spoke next, another short phrase that drew Paul around and sent his eyes traveling up the face of the mansion. Within a moment, he found her, a smile breaking across his lips. Charmaine shook her head. John must have known she was standing there, watching them. How had he known? Or had he? He was probably playing Paul for the fool and got lucky.

John disappeared into the stable, emerging minutes later with a great black stallion in tow: Phantom, according to the twins. The proud beast fought the bridle, his sable coat shimmering in the late morning sun.

A groom led another horse out. When George took the reins, Paul threw his hands up. "I won't be long!" George called from the saddle.

Everyone seemed to be waiting for John to mount up as well. No one, not even Paul, rode the "demon of the stable," so dubbed because he was constantly breaking out of his stall, jumping the corral fencing, evading stablehands or nipping the other horses. Great care was taken to segregate him. Clearly, John intended to do what his brother had the good sense to avoid, and Charmaine planned to laugh loudly when the stallion threw him onto his conceited rear end.

The steed was growing zealous for the freedom of the road, pulling fiercely at the bit, but John appeared oblivious as he conversed with George. He casually produced something from his shirt pocket and raised it to the animal's large muzzle. The horse gobbled it up. John stroked his satin flank and then, with one fluid motion, swung into the saddle. The horse bolted, but John reined him in, his momentum ending in a lunging halt. With a loud whinny and a violent shake of his huge head, the horse began to circle in place. Charmaine snickered; the man was no horseman. Finally, a weakness to exploit when the moment was ripe!

"He's rarin' to go!" George averred. "He hasn't been ridden in ages."

John concurred. "I see my brother wasn't brave enough to work him out!"

"No, John, I value my neck too much!" Paul called back. "If he throws you, it will be your own folly. You won't control him until he's had a good long run!"

"We'll see, Paulie," John countered. "It won't take him long to remember all the tricks."

As if to fortify his contention, he leaned forward and patted the animal's sleek neck. A nudge to the flank, and the beast trotted toward Paul. John reached out and ruffled his brother's hair, laughing heartily as the horse completed a wide sweep of the area, hooves tapping out a perfect rhythm on the cobblestone drive. John snapped the reins hard, and the steed shot forward, speeding past George and exiting the compound, his legs a blur, tail and mane sailing in the wind. George spurred his own mount into motion and followed in hot pursuit, disappearing in a cloud of dust kicked up by the vagabond stallion.

Charmaine stepped out of the house and felt liberated. The children were gay, chasing butterflies and picking exotic flowers that grew with abandon in the grassy fields. Though it was hot, the sky was a deep azure and the breeze carried the sweet scent of ocean spray. The tropical paradise was a balm for her turbulent mind, a welcome respite from days of sequestration in the nursery.

They traipsed northwest through three fields, their destination a special picnicking spot the twins had chosen. Ahead was a wooded area, breached only by a dark, narrow path of craggy rocks that appeared to lead nowhere. They entered the copse, trudging up an incline that wasn't quite as treacherous as Charmaine had at first imagined. Soon the path leveled off and quite unexpectedly, opened onto a lush, grassy bluff that was enclosed on three sides by thick foliage. The western edge offered a lofty view of the ocean, a breathtaking vista.

"Oh, girls, this is just beautiful," Charmaine sighed, returning their ebullient smiles. "Look at the flowers! And the sea—look how it shimmers in the sun!"

They giggled in reply, setting down the picnic basket. With her help, they spread a blanket in the shade of a tall cotton tree and laid out the bounty Fatima had packed for them: fried chicken, crusty bread, fresh oranges and bananas, cookies, and lemonade. Charmaine remembered many an evening in her impoverished home where soup and bread were the main course, portioned over a few days to make it last. If she were lucky, a feast such as this would adorn their Christmas table. She silently thanked God for her good fortune and prosperity this day. If only her mother could know how happy her life had become.

They delved into lunch, famished after their long hike. Even Pierre ate heartily, and Charmaine chuckled as he stuffed a third cookie into his greasy mouth. She wiped his face and hands clean as he squirmed away. Then he settled on the other side of the blanket and fell asleep from sheer exhaustion, content to take his afternoon nap in the open air.

John meandered into the kitchen in an attempt to shrug off the boredom that pervaded the study. The afternoon was drawing on, and there was no sign that lunch would be served any time soon. He had declined George's invitation to eat at Dulcie's. He wasn't in the mood to mingle with the men who caroused there. So, he returned alone. He'd grown accustomed to being alone, and most of the time, he preferred it that way. But now he was hungry.

"'Afternoon, Master John," Fatima greeted as she bustled around the sweltering room, setting a tray of warm muffins on the kitchen table.

"Good day, Cookie," he returned as he sat down. "God, it's hot in here! I still say that stove should be out in the cookhouse where it belongs."

"Mind your mouth and don't be giving your pa any ideas," she warned. "I like it right here. Saves me a lot of running. And don't go touching those muffins!" she threatened, catching sight of his avid eyes on them. "They're for dinner."

"I'm not after your muffins, but it's nearly two. Where's lunch?"

His question drew a grumble from Fatima, who was now stoking the oven. As she bent over, John snatched a muffin and concealed it under the table.

"There ain't no table lunch today, Master John."

"And why is that? Are you holding out for a raise in wages?"

"You know me better than that," she chided, well aware he teased her. "I already sent a tray of food up to your pa and Missus Agatha. I didn't expect you back for lunch."

"What about the children and their governess?" John asked,

stealing a bite of his muffin when Fatima visited the pantry and dropped potatoes into her apron.

"Miss Charmaine took the children on a picnic," she explained, turning back to the table to dump them there. "I fixed them a basket of food before they left."

"A picnic?"

Fatima eyed him suspiciously. "I know what you're thinking, Master John."

"What am I thinking?"

"If you're hungry, I'll fix you something, just leave Miss Charmaine alone."

"Leave her alone?"

"I heard you picking on her last night. She's a nice girl, and she don't know you. So you leave her be, before you frighten her right out of this house."

Fatima fetched a loaf of bread to make him a sandwich.

"A nice girl, eh?" he asked skeptically, grabbing another muffin and raising it to his mouth. "I keep hearing that. George is sweet on her, and my brother—"

His words were cut short when Fatima caught him red-handed. "My muffins!" she bellowed. "Now you put that back before I take a stick to you!"

John scrambled from the chair and was out the back door before she could maneuver her wide girth around the table. He sidestepped several frantic chickens that squawked as they scattered out of his way, then he nearly got tangled in the laundry on the clothesline. But he laughed loudly, knowing he'd escaped her.

"Go on, now," she scolded from the doorway, shaking a knife at him, "and don't you come back here 'til dinner!"

He tipped his cap, bowed cordially, and walked down the back lawn, chewing on the warm muffin he'd nearly swallowed whole. It only whetted his appetite; now he was really hungry. He knew where he could eat—and a fine lunch at that! He laughed again, realizing the afternoon would not be boring after all. Poor Miss Ryan! She'd be alone with him; no Paul to come to her rescue. Well, at least the children would be pleased to see him. His destination was simple, since he knew exactly where they'd be enjoying their picnic.

Charmaine removed her bonnet, relaxed on the blanket, and took in her surroundings again. "How romantic," she murmured, imagining herself in this paradise with Paul. "How ever did you girls find this place?"

"We didn't," Yvette replied matter-of-factly, "Johnny did. A long time ago."

At the mention of the man's name, Charmaine's eyes darted around, searching the shaded areas. *He's not going to jump out at me,* she reasoned. *He rode off to town, and we were gone long before he returned. He has no idea where we are . . .*

"What's the matter, Mademoiselle Charmaine?" Jeannette asked.

"Nothing. Tell me more about this spot. When did John show it to you?"

"When Mama was well. When we were little."

"And if we close our eyes," Yvette said, "we can pretend she is with us . . ."

Jeannette did as her sister suggested, and Charmaine indulged their poignant fantasy. "You mentioned John," she finally said. "He discovered this place?"

Yvette nodded. "When he was a boy, he used to go on expeditions with George. That's when they found these cliffs. Johnny swore George to secrecy. He told us, from then on, whenever he got angry with Paul or Papa, he would come to this hideaway because it was the one place on the island Paul didn't know about, the one place where he could be alone. When he knew we could be trusted, he brought us here, too. But we had to promise *never* to tell Paul."

Charmaine gritted her teeth. The gall of the man—setting the children against Paul.

"I decided you could be trusted, too," Yvette added thoughtfully. "And if . . ."

"And if what?" Charmaine asked suspiciously.

"And if Johnny wants company today, he's sure to look for us here."

Wants company? First he has to return from town, then discover we've left the house. Certain both could not possibly happen, Charmaine dismissed the thought, pleased when Yvette suggested a game of hide-and-seek.

She and her sister scurried off, declaring their governess the seeker and the blanket, "home." Charmaine covered her eyes and counted to fifty. Then she scanned the far edges of the encroaching forest, searching for any movement that would betray the girls' hiding places.

The crunch of leaves caught her ear, and she headed down the path by which they'd arrived. A snapping twig pointed to the brambles straight ahead. Determined to surprise them, she broke into a run and rounded the brush at top speed, lunging to a sudden halt when she nearly landed in John's arms, her bun falling loose and spilling its bounty onto her shoulders.

"Well, now," he exclaimed, "I didn't expect you to be *that* happy to see me!"

Fuming, she snubbed him, making a great show of turning away.

"Aren't you going to tag me?" he pressed.

"No!" she threw over her shoulder as she stomped back to the clearing, pulling pins free of her hair. Unfortunately, the man fell in step alongside her.

"Johnny!" Yvette and Jeannette called in tandem, running from opposite sides of the bluff to greet him. "You did find us!"

"I was looking for lunch, and Cookie told me she packed a picnic for you."

"You can have some!" Jeannette offered, pointing to the leftover food.

John walked over to the blanket and stared down at the slumbering Pierre. After a moment, he lifted a discarded plate and piled it high with food. Then he settled against the trunk of a tree and delved into his meal. Yvette sat next to him, while Jeannette prepared him a plate of cookies.

They ignored Charmaine, who continued to simmer as she coifed her hair. He obviously intended to stay. After an interminable silence, she found the nerve to speak. "Do you always intrude upon people uninvited?"

"Only when it's worth it. And always when they're unsuspecting."

"And what exactly does that mean?"

"Let's take you for example: My, my, the secrets I've uncovered by intruding on you!" His eyes twinkled, but he waved away her displeasure with the chicken bone he held, tossing it over his shoulder. "Today I'm only intruding for lunch. This is delicious. The blisters I got on the journey here were a small price to pay."

Charmaine bit her tongue and focused on cleaning up, grateful when the twins engaged his attention, asking him for stories about America.

Their voices woke Pierre, who sat up, rubbed his sleepy eyes, and smiled when he recognized John. Yawning, he left the blanket and walked deliberately toward the man, made a fist, and plunged a targeted punch into his shoulder.

"Pierre!" Charmaine cried in disbelief. The boy had never raised a hand to anyone before. She feared John's reaction, certain he'd use the child's bad behavior to discredit her. Instead, he doubled over as if seriously injured and, with a loud groan, flopped to the grass, where he lay perfectly still.

With great trepidation, Pierre stepped closer, oblivious of his sisters, who were winking at one another. No sooner had he crouched down, and John's eyes popped open with the cry: "Boo!" Pierre jumped, then chortled in glee, not satisfied until he'd played "boo" three more times.

When John tired of the game, he drew the boy into his lap, pulled his cap from his back pocket, and placed it on Pierre's head. It was too large and slid over his eyes and nose. Only his grinning lips were visible.

Charmaine leaned back against the tree and watched them guardedly. Pierre was warming up to his elder brother. Just what she needed, a third child begging to see John all day long.

"How'd ya get here?" the boy asked, peering up at John from under the cap.

"On Fang, silly!" Yvette interjected, casting all-knowing eyes to John.

"Fang?" Charmaine asked.

"Johnny's horse," Yvette replied presumptuously.

"Horse?" Charmaine expostulated, turning accusatory eyes upon the man. "I'm sure you'll never recover from your large *blisters.*"

"I said I had blisters," he rejoined, "I didn't say where."

The girls bubbled with laughter.

Charmaine was not amused. "Your horse's name is Fang? If it's the horse you were riding this morning, I thought his name was Phantom."

"The grooms call him that because of his bad manners. A phantom stallion. Surely you've heard that expression before, my Charm?"

"Of course I have!" she snapped, thinking: *like master, like horse.*

John's smile broadened. "Anyway, his real name is Fang."

"Fang," she repeated sarcastically, "why, that's a dog's name."

"Dog or horse, it's still an animal's name." John winked at Yvette when Charmaine turned away. "And he was given the name for a very good reason."

On cue, Yvette skipped to Charmaine and grabbed her hand, insisting she examine the horse so she would understand his bizarre name. "Come, Mademoiselle Charmaine, we'll show you."

Unwittingly, she was drawn into the girl's enthusiasm, and before she could object, was trekking the pathway with Yvette. She glanced over her shoulder to find John close behind, Jeannette at his side and Pierre on his shoulders.

The boy attempted to wave from his lofty perch, but quickly changed his mind, clasping both hands over John's eyes. John peeled them away with the complaint: "I can't see, Pierre! If I trip, we'll be like Humpty Dumpty and all fall down." Charmaine giggled when the three-year-old let go of John's face only to grab fistfuls of his hair.

"That's not Humpty Dumpty," he declared, "that's Ring a Ring a Rosy."

Moments later, they found "Fang" grazing in the middle of a wild field, his great head bent to the long grass, his tail swishing in the breeze.

"Come quickly!" Yvette urged, breaking into a run.

"Yvette!" John shouted. "Wait for me."

She stopped immediately, arms akimbo. "Then hurry up!"

When he reached her, he set Pierre down and squatted, looking her straight in the eye. "I've told you never to go near Fang without me. I thought you understood."

Yvette bowed her head. "But—"

"There *are* no buts, Yvette. The horse can be dangerous if he's startled. You are not to go near him unless you are with me. Agreed?"

"Agreed," she replied meekly.

John's genuine concern surprised Charmaine. After patting Yvette's back, he placed his cap on her head, a privilege that regained her friendship. Now she tugged at his hand and called for Charmaine to follow.

"So, this is Fang," Charmaine remarked apprehensively, jumping when the horse shook its head.

"Yes," John acknowledged, stroking the black mane, "this is my horse." He threw an arm over the animal's neck and proceeded to introduce them. "Fang, this is Miss Ryan, formerly of Richmond, Virginia. Miss Ryan, this is Fang, my loyal steed."

The twins were giggling, and Pierre joined in.

Suddenly, the horse stepped forward and, to John's delight, neighed a greeting that petrified Charmaine. "That means 'pleased to make your acquaintance' in horse talk," he explained, drawing more laughter from the children.

Charmaine smiled in spite of herself.

"Do you like him, Mademoiselle Charmaine?" Jeannette asked.

"He is quite remarkable," she replied nervously, "however, I have yet to see why he's named Fang. I still say that's a dog's name."

John stepped closer. "You use the perfect word to describe Fang, Miss Ryan," he replied, taking hold of her wrist to lead her nearer the steed. "You see, Fang has a *remarkable* characteristic that distinguishes him from other horses."

She cringed with the contact of his warm hand and pulled away quickly.

"He was born with one overly large, very sharp, front tooth. Right, girls?"

They nodded vigorously.

"One overly large front tooth?" she asked. "Surely you jest."

"No, I do not. Fang has a reputation for nipping fingers and other horses. That's why they all steer clear of Fang. He uses his tooth as a weapon."

The twins hadn't stopped laughing. How had she been drawn into this ridiculous conversation? If the children weren't enjoying themselves so immensely, she'd be walking back to the blanket.

"You don't believe Johnny, do you?" Yvette demanded. "It's really true!" She looked up at her brother. "You better show her."

John pulled the stallion's head up from the grass and grabbed his muzzle. When Fang whickered in objection, Charmaine stepped back.

"Why are you moving away?" he asked. "Don't you want to see the oddity of the century? You'd pay a fee to glimpse something like this at the circus."

"Actually," Charmaine faltered, "I'd hate to put you through all that trouble. I'm sure I can do without seeing the 'oddity of the century.'"

"Go ahead, Mademoiselle," Yvette implored. "He won't bite you."

Charmaine wondered whether the girl was referring to the horse or John. She decided to placate them and be done with it, or she'd never hear the end of it.

John produced a lump of sugar from his pocket. The stallion's lips curled back, and the treat was devoured, but Charmaine witnessed nothing unusual.

"Did you see it?"

"Well, actually, no."

"How could you miss it? It was right there, plain as the nose on your face!"

"Now, Yvette," John chided, "give Miss Ryan a chance. She doesn't know where to look like you do. Perhaps if she stepped a bit closer, she'd see better."

This time when John held out the sugar, he drew back the horse's lips and Yvette pointed to the area of interest. "Look! See it there? See that big fang?"

Charmaine didn't see a thing, but the girl's huff of frustration prompted her to scrutinize the animal's mouth further.

John let go of the huge head and pressed his brow into the steed's neck. Charmaine frowned. *Is he ill?* He looked heavenward, his entire face one tremendous smile. Tears were welling in his eyes, and in a flash, she realized he was laughing. The twins rivaled his mirth, doubling over in painful glee, unable to speak. Even Pierre was giggling.

"You are the first grown-up that prank has worked on!" Yvette gasped.

Charmaine's heart plummeted. They were enjoying themselves at her expense! Suddenly, insidiously, her throat constricted with tears. Why was this man so determined to make a fool of her? Now he had the children ridiculing her! In great despair, she grabbed Pierre's hand and set a brisk pace back to the bluff.

"Mademoiselle!" Jeannette called after her, running to catch up. "You're not angry, are you? We didn't mean to make you angry. It was only a prank, but we wouldn't have done it if we thought you wouldn't find it funny, too!"

Charmaine struggled not to cry and was comforted when she received an affectionate hug from the gentle twin. Yvette and John were fast approaching, and she quickly composed herself, not wanting the man to know he had once again reduced her to tears.

He saw her dab at her eyes. *Such a deft little actress. Now I'm supposed to feel guilty because I made the little lady cry.* He shook his head derisively and chuckled to himself. *She is quite fetching with her curvaceous figure and wild hair—her best assets by far. And she uses that sidelong glance to disarm a man. No wonder Paul and George have fallen for her. Well, George is Mr. Earnest, and Paul likes to be the hero so he can seduce her. And Johnny? Well, Johnny isn't taken in so easily. Still, if she wants to play, then why not? Johnny has nothing to lose. With Paul in her pocket, she thinks she can take on the best of them. But she hasn't played with the likes of Johnny. Well, Miss Ryan, you shall see what it's like to play with Johnny.*

"Race you back to the blanket!" Yvette challenged. "The last one there has to carry the picnic basket home!" The girl broke into a run and bounded into the path, Jeannette and Pierre in hot pursuit.

John drew alongside Charmaine. "Don't you have a sense of humor?"

She was determined to ignore him and stared off into the distance. But he wasn't about to be dismissed, so he stepped in front of her. When she turned her face aside, he grabbed her chin and forced her to look at him. She slapped his hand away. "Don't touch me!"

He only chuckled. When she sidestepped him, he hastened to catch up. "I'm sorry if my jest offended you," he apologized, garnering her utter astonishment. "It's a prank the twins enjoy playing. I thought you'd go along with it."

Doubting his sincerity, Charmaine withheld comment, relieved when they reached the bluff.

"You didn't even try to catch us!" Yvette complained.

John scooped up Pierre, who had run to greet them, then set him down again. "Now, Yvette, you would pout all day if I had outraced you."

"You couldn't have done that if you tried!"

Pulling his cap off her head, she brandished it before him. "I still have this! Let's play 'keep away' from Johnny!"

When John lunged at her, she darted out of reach. As he closed in, she sent the cap sailing through the air to her sister.

He grinned. "All right, Jeannie, now give it back."

She hesitated, then squealed as he dove at her, scurrying away with his cap in hand. Then she, too, sent it flying.

John played along, indulging their tossing escapade. With hands on hips, he strategically placed himself between them. But Yvette recognized the ploy and threw the cap to Charmaine this time. She caught it and was drawn into the game as well. Now John was tracking her.

"Are you going to give me the cap, my Charm?" he asked, arm extended.

"Don't give it to him, Mademoiselle!" Yvette cried. "Throw it to me!"

Charmaine launched the cap in Yvette's direction, breathing easier when John swung away. When it eventually came sailing back, it fell short of its mark, hitting the ground near Pierre. He picked it up, giggled, and clumsily shuttled it to her, enabling John to close in. Charmaine tucked it behind her back and blindly retreated. John steadily advanced, blocking her view altogether. Her foot struck the trunk of the tree. She was trapped!

He was only inches away, and as her eyes traveled up from the buttons on his shirt, past his neck to his clean-shaven face, memories of their first encounter rushed in. Somehow, he seemed taller than that night, even more imposing than the morning he'd barged into his room and found her reading Colette's letter. But he wasn't angry now. He leaned in close and, with a victorious grin, placed his hands flat against the tree trunk, imprisoning her there. His eyes were magnetic. At that moment, he struck her as being very handsome, his wavy hair falling low on his brow, his usually stern features turned boyish. He seemed to read her thoughts, and the rakish smile widened, boring deep dimples into his smooth cheeks. All at once, the blood was thundering in her ears, and she felt her face grow crimson.

"May I have my cap back, my Charm?" he asked huskily, "or must I remove it from your backside forcibly?"

Her limbs were quaking as she handed it over. He stood there a moment longer, restoring it to its original shape, complaining of the damage done. "I'm afraid it hasn't fared well in the battle. It will never be the same."

Yvette was outraged. "You're lucky you even got it back!" She turned on Charmaine. "You're no fun! You didn't even try to keep it away from him!"

"Well, Yvette," John said, "all good things must come to an end. *Even games.*" Though he spoke to his sister, his eyes remained fixed on Charmaine, who was still leaning against the tree. He fixed the cap on his head and walked over to Pierre, affectionately ruffling his hair.

The twins sneaked up behind him, bent upon dislodging the cap and engaging him in the game again. But he stepped out of their reach. They danced around him still, trying to jump high enough to snatch it. Charmaine had never seen them so gay.

"Up to no good again, eh?" he accused mischievously.

"Just like you, Johnny!" Yvette rejoined.

"Just like me? When am I up to no good?"

"You're always up to no good," Yvette exclaimed, as if it were common knowledge. "That's what Father says."

A black scowl darkened John's face. Impulsively, Charmaine took a step closer to Yvette, fearful he might strike the girl. Instead, he demanded more information. "He told you that?"

"No, not me. Just Paul."

"But you were there."

"Not exactly. Paul had something important to discuss with Father, and I wanted to know what it was. So, I went to the kitchen and took a glass from the cupboard and listened through the wall of the water closet next to Papa's dressing chamber. It worked fine, because I could hear every word they said. Paul was angry about something you did, something about sending a ship here without papers. Anyway, that's when Papa said you were up to no good."

Suddenly, John was laughing heartily. "A glass against the wall," he murmured, shaking his head in amazement.

Yvette nodded, pleased with his reaction. "You remember when you showed me how to do that, don't you?"

"Ah yes," he sighed. "You are an astute pupil, Yvette."

Charmaine was both astonished and irate. "So, her eavesdropping on Saturday was my fault, but this incident is just splendid because the instruction came from you, is that it?"

John laughed harder and spoke to Yvette. "My advice to you,

my little spy, is: keep up the good work, but take care *not* to get caught. If Paul finds you with that glass, he'll lock you up in the meetinghouse cellar with all the drunkards."

"Where you belong, no doubt!" Charmaine snapped.

"What do you mean by that?" John asked.

"You had better think twice before you teach the children your antics. They may come back to haunt you."

"I'll make a note of that," John replied in overemphasized seriousness. With a theatrical flourish, he produced an imaginary paper and quill and pretended to write. "Miss Ryan, an authority on high morals and untainted virtue, warns me I had better watch my step, or else!"

"Or else what?" Yvette asked.

"Paulie will give me a sound thrashing. Isn't that right, Mademoiselle?"

Charmaine's eyes narrowed, but she refused to answer, as once again her caustic retort failed to meet its mark.

When John saw she had nothing more to say, he chuckled softly and bade the children a farewell. He turned back to her, pulled the cap off his head, and held it over his heart. "Thank you, Miss Ryan, for graciously allowing me to join your picnic luncheon. I'm sure you'll agree it was most enjoyable, but please don't beg me to stay any longer, since I really must be leaving now."

Enjoyable, indeed! She almost laughed outright at the absurd statement. Still, she sighed with relief when she realized he really meant to depart. Not even the children were able to change his mind, and he soon disappeared down the pathway. Not long afterward, they, too, headed for home.

Chapter 2

IT was an hour past daybreak and Charmaine and the children were already out of the house. Late last night, George had informed the twins Chastity would finally foal. And so, they were up and dressed at the crack of dawn, pestering Charmaine to visit the stables. Once there, they reveled in the miracle of new life. But Pierre had quickly tired of the spectacle.

Presently, he giggled uncontrollably as Charmaine spun him round and round in wide circles. Dizzy and exhausted, they collapsed onto the dewy lawn, where Charmaine affectionately kissed the top of his head. He scrambled away and stood before her, his cheeks rosy. "I wanna do it again!" he demanded, presenting his back to her and throwing his arms up into the air.

"Pierre," she complained breathlessly, "you are going to be ill!"

"One more time!" he pleaded, turning his baby-brown eyes upon her.

"That is what you said the last time," she replied, placing a finger to his protruding belly and marking her words with a tickle. He squirmed and giggled. "Very well," she sighed, rising again. "But this will be the last time, yes?"

He shrugged with head cocked, an adorable pose that made it impossible to say "no." She chuckled and gave him a fierce hug, then twirled him again. His glee echoed off the façade of the manor. When she set him down, he scrutinized her with another tilt of the head. Spontaneously, he threw his arms around her waist and hugged her as tightly as she had him moments ago.

Tears sprang to her eyes. "I love you, Pierre—so very much!"

As she released him, he espied a butterfly flitting over the flowers in the lawns and was off, chasing it down. He stopped to examine it each time it alighted. Charmaine sat in the grass and watched his carefree pursuit.

John strode back into his bedchamber, perplexed. Laughter had awoken him, drawing him out onto the veranda. He stood in awe of Charmaine Ryan's gentle play and genuine affection for Pierre. Quite unexpectedly, he felt reassured the orphaned boy had found the surrogate mother he needed. Perhaps the young governess was not just another of Paul's hussies. He rubbed the back of his neck. Perhaps he had misjudged her.

The butterfly forgotten, Charmaine watched Pierre toss pebbles across the cobblestone drive. Though she appeared a tranquil figure in the cool morning breeze, her thoughts were turbulent.

The week had ended less eventfully than it had begun. After Tuesday's picnic, she came to accept the futility of hiding from John. Though the past three days had been a tedious exercise in self-control, she was getting better at holding her tongue, learning the hard way it was impossible to win a war of words with him. He was far too quick on the comeback, another trait that rankled her.

As for Paul, he'd grown aloof, resuming his hectic work schedule on Charmantes. They hadn't shared another moment alone. It was for the best, she reasoned. The last thing she needed was for John to catch her in his brother's arms again. Nevertheless, Paul had been at dinner every evening, and for that, she was grateful. Tonight would be different. He had headed for Espoir before daybreak and wasn't expected back from the other island until late. This evening, she would have to face John alone.

The twins scampered through the stable doorway, shattering the serenity as they raced up the lawns shouting and waving. "Mademoiselle Charmaine, don't you want to pet the new foal?"

"I think he and his mother need to be alone, and we must go inside to eat."

"Only for a little while," Jeannette pleaded as they reached her.

"And we can tell Johnny that Phantom sired a colt!" Yvette exclaimed.

"Johnny?" Charmaine queried quizzically. "Phantom sired?"

"Well, of course! Why else would his coat be so very black?"

"Why else, indeed?" she murmured.

It wasn't until they had eaten, and Pierre, who'd grown cranky by the end of the meal, was settled for an early nap, that Charmaine accompanied the girls back to the stable. The foal was a sight to behold: jet black, long of leg, and fuzzy all over. He began nursing just as George returned. Confident the twins were in safe hands, Charmaine left them in order to check on Pierre.

The boy was not in his bed. She entered the playroom, but it, too, was empty. She checked her own room next. Nothing. Where could he be? She headed toward the stairs, counseling herself calm. Pierre was fine. He'd awoken and left the nursery looking for her. Perhaps he was in Paul's chambers again.

The sound of shattering glass told her she was wrong. It had come from farther down the corridor, from Colette's sitting room, a place where Pierre had often played, a place now forbidden to him. Instantly, Charmaine was at the door, cursing her ill fortune when the opposite door was yanked open and the mistress of the manor swept out of her husband's quarters.

Agatha's eyes narrowed, but when a child's giggle drew their attention, those eyes turned evil. In a rush, she pushed past Charmaine and threw the door open. Pierre was crouched amid shards of glass and fresh flowers.

"You spoiled little brat!" she hissed, descending upon him in a fury. She grabbed him by the arm and lifted him clear off the floor. "I'll teach you not to touch what doesn't belong to you!"

Charmaine flew at the woman. Stunned, Agatha let go, and Pierre scrambled behind Charmaine, where he pinned his quaking body against her legs and buried his face in her skirts.

"How dare you?" Agatha demanded.

"I—I'm sorry—"

"*Sorry?* Is that all you have to say? You allow him to escape your supervision, enter my private chambers and break a priceless vase, presume to interfere, and then assume an apology will suffice?"

"It was an accident. You can take the cost of the vase out of my wages."

"Take the cost out of your wages?" Agatha echoed snidely. "You underestimate the value of that piece. But even if I were able to replace it, I refuse to tolerate your insubordination. For some reason you think you can speak to me as if you are a member of this family—initiate an assault of my person! Well, let me remind you who you are—an employee, an inferior!"

"I did not mean to be insolent—"

"Step aside, Miss Ryan, and hand the boy over. Since you are unable to discipline the children, it is time somebody taught you how."

"No, please!" Charmaine begged, shielding Pierre with her arms.

"I said, step aside," Agatha ordered, incited by the boy's whimpers as she tried to pry him from Charmaine, "or I shall dismiss you!"

Charmaine had no choice. Agatha had the authority to carry out her threat, especially today, with Paul gone. In great shame, her arms dropped away.

"Mama! Mama!" Pierre desperately cried, clutching her legs.

Agatha yanked him free and carried him across the room to her dressing table chair, where she sat, laid him across her lap, and bared his bottom. She grabbed her hairbrush and struck him with it.

"Don't!" Charmaine shrieked. "Please, don't!" But her horror was muffled beneath Pierre's wails, which grew louder with each brutal whack, spilling an ocean of tears on the carpet. She finally dove at the woman. "Let him go!"

"What in hell do you think you're doing?"

Startled, Charmaine broke away. But Agatha cowered, for a livid John stood over them, beholding her defenseless victim. The boy's bottom and lower back were covered in purple welts. Repulsed, he turned acid eyes on his aunt.

"By God, woman, what is the matter with you?"

Ashen-faced, Agatha abruptly released Pierre, who ran to Charmaine. Then, she rose regally from her chair and smoothed her rumpled skirts, a pathetic pretense at dignity.

"The boy needed a firm hand," she replied imperiously, attempting to conceal the hairbrush in the folds of her skirt.

"A hand?" John snarled, seizing her arm and ripping the brush away. "You nasty bitch! I should take this to you!"

Agatha flinched when he hurled it across the room, then gasped at his profanity. "How dare you? I am mistress of this manor! I demand your respect! You will not speak to me like that! You will apologize!"

"Hell will freeze over before I apologize to the likes of you!"

"How dare you?"

"How dare *you* abuse the boy over a vase that can easily be replaced?" he shot back. "I warn you now, Agatha, if you ever raise a hand to any child in this house again, I will tear it off and cast it to the dogs!"

"How dare you? How dare you?" she shrieked.

John ignored her, turning to Charmaine, who cradled Pierre to

her breast, the boy's grip tenacious, face buried in her hair, his muffled sobs little more than shuddering whimpers. John placed a comforting hand to his back, then grasped Charmaine's elbow. "Come
with me, before I strangle her."

He nudged her forward, faltering momentarily. Frederic stood
in the corridor doorway, his face grim. John pressed on, and the elder immediately stepped aside. Charmaine felt a frigid gale of resentment pass between them, the icy tentacles made manifest by
Agatha's cries of indignation. "He has abused me, Frederic! You
didn't hear what he called me in front of the house staff! I am . . ."

They continued down the south wing corridor. When they
reached the nursery, Charmaine looked at John askance, bracing
herself for a battery of irate questions. "Where are the girls?" he
asked instead.

"In the stables with George, watching the new foal."

She was surprised when the inquiry ended there. John was already at the bell-pull, summoning a maid.

Charmaine placed Pierre on his bed and sat down next to him.
He cuddled his pillow for comfort, compounding her misery. She
had failed him, and her heart was heavy with guilt. "Pierre, I'm
sorry—so sorry," she whispered.

He shoved a thumb into his mouth and closed his eyes to the
world.

A hand came down on her shoulder, and Charmaine looked up
at John. He had rescued them both. "Thank you," she choked out,
uttering words she never thought she'd say to him.

"For what?" he asked softly, his eyes earnest.

"For stopping Mrs. Duvoisin, for—"

"I was a bit late."

Charmaine gazed down at the boy, silently shouldering her cul-
pability; she should never have handed him over to the wicked
woman. "How could she do that to an innocent child?" she lamented.

"It is beyond reason," John snorted. "Horsewhipping is too good for her."

A knock fell on the outer door, and John opened it to Anna. "We need a basin of cold water and fresh washcloths," he directed.

With a bob, the maid disappeared, returning minutes later with the requested items. Rolling up his sleeves, John dipped the cloth in the water and wrung it out, gently laying the cool compress across Pierre's buttocks.

"This should keep the swelling down."

Pierre awoke with a start, not at all pleased with the comfort placed upon his bruised posterior. He moaned, and Charmaine knelt beside him, massaging his back while John continued to apply the cloth.

"I'm sorry, Mainie."

"I know you are, Pierre, but you mustn't go near those rooms again."

"I won't go there no more."

"Good," she murmured and placed a kiss on his forehead.

Pierre turned his head deep into the pillows. Charmaine took the cloth from John. The welts had already gone down, but she feared he wouldn't be able to sit for the next day or two.

"Don't worry, Miss Ryan," John reassured, reading her mind. "Children heal quickly. I'm sure we can find a soft pillow for Pierre's bottom."

"This should never have happened. I should never have left him alone, and I should never have allowed that woman to raise a hand to him, threats or no."

"You're being too hard on yourself, Mademoiselle. It would have been far worse if you weren't there. You saved Pierre from Agatha, and he knows that. There is no sense in punishing yourself over it."

She was astonished; his words were compassionate and comforting. Just as amazing, he hadn't taken her to task for allowing Pierre to escape her supervision.

"Better?" he queried.

She nodded, nonplussed.

"Good. Then I'll be on my way. Take care of him for me now, will you?"

When she nodded a second time, he smiled at her—a genuine smile, devoid of mockery. Then he was gone, leaving her in stunned disbelief over all he had done for them.

Sunday, August 27, 1837

John and Pierre sat at the dining room table. Almost everyone, family and servants alike, was at Sunday Mass. But the wooden pews of the chapel were too hard for the boy's bruised buttocks, so John had suggested Pierre remain behind with him. Thus, the boy's injury had allowed them this time to be alone together.

John leaned forward, pretending to study Pierre as raptly as the three-year-old studied him. A fine boy, he decided. "Well, Pierre, what are we going to do for the next hour?"

"Go fishin'."

"Fishin'? How do you know about fishin'?"

"Jawj said you fish-ed wif Gummy off'a the dock, 'member?"

John chuckled, amazed by the boy's recollection. "One day we shall go fishing," he promised, "but we will use a rowboat."

Pierre tilted his head to one side. "What's a woeboat?"

"It's a small boat that only a few people can sit in at one time," John explained patiently. "It's the best way to fish in a lake or on a river. Maybe I'll purchase one for your birthday, and we can go fishing then. Would you like that?"

"Uh-huh," Pierre nodded emphatically.

"Good. In fact, where I live, there's a large river called the James. Do you think you'd like to go fishing there?"

Pierre puzzled over his elder brother's words. "Where you live?"

"Yes—in Virginia. I'll have to travel back there soon."

"Why?"

"Because I have work to do there."

"Why?"

"Because . . ." John was at a loss and chuckled again. "Because I just do. Do you think you'd like to come with me? We would captain a giant ship across the ocean and sail right up the James River. And when we landed, you could see the buildings in the big city and my house. Do you think you'd like that?"

Pierre studied him speculatively. "Would I live in your house?"

"Would you like to live with me?"

"Only if Mainie could live there, too."

"Only if Mainie could live there, too," John mumbled under his breath. "Well, Pierre, we'll have to see about that." He ruffled the lad's hair affectionately.

Father Benito droned on, and Charmaine caught herself daydreaming. Agatha sat directly in front of her, a constant reminder of John's profanity. *Bitch* . . . the label had had an effect. Agatha had kept to her boudoir until this morning, and Charmaine could thank the man for that, too. Nevertheless, she anguished over Frederic's reaction. He hadn't confronted her as yet; surely he would.

John. By no means did his blessed intervention excuse his reprehensible behavior, but it had brought about a most unexpected cease-fire. For this reason, she bowed her head and said a prayer for him. It was as if her mother were there, telling her it was the right thing to do. Even at dinner last night, he had been pleasant. With Paul and Agatha absent, the mood had been relaxed, and to the children's delight, he and George carried on throughout the meal, telling jokes, playing tricks, and acting silly. Not once did he send a cutting remark her way, and so it had been easy to place Pierre in his care this morning. Perhaps the worst was behind them; perhaps they had reached a truce.

When the Mass ended, Stephen Westphal approached Paul.

"What brings you to services here?" Paul asked.

Westphal, who hadn't returned to the manor since that terrible dinner last December, glanced at Charmaine. "It is difficult to track you down during the week, so I had hoped to catch you at home."

"What is it?"

Agatha moved to Paul's side, and Stephen nodded a greeting. "Perhaps we should go to the library. This is a business conversation, private in nature."

"You can tell me here," Paul replied, suspicious of the man's reticence.

Westphal plunged in. "Some of the Richmond accounts you attempted to liquidate were closed out earlier this year."

"Closed out? What do you mean, closed out?"

"The funds were withdrawn in March—" Westphal cleared his throat "—by John. By all indications, there are no monies left in the Virginia State Bank."

Paul massaged the back of his neck, perplexed.

"This is outrageous!" Agatha exclaimed.

Westphal rushed on. "Don't worry, I had Edward Richecourt contact the Bank of Richmond. Those accounts are still intact, and the shipping firm has been paid; however, it would be prudent to find out whether other accounts have been terminated before future notes are written against them."

"We can find that out right now," Paul replied, "that is, if I can locate John. He's probably still sleeping."

"No, he's not!" Yvette piped in. "He's in the dining room with Pierre."

"Pierre?" Paul queried, noting for the first time the three-year-old's absence. "Alone?" he added, his anxious eyes now leveled on Charmaine. "You left the boy alone with John?"

"Yes—" Charmaine faltered "—but I'm certain he is fine."

Paul rushed from the chapel. Stephen threw a quizzical look at Agatha and hastened after him. Trembling, Charmaine and the girls did the same. She worried over the expression on Paul's face, the implication Pierre was in some sort of peril. Surely John wouldn't endanger his own brother.

They found Pierre seated in John's lap, giggling.

"What's the matter, Paul?" John asked as his brother stepped up to the table, a small entourage behind him. "You look as if you've seen a ghost."

Paul exhaled.

Greatly puzzled, Charmaine studied both men, but their faces bore no answers. *Pierre is fine—so why the alarm?*

Stephen broke the perplexing tableau, stepping forward with hand extended. "John, how good it is to see you again."

John made no move to rise. "It is?" he asked, ignoring the proffered hand, which hung suspended in midair long enough to become embarrassing.

"Of course it is," the banker rejoined in confusion, his arm dropping to his side. "Anne has written a great deal about you of late. I'm pleased to hear you've been getting along so famously."

John snorted. "Famously? Is that how she describes it?"

"Well, yes."

Westphal began fiddling with his collar. He'd forgotten how brutally blunt John could be. Ten years in America hadn't smoothed the man's rough edges.

"Did your daughter write she was chasing me all over Virginia and I traveled to New York to get away from her?"

"No—no, of course not!" Westphal blustered, then laughed pretentiously as if John were only joking. "She led me to believe that—that—well, that—"

"Well, Mr. Westphal, it appears your daughter has *misled* you. So let me clear the matter up for you right now: I have no intention of ever proposing marriage to her. Is there anything else you've been led to believe?"

To Charmaine's delight, the banker's face reddened in disgrace. "I don't know what to say," he jabbered further. When John held silent, he beat a hasty retreat toward the foyer.

"I know he's annoying," Paul commented as everyone took their seats, "but you didn't have to break it to him quite like that."

"No? Trust me, Paul, it is for the best. Unlike Mrs. London, he got the message, so perhaps he will convince her she is wasting her time. I'm tired of her incessant pestering and would see an end to it."

Paul shook his head, but didn't pursue the matter. "I need to speak with you about the Virginia bank accounts. You closed two of them. Why?"

John leaned back in his chair. "I thought it unwise to have all our money in the South, so I transferred funds to New York. Why do you ask?"

"I wrote notes against those accounts. Why didn't you let me know they'd been moved?"

"I didn't know about the notes. Why didn't *you* let *me* know?"

Paul didn't answer. He grabbed a journal, sat, and began to read.

The children had just finished changing out of their formal Sunday attire and into clothing suited for the stable when a knock fell on their nursery door.

Jeannette opened it. "Papa!"

Charmaine finished tying Pierre's shoelace and stood slowly, bracing herself for the man's upbraiding.

"Good morning, Jeannette," he greeted. "Where are you off to today?"

"The stables, Papa. We're going to check on the new colt!"

"Chastity foaled yesterday," Yvette added. "We've spent so much time at her stall, the colt thinks we're his masters. Maybe he could be mine?"

"I don't know, Yvette," her father answered seriously. "If the foal grows to be anything like his sire, he may be too much stallion for you to handle."

Yvette grumbled, but he chuckled softly. "Why don't you and your sister run along to the paddock now? I'd like to speak with your governess."

They needed no further encouragement. Other than Pierre, who was on hands and knees playing with his blocks, Charmaine and Frederic were suddenly alone.

He must have read her apprehension, for he spoke directly. "Miss Ryan, I apologize for my wife's conduct yesterday morning. It won't happen again." Charmaine was dumbfounded, but he didn't seem to notice, his attention on Pierre. "How is he?"

"Recovering," she said, and then, by way of justification, "I thought he was napping, sir. When I returned to check on him, he was gone. I suppose he went into Mrs. Duvoisin's chambers because they used to belong to his—"

"Charmaine, I'm not asking for an explanation. I am quite pleased with your care of my children. It is the single thing I don't worry about."

Amazingly, the ugly episode was closed, Frederic calling to the boy and requesting a hug, which the child eagerly bestowed.

That evening, John came to the nursery to say goodnight to the children. He hesitated on the threshold, his eyes resting on Charmaine, who was struggling to dress Pierre for bed. The boy giggled up at him, squirming against the garment.

"He's improved throughout the day," she commented with a tentative smile.

"Johnny," Yvette interjected before he could respond, "is it true you're not going to marry Mr. Westphal's daughter?"

"I'm not going to marry her," he reassured.

"Good," she said. "I don't want you to marry *anyone,* especially her!"

John smiled at her naked honesty.

"Is she really rich like her father says she is?" she pressed.

"Her husband was a wealthy man, and she'll most likely inherit her father's money some day, too." He eyed her quizzically. "Why do you ask?"

"If she is already rich, why would she want to marry you?"

John laughed heartily. "Because I'm so charming, of course!"

Charmaine rolled her eyes, not caring that he had turned to see her reaction.

"I don't think so!" Yvette refuted. "That's why it doesn't make sense."

"For some people, no matter how much money they have, it's never enough, so they make their fortunes bigger by marrying someone with even more."

"But you won't do that, will you, Johnny?" she asked.

"If I marry, Yvette, it will be to a woman who won't care about the size of my fortune; a woman who is happy just to be married to me. And someday, that's how it should be for you, too."

Charmaine was stunned by his declaration and bowed her head, not wishing him to see she approved of the values he was imparting to his sisters.

"Like Cinderella?" Jeannette interjected, bright-eyed.

"Like Cinderella," John nodded.

"Only the wicked stepmother will belong to the prince's family," Yvette added. "But she'll never get you to sweep the floors, will she, Johnny?"

John sniggered. "I wouldn't dream of taking her broom. How ever would she travel?"

Monday, August 28, 1837

With Fatima at market and the children hungry, Charmaine prepared a snack tray in the kitchen. She looked up when Anna and Felicia entered the room, then set knife to bread and tried to ignore them.

"Like I was sayin'," Felicia began pointedly, chafed by Charmaine's aloofness, "I'll satisfy him. Just you wait and see, and it won't be by pretendin' to be some innocent virgin. He don't want some backward chit, anyway. What do you think, 'Ma-de-mwah-zelle'? Do I got a chance?"

Charmaine began buttering the slices. "A chance at what?"

Felicia laughed spuriously. "There you go again, actin' all naïve, with your high-and-mighty airs. You think you're better than me, don't ya? Ever since you got your room moved to the second floor. Well, you might think you're somethin' special, but you ain't. You're still hired help, just like me and Anna. So you oughta stop pretendin' 'cause everyone knows you're just the riffraff daughter of a murderer! Worse than us, in fact."

Charmaine grimaced, hurt, yet perplexed. The maid's verbal abuse had died down long ago, so why this?

"What I'd like to know is what you're up to," Felicia proceeded. "You've been stringin' Paul along for a year now, and that ain't worked. So maybe you think you can make him jealous by fishin' for a bigger catch. Is that what she's up to, Anna?"

Anna nodded, bolstering Felicia's fantastic theory.

The jaded woman smiled wickedly and continued to speak to Anna as if Charmaine weren't there. "Ma-de-mwah-zelle Ryan will have her hands full if she thinks she can mewl after John the way she's mewled after his brother."

"*John?*" Charmaine gasped. "I leave him to you, Felicia!"

"Ain't that generous of you!" the maid exclaimed, eyes hard as granite, voice cold as ice. "But I've seen the changes 'round here—enemies one day, friends the next. What did ya do, lift your skirts behind Paul's back?"

Revolted, Charmaine grabbed the tray and rushed up the servant's staircase.

"That's right, Ma-de-mwah-zelle," Felicia called after her, "you run back to the children and leave the men in this house to me. But if you're gonna keep playin' your games, stick to Paul and stay away from John!"

Charmaine was still simmering when she reached the nursery. She forced a smile for Rose and Pierre, offered them the snack, then settled next to Jeannette, who was absorbed in a book. "It must be interesting," she commented, pushing Felicia from her mind.

"Hmm?" the girl queried, her eyes rising slowly to Charmaine. "Oh yes, it is! Mademoiselle, do you really think a person can become a vampire?"

"A vampire? Is that what your book is about?"

"Yes! They're terrible creatures that awaken from the dead," Jeannette explained, her eyes wide with wonderment and fear. "By day, a vampire's body remains asleep in its tomb, but at nightfall, the vampire rises up and stalks the earth, searching for victims—"

"Jeannette, you'll frighten your brother! Why ever would you want to read such a novel, anyway?" She took the book and leafed through the pages of folklore. "Wherever did you get this?"

"Yvette found it in the library a couple of days ago," Jeannette explained. "She's going to read it after she finishes *Frankenstein*."

"*Frankenstein?*" Charmaine asked, her eyes going to Yvette, who lay on the floor next to the French doors, also reading.

"This is even more frightening than vampires," the girl imparted. "Just listen . . ." and she began reading excerpts from the ghastly story.

Having heard enough, Charmaine walked over to the girl and wrenched the book from her hands. "Mary Shelley . . . Where did you get this?"

"From Johnny. And Mary Shelley claims a corpse stood over her—"

"*Corpse?*" Charmaine gasped. "Why would anyone, let alone a woman, want to write something like this?"

"To win a wager," Yvette replied.

"A wager?"

"Johnny said Mary Shelley and her friends were trying to see who could write the most frightening story."

"And did she succeed?"

"I think so. After all, wouldn't you be frightened by Dr. Frankenstein's experiments to bring the dead back to life?"

"Bring the dead back to life? Yvette, this story is sacrilegious—"

"—and he collected the bodies from graves—"

"That's enough, Yvette!" Charmaine scolded, snapping the book shut.

Rose concurred.

"No more talk about desecrated graves or reanimated corpses," Charmaine decided. "And just to make certain, I'll hold on to this until you are a bit older."

"But you can't! I have to finish reading it or else—"

"Or else what?" Charmaine pressed, noting the glance Yvette threw Jeannette's way. "Out with it, or you won't be seeing this book *ever* again."

"That's unfair!" she replied in a huff, and then: "Joseph was teasing me. He called me a ninny and said I'd be crying before I finished it. So now I must!"

"Yvette, why do you allow that boy to taunt you? He is five years older than you are. He knows he can get the better of you."

"Well, he can't! And once I've won the wager, I can call him a ninny!"

"Wager?" Charmaine asked. "I hope this doesn't involve money."

Yvette shook her head emphatically, but Charmaine remained unconvinced. Nevertheless, she relinquished the book with the agreement that once Yvette had proven her point to Joseph, the macabre storytelling would cease.

Tuesday, August 29, 1837

"Rose isn't feeling well," John explained from the nursery door.

"Yes, I know," Charmaine replied timidly.

"She mentioned the girls' lessons. I thought I might lend a hand with Pierre."

Charmaine nodded warily, allowing him to enter, and so it was settled. John hadn't spent thirty minutes with Pierre before the twins coaxed him over to their desks, and soon, he was dividing his attention amongst all three children.

She had been loath to reveal the subjects they had covered thus far, certain he'd scorn her limited knowledge, but he didn't seem to care at all. He took them on imaginary journeys to uncharted places filled with curious facts, weaving a treasure trove of information into a spellbinding tapestry. They rode a train pulled by a locomotive steam engine from Richmond to Washington, where they climbed into a hot-air balloon and floated all the way to New York. There they watched a baseball game and ate ice cream in the middle of August, rode an omnibus to the circus and saw a mermaid and a man with two heads. Next he launched into silly stories that he told in clever verse, and when he couldn't think of a word that rhymed, he made one up. The children's giggles bounced off the walls, their faces radiant with wonder.

As the second hour neared its end, Charmaine began to fathom John's subtle, yet artful tactics. She had never known a man to seek out children as he did. If it were possible, he had won them over again, and she realized this would be the first of many such lessons. They would benefit from his knowledge, and he, in turn, could escape to this oasis of acceptance in a home where he was mostly spurned.

She marveled at how effortlessly he captivated them. She'd never seen them so happy, not even when Colette was alive. Begrudgingly, she acknowledged he was a better tutor than she could ever hope to be. How could she compete? Did she want to? Age, experience, travel, and the privilege of wealth gave him the undisputed advantage. This was a fortuitous opportunity for the girls, even Pierre.

When the twins pleaded him to visit the next day, John awaited her consent. *Her consent!* She almost laughed aloud at the idea. He didn't need her permission to return, and she wondered why he had even bothered to look her way. Why was he suddenly showing her respect? What had happened to bring about his drastic change in attitude?

The more she pondered the question, the more perplexing it became. Was it the spanking incident with Pierre? That seemed to be the turning point, but she quickly dismissed the notion. Since the night of his arrival, he hadn't disguised his belief she was promiscuous—his brother's paramour. So how could Pierre's spanking have changed *that* opinion? Yet now, he was treating her like a lady!

Whatever the reason, she wouldn't lament her good fortune, and she certainly wouldn't jeopardize it by barring him from his sisters' studies. As long as he treated her amicably, she'd reciprocate. Today's turn of events heralded good times at last, good times indeed!

Friday, September 1, 1837

It was close to midnight when the French doors began opening again. Jeannette was frightened and stood quaking at the foot of her governess's bed.

"Yvette probably opened them," Charmaine reasoned. "It was hot today."

"I did not!"

Yvette's denial from the room beyond seemed a bit too vehement. They'd been through this same scenario two weeks ago. Clearly, a hoax was being perpetrated. The girl's fascination with the morbid had continued to grow: monsters, vampires, and now ghosts.

Charmaine sighed and ushered Jeannette back to her own room, fixing a pointed stare at Yvette once Jeannette was settled back in bed.

"You think *I* opened them?" Yvette demanded.

"I thought you wanted to prove Joseph the ninny, not your sister."

Yvette folded her arms in a huff, denying any hand in the opening doors.

Charmaine did not believe her; unfortunately Jeannette did and could not be reassured. When footfalls resounded in the hallway, Charmaine was ready to seek assistance. "If your brother tells you there's no such thing as ghosts, will you believe him?"

Jeannette nodded halfheartedly.

Charmaine looked down at Pierre, clutching his stuffed lamb. He slept soundly, oblivious to it all. She slipped on her robe and departed.

Paul's dressing room door stood slightly ajar, soft light spilling through the crack. Charmaine raised her hand to knock, but hesitated.

"Second thoughts?"

She jumped, heaving a sigh of relief when she pivoted around to find John ascending the last steps of the staircase. "You startled me."

"I'm sure I did," he commented wryly. "Next time, use the French doors. They're less conspicuous."

"French doors?" Charmaine queried innocently. The light dawned. "Oh, you don't understand! I was only going to ask your brother for a favor."

"A favor?" he snickered, his lips curling into a lopsided smile. "Shouldn't he be asking you?"

"Sir, you misunderstand."

John shook his head, chuckling this time, and stepped toward his bedchamber door mumbling, "I don't think so."

"Sir?"

"Mademoiselle?"

There was no turning back. He was the preferable choice for comforting his distraught sister. "Do you have a moment?"

"I have a whole night."

Her cheeks grew warm. "Oh, never mind! I'll see to it myself."

He curtailed his japing and met her at the nursery door. "What is it you actually wanted, Miss Ryan?"

Once she'd explained, he entered the children's bedroom, crossed to Jeannette's bed, and set his efforts to comforting her.

"Miss Ryan tells me you're frightened."

"The French doors keep opening all by themselves," she moaned, glancing toward Yvette, who remained awake, but silent.

John's gaze followed. "And you don't know who opened them?"

"No, but when it happened the last time, I saw somebody. This time, I only heard a noise."

"It was just your imagination—the result of all the ghost stories you've been reading."

"No, it can't be," she countered. "The first time it happened was before I started any of those books. Besides, doors don't open by themselves."

"Sometimes they do," John replied.

"They do?" both girls asked in unison.

"They do," he affirmed, demonstrating how a draft could cause a door to swing open. Jeannette smiled at last, admitting she was no longer afraid.

"But how did the latch come undone?" Yvette asked.

"These doors don't lock, Yvette. Sometimes a latch doesn't catch properly. That's probably what happened tonight. Wouldn't you agree, Miss Ryan?"

"Absolutely."

Yvette only grunted and stretched out once again on her bed.

He walked over to the French doors to reopen them. "It's going to be hot again tomorrow. Best to enjoy the breeze while it lasts."

"No!" Jeannette cried. Then seeing she'd disturbed Pierre, she continued more softly, "Please close them—the right way, Johnny. I'm still frightened."

"But you told me you weren't."

"Not of the doors, just of someone creeping in here, like the last time."

"The only person creeping around the house at this late hour," John remarked lightheartedly, "is George, pillaging treats from Cookie's kitchen."

The girls giggled, as he knew they would, but their laughter succeeded in waking Pierre.

Charmaine sighed. The disruption had turned into a midnight party.

John read her displeasure and stepped over to the boy. "Back to sleep," he gently admonished, ruffling the lad's hair. "There is nothing to be afraid of in here. You have Miss Ryan in the very next room, and if you need me, I'm close, too. All you have to do is call."

"Thank you," Charmaine whispered as he reached the door, disconcerted by his nearness.

"Any time at all," he replied.

"Johnny?" Jeannette called. "Do *you* believe in monsters?"

He faced her again. "Definitely."

"Have you ever seen one?"

"Saw one this morning at breakfast."

"You did?"

"Didn't you?"

"No."

"I don't know how you could have missed her," he continued with a straight face, giving them a moment to absorb his irreverent humor. "She was sitting right at the foot of the table with her great big nose in the air."

They burst into laughter, and Charmaine stifled a giggle of her own.

"You know," he offered, stepping toward their beds again, "Paul was frightened of Cookie when she first came to work here."

"Why?"

"Well, we were very young when she became our cook—only about five or six years old. But Paul thought she was the boo-bock."

"The boo-bock?"

"Yes, the boo-bock—a monster," John explained, delving into an extended story of how he had tricked Paul into believing the jovial and kindhearted cook was attempting to poison him. The children hung on his every word, chortling more than once, and especially when their disgruntled father threatened Paul with the switch if he persisted in his disrespect. Although Charmaine knew the tale was meant to be a diversion, she was certain every word was true and found the deception cruel.

John read her disdainful expression. "Surely you can find humor in a childhood prank, Miss Ryan. I assure you Paul played his fair share on me."

"Well taught at your hands, no doubt."

"No doubt," he agreed. "I apologize if my inadequate stories offend you."

Charmaine regretted the remark. "I'm sorry. I·never had brothers, so I suppose I'm not a fair judge of how boys behave. I do appreciate your help."

"Very well," he replied, winking at the children, "we'll leave it at that."

"You know, Johnny," Jeannette mused, "I'm not afraid when you're here. Do you think you could sleep with us tonight?"

"And where would I sleep, Jeannie?"

"With Pierre. He wouldn't mind. Would you, Pierre?"

The boy immediately lit up. "No, I wouldn' mind!"

"*See?* Please stay!"

John canted his head as if considering the request, and Charmaine cringed at the begging chorus that followed, mindful of the adjoining door and its easy access to her room.

"You're not being fair to Pierre," he said. "You've talked him into this."

"No they hav'n," the child replied, his chubby cheeks rosy in the lamplight. "I want you to stay wight here, too!"

Charmaine waited for John's response, struck by the tenderness—vulnerability perhaps—that fleetingly crossed his face. "It seems I'm outnumbered. If Miss Ryan has no objections," and he looked at her, "then I suppose I must stay."

"I've no objections," she murmured, hugging herself against his perusal.

He nodded and turned away, the resemblance he bore to his father at that moment, striking—mostly in the magnetism he radiated. It was uncanny. *John and Frederic are alike in so many ways . . . and both of them would vehemently deny it if they heard me say so.* No wonder they clashed; two such intense personalities in one family couldn't possibly coexist without someone getting hurt.

This revelation impelled her to study him more closely. He sat next to Pierre now, pulling off his boots. Even the physical traits were strong: the thick head of hair, squared jaw, curved nose, and thin lips. Although Paul was unmistakably a Duvoisin, with John, the similarity to Frederic went beyond appearance. John was so self-assured, directed himself with such purpose, that Paul couldn't hope to compete. Suddenly, she was ill at ease with her mutinous musings.

"Will you monitor my bedtime preparations like you do Pierre, my Charm?" he quipped as he worked at his belt buckle. "Or must I beg for some privacy?"

The twins giggled, and Charmaine's cheeks flamed red, realizing she'd been absentmindedly scrutinizing him. "I—I'm terribly sorry!" she sputtered. "I didn't mean to—I mean I was—"

"I'm sure you didn't," he interrupted with a chuckle.

Realizing the shirt was coming off next, Charmaine hurried to the door. But when she looked over her shoulder to bid them one last goodnight, she saw he'd merely untucked it and was already stretched out alongside Pierre.

"I'm bunking with you tonight, Pierre," he said, unaware of her nettled regard.

She'd show him she wasn't embarrassed! She marched to Jeannette's bed. "Let me tuck you in, sweetheart," she said, pulling the coverlet up and giving her a kiss. She did the same to Yvette. "No talking," she ordered mildly, walking over to Pierre next. She picked his lamb off the floor and placed it in his arms, giving him a kiss on the forehead.

"Don't I get one?" John asked in feigned disappointment.

The twins giggled.

"I only kiss good boys."

The twins giggled again.

"Bad boys are more fun to kiss."

The giggles grew louder.

"Goodnight, *Master* John."

The children's glee followed her into her bedchamber.

"You two had better stop laughing," he warned, "or else Mademoiselle Ryan will tan my hide. Kissing I can take. A spanking? Never!"

Paul was exhausted, but couldn't sleep. The day had been blisteringly hot and his chambers were uncomfortably warm. Presently, he stood on the balcony taking in the cool night air. It was impossible to keep up the exacting pace of running Charmantes and developing Espoir at the same time. Thankfully, George was back, but even so, critical problems ultimately fell into his lap, the biggest of all, the infant tobacco fields. Not so terrible if he wasn't needed on Espoir, but he was. Supplies had arrived, new construction had commenced, and fresh cane tracts were planted. It demanded a week of his time. His brother had experience with tobacco. Paul wondered if John would agree to help out while he was away.

Voices seeped into Charmaine's dreams, melded, then abruptly broke away, snapping her awake. It was dark, but the voices came again—from the children's room—one of them deep and irate. She jumped up and opened the door.

John stood in the center of the room, holding a distraught Joseph Thornfield by the scruff of the neck and pointing to a crumpled sheet that lay at his feet.

"I told you, sir," the boy stuttered fearfully, "I didn't mean any harm!"

"*Didn't mean any harm?*" John expostulated. "You come creeping through the French doors in the middle of the night, draped in a white sheet, and you're telling me you didn't mean any harm?"

"No, sir."

"John—I mean, sir," Charmaine corrected, "please—let him go."

"*Let him go?* Can't you see what he's been up to tonight?"

"I can see, but it's not all his doing. Is it, Yvette?"

John's brow knitted, befuddled, but when Yvette threw Joseph a murderous scowl, he understood.

"It was only a wager," she replied defensively. "And I tell you now, Joseph Thornfield, you did not frighten me, so you have not won the bet."

"*A wager?*" John railed, shaking the lad hard. "You're telling me you've crept into this room—God knows how many times—just to win a wager?"

"It was only tonight, sir!"

"That's a lie!" Yvette blazed. "You've frightened Jeannette before!"

"I have not! I swear I haven't! This was the very first time!"

"You're just saying that so you won't lose your dollar!"

"No, I'm not! Here, take the money and see if I care." Joseph fished a crumpled dollar from his pocket and shoved it toward Yvette.

John quickly snatched it away, knowing it was a great deal of money for the boy. "Is this your half of the wager?"

"Yes, sir, but—"

"And you think you've lost your stake because you failed to frighten her?"

"No, sir, but—"

"Then why in hell are you handing over your money? Never mind. I'll just hold on to this." He waved the note under the boy's nose. "When you've shown me you won't throw away a month's wages on a ridiculous gamble, you can have it back. Now pick up that sheet and get out of here before I change my mind!"

"Yes, sir!"

The boy grabbed the linen and dashed through the French doors.

John raked his fingers through his tousled hair, pausing at the base of his neck when his eyes lifted to Charmaine. Her hair was plaited in a thick queue that hung over one shoulder and past her breast. She'd forgotten her robe in her haste to reach the nursery, and the thin nightgown highlighted her unbridled curves and heaving bosom. No wonder Paul found her attractive. He couldn't have conquered her yet. She was too wide-eyed and innocent to have been with an experienced man.

"He's just a boy," she was saying, unaware of his sensate thoughts.

"Yes, he's just a boy," John agreed, "but he startled the life out of me creeping over to Jeannette like that. *I* should be paying him!"

Charmaine smiled, and Yvette snickered.

"Too bad he didn't find the right bed."

"He wouldn't have frightened me even if he had," Yvette objected haughtily.

"I'm sure," John laughed, finally seeing the humor in the whole affair. "Let's get back to bed. Move over, Pierre, and make some room for me."

"Johnny?"

John regarded Jeannette, who'd remained quiet.

"Joseph said he didn't come into our room until tonight. So who was it that other time?"

"It was Joseph. He was just too afraid to admit it."

"I don't think so," Jeannette reasoned. "Because the first time it happened was before Yvette and Joseph made the wager."

John frowned skeptically. "You've confused the dates, Jeannette."

"I'm sure I haven't. The first time was the night you came home—the night of that terrible thunderstorm. Remember, Mademoiselle?" Jeannette looked to Charmaine. "The storm was so bad, it even frightened you. That's when you went to fetch us cookies and milk. You remember, don't you, Mademoiselle?"

"I remember," Charmaine whispered, conscious of John's eyes upon her, worried her heady memories were publicized on her burning cheeks.

"That explains a few things I was wondering about," he murmured thoughtfully. "But it doesn't tell us when the wager began."

"Yes, it does," Yvette interjected. "You gave me *Frankenstein* the first morning you were home, and Joseph challenged me *after* he saw me reading it."

"*Frankenstein,*" John grunted. "So, it's my own fault I'm not getting any sleep tonight."

Charmaine was tickled with his assessment.

"All right. Back to my original theory," he concluded, "the breeze and a faulty latch, which I'll fix in the morning."

"But, Johnny, I really did see someone else in here!" Jeannette pressed.

"No, Jeannette, you didn't. You were dreaming. I promise, nobody has been creeping into this room at night."

"Somebody has," Pierre piped in.

"Really?" John smiled. "And who would that be?"

"I'm not 'apposed to tell," he averred.

"Please?"

"Well . . . sometimes . . . Mama comes to see me."

Everyone inhaled in unison, a huge sibilant sound that held.

John grasped the boy's shoulders, stern in disbelief. "What did you say?"

Pierre remained unaffected, a winsome smile on his face.

"Pierre," John persisted, "who did you say visits you at night?"

"Mama," he reiterated happily. "She plays with me and tells me things."

"He's lying!" Yvette protested, but when Charmaine told her to hush, she grumbled under her breath: "Well, he is."

"What does she tell you, Pierre?" Charmaine asked, stepping closer.

"Can't tell. I'm not 'apposed to."

"Why aren't you supposed to?" John asked.

"Mama . . . she says never to tell."

"Pierre," Charmaine offered, "maybe you've been dreaming."

"Oh no," he replied resolutely. "She wakes me up, and sometimes she visits me when I take my nap. She took me to her big room that day when that auntie spanked me . . . ."

Jeannette began to weep, her wounds reopened.

With an instinct born of love, Pierre crawled from his bed and cuddled next to her. "Don' cry, Jeannie. I sorry I made you cry."

Charmaine was at a loss and turned to John, but one look at his face—the pallor that rivaled the goose flesh that crawled up her neck—and she knew he'd be of little help. What was wrong with him? Men were supposed to be strong.

"He's obviously been dreaming," she reasoned with weak con-
viction.

Sometime later, she climbed back into bed, but Pierre's bizarre
story kept her awake, amplified by John's grave eyes staring at the
French doors, as if he fully expected the ghost of Colette Duvoisin
to float through them.

Saturday, September 2, 1837

Surprisingly, Charmaine awakened early the next morning, so
early in fact, she heard Paul descend the stairs at the crack of dawn.
Coming to an abrupt decision, she threw back the covers. She'd
breakfast with him. Perhaps he could make some sense of last night
and the fantastic chain of events that had shaken all of them. Unlike
John, Paul would prove sensible: laugh at her and then supply some
logical explanation.

As she dressed, she wondered if John had remained in the children's room the entire night. She crept to the connecting door and
gingerly opened it. All four occupants were sleeping soundly. Pierre
was cuddled in the crook of John's body, his back pressed against
John's chest. He clutched his elder brother's hand, a substitute for
the stuffed lamb, which had fallen to the floor again.

Charmaine was captivated, the similarities between man and
boy remarkable. Though Pierre's hair was a shade closer to his mother's, the cut of his face, the almond shaped eyes—Frederic's eyes—
were the same. Even in sleep, they worked beneath closed lids. So,
too, did John's, though the movement ended there. He was totally
relaxed, his face youthful. He was rather handsome now, his even
breathing stirring the fine locks atop Pierre's head. Her gaze roamed
further, to the two arms, juxtaposed, Pierre's creamy white against
its swarthy counterpart. Paradoxically, the limbs drew strength and
comfort from each other.

She closed the door, freezing when it creaked on swollen hinges.
It roused Pierre. He turned over, found John in his bed, and sat up.

Yawning, he leaned forward until his face was only an inch from his brother's and tried to pry open an eyelid. John turned onto his stomach and buried his face in the pillow. The three-year-old immediately straddled his back.

"Have mercy on me, Pierre," the man groaned as the boy began bouncing. "If I were a horse, I would have slept in the stable last night."

Charmaine stifled a giggle, watching as Pierre slipped to John's side and squeezed into the space between man and wall. To her surprise, he stuck a thumb in his mouth and closed his eyes. She shut the door and finished her toilette.

Paul sat alone at the table, sipping his coffee and reading a newspaper. When Charmaine stepped closer, his eyes slowly lifted, and a smile broke across his face. "This is an unexpected surprise. Why are you up so early?"

"I don't know," she fibbed, dissembling under his charismatic charm. "I guess I just couldn't sleep." *Stupid answer! Tell him the truth . . . that is why you came down here!*

"Well, then," he said, "your insomnia has become my good fortune."

He stood and helped her with her chair. She breathed deeply, intoxicated by his presence, the light scent of shaving lotion and cologne that lingered in the air. Impressions of last night's haunting receded.

Fatima broke the spell, bustling into the room to lay a plate before him, taking Charmaine's breakfast order as she poured two cups of coffee.

"I'm glad we have this quiet moment," he said. "I have a few things I need to discuss with you."

"Yes, so do I . . ."

Again he smiled, and she hesitated, waiting for him to speak first.

"I'll be leaving for Espoir on Monday," he continued.

"*Leaving?*"

The word erupted with childish fervor, yet he seemed pleased.

"Only for a week or two. I've neglected her for a while. But there are important matters that can't be postponed any longer."

"Two weeks?" she asked sullenly. The day had quickly turned dismal.

"The time will pass rapidly, and I'll be home before you know it. Why the glum face? This isn't about John, is it? He hasn't been troubling you, has he?"

"No, he's been unusually courteous this past week."

Paul scowled. "So I've noticed. What is the matter, then?"

She was about to tell him, but faltered. "It was nothing."

"Are you certain?"

"Yes, quite certain. I'll be fine while you're away. We'll all be fine."

He cocked his head to one side, his expression thoughtful while Fatima served Charmaine's food. "How are the children?" he asked.

"Lately, they've been very happy, especially with John entertaining them."

"John?" he queried, rankled by her use of his brother's Christian name, which fed his growing unease. *In that case, she is fair game. We shall see who is the better player.* "I don't like it," he objected. "He shouldn't be 'entertaining them.' He's a bad influence."

Not one week ago, Charmaine would have readily agreed, but John's conduct had been exemplary over the past few days.

"I will put a stop to it. I don't want him taking advantage of my absence."

"Put a stop to it?" she exclaimed. *Easier said than done!* John had gone from minding Pierre, to helping with the girls' lessons, to sleeping in the nursery with them. One look at Paul's face, and she prayed he'd not find out. "I don't see how you can possibly order your brother around," she reasoned. "He comes and goes as he pleases."

"I will speak to him. He shouldn't be interfering."

"But you can't do that!"

"Why not?" he asked, puzzled by her vehemence.

"What I mean is—that won't be necessary. There is no sense in stirring up a hornet's nest. He's been cordial to me of late, and the children enjoy his visits. Besides, if you tell him not to pester us, he is sure to do just that. I'm certain if we do nothing, he will tire of visiting the nursery all on his own."

Paul considered her comment. "You are likely right," he said, allowing her to breathe easier. "At any rate, Charmantes must be managed while I'm away. That should keep him occupied during the day. Even so, you should remain wary of him, Charmaine. I know him well, know how he operates, the little games he loves to play. He will use the children to toy with your affections. I'll not allow him to hurt you."

Charmaine was certain his gallantry was sincere, but she smiled halfheartedly, ate quickly, and left his company.

She had just reached her room when John stepped out of his own chambers, bleary-eyed. Clearly, he'd be glad to be back in his own bed tonight.

"Good morning . . . I think," he said, securing the last button at his collar. "Did you get any sleep last night?"

"I eventually drifted off, close to dawn. Are the children still asleep?"

"Surprisingly, no, but they appear well rested and are already begging to visit the stables to curry the foal. They are working on a surprise for you. We thought you were still asleep, and I suggested they not disturb you. So they're attempting to dress themselves, Pierre included, though I think his knickers might wind up on backward. When I left, he had a leg in the arm of his shirt, but refused help."

"I see," she replied with a chuckle.

"I'll take them down to breakfast if you'd like to rest for a while."

He shouldn't be interfering. Charmaine cringed. Paul might still be eating. "That won't be necessary," she replied a bit too adamantly, then quickly added, "but, thank you all the same."

"Is there a reason why I shouldn't take them down to breakfast?"

"No," she lied, not wishing to kindle *his* suspicions. Would she now be forced to effect a balancing act between Paul and John? She groaned inwardly. "I couldn't possibly impose on you again this early in the day. Of course you're welcome to join us. It is just that the children are my responsibility."

"Yes," he pondered aloud, but his knitted brow indicated doubt.

"He's so beautiful!" Jeannette exclaimed, petting the colt's sable coat.

"Not beautiful," Yvette countered, "handsome. Johnny, do you remember Rusty?"

"Yes," the man answered, throwing a saddle over Phantom's back. "Why?"

"Remember how you taught Jeannette and me how to ride him?"

"Mm-hmm."

"It's a shame he died, because we never go riding anymore. All the other horses are too big for us, and Mademoiselle Charmaine doesn't know how."

"So they are," John agreed, securing the saddle straps.

"If only there was another pony . . ."

"What are you hinting at, Yvette?" he asked, turning to study her. "Are you hoping I'll purchase one for you?"

"Oh, could you, Johnny?" she cried, her face transfused with excitement. "Two would be nice! One for me and one for Jeannette. *Please?"*

Jeannette's face mirrored her sister's, and John couldn't help but smile. "We'll see," he said, taking hold of Phantom's reins. "Now, step aside. I'm off to town. I have some business to take care of at the bank."

"Do you really have to go on Saturday and so early in the morning?"

"I'm hoping to inconvenience the clean Mr. Westphal into opening his bank before nine. If I time it just right, I may catch him in his nightgown and cap."

Jeannette and Yvette sniggered.

John had just reached the stable doors when Charmaine and Pierre appeared. She carried a letter she'd written to Gwendolyn Browning the day before and, realizing John was leaving for town, bravely asked him to post it.

"What is this?" he chuckled. "You'd entrust me with so *personal* an item?"

Instantly, she regretted her impulsive request. "I'm sorry I asked!"

"Just a minute," he laughed again. "There's no sense in storming over nothing. Let me have the letter. I'll see it gets to the mercantile intact."

Her eyes shot daggers at him, for he never missed an opportunity to bait her, but he was further entertained as he took the correspondence from her hand.

The morning wore on, and the children grew cranky. After lunch, Charmaine suggested a nap. Though Yvette objected, in five minutes, even she was sound asleep. Charmaine picked up the discarded vampire book and tiptoed from the room. She'd return it to the library and choose another for herself.

The study was occupied. John sat at the desk with his head buried in his hands, so deep in thought he was unaware of her presence.

"Sir?" she queried.

He came up immediately from his contemplation, but quickly

averted his gaze, wiping a forearm across his eyes. They appeared glassy, red even, undoubtedly the result of his restless night. She wondered whether the strange events were still on his mind.

"Sir, are you all right?"

"Sir?" he mimicked, finally looking at her. "I thought we'd dispensed with that formality last night. I prefer John."

"Very well," she replied guardedly, recalling Paul's warning.

"I returned from town two hours ago," he said, "but I've yet to see our resident ghost, Joseph Thornfield. Does he only come out at night?"

"Why do you want to see him?"

"I visited the bank on his behalf this morning, and I want to give him this account voucher before he complains I stole his money."

"A bank voucher?" Charmaine asked in astonishment. "Have you placed his dollar in the bank for him?"

His expression turned cross. "For safe keeping."

"Of course," she nodded, smiling buoyantly now.

"You think I'm being too lenient with the lad, don't you?"

"Oh, no, sir. I mean, John."

She was laughing at him, and he didn't like it. "Are you here for a reason, Miss Ryan?"

She considered the book she held and sobered. "I'm glad you were lenient with Joseph. Yvette is a different matter."

His frown deepened. "Yvette? Why?"

"You may think she's clever, but her escapades are getting out of hand. After her mother's death, I indulged her. Her precocity was preferable to lethargy, and her antics had a positive effect on Jeannette. They were smiling again. But lately, she's lost all sense of decorum."

John snorted. "I'd be more concerned about Jeannette."

"Jeannette?"

"Yes, Jeannette. She's far too good, far too kind. Unlike Yvette, who's learned to stand up for herself, who will never be manipulated, Jeannette is a sweet innocent who might easily be destroyed one day."

Charmaine's bewildered expression gave him pause; he hadn't meant to say so much. "Yvette was born into money," he quickly added. "She is playing the part of a little rich girl."

The final remark chafed Charmaine. "A *spoiled* little rich girl," she corrected defensively. "Her mother would not approve. Colette demanded good manners of all three children, grace and charity taking precedence over wealth. Yvette respected that, responded to her mildest of reprimands."

John's eyes turned dark. "Each to his own opinion, Miss Ryan. But I hold it is wiser to be bold than meek."

Monday, September 4, 1837

John sat slumped in one of the study's large leather chairs and fiddled with one of Pierre's blocks, lacing it through his lean fingers, waiting for Paul, who held his position behind the huge secretary, to finish speaking. His brother had requested this meeting last night, but John had brushed it off until the morning, saying he was too tired and would be up before seven. Thus he sat, the early riser, if not the serious businessman Paul expected him to be.

"That is the state of our financial affairs. Any comments?" Paul looked up from his ledger, instantly losing his patience. "What are you snickering at now?"

"You, Paulie. You take this all so seriously."

"You're damned right I do—"

"I don't know where Father and I would be without you," John interrupted blithely. "In the militia, perhaps."

"You sit there and laugh, but this is not some trivial game to be scoffed at. You're in for a rude awakening someday. By then, it may be too late. Don't come crying to me when you find a fortune has slipped through your fingers."

"Whose fortune, Paul? Father's or mine?"

"You know when Father dies it's all yours."

"The only fortune I'm worried about is mine, the one I acquired on my own."

"On your own?" Paul scoffed. "Beyond your salary, I think you're overlooking all the other conveniences Father's shipping, plantation, and good name have afforded you in making your *own* fortune."

"I'd have been a fool not to take advantage of them," John replied in kind, "but Father's enterprises benefit from my charity as well."

"Charity?"

"Let's start with the staples I ship to the island on a regular basis at no charge: feed, flour, corn, tobacco—"

"Grown on Duvoisin land, John, land that has belonged to the family for three generations—"

"And farmed by workers whom I pay out of my own pocket. I haven't been reimbursed for that."

"That is your own folly!" Paul bit back. "You weren't forced to free your slaves. The land could be farmed for a pittance of what you pay your tenants!"

"Yes, Paul, my folly and my conscience."

"Conscience?" Paul snorted in derision. "Since when has conscience concerned you? They're only slaves."

"Yes, Paul, they're only slaves. And Cookie is only our cook, and Buck only your foreman. You've never been to a slave auction. If you had, you'd be revolted, and you certainly wouldn't abide such degradation, free labor or no."

Paul exhaled. The argument was moot. He'd learned long ago, starting with Colette: the abolitionist could never be persuaded to think logically.

"Never mind, John. I've not called this meeting to debate with you. Obviously, we view things differently. You, of course, know that and have led me far from the point."

"I didn't know there was a point to all this rambling."

Paul ignored the remark. "The island is short of supplies. For all your so-called *charity,* we haven't received a shipment of staples for months now."

"You must be mistaken. Before I left for New York, I left instructions at the Richmond warehouse that your last order be shipped no later than mid-April. I couldn't have spelled it more clearly—"

"Well, no such packet arrived."

"—if I had drawn a picture for them."

Paul's eyes narrowed. "Don't tell me that was the vessel with the missing invoices!"

"Missing invoices? I don't handle the paperwork."

"No—you only draw on it!"

John chuckled. "Now, Paul, don't lose your temper over a harmless joke—"

"*A harmless joke?* Is that what you call it?"

"When did you lose your sense of humor, Paul? You're no fun anymore. Anyway, you received the supplies, so why the scolding?"

"Because, dear brother," Paul snarled between clenched teeth, "I sent the vessel back to you!"

"Back to me? In God's name, why?"

"It was your confounded mess. I don't pay my crews to dig through holds, break open casks, and take inventories!"

"What are you talking about?"

"The ship arrived here, all right, via Liverpool, with a cargo for Richmond. Your incompetent captain insisted that—under your orders—he stacked our supplies at the very back of the hold, instead of off to one side. Once he took on the European wares, our casks were buried!"

"I don't give loading instructions," John replied. "Stuart does, and he knows what he's doing, so the mix-up must have occurred in Britain."

The response was sincere, and Paul surmised the new captain had been pressed to weigh anchor and leave port, so to save time he'd cut corners and ordered the European goods loaded haphazardly.

"The British invoices were legitimate," John continued, scratching the back of his head, "and the casks for the island were marked with the Duvoisin crest. So between the European invoices, your original order, and the crest on the barrels, how difficult could it have been to locate your cargo?" John's deep chuckle erupted into a hearty guffaw. "And you sent it all back!"

"It isn't funny, John!"

"Yes, it is!" he averred, wiping a tear from his eye. "Tell me, Paul, were you wearing trousers or a skirt the day you made that decision?"

Paul's face blackened. "Laugh all you like, John, but you couldn't have been happy when the ship returned to Richmond. In the end, it was your loss."

"What loss? I wasn't in Virginia to receive the ship. I was in New York."

"Jesus Christ!" Paul exploded. "Do you realize what that means?"

"Yes," John snickered, "either the cargo is sitting in my warehouse losing market value—which doesn't affect me, since I wasn't selling it, anyway—or, Stuart figured you didn't need it, and put it up for auction. That brings in money I hadn't counted on. If I were you, Paul, I'd pray it's stored in the warehouse, but I wouldn't bank on it."

"Damn it, John, your bright idea for these new shipping routes is just not working! Now, you're going to set this matter right before the day is out!"

"And how do you suggest I do that?"

"You are going to write to Edward Richecourt and have him arrange another shipment of the staples we need, straightaway. No stops in New York or Baltimore, no stops in Europe. It's leaving Richmond and coming here directly, within the month, with accurate invoices. And from now on, I want a dedicated packet running a Charmantes to U.S. circuit at least once a month."

"*Edward Richecourt?* That stiff ass wouldn't know the first thing about handling this," John replied. "I'll take care of it my own way. But since I'll have to pull a ship off its normal route, I'm going to charge all the associated expenses to the island's account, not mine. And if you want a dedicated bark running half-empty between here and the States, weighted down with blocks my crew will have to load and unload for ballast, why not use one of *your* new ships? That way the family business can benefit from your charity, too."

"Just be about it, John. I'll see to it you're paid."

John stood to leave, but Paul stopped him. "I'm not finished yet."

"No? What more could you possibly have to say?"

Paul ignored the gibe. "I'd appreciate your help while I'm on Espoir, looking in on operations, especially the tobacco. We're new at it."

"Why in the hell did you plant that?" his brother continued in the same vein.

"I don't know. Now that I've seen all the additional work it has caused me, I wish I'd gone with cocoa instead. But that's neither here nor there. Harold, Wade, and George handle day-to-day production well enough, but Charmantes requires capable— practiced—hands. Things always run smoother when I'm around."

"Then can you really afford to place her in my *incapable* hands?"

"I never said you were incapable, John, just bent on irritating me. You have more authority than George if a crisis erupts, which always seems to happen when I'm away."

"Don't worry, Charmantes will be shipshape when you return."

"Good," Paul nodded, feeling at ease for the first time that morning.

Then he remembered something else. Despite Charmaine's request he leave well enough alone, he forged forward. "There's one more thing, John. I'd like to talk to you about the children."

John's expression turned stern. "What of them?"

"I don't want you annoying them."

"Annoying them?"

"You know what I mean, distracting them from their lessons, seeking them out in the afternoon, playing nursemaid."

"I didn't realize you had such a sharp eye," John replied curtly, "especially when you're away from the house all day. So how *would* you know what's going on? Unless, of course, you have an informant."

"I have no informant. I see for myself what's happening. You know Father wouldn't approve. He doesn't want you around them."

"Approve?" John queried derisively. "I don't give a damn what he wants, and I certainly don't care if he approves. I will seek out the children whenever and wherever I like, and you can tell him that."

"Damn it, John! When will you desist from this need to hurt him?"

"*Hurt him?* What about me? There was a time when you were sympathetic to me." Disgusted, he added, "Just remember, Paul, he started it all."

"And he's paid."

"Has he? Well, then, so have I."

Chapter 3

Sunday, September 10, 1837

An hour before Sunday Mass, Yvette announced she was not going. "The benches are too hard, and Father Benito talks gibberish. If Johnny doesn't go, why should I?" Charmaine had reasoned, cajoled, and threatened to take the matter to Frederic—all to no avail.

John! She simmered. *This is all his doing!* He hadn't set foot in the mansion's chapel since he'd arrived. Plainly, Yvette was utilizing Paul's absence to pit her governess's authority against John's. *Well,* Charmaine fumed as she headed toward Frederic's chambers, *we'll just see about that!*

She didn't get far. Agatha emerged from the south wing corridor, blocking her path. Few words had passed between them since Pierre's spanking, and Charmaine wasn't about to strike up a conversation now. With a cursory nod, she changed direction and scooted down the stairs.

As her initial fury ebbed, common sense took hold. To whom could she turn to convince the headstrong eight-year-old attending Mass was essential for her moral welfare? Rose? Possibly. John? She almost laughed aloud at the thought; he was the root of the problem.

Still, he didn't know a thing about it. Perhaps if he did, he'd accompany them to the chapel, and Yvette would abandon her protests. Hadn't he lent a hand before?

She found him in the dining room, alone, eating a large breakfast, even though the rest of the household observed the Church's decree of a strict fast before Communion. She had seen less of him this week. With Paul gone, he'd assumed the reins of responsibility. Nevertheless, he had managed to spend time with the children before he left the house or directly after dinner. It was becoming less difficult to speak to him. Even so, she stepped forward gingerly.

"Excuse me, sir."

John's eyes left his newspaper. "Miss Ryan," he returned, irritated by her persistent formality. "Is there something I can do for you?"

"Yes, there is," she jumped in, mustering a radiant smile.

She was rewarded for her efforts, for he smiled in return, apparently disarmed by her ebullience, and she braced herself for a suggestive remark.

"What would that be?" he asked instead.

"I'd like to invite you to attend Mass with us this morning," she said, carefully choosing her words. "I know the children would enjoy your company."

His smile vanished. Still, he hadn't refused.

She took courage and pressed on, hoping to fan his enthusiasm again. "And then there's Pierre. He can be quite fidgety in church, but I thought if you were there—well, you're so good with him and—"

"Really?" he interrupted, fixing steely eyes upon her. "You know, Miss Ryan, your tactics are duplicitous, yet rather transparent. You play the helpless heroine to a fault, seeking out my aid when it suits you, then complain to my brother afterward."

"I'm afraid I don't understand."

"Don't you? Well, no matter."

The seconds gathered into an uncomfortable silence.

"Was there something else, Miss Ryan?"

"Something else?"

"Yes. I'd like to return to my meal."

Dumbfounded, she dropped her hands to her sides and blurted out, "Won't you even consider accompanying us to the family service?"

"Miss Ryan," he replied slowly, "as a boy, I heard enough of Father Benito's fire-and-brimstone sermons to last me well into eternity. I had no choice then. I do now and have no intention of suffering through even one more. I need no pretentious priest to measure my pain. I do that well enough on my own. Does that answer your question?"

"Surely you can't mean that!"

"Haven't you learned by now I always mean what I say? Apparently not. So, let me spell it out for you: I will not accompany you or the children to Mass. Not today, nor next week—not ever."

"But you must!" she objected, anger eclipsing her dismay. This man was wreaking havoc in the household with his heathen ways, and it was time someone told him so. "You may not care a farthing about your own soul, but it is unforgivable you've neglected the children's!"

Bemused now, his brow arched. "What have they to do with it?"

"Everything and more! You ought to consider the effect your bad example has on them. What do you think crosses their impressionable minds when week after week, they see you reject God by refusing to partake of His son's holy celebration? How do you propose I explain it to them?"

"So," he scoffed, "this has nothing to do with an invitation to join you after all. And here I thought you worried over my sooted soul."

"Have no fear about that!" she rejoined pointedly. "I'd be a fool to think I could ever sway the likes of you!"

"A very Christian attitude," he replied mordantly.

"How dare you mock my values?"

"Your values, my dear, are not, by my estimation, worth holding."

"Oh, you—you—"

"Scoundrel? Infidel?" he offered. "No, I think *demon* would be more to your liking."

"Yes, demon is perfect!" she exclaimed furiously, but instantly repented the words. "I'm sorry. I didn't come here to call names."

"No? A lecture in morality then?" he pressed, annoyed she felt at liberty to confront him this way. Wasn't *she* the hired help and *he* the family? When she refused to answer, he continued. "Miss Ryan, let me clear something up right now. I don't take kindly to people—especially righteous women—who nurture a bit of good will with me and then assume I can be manipulated into doing their bidding. For the moment, I'd like to think you and I have come to a truce of sorts; however, I guarantee I will put an end to that truce within the hour if you persist in attempting to bend me to your will."

His deadly tone left no doubt she had pushed him too far. Even so, she felt unjustly accused. She had approached the situation from the wrong angle and had to find a way to salvage her self-respect and regain the ground of civility they had cultivated over the past fortnight. "Sir, that was not my intention."

"Then what is this all about?"

"I've told you—the children, specifically Yvette. She refuses to attend Mass because, as she puts it, 'If Johnny doesn't go, why should I?' I thought if you accompanied us, she would forsake this stubborn nonsense."

He did not immediately respond, though Charmaine could tell a barrage of retorts raced through his quick mind. When he did speak, she was aghast.

"Leave her behind with me, then. The Mass is, after all, a ritual for which the soul is supposed to yearn, is it not?" Sarcasm laced his query. "If Father Benito's preaching leaves her empty, what is the point in forcing her?"

"*The point?* The point is we are speaking of a child's soul, a soul that will not reach its Maker if it does not partake of the sacred ceremony you ridicule! I cannot believe you're suggesting she is old enough to decide this for herself!"

He remained calm in the face of her resurrected rage. "And what need does an innocent eight-year-old have of that damned doctrine? Perhaps your comprehension would not be so limited, so obtuse, if you answered that question without prejudice, Miss Ryan. What terrible sin has she committed, is capable of committing, that would damn her to your godforsaken hell for all eternity? What morality need she learn that her own family cannot teach her?"

"What morality, indeed!" she rejoined contemptuously. "If her mother were still alive, I might agree with you. But even the mistress Colette did not limit her Christian example to good deeds alone. She marched the children to the chapel each and every Sunday. Can't you see? It is what *she* wanted."

"By God, woman!" he exploded, slamming a fist into the table. "What makes you think I give a *damn* about what the mistress Colette wanted?"

"Because—" Charmaine stammered, wide-eyed and trembling "—because she was a kind and decent woman who lived her faith, a faith she wanted her children to embrace." Foolishly, inexplicably, she babbled on, even though her mind screamed: *flee.* "Besides, she was your father's wife and mother to your siblings. Surely, as such, you should respect her wishes!"

"Miss Ryan," he snarled, "the mistress Colette was a very different woman than the one you have painted, and my feelings toward her were far from noble. She should *never* have become 'Mrs. Frederic Duvoisin.' In fact, I approved of her less in that role than I do the third Mrs. Duvoisin. So keep your angelic apparitions to yourself. I cannot stomach such a large dose of piety and virtue this early in the day!"

With his last words, Charmaine did indeed flee, her dignity in tatters.

Colette, dear sweet Colette! How could the man degrade her so? Charmaine couldn't understand it! Paul's assertions echoed in her ears: *Even Colette, as good and kind as she tried to be to him, suffered at his hands.* It was true! True! How could she have allowed her guard to slip these past weeks? How could she have thought there was anything more to the man than her initial impression of turpitude? What a fool she had been! Paul had warned her, and still, she had discounted his wise judgment and allowed John to ingratiate himself to the children. No wonder Paul was wary! John *was* depraved! Thank God she had seen him for what he was before it was too late!

Yvette faltered when she entered the nursery. "Did you speak with Father?"

"No, I did not. I spoke to your brother instead."

"Johnny?"

"I'd hoped he'd reason with you, but he refused. In fact, he scorned your mother's beliefs. What a shame you've chosen his bitterness over her goodness."

Jeannette stood from her bed. "Yvette is hurting Mama by not going to Mass, isn't she, Mademoiselle?"

"Yes, I'm afraid she is," Charmaine whispered.

"See, Yvette, I told you so. You mustn't hurt Mama anymore. She won't rest in peace unless she's pleased with everything we do."

Rose walked in. "What is this?" she asked, taking in their somber faces. "I've seen happier people at a funeral."

It was too much; Jeannette erupted into tears, and Yvette's frown deepened.

"Whatever is the matter?" Rose clucked. "There now, child, don't cry."

"Yvette won't go to Mass!" she sobbed. "She doesn't care Mama—"

"I didn't say that!" Yvette countered. "And I've changed my mind. I'll go, Jeannette—only please stop crying!"

The night was black. An open carriage swayed as it gained momentum. The dark, dusty road was barely negotiable, treacherous to the inexperienced hand, and fear suddenly gripped the driver. She pulled back on the reins and the horse shied and whinnied, then slowed to a steady prance. Although the buggy's lamp would help illuminate the way, it was wiser to leave it unlit. The deserted road leveled off, and a dim light appeared through the trees off to the right. The driver yanked on the reins, and the horse all but stopped. Locating the turn, the animal proceeded gingerly, and the conveyance moved toward the beacon, squeaking to a halt before a solitary structure nestled in the dark forest. Still, the real journey had yet to begin, and she steeled herself against the impending trial, descending the coupe, her black skirts cascading to her ankles as she reached the ground. Although she stepped stealthily, gravel crunched underfoot, signaling her trek. As she mounted the steps, the door cracked open.

"You are late," a deep voice accused from within. "Six hours late."

She crossed the threshold, and the door closed behind her. With an air of indifference, she ripped off her gloves, pushed back the hood of her cloak, and faced the enemy. "I told you I would come, and I have."

She was angry. He could see it in her set jaw and piercing eyes, but she was worried too, her discomfiture poorly concealed beneath a mask of cool contempt.

"You seem to believe you can keep me waiting," he stated coldly, "and I have never tolerated waiting for anyone, least of all the likes of you."

"How dare you—"

"Mrs. Duvoisin," he admonished, irritated by her outrage. "Don't play games with me. You are here for an unseemly reason, one that you hope will go away if you just ignore it, a supposition you thought to test by arriving late today. So let me spell it out for you. I never forget, and I am not a tolerant man. Next time, don't be tardy, or my patience will reach its limit before the first hour has passed."

"Next time? I assure you, there will be no next time," she hissed. "You are mad if you think this will continue!"

"On the contrary. Not only will you continue to pay me, but as of today, my silence costs twice as much."

"You have been paid enough already!"

"If that were the case, you would not be here tonight, would you?" He paused, letting his remark sink in. "Let me decide when I have been paid enough. Even at double the price, my fee is not at all unreasonable for the wife of Frederic Duvoisin. After all, look at the heights you have scaled thus far. And isn't that what this is all about—how you've benefited from plotting and planning? So why not share the wealth with someone who understands you?"

"I've no idea what you are talking about!"

"No? Your husband might be interested in learning of the duplicitous life you've been leading. And then there's a theory I've been toying with. Frederic might find a visit from me most . . . 'revealing,' shall I say?"

"There are ways to deal with you!"

His eyes turned evil. "Do you take me for a fool, Madame? I hope not. Because if you try to get rid of me, the truth *will* come out."

He watched her fear deepen and nodded. "Yes, I have taken precautionary measures. Now, let me relieve you of this."

He stepped forward and slipped the reticule from her fingers. Loosening the cinches, he fingered the cold cash within. Satisfied, he pulled the strings closed. "Very good. Very good indeed. From today forward, we will meet every other Saturday at three o'clock sharp. I do so enjoy your visits. Goodnight, Mrs. Duvoisin."

"Saturday? Why Saturday?"

"Surely you can see the wisdom of a Saturday rendezvous. If you fail to keep that appointment, I can kill two birds with one stone come Sunday morning." He chuckled wickedly, pleased with his pun. "At any rate, I doubt your husband will be pleased to see me. Our last private meeting was disastrous enough. Another could prove fatal." His keen eyes rested pointedly on her, and for the moment, she ceded defeat.

Monday, September 18, 1837

The children were asleep, and Charmaine climbed into bed, exhausted. Last week had been difficult, and this one was off to a bad start. It had rained every day, and they had been housebound. To make matters worse, John hadn't come near them, his absence feeding the children's boredom and restlessness. Of course, they begged for his company, but he used Paul's trip to Espoir as an excuse: he was busy with work, a justification that acquitted him while branding Paul the despot. Nevertheless, Charmaine hid behind the same white lie when they complained to her, and wondered what fib she would use when Paul returned. She didn't have to worry about that yet. Paul had sent word he'd be detained on Espoir a week longer. If the rain persisted, it meant another seven days cooped up in the house, another week that would consume John's time. She suspected he was avoiding them out of spite to prove some enigmatic point. For all his preoccupation with "work," she was certain those responsibilities wouldn't have prevented him from setting time aside for the children if he had been so inclined.

Once John passes judgment on somebody, he rarely changes it. Obviously, his unfavorable opinion of her hadn't changed, despite his conciliatory comportment in the days leading up to last Sunday.

What had he called it? A truce? A truce was a suspension of fighting between enemies. So, John still viewed her as an enemy. But why should that matter to her, anyway?

She'd considered forgiving his unholy remarks—words spawned in the heat of the argument—but abandoned that idea yesterday when they crossed paths with him on their way to the chapel. "So, Miss Ryan," he'd observed wryly, his eyes on Yvette, "I see you have risen from the battle victorious." It was too much! She seethed throughout Mass. The man was incorrigible, no, worse, barbaric, without principle, unable to communicate on a level shared by the whole of civil society. He didn't deserve her clemency.

Still, he.dominated her thoughts, and her mind lingered on something Millie Thornfield had said earlier when she had drawn her bath. "My Mum likes him. She claims that any man who loves children the way Master John loves his sisters and brother has to have a kind heart." Charmaine wondered. Was his affection for the children genuine, or were his motives perfidious? Did he cultivate the work of the angels or of the devil? She fluffed her pillow, resolved to travel the path of caution.

Thursday, September 21, 1837

Pierre trained his weary legs on the portico steps, teetering when he reached the summit. He hardly appeared the youngest lord of the island, rather a guttersnipe without family or home: his face smudged black, his fine clothes soiled, and his shoes muddied beyond repair. Yet, he drew a triumphant breath and trudged along the wide colonnade, dragging a fishing pole twice his height behind him.

The day turned black. Suddenly, the sky ripped apart, sending torrents of rain soaring toward the anxious earth. Certain her worst possible fears had come to fruition, Charmaine recommenced her pacing. A commotion in the foyer drew her out of the drawing room.

"Oh, Miss Ryan," Travis Thornfield lamented as he ushered the little ragamuffin toward her, "look what the wind has blown in! I'm afraid he is in dire need of your tender care."

"I'll see to him immediately," she replied, her eyes never leaving Pierre. She was shaking all over, a palpitating surge of relief that surpassed her receding distress. "And just where have you been, young man? Do you know how upset I've been?" The boy's eyes welled with tears. "Oh, Pierre!" she sobbed, instantly regretting the trenchant reprimand and hugging him close, unmindful of his soggy state or that his clothes reeked of dead fish. "I should spank you for frightening me so." She did not notice John, who towered over her.

"If you must scold somebody, Miss Ryan, it ought to be me."

She straightened up. "How dare you take him away without my knowledge?"

"Miss Ryan," John attempted to placate, appreciating her concern, if not the tone of voice, "didn't Rose tell you he was in safe hands?"

"Yes, she told me!" Charmaine snapped. "But you had no right to take him anywhere without my permission!"

"Permission?"

"Yes, permission! The boy is my responsibility, not yours! He was out of my care the entire day. God only knows what harm could have befallen him!"

"Miss Ryan," John snarled with set jaw. "I am not a pestiferous beast. I have feelings just like you, I am capable of—" He shook his head and forced himself calm. "I apologize for your distress, but I didn't think you would worry over Pierre's welfare."

"Then why did you go behind my back to abduct him?"

"I didn't abduct him," John answered in exasperation. "I went to Rose in the hopes of avoiding the nasty dispute we're having now."

"And how would I have explained Pierre's whereabouts if your father had visited the nursery today?" Charmaine retaliated. "I'm certain he would be displeased with my lax guardianship—that someone was able to take his son from the house without my knowledge."

John clenched his fists, and it was a moment before he trusted his response. "He didn't 'visit the nursery,' did he?" When Charmaine held silent, he relaxed. "I hope you've learned a lesson today. Maybe now you will admit I can be trusted with the children. For all of your worry—fed undoubtedly by my brother—I have returned Pierre safely. Yes, he's filthy, but happy. At least he was until you dampened his gaiety." John looked down at the boy, who stood mute at Charmaine's side, eyes wide as saucers.

"Don' be angwee, Mainie," Pierre sniffled. "Johnny took me fishin'. We had fun. We didn't do nothin' bad."

His beseeching voice mollified her. "I'm not angry with you, Pierre," she whispered, clasping his hand and throwing John one last meaningful glare as she turned toward the stairs.

Pierre pulled away. "I don' wanna go to the nulswee. I wanna see my fishes."

"Your fish?" Charmaine asked, noticing for the first time the discarded fishing pole and the repugnant odor.

"Yes, my fishes I caught in my fishin' boat," he explained.

"Your fishing boat?" Charmaine looked to John, who was smiling now.

"Johnny bought it for my birfday, and we went fishin' today."

"How very generous," she replied tightly. "Only it's not your birthday."

"I know," Pierre agreed, "but the boat didn't, so we be-tended it was."

Charmaine read the approving twinkle in John's eyes, then Pierre's pure joy. His innocent charm vanquished her ire. "And where are these fish you caught?"

"Right here," John said, dangling a variety of dead specimens from a hook.

"I wanna put 'em in some water and see 'em swim," Pierre insisted.

"Oh no," John chuckled, holding them out of the boy's reach. "We're giving these to Cookie so she can fix them for dinner."

"You mean eat 'em?" Pierre asked apprehensively. "I don' wanna eat 'em. I wanna see 'em swim."

"But they can't—" John began, and then "—come with me."

Minutes later, they were in the kitchen, staring into the large tub of water John had placed on the wooden table. Pierre poked a finger at one of the floating fish, perturbed when it did not dart away like the others in the lake.

"Why ain't he swimmin'?" Pierre asked.

"Why *isn't* he swimming," John corrected.

"Why isn't he swimmin'?" Pierre repeated, his eyes fixed on John.

"Because he's dead," John replied levelly.

"Did it hurt?"

"I don't think so. Anyway, he's mighty happy to know he's going to be a delicacy dinner tonight, cooked by the world's greatest chef—"

"Oh go on with ya, Master John," Fatima exclaimed bashfully.

"—and devoured by the likes of George, a man renowned for his discriminating taste in fine cuisine—and anything else that's edible."

As if on cue, George stepped into the kitchen, eliciting Pierre's giggle. "What is he laughing at?" George asked, looking from a smiling Charmaine, to an embarrassed Fatima, and a mischievous John.

"Dead fish, George," his friend answered. "Only some dead fish."

Sunday, September 24, 1837

When Frederic appeared at the nursery door at noon, Charmaine wondered if the outing she had planned would be spoiled. But he only nodded when the girls told him they were going into town for the remainder of the day.

"I'll only visit with you for a short while," he said.

Charmaine retreated to her room, allowing them some private time together.

John had slept late and it was early afternoon when he left his chambers. Assuming the children would be in the nursery, he headed there, but as he lifted his fist to knock on their door, his father's voice stopped him. He quickly lost his desire to see them and changed course. Lunch . . .

He was halfway down the stairs when he noticed the tall stranger standing in the foyer. Though dressed in Sunday attire, his clothes were threadbare. Yet, his stance was confident, arrogant even, as he studied the portrait of Colette. John bristled at his perusal, the seeming right he had of being there.

"Excuse me," John called gruffly, continuing his descent. "Can I help you?"

The stranger tore his gaze from the painting and focused on him. "Yes."

The dark eyes grew intense, so much so John was confounded. "Are you John?"

"I am. And who might you be?"

"Wade Remmen," he replied casually, extending a hand in greeting.

John stepped forward to take it. "Ah yes, the illustrious Mr. Remmen," he derided. "I've heard a great deal about you."

"And I you," Wade returned, "more than you could ever imagine."

John's brow raised, intrigued. *Very self-assured,* he thought. *No wonder Paul has placed him in charge.* "What can I do for you, Mr. Remmen?"

Wade looked down at the papers he held in his other hand. He passed them to John. "Your brother told me you'd be taking over while he's on Espoir. I expected him back by now, but, as you know, he's been detained. These are for him. It's a tally of the wood delivered into town over the past two weeks as well as the shipments sent to Espoir."

John scarcely glanced at the invoices. "I'll see he gets them."

"Actually, I'm to deliver them back to the warehouse with a signature. If you could look them over now, I'd appreciate it."

"Mr. Remmen, today is the Sabbath. I always honor the Sabbath."

Wade frowned momentarily. "Very well. If you could possibly get them to me at the mill tomorrow, I'll take them into town after I've finished work."

"I'll do better than that," John said. "I'll deliver them to the warehouse tomorrow morning. How would that be?"

"That would be fine."

John saw Wade to the door, then stared down at the documents. Inspired, he took the steps two at a time and, without knocking, entered the nursery. He found Jeannette on his father's lap, Pierre playing at his feet, and Yvette reading a story to them. Charmaine was nowhere to be seen.

Frederic looked up in surprise as Yvette greeted him with, "What are you doing here? Joseph said you were still sleeping."

"I have something for Father," he answered curtly, stepping into the room and depositing the invoices on the desk nearest the man. "Wade Remmen delivered these. They need to be signed by tomorrow morning."

"Wade?" Jeannette queried excitedly. "Is he still here?"

"He just left."

She jumped from her father's lap and scurried across the room.

"What is this?" her father called after her, but she paid him no mind as she raced out onto the balcony in the hopes of catching a glimpse of the man who had caught her fancy.

Yvette rolled her eyes. "She's in love."

Frederic chuckled. "Is she now? With Mr. Remmen?"

"All because Mama told her how very handsome he is."

Frederic's eyes turned black.

"What is the matter, Papa?" Yvette asked.

"Nothing," he bit out.

John was just at puzzled, but he quickly discounted his father's strange reaction when it looked as if the man were about to speak to him. A second later, he was out the door, ignoring his sister's calls for him to stay.

"Will there be something else, Miss Ryan?"

"No . . ." Charmaine hesitated, stroking the more expensive bolts of yard goods. As Maddy Thompson returned them to the shelves, Charmaine bit her bottom lip. "On second thought, I *will* take the paisley taffeta and blue muslin."

"It will raise the amount of your purchase considerably."

"Yes, I know," Charmaine murmured.

A short while later, she stepped out of the mercantile, package in hand. Though she was light of coin, she did not regret her extravagance. The twins' birthday was only four days away, the first without their mother. Charmaine intended to make it the happiest of occasions, much as they had hers only nine months ago. The unexpected memory evoked an untenable sense of loss and loneliness. She missed Colette and sighed deeply, hoping to shake off the melancholy. She thought of the girls again. She'd spend the next few evenings sewing, a labor of love made possible by the wages she had saved.

She squinted against the bright sun and headed toward the livery. George was where she'd left him, on the boardwalk, amusing

Pierre, who sat on his lap, and the girls, who were climbing on the casks beside him. Clutching her parcel, she picked her way past buckboards and carriages and the strolling townspeople.

"Get everything you needed?" he asked when she reached them.

"Yes, and thank you for minding the children."

"I was happy to do it," he replied, standing to lift Pierre into his arms. "And a good thing, too, the mercantile is open on Sundays," he finished.

Charmaine reserved comment, having refused to shop on the Sabbath on more than one occasion, doing so only today because he had offered his nursemaid services. It had been an ongoing dispute—*Keep Holy the Lord's Day.* Charmaine embraced the Third Commandment and stood as the exception among the churchgoing islanders who, every Sunday, directly after noon Mass, discounted Father Benito's vehement threat of eternal damnation and patronized the many businesses that opened their doors.

"Would you like me to drive you back to the house?" George asked. "Or would you prefer to visit Stephen Westphal?"

His teasing induced a frown and then a giggle. "We had better head home, or we will be late for dinner."

"Not yet," Yvette protested. "We've been waiting to see Gummy."

"Who?"

"Gummy Hoffstreicher," the girl reiterated. "You remember—the boy who stole sandwiches from Johnny and George. He comes past here every day."

"Yvette, he's just a man," Charmaine reasoned. "There will be other chances to meet him, and when you do, I hope you remember he is a human being, and should be treated as such, no matter what stories you've heard."

Yvette rolled her eyes, prompting George to intercede. "Charmaine, I'm sorry. We were just jesting a bit."

"I know, George, and I don't hold *you* responsible—"

She was interrupted by shouts from the dock and the push of bodies gravitating to the wharf. "What is it?"

"A ship must be arriving," he replied, shielding his eyes to look.

Charmaine did the same, concentrating on a smudge of white passing into the cove. They, too, pressed nearer the quay.

"Can you see it?" Yvette asked excitedly, tugging on George's shirt. "Where's it coming from? Can you tell by the mast? Is it flying our flag?"

"Yes," George replied. "It must be the *Gemini*. The *Raven* isn't due in port until next week. Paul will most likely be aboard."

"Wonderful," Yvette mumbled in sudden disgust.

The girl's reaction did not dampen Charmaine's soaring spirits as she peered longingly at the white masts that were steadily growing larger. Finally, everything would be right again.

Not ten minutes later, the creaking vessel thumped against the dock. With admiration, Charmaine watched Paul command her crew, throwing himself into the mooring, much like the day she'd arrived on the *Raven*, one year ago. He was even more handsome now, the finest figure of a man she had ever beheld, and her quickening pulse forced her to look away.

Paul donned his discarded shirt and left the sailors and longshoreman to finish up. As he descended the planking, he noticed the welcoming party, Charmaine in particular, a bit of loveliness he hadn't expected to see until he got home and a painful reminder of his lack of female companionship for the past three weeks. When he reached them, their eyes locked. *Is that lust in her gaze?* It ignited his passion. As if perceiving his need, she averted her face. He focused on George, determined to quell his rutting instincts.

"Good afternoon, weary traveler," that one greeted jovially, "and how is the work coming along on Espoir?"

"Quite well, and what a nice greeting this is," Paul returned, putting an arm around Jeannette, his eyes traveling to Charmaine again. "Charmaine, you are looking lovely."

"So are you," she blundered. "I mean—you are looking well."

The girls laughed, bolstering the deep blush that rose to her cheeks.

"I *am* well," he replied, "though I'm looking forward to Fatima's cooking. I won't even tell you what the men prepared at the camps. Some of it wasn't fit for consumption. I'm glad to be back. Espoir doesn't have the feel of home."

"One day it will," George replied, "just give it a little time."

"I suppose so," Paul concurred. "Have you missed me, Pierre?" he asked, gesturing for George to hand the boy over.

"Uh-huh. But I wanna go home. I'm hungwee."

"So am I!" Paul agreed, holding Pierre high in his arms. "Home it shall be."

George ran ahead to the livery, leaving Paul, Charmaine, and the children to walk slowly down the boardwalk. "Well, then," Paul mused, "you'll have to tell me everything that's happened while I was away." His words were directed at the children, though his eyes remained trained on their pretty governess.

Frederic paced his chambers for the remainder of the afternoon and well into the evening, his quandary mounting in the dark. So, Wade Remmen had been Colette's lover. Or had he? Should he bring the man in and question him? He snorted at the thought. The young man would admit nothing. Nevertheless, Frederic knew he would be able to read the truth in Wade Remmen's eyes. And then what? What could he do? What should he do? And what of his children? Did he want his children to know? They would certainly find out if he pursued it. They loved their mother, thought of her as an angel. Sadly, he realized he still loved her; even in her infidelity, he still loved her. Paul was right: Colette *was* good and kind. If she had taken another lover, it was because of him and his deplorable disposition. He was through blaming her for every miserable thing that had befallen him, and he refused to torture his children with assertions about her unfaithfulness. Let them hold on to their precious memories. Colette was dead and buried, and this nasty affair would be as well. Reaching that resolution, he stretched out on his empty bed and slept.

Charmaine had intended to sew tonight, but after three aborted attempts, she set the fabric aside. Her mind was not on the task. It ran rampant with images of Paul and the overwhelming feelings his arrival home had incited, foreign desires that tingled her fingertips one moment and drained her limbs the next, leaving her strangely agitated. She recalled the indescribable look he had leveled upon her at the harbor, the rush of blood that had left her lightheaded. Even now, she shuddered in wanton yearning. Dear God, what was wrong with her?

It had been difficult to converse with him for the remainder of the day. She was grateful when he, John, and George retired to the library after dinner, and she and the children were able to slip upstairs unnoticed. Thankfully, they crawled into their beds without so much as an argument and fell asleep earlier than usual.

Right now, she longed for a walk in the gardens, but quickly dismissed that idea. Though it might help clear her mind, she couldn't chance meeting up with him. She no longer trusted herself. No, until these inexplicable sensations dissipated, she would avoid Paul at all costs. Thus, she said her prayers and climbed into bed.

Paul stepped out onto the balcony. It had been a productive evening. Come morning, he would see if his brother had accomplished all he purported. According to George he had, lending an invaluable hand—with the tobacco in particular. If that were true, Paul wouldn't be swamped tomorrow.

Thoughts of Charmaine took hold again. He longed to corner her alone and finish what he'd postponed for far too long. She wanted him, perhaps as much as he wanted her. But she had escaped to her room, leaving him to chomp at the bit. *Is she sleeping?* On impulse, he decided to find out . . .

The nightstand lamp burned low, but his eyes quickly adjusted to the dim light. She was asleep. He stepped up to the bed and stared longingly down at her. Lovely . . . she was so lovely, with dark lashes fanned against creamy white cheeks, kissable lips slightly parted, a stray hand raised beside her pillow, and her luscious breasts rising beneath the thin fabric of her nightgown. How he yearned to make love to her. What would she do if he awoke her with a kiss? His pulse accelerated as he imagined any number of reactions. She might struggle, and he found that possibility highly sensual. But no, it would be her first time, and he wanted the experience to be exquisite, an awakening she would agree, perhaps even beg, to engage in again. With that thought, he backed out of her room. He would never sleep tonight—*Never!*

Charmaine's eyes flew open, and she grabbed hold of her coverlet for support. How long had she held her breath? *You weren't holding it, silly! You feigned absolute serenity. And all the while, your heart was thundering in your ears.* Surely he had heard it! How could he not? She had waited for the kiss that never came. Prayed that he wouldn't—longed that he would. Then he was gone . . . *Gone!* With a moan, she turned over and attempted to breathe, to sleep.

Chapter 4

"WILL you marry me, Charmaine?"
The words were soft in her ear, caressing her neck, and at first she was certain she was dreaming. Yet Paul pulled her closer, his plundering mouth returning to her lips, his desperate plea speaking to her body as well as her heart . . .

Charmaine woke with a start, and it was a full minute before her erratic breathing lulled. Then, as the euphoria of impassioned sleep waned, piercing reality took hold, and she groaned. Paul had disturbed her slumber for four consecutive nights, ever since he'd crept into her chamber and stood over her bed. The recurrent dream was so vivid it plagued her waking hours as well.

A dream, only a dream! Dare she hope for more—for the ardent proposal whispered only in sleep? Or was she doomed to stand on a summit of uncertainty, expectant one day, disappointed the next? There were no answers, only a wistful wish spun upon one word: perhaps. She rose and began her daily routine.

The clip-clop of horse's hooves drew her to the veranda. She watched Paul lead his white stallion from the stable, mount, and gallop away. Since his return, he'd been so busy, it was no different than when he was on Espoir, almost as if he were avoiding her. But that was silly. She knew what he demanded of himself. It was only six in the morning, and already he was gone, probably for the day. Once again, she'd have to wait. But, for what? Another indecent breach of her bedchamber? It was just as well he kept away.

Forget him, she told herself as she turned to dress. *It's the twins' birthday. Use the occasion as a distraction.* She had promised they could spend the day in any manner they wished, and that would certainly keep her mind occupied.

She had been quite sly in her preparations. They knew nothing of her late-night efforts with needle and thread, nor the presents she had wrapped and neatly stacked on the dining room table only a few short hours ago. Jeannette would be delighted with the dresses for her china doll. Yvette was a different matter. Charmaine hoped the girl would be pleased with the feminine breeches she'd concocted. Certainly, Agatha would disapprove. However, the damage was done; best not to fret over the consequences now.

A rap fell on the connecting door, and Charmaine opened it to a sleepy-eyed Pierre. "Good morning, my little man," she greeted, scooping him into her arms. "What do you think of your lazy sisters? Should we let them snooze their birthday away, or should we wake them up?"

"Wake 'em up," he directed, squirming from Charmaine's embrace and bouncing on Yvette's bed.

The girl groaned. Then, realizing her birthday had indeed arrived, she was across the room, coaxing her sister to rise. When Charmaine mentioned presents in the dining room, they dressed hastily and were gone.

Ten minutes later, she and Pierre found them seated empty-handed at the table, their presents nowhere in sight, their angry eyes on their elder brother.

"That's unfair!"

"Ah, but it is more fun," John replied, sipping his coffee.

Charmaine stepped up to the table, annoyed. "What is this?"

"Good morning, Miss Ryan," he responded, ignoring her displeasure.

"Good morning," she returned stiffly, helping Pierre into his chair.

John's eyes traveled to the three-year-old. "How are you, Pierre?"

"Good," the boy answered. "Can we go fishin' again?"

"Not today. Today I have other plans."

Charmaine interrupted. "Where are the presents I wrapped?"

"They're hidden," John replied.

"Hidden? And who hid them?" she demanded, as if she really had to ask.

"Now, my Charm, please allow me to explain. First, seeking them out can be as much fun as opening them. And second, your gifts aren't the only ones hidden. Rose supplied me with a few, and there were the two large ones I—"

"*Truly?*" the girls exclaimed in tandem. Sanguine anticipation replaced anemic disappointment, and Charmaine was forgotten as Jeannette and Yvette bombarded their elder brother with questions.

"I'm not about to tell you where they are," he chuckled. "It took me the whole night to hide them. It is up to you to conduct a treasure hunt."

"Treasure hunt?" they queried, the words echoed by Charmaine.

John noted her smile. "I take it you approve of this innovation in gift giving?"

"I suppose so," she answered honestly, unable to remain hostile, her attention snared by Yvette, who had pushed away from the table. "Oh no, you don't, young lady. Breakfast first."

"But—"

"No buts," John admonished, enforcing Charmaine's edict. "Besides, I have a few clues you might be interested in hearing while you eat."

Yvette eagerly complied, and they ate quickly. The girls' alacrity was contagious, and even Charmaine was caught up in it, fed by John, who committed to nothing, but seemed to promise everything. She began to worry they would be disappointed. Her presents were sadly lacking next to the picture he was painting, and though his gifts also awaited discovery, she doubted even they could measure up to the twins' expectations.

"Now, remember," he warned when they rose from the table, "with every treasure hunt, there is always an adversary—a rival—who is searching for the treasure as well. So, you must be careful not to be caught."

"Caught? By whom?"

"Who else?" he snickered. "Auntie Agatha—the deadliest enemy of all!"

The ease with which he garnered their mirth still astounded Charmaine.

"Don't laugh," he chided seriously. "If she catches you, the fun is over."

"Yes, yes," Yvette said, and tugging her sister's arm, they bounded off.

"Me, too!" Pierre declared, pushing away his bowl of half-eaten porridge.

"You, too, what?" Charmaine asked, tucking in the napkin that had come loose from his collar.

"I wanna look for them presents, too."

"When you've finished," Charmaine answered, lifting a spoon to help him.

He grabbed at it, insisting, "I do it myself!"

Charmaine relinquished the utensil with a squeeze of his shoulder and a kiss on his head. But as she turned back to her own food, she caught John's warm gaze upon her, a self-conscious moment when their eyes locked. To her surprise, John broke away first, returning to his newspaper.

"Good morning, everyone!" George hailed from the hallway. He espied the serving bowl of porridge, sat down, and pulled it in front of him. "Is anybody eating this?"

John snickered. "Have all you like, though the hogs will be disappointed."

George ignored John's japing and poured liberal amounts of cream and sugar atop the oatmeal, and then, to Pierre's delight, ate from the large dish using the serving spoon.

"I suppose, George, you have come to the table for another reason?" John interrupted. "Aside from a second breakfast, that is."

"Reason? Oh yes. I'd almost forgotten. The children's birthday . . ."

He caught John's swift shake of the head and fell silent. *Too late!* Charmaine's attention had been snared, her inquisitive eyes on him. "It is the twins' birthday," he repeated, attempting to mask his blunder, "isn't it?"

"Yes," she agreed suspiciously, "but you knew that."

"And I was just wondering how you were celebrating it. Do you have something special planned for the day?"

"Only their presents and now this treasure hunt. But I did promise them no lessons. They can decide what they'd like to do, within reason, of course."

"Of course," George nodded, his brow arched in John's direction.

Though Charmaine's curiosity was piqued, John smiled passively in return; the strange exchange yielded no clues.

"So George, did all go well?" John asked.

"I moved the shipment early this morning, if that's what you want to know."

"Then everything is settled?"

"Everything is in order, just the way you wanted it, except—" George held up one finger "—there is the matter of finances."

"Finances?" John queried. "I gave you the money weeks ago, or have you forgotten?"

"No, John, I haven't forgotten. But neither am I a fool. That money was for the payment of the p—eh . . . the merchandise. It did not cover *my* fees. Now, I do admit I am your friend, but after I spent a good portion of yesterday avoiding Paul to work on this project for you, I do believe you owe me something in return, and I don't mean gratitude." With that, he held out his hand, palm up.

Charmaine giggled, for he looked like a beggar. Intrigued, she watched John pull out a wallet and hand him a sheaf of bank notes, a sum that rivaled her week's wages. What favor could have merited such a hefty allowance? George straightened the bills, counted them meticulously, and smiled at her as he tucked them into his pocket. She was oddly disconcerted by that smile, as if she were an involuntary participant in the transaction. Her eyes traveled to John for an answer, but he was reading his newspaper again. She did not trust him. George, however, was her friend and wouldn't lead her to harm. Neither would he lie to her. She'd question him about it when they were alone.

Pierre scattered her thoughts when he began banging his spoon on his empty dish. She quickly confiscated it, sending him into a fit of tears.

"I'm sorry, Pierre," she said, "but it's impolite to make such a racket."

He continued to wail, refusing the milk she offered him and turning his face aside when she tried to wipe it.

John abruptly stood and stepped behind the boy's chair. Certain he intended to usurp her authority and seize the utensil, her grip tightened on it. But he ignored her completely and lifted Pierre from his seat, holding him high in his arms. "What is all this fuss about?" he asked. "Surely you're not crying over a lost spoon? Or maybe you are not the Pierre I know. Could that be it? Maybe you're some other lad come to take his place, because the Pierre I know never cries. He is always smiling, especially at Mainie. Isn't that so?"

The tears stopped. "I'm Pierre," the boy declared. "But I have to go potty."

"No," John corrected wryly, "you *had* to go potty."

"Oh my!" Charmaine groaned, immediately comprehending the boy's crankiness. "Come, Pierre, let's go to the nursery and change you."

But John drew back as she reached for the child. "Let me carry him. There's no point in soiling your dress as well."

Before she could object, he headed into the hallway. There they found Jeannette, sitting on the landing, knees drawn up to her chin, shoulders sagging.

"What is this?" John asked. "Have you uncovered all your gifts already?"

"No," she pouted, her eyes fixed on the floor. "I've only found one . . . a rock! Yvette found three of hers, and they were all real presents: candy, a book, and some funny-looking knickers. But all I got was a wrapped-up rock!"

"Well, perhaps that's all there is for you," he jested.

"Don't say that!" Charmaine hissed. "You'll have her crying as well!"

He took her point to heart. "Don't give up so easily, Jeannette. There are just as many presents for you."

"But where can they be? I've searched everywhere!"

"Everywhere?" he probed.

"Everywhere but out—" Her words gave way to comprehension, and her face brightened. "They're not in the house, are they?"

"One clue is all you get."

It was enough. Jeannette stormed the front portico, leaving John to chuckle all the way to the nursery.

He's having as much fun as the girls, Charmaine thought.

"Put him on his bed," she directed over her shoulder, retrieving a set of undergarments, knickers, and a towel from the armoire.

John deposited his wet charge, then stood with arms spread wide, surveying his saturated shirt and damp jacket. Charmaine stopped in her tracks, dropping everything but the towel on a nearby chair. "Oh, no! Your jacket is ruined! And your shirt! Oh, I'm sorry!" Without thought, she began to wipe vigorously across his shirtfront and down to his waist, blotting the fabric dry. Suddenly, she realized her impropriety, and her hands dropped to her sides. Cringing, she looked up at him, then slowly stepped away. "I—I'm sorry."

He didn't move, his raised arms mourning the space she had vacated, his crooked smile nourishing the blush that was deepening upon her cheeks.

"I—I'd better see to Pierre."

"Yes," he agreed, his smile broad now, "and I had better leave before I develop a further complication that won't be remedied with a dry cloth."

Once Pierre's clothes had been changed, Charmaine led him out onto the balcony to look for Jeannette. The main doors opened below and George and John came into view. John had changed into a white shirt, fawn colored pants, and high boots. Completing the ensemble was the leather cap he wore, the garb lending itself to a day in the saddle. Evidently, he and George planned on riding out together.

They were absorbed in conversation, and although Charmaine couldn't catch the phrases, their easy banter bespoke a deep-rooted friendship. Even after six weeks, she puzzled over their camaraderie: a chuckle here, the shake of a head there, a raised hand to emphasize a point, or an arm clasped around the other's shoulder. Most brothers would envy such a bond.

A squeal of delight punctuated the air, and the twins bounded from the stable, racing to their brother. Yvette reached him first, hugging him fiercely. "Oh, they're beautiful, Johnny! Wherever did you get them?"

His response was too soft to hear. Then both girls were dancing around him, grabbing his arms and pulling him toward the paddock. "We can go right now!" They stopped when he spoke again. "Yes!" Jeannette laughed.

"Let's get her!" Yvette added, turning toward the house, espying Charmaine in the process. "There she is!"

The troop took a few steps in her direction. "Mademoiselle Charmaine!" Jeannette shouted. "Wait until you see what Johnny gave us!"

"Stay right there," Yvette interjected, "and we'll bring them out!"

Charmaine surmised what the presents were, and she watched as the girl disappeared into the stable with George. Jeannette continued across the lawn with John, her face radiant. "Just wait until you see!" she reiterated. "They are the most wonderful presents in the whole world! Better than anything I expected this morning! Better than any treasure!"

George led two ponies through the stable door. They were gorgeous creatures, meticulously groomed for the occasion and perfectly matched to the twins' dispositions. One was coal black, a proud animal, prancing wickedly against the bit in its mouth, its head held high. The other was powder white, docile, but no less handsome.

"They're beautiful, girls," Charmaine said, anticipating their next request.

"Johnny said he would take us riding if you gave your permission."

"There's no point in owning a pony if you cannot ride him, is there?"

"No!" Jeannette agreed. "And will you come along, too?"

"Me?" Charmaine asked in flustered surprise. "No, I'm afraid you'll have to enjoy your ride without my company. I'll just remain behind with Pierre and worry over your safety."

"Oh, please come, Mademoiselle!" the girl implored. "It won't be fun without you, and you promised to spend the day any way we wished."

"And I will," Charmaine reaffirmed, "as soon as you return. Now don't look so glum. It is you who have received such fine animals, not I, therefore, you should enjoy them."

"But Johnny purchased a horse for you, too!"

Charmaine paled. "I'm afraid I don't understand . . ." But she understood all too well, and already her mind was racing for a suitable excuse to extricate herself from the promises she had made over the past two days.

John read the turmoil on her face. "Miss Ryan," he called up to her, "I took into consideration your diligent supervision of the children and knew you would insist on joining us today."

When George stepped out of the stable this time, he led a speckled horse over to the corral. The dappling gray was just as majestic as the ponies, its silver coat shimmering in the morning sun, its dark mane and tail rippling in the breeze.

Charmaine was dumbfounded. All that had passed between the two men at breakfast was suddenly clear: the raised brows, the riddle conversation, and the monetary transaction. "I cannot accept such a gift from you! It is quite inappropriate."

"Do not think of it as a gift," he replied. "Think of it as a tool, one required for your job. Then it becomes entirely appropriate."

"*What?*" she fumed.

"The twins will want to ride frequently, and I won't always be around to accompany them. As you've often reminded me, the children are your responsibility, so you will need a horse if you are to go with them."

"You must hurry, Mademoiselle Charmaine!" Yvette beckoned from below. "You can't stand there all day. The horses will grow impatient!"

"And so will we!" Jeannette added.

"That's right," John concurred. "Change into something more comfortable, a dress you can afford to soil, and come down quickly."

"I can't!" Charmaine protested, angry at his matter-of-fact attitude, his confidence she would do his bidding. "I have to stay with Pierre." She looked to her young charge, who had grown bored and was now running up and down the length of the balcony.

"Pierre is coming with us," John asserted.

"Really? And where do you propose we put him?"

"He can ride with me. Now, we are wasting precious time. Find a suitable garment and get down here before dusk is upon us and the day is gone."

"I'm sorry to disappoint you, but I am not going anywhere on that animal. I won't be held responsible for him."

"Her," John corrected, "and I told you, the horse is yours."

"I don't believe you. No one in their right mind would purchase an expensive animal like that for a governess."

"Whether you believe me or not, Miss Ryan, I have, and you *are* going to accompany us on this outing," he persisted, matching stubbornness for stubbornness. "As the children's governess, you are obliged to supervise them throughout the day. Isn't that right?"

"Yes, but—"

"But what?"

"I don't know how to ride!" she blurted out, stung by the twins' laughter and Yvette's exclamation of: "I told you!"

John's frown struck them mute. "We shall teach you," he said, his manner thoughtful and persuasive. "The mare is gentle. So, no more excuses. We will wait at the stable. If you haven't joined us in ten minutes, I shall come for you." He grasped the girls' shoulders and walked them back to the paddock.

Charmaine sighed. "Now what are we to do?" she asked Pierre as he scurried past her.

He stopped and looked up at her. "Go."

She chuckled ruefully. "Then go, we shall."

Millie Thornfield hesitated before knocking on Frederic's ante-chamber door, drawing a deep breath and tightening her grip on the basket she carried when he bade her enter. He looked up from the periodical he was reading and beckoned her to come closer. "Well?"

"I have them, sir," she whispered. "The prettiest two of the litter."

"May I see?"

She set the basket down and uncovered it, revealing two kittens, one gray, the other orange. They immediately awoke, and as the marmalade feline yawned and stretched, the gray tabby pounced on her, igniting a fierce tussle. Millie giggled despite her surroundings. Then, remembering where she was, she reined in her sudden joy and looked back at the master of the house, surprised to find him smiling as well.

"Thank you, Millie. You had an excellent idea. My daughters should be pleased. Even Pierre will enjoy watching them play."

Charmaine arrived at the stable with Pierre, clothed in a time-worn dress. Jeannette was ecstatic, exclaiming it was going to be a marvelous day. Charmaine shuddered, knowing John would return and the real disaster would begin. If only Paul were around; he would put a stop to such folly. But no, her fate rested in his brother's hands.

The twins had named their ponies Spook and Angel, and were asking George about their gender when John appeared with Phantom. "Angel is female, and Spook is male," George said. "I believe they will be serving more than one purpose."

"And what is that?" Jeannette innocently asked.

Yvette clicked her tongue. "Now what do you think? Making foals like Phantom and Chastity did. Isn't that so, Johnny?"

"Exactly."

"And can we watch this time?" she inquired, eliciting an embarrassed frown from Charmaine. "I don't understand what happens, and I'd like to find out."

"You would, would you?" he queried, unfazed.

George, however, pulled at his collar, which bolstered Charmaine's fear an explanation of conception and birth was at hand.

"It will have to wait, Yvette," John said instead. "The day is wasting away. Fetch the picnic basket while I help Jeannie and Miss Ryan into their saddles."

"Picnic basket?" Charmaine exclaimed.

"Now, my Charm, what would a picnic be without a picnic basket?"

"It wouldn't be a picnic," she supplied. "I don't want to go on a picnic with you. One was quite enough, thank you. And I've forgotten my bonnet."

"You'll disappoint the children . . . on their special day."

Trapped! John and George's clever interrogation at breakfast had uncovered her plans for the day. She had played right into John's cunning hands. "I'll not ride far from the house," she stipulated.

"Not far at all," he reassured, though she was certain he lied. "What are you waiting for, Yvette?" he pressed. "Go and fetch the basket!"

She immediately jumped to do his bidding.

The nursery was unusually quiet, both bedchamber and playroom empty. "Set the basket on the floor, Millie," Frederic directed. "I thought they'd be here for lessons."

"Would you like me to go and find them, sir?" she offered.

Laughter wafting off the front lawns drew him to the French doors. "That won't be necessary," he muttered, hobbling out onto the balcony. There he stood, inconspicuous in the shadow of the large oak, watching the drama unfold below.

John finished adjusting the girth strap on Jeannette's pony. Once secured, he motioned to her. In the next instant, she was seated squarely on Angel's back, laughing gaily. He raised her stirrups a hair higher, then stepped back. She knew what she was doing, for she nudged the animal, and it loped away.

John turned to Charmaine next, and a violent panic rose up inside her. There would be no escape now, and wide-eyed, she looked to George for reassurance. He smiled in return, stroking the mare's speckled neck. "Don't be alarmed, Charmaine. She's quite complacent and easy to ride." He led the horse to her side and relinquished the reins to John, taking charge of Pierre while the man worked the mare's saddle straps.

"Are you ready?" John asked when he was finished.

Her mouth was so dry she was unable to reply. Though the animal was not as large as Phantom, it was imposing. "It's so high," she whispered, her eyes fixed on the saddle that was level with her anxious gaze.

"Yes, it is," he conceded, his regard assuasive when she faced him, "but it's quite easy to mount."

"I've never ridden before," she pointed out again, trembling. "I have no idea how to get up there."

"There's a first time for everything," he reasoned devilishly.

She glared at him, finding no humor in her present predicament.

He ignored her disdainful air. "Don't worry, my Charm, I'll not allow your first ride to end in failure."

She caught sight of George's snigger. "I don't intend to be patronized! If that is your game, then you may prey upon some other woman!"

"But Miss Ryan, you do me a great injustice," he protested

mildly. "I am merely attempting to assist you in a new undertaking. Allow me to demonstrate." He did so, offering step by step instructions as he swung up and into the saddle. "Easy enough," he concluded. "Do you understand?"

She nodded, even though she knew her struggles were just beginning.

Then he was off the horse and standing beside her again. "Well?" he queried brightly, entertained by her apprehension, his audacity maddening.

"All right!" she snapped, tearing her eyes from his mocking face. Without hesitation, she took hold of the dark mane and the rim of the saddle. To her amazement, the horse did not move.

"Very good," he observed, "but you need to place your foot in the stirrup."

"I know that!" she shot back. But as she lifted her leg, her undergarments were exposed, and in her haste to veil them, she missed the iron. She tried again, releasing the mane to steady it, and still her contorted efforts proved futile. She burned in shame, aware the men were exchanging smirks behind her back.

"Miss Ryan," John reproved, arresting yet another pathetic attempt. "I am past the age of lusting after your petticoats. If you worried less about your underskirts and more about getting into that saddle, you'd have already mounted!"

"Stop taunting me! If it weren't for your rude jests, I'd be able to do this."

"Really?"

"Yes, really! Besides, it is not proper for me to ride a horse this way. No wonder I'm finding it difficult. A lady should ride sidesaddle!"

"There you are mistaken, Mademoiselle," he contradicted with a laugh, amused by her numerous excuses to avoid the inevitable. "In Paris or London ladies ride sidesaddle, but here on Charmantes, women straddle their mounts . . ." His words trailed off as his thoughts turned ribald, his eyes going to George. "You're less likely to fall off that way. Besides, this *position* is quite *natural*, and worlds more *comfortable*, especially to the inexperienced horsewoman."

George chuckled softly.

"I'll take no assurances from you," Charmaine rejoined.

"Do you doubt my riding experience?" he queried in pretended offense. "I've been proficient in the art for quite some time now, and some—those who've had the *pleasure*, that is—have congratulated me on my skill."

She eyed him speculatively, unable to fathom George's mirth. Obviously, the man was speaking in riddles, and only George understood what he really meant. Wishing only to place the entire ordeal behind her, she gestured to the stirrup. "It is far too high. Could you at least lower it for me?"

"Why, my Charm, I'm afraid that wouldn't do at all."

George roared with laughter and John joined in, all at her expense.

Miserable, she stepped away from the horse, reliving the incident with "Fang," a thick lump lodged in her throat. She was about to flee when Yvette returned lugging a picnic basket, protesting her governess had yet to mount up.

"I'm sorry, Charmaine," John apologized, taking in her forlorn face. It was clear how very innocent she was, and he suffered a pang of contrition. "We're not laughing at you. The stirrups have to be high so you can pull yourself up and into the saddle."

His vulgar mien was gone, leaving Charmaine confused.

"I offer my shoulder. Lean on me while you put your foot into the stirrup, and you'll be atop the mare in no time."

She couldn't object; he was already crouching next to her. She rested her right arm tentatively across his back. Oddly secure, her foot found the iron.

"Grab the saddle and mane," he directed. "That's it. Now, pull up."

She barely left the ground, her attention riveted on the warm hands that encompassed her waist.

"Try again," he coaxed before she lost courage.

This time, she pushed off, and somewhere between earth and saddle, John's strong arms propelled her upward. When she exhaled, she was astride the mare, looking down at him. Though she focused on his smiling face, her mind lingered on her waist where his hands had branded her.

In the next moment, a wave of paranoia seized her—her familiar surroundings turned perilous from the lofty perch, and she clutched the horse's mane desperately, letting go only when John pulled the reins over the mare's head and handed them to her. She hardly noticed his familiarity when he shortened the stirrups and took hold of each ankle to test the length. To her horror, he turned away, tending to his own mount.

Instantly, the horse shifted. "Where are you going?" she cried.

"One moment," he assured her.

"You can't leave me here! I've no idea how to control this animal!"

As if on cue, the mare ambled toward the grassy knoll where the ponies grazed. "She's moving!"

"Let her go," John replied, as he hitched the surcingle about the small picnic basket and fastened it to Phantom's saddle, "she just wants to graze."

As predicted, the mare stopped when she reached the ponies, and her head plummeted to the lawn. Petrified, Charmaine held on to the reins for dear life, certain she was going to slide down the horse's neck, breathing easier only after some minutes had elapsed and she remained in place.

John untied Phantom and swung up into the saddle. The horse snorted loudly and shook his head, fighting the bit and the iron hand that held him in check.

"Are you more at ease now?" John asked as he drew even with her, eyeing the leather straps entwined in her white-knuckled fingers.

"Yes," she replied, pushing the inconsequential inquiry aside. "Do you still plan on having Pierre ride with you?"

"Of course. Why do you ask?"

"I think we should leave him with Rose."

John's brow furrowed and his eyes grew stormy.

"I'm concerned for his safety," she added. "That beast is so fierce."

His visage softened, then the anger was gone altogether. "Mademoiselle, for all those who would love to see me land on my backside, he has yet to throw me. Pierre will be fine. Besides, you wouldn't want to disappoint him, would you?" His eyes traveled to the patiently waiting boy, whose face was alight with anticipation.

Charmaine knew she had been manipulated, emotion pitted against common sense. She could also tell John's mind was made up.

"This day belongs as much to him as it does to his sisters. Do you think we could leave him behind in tears and then hope to enjoy the afternoon ourselves?"

"I suppose not," she conceded. "But sometimes things are beyond our control and—"

"Charmaine, must I give my solemn word? Pierre is the *last* child who will come to harm because of me." Dismissing further protest, he nudged the stallion toward George, and the boy was placed in front of him.

As John prodded Phantom into motion, Pierre squealed with glee. Now, she was glad they had not left him behind. He would have been miserable cloistered in the house all day.

Yvette balked at her elder brother's riding instructions. "I mounted all by myself didn't I?"

So, once again, John drew up alongside Charmaine and gave her a brief demonstration on how to prod the horse and use the reins. It seemed too simple to work. He cautioned her to loosen up on the straps, warning that clutching them too tightly wouldn't prevent her from falling off, but could provoke the animal into throwing her. "The mare doesn't need to be broken. That has already been done for you," he finished, chuckling at her renewed anxiety.

Yvette tugged on her reins and Spook abandoned his grazing for the cobblestone drive. Jeannette quickly followed suit. Their unquestionable ability left Charmaine shaken, and she breathed deeply when John nodded to her.

"Your turn," he said.

In imitation of the twins, she steered her horse in the same direction, awed when the beast complied. They were on their way, bidding George goodbye and clopping through the iron fencing to the dirt road. Charmaine's tension faded with the rhythm of the animal beneath her. As long as the route remained straight, the mare walked steadily along, obediently following the ponies.

Frederic remained on the veranda, haunted by fragmented memories. *You're never home to spend time with them . . . I'd much prefer to have a horse . . . It wouldn't have to be in a box, Papa . . . You could have him hidden in the stables with a big blue ribbon around his neck . . . John loves them . . . He'll see they are cared for . . . The colt thinks we're his masters, maybe he could be mine . . . Colette wrote to me . . . to supply the children with the love and affection they'd never get from you . . . Pierre is the last child who will come to harm because of me . . .*

The riders were long out of sight when Frederic turned back into the nursery. He was alone and had only himself to blame. With a plaintive sigh, he looked down at the basket. The kittens were once again sleeping.

Kittens . . . Yvette had begged for a horse on her last birthday, and he had decided to give her a stray kitten instead. Why did he think such a gift would please her? He knew what she longed for. But had he listened? John, on the other hand, had been home less than six weeks and already knew her deepest desires. His son was fulfilling Colette's dying request.

Then there was Pierre. He was too young to lament what he could never receive from his sire—what his childhood and the circumstances surrounding his birth would deny him. But it wouldn't be long before he, too, was turning nine and, like his sister, would grow disenchanted and unhappy.

Nine . . . was it possible Yvette and Jeannette were already nine? Frederic stared across time. Nine years ago today, his prayers had been mercifully answered; his young wife had survived the difficult labor and birth of twins.

Twenty-nine years ago tomorrow, he had not been so blessed, and he trembled with the memory. Images of that bleak night, just past midnight, assaulted him as if it were yesterday, and his chest tightened with the overwhelming loss of that first delivery.

"John," Elizabeth had moaned, suffering another violent contraction. "If it's a boy, Frederic, name him John." They were her dying words.

Colette's labor had mirrored Elizabeth's, and though he'd always been stalwart, Frederic had been terrified the night the twins were born, certain he was going to lose his second wife as surely as he had lost his first twenty years earlier.

But God had been merciful, and Colette was spared. *Why?* Had the Good Lord heard his petition in those last few hours before midnight? Was Colette's recovery a result of the vow he had made to the Almighty and to himself? He realized, if nothing else, it had propelled him to this point, scripting the present and marking the lives of his children in the most disastrous way. He sat down hard on Yvette's bed and rubbed his throbbing brow. Would he allow the past to dictate the future? *Dear God,* he murmured, *what am I to do?*

"Do you like the ride, Pierre?"

John's voice interrupted the thud of hooves in the dust.

"Yes!" the boy giggled. "I like this big horse!" He craned his neck back to regard his saddlemate and exclaimed, "You're upside down!"

"No, I'm not, you are."

Pierre looked down at himself thoughtfully. "No, I'm not!" he disagreed, eventually noticing Charmaine. "I like this ride, Mainie!"

"I can tell," she replied with a smile.

John smiled as well. "Have you put aside your misgivings?" he asked.

"Most, but not all. I'm becoming used to her movements. However, I'm not looking forward to getting down."

"Don't worry. It is much easier than mounting."

Their short conversation lapsed into silence, and Charmaine began to enjoy the scenery around her. She directed her gaze away from John, taking in the foliage and wild birds, turning back to him only when her neck began to ache. She found him studying her thoughtfully and braved his unnerving regard. "Is something wrong?" she asked.

"Wrong?" he queried with arched brow. "Why should anything be wrong?"

"The manner in which you are staring at me leads me to assume the worst. Perhaps I've grown a wart on the end of my nose?"

"A wart? No, my Charm, your nose is just fine . . . perfectly shaped." His gaze came to rest there.

"What then?" she pressed.

"Am I not permitted to admire your accomplishment? I do not mean to ogle you, Miss Ryan. It's just, I never thought to see you sit a horse so well. Quite an accomplishment for a beginner."

"Compliments are of no use," she remarked, certain he mocked her.

But his next words were quick and sure, leaving her befuddled. "No compliment intended, merely an observation that answers a score of questions."

"Such as?"

"Why you were employed as the children's governess."

"Surely you are not suggesting riding a horse has led to my present occupation? But then, the workings of your mind never cease to amaze me."

His lips broke into a rakish grin. "I'm glad to hear that, no matter what else I might be, I haven't been a bore."

"You haven't answered my question," she rejoined.

"I wasn't aware you had asked one."

"What exactly is the connection you've made between my employment as the children's governess and my achievement upon this animal?"

"Oh, that question. Well now, I was contemplating your ability to conquer a new endeavor, in this case, riding the mare. That particular facet of your character led me to understand how you gained the position you now hold. Even in fear, you pressed on. I commend you on your determination."

"You mock me, sir," Charmaine replied sheepishly.

"No, Miss Ryan, I do not mock you. That *was* a compliment. You play a very important role in the children's lives."

"You've just now realized that?"

"No. In fact, it was the reason I doubted your capabilities at first."

"At first?" she asked in great surprise. "And you don't now?"

"No, not anymore, not since I gave you a chance—watched you with them."

She was too astounded to speak.

"You enjoy your job, don't you?"

"Yes, I do. I love the children."

"Do you?"

Though his words were not unkind, they rattled Charmaine. "Yes!" she averred. "Don't you believe me?"

"I believe you," he answered resolutely. "I just wanted to hear you say it again, to reassure me perhaps."

"Reassure you? Certainly that's a curious remark?"

"Why should it be curious, considering the state of their lives? My father is a recluse, their mother is dead, and their stepmother hates them. They need somebody to love them."

He grew pensive, his gaze traveling to the edge of the forest. She preferred the silence to his disturbing statements. Their odd discourse had taken its toll. She was certain of only one thing: she'd never in a million years understand him.

John Duvoisin. The man *was* an enigma, and more often than not, a thorn in her side. Life on the island, in the house, hadn't gotten back to normal since his arrival. Granted, the great storms that had shaken the manor that first week were all but gone, and yet, his presence affected everyone.

Thoughts of his departure, one that had grown less likely with each passing day, came unwittingly to her lips. "When are you planning to leave?"

John's attention was snared, his expression sharp, then devilish. "I'll bet you can't wait until that day arrives, can you?"

"I—I didn't mean for it to sound that way," she gushed.

"Forgive me if I refuse to believe you this time. No," he laughed, "I'll wager you meant every word."

"I just wanted to know—"

"Know what? When you can expect things to get back to normal on Charmantes? When you and my brother can recommence your love affair?"

"It's not a love affair!" she objected fiercely.

"No? I suppose I just imagined the passionate scene I walked in on that night. The question is, how much further has it all gone?"

Charmaine turned away in heightening embarrassment.

"Your red face would lead me to believe the worst. However, my growing faith in you would not." He paused a moment as if in deep thought. "I'm feeling generous today, so I'll offer you a word of warning concerning my brother."

"Don't bother!"

"Oh, but I feel it is my obligation."

"Your obligation?" she queried incredulously. "Since when have you become so noble? Or do you think by maligning your brother, you'll promote yourself?"

"I'm the first to admit I'm beyond redemption, Miss Ryan." He chortled anew. "Now, don't lead me off track. We were speaking of Paul and all the trouble—"

"And I told you, I've no interest in what you have to say."

"Interest," he repeated. "A perfect word, for it's at the heart of my very next point. You should be *interested* to know, Paul has but one *interest* in you."

Charmaine gaped at him.

"Don't be offended. I'm only stating the facts as they are."

"Facts? What would you know of facts?"

"Plenty. If you would like to—"

"I would like nothing, and I'll not believe a word of it, anyway."

"I assure you my facts are not fabricated," he pressed on. "But perhaps you'd prefer a more reliable source, someone who could provide concrete evidence. I'm certain the maids of the manor could tell tales that would shock even me. You see, Paul has quite an affinity for the young ladies in my father's employ. He must have been quite disheartened when your more distinguished position of governess placed an unusual obstacle in his one-track path."

"What is that supposed to mean?"

"Must I be more explicit, my Charm? My brother is a Don Juan with an insatiable appetite for women. Not that I'm condemning him morally. What is a man to do when the mansion is so well 'stocked'? Before I left a few years ago, there was many a night when some young maid, who should have been sleeping virtuously in her own bed on the third floor, found *comfort* in my brother's bed one floor below. I doubt those fair times have changed, especially if you are holding him at bay."

"If?" she choked out, even as a distant memory surfaced. *I'm speaking of comfort—yours and mine.* "Well, if you're hoping to trap me into confirming your crude speculation, allow me to dash those hopes right here and now! I have no intention of carrying this conversation any further."

"I'm not speculating. I grew up with him. My brother is many things, but celibate is not one of them. He's sampled the fruit many times, in assorted varieties. I know."

"Really? And how do you know? Did you place a glass against the wall?"

"I didn't have to," John chuckled softly, amused by her feisty reply. "Paul never guarded his liaisons. In fact, he often boasted about them."

"Many people boast," she reasoned, "I'd hardly call that concrete evidence."

"My, you are determined to defend him, aren't you?"

"I'm not defending him!"

"No?"

"No!"

"Then why turn a deaf ear to information that is in your best interest to know?"

"Whatever went on between Paul and someone else is none of my business."

"Why do you use the past tense?"

She was appalled by his tenacious debasement of his own brother. "I refuse to believe your lies."

"Believe what you will," he snorted, certain she could not be *that* naïve, "but don't cry into your pillow later on, for I did warn you."

"I don't need your warning!" she retorted, ripping her gaze from him.

"That maid," he pursued, forefinger to lips, "Travis's daughter, Millie . . ."

Charmaine's eyes shot back to his taunting face.

"The voluptuous Felicia was his favorite, but I believe he's allowing that field to lay fallow for a while, a good guess considering how she's been acting toward me lately. If Paul gets nowhere with you, I'd place money on Millie."

"But she's only sixteen!"

"The perfect age—no diseases."

"Enough!" Charmaine cried out. "I've heard enough!"

The twins turned round in their saddles. But John only smiled and waved to them. A moment later, he and Charmaine were forgotten.

"Of course," he pressed on, "Paul may have a bit of trouble seducing Millie with her father about. Therefore, Miss Ryan, you'd best be on guard, unless of course, you are willing . . ."

"You are positively crude," she hissed. "As for your *chivalrous* warning, it was unnecessary. I'm not some trollop who'd give herself to a man without sacred vows exchanged before a priest and God, so take your lecherous insinuations elsewhere!"

"Marriage?" he laughed derisively. "You think he would marry you?"

His boisterous reaction gained the twins' sidelong glances a second time.

Crushed, Charmaine bowed her head to the decimation of her most cherished dream. How foolish those girlish fancies suddenly seemed! Marriage. Of course Paul wouldn't marry her, a lowly servant girl. Oh, yes, she was the governess, but as Felicia had said only a week ago, an employee just the same.

"I'm sorry if you were misled," John proceeded, "but my brother could never marry you, even if that were his most ardent desire. You see, money marries money, especially when the money is limited. Paul isn't heir to my father's estate. Not yet, anyway. So, if he marries, he'll invest any money he has in a rich wife."

Her pain diminished. This man, in his great analysis, had never touched upon love and all its glorious possibilities. Unable to love, having never loved, he thought of marriage only in terms of capital and investments, of buying a wife like one would a mare or a new ship. He could never hope to appreciate an emotion so strong it could impel a decent man to snub convention and break society's code by choosing a partner lowly born and financially poor, yet rich in love.

"Yes, Paul will be forced to seek a wealthy wife," John continued, "I, on the other hand, can marry whomever I choose." He chuckled wryly, a laugh born of pain, not pleasure.

Charmaine regarded him again, perceiving the irony in his voice. Was he afraid his father would disown him? But as she searched his face for an answer, he turned away, leaving her to puzzle over the cryptic remark.

Yvette's shout drew their eyes to the road ahead. "Look Johnny— a rider!"

"Speak of the devil," John muttered.

Though not the devil, it might well have been. Atop his white stallion, Paul was quickly approaching, and Charmaine worried over his reaction. Surely if he didn't like John pestering the children during lessons, he'd find their late morning excursion intolerable. She was grateful when Jeannette greeted him enthusiastically.

"Good day, Paul! How do you like our presents?"

"Very nice," he said, reining in Alabaster shoulder to shoulder with Phantom.

"Johnny purchased them for us," she added, unmindful of his twitching jaw.

"So I imagined," he replied tenderly, his cold eyes reserved for John.

Charmaine waited with bated breath. It would be wise to proceed with caution, but she knew John would never do that.

"What brings Paulie home so early today?" he asked merrily.

"Yes," Yvette echoed, "what brings Paulie home so early today?"

Ignore them, Paul thought as he tore his gaze from his heckling brother. "Good morning, Miss Ryan," he greeted debonairly.

"Good morning," she returned, relief rushing in.

John couldn't restrain himself, the endearing exchange fanning his knavery. Leaning forward, he addressed Yvette. "Good morning, Miss Duvoisin."

"Good morning," his young sister mimicked, catching on quickly.

Satisfied he commanded Paul's attention once again, John continued. "You didn't answer my question, Paul. Aren't you feeling well?"

"I'm fine, John."

"Then why have you rushed home so early in the day? There must be a score of projects just waiting for your—how did you put it—'practiced' hands?"

"They're finished, John. I was out of the house early—"

"Mr. Proficiency."

"—with the intention of celebrating the twins' birthday this afternoon." His eyes rested on Charmaine, a hint of a promise reflected there.

"What a shame," John sighed with the snap of his fingers.

"And why is that?"

"Isn't it obvious? You are hours too late! We're on our way to a picnic. You're welcome to join us, of course. Not even I would be so cruel as to exclude you from the outing." *Besides,* John thought, *it will be entertaining to watch Paul in action with the governess.*

Paul's demeanor hardened. "I'll see you later," he told Charmaine, "at the house." He yanked on the reins, drawing his stallion away.

As he galloped off, Charmaine experienced a pang of regret; Paul's companionship had slipped through her fingers. But there was no point in crying over spilled milk.

"I think someone's in trouble," John teased in a singsong children's chant.

She ignored him.

They nudged their mounts into motion again, leaving the dusty road and trekking south across a wide meadow, its tall grass speckled with wild flowers. As they meandered along, Yvette asked to race her pony, but John set aside the petition; Spook could step into a hole and break a leg.

"Like Charity?" the girl asked.

"Possibly."

"Not like Charity," Jeannette corrected, "because Charity didn't really break a leg. I remember Mama crying and saying Dr. Blackford destroyed her horse for no good reason."

"You never told me that, Jeannette! Is that true, Johnny?"

"Yes," he pronounced flatly, "it's true."

"But why? Why would Dr. Blackford do that?"

"Because the man is a pompous imbecile. He calls himself a doctor and can't diagnose a fracture correctly . . ." Then he mumbled under his breath, "I could be dying, and I wouldn't let him near me."

Charmaine shifted uneasily in her saddle, relieved when she realized the girls hadn't heard the last comment. The man was criticizing the physician who had ministered to their mother. Even so, she was curious about the story. At first, she had assumed they were talking about Chastity, the mare that had foaled only weeks ago. Now she realized they were talking about an entirely different animal.

John explained that Paul had purchased Chastity for Colette some weeks after Charity was destroyed in the hopes of brightening her spirits. "But Colette loved Charity," he concluded, "and Chastity never quite took her place."

They came to a wooded area, and John prodded Phantom to the front of the entourage, leaving Charmaine to take up the rear. He uncovered an obscure trail hidden in a dense copse. The horses entered single file, and the leafy lane closed in around them. Though it was cool here, Charmaine would have preferred the heat of the meadow. Now she had to work at guiding her mount, lest she stumble over a dead branch. The heavy vegetation offered its share of obstacles as well. Low-hanging twigs accosted her, scratching her face, catching at her dress, and loosing strands of her hair. Dodging them, she soon forgot about the horse beneath her, and the mare abruptly stopped. Charmaine nudged her sides, but the animal was already chewing on a patch of tall weeds and refused to budge. Frustrated, she looked to John, but he was nowhere in sight. Yvette and Jeannette disappeared next, directing their ponies around a bend up ahead.

"Come on, you silly horse!" she scolded. "You can't eat now! Move! Please move." The mare, however, chewed away, its reins pulled taut against its craning neck. Gritting her teeth, Charmaine yanked on the leather straps. The horse only whinnied, then returned to the vegetation. "Oh no, you don't!" she hissed, jerking the reins again and nudging the beast's flanks. The animal shook its head and stepped backward. Paralyzed with fear, Charmaine pulled harder. The mare trumpeted loudly and began prancing in place, then turned, wedging herself on the narrow path, her wide neck bowed sideways, head pointed in the direction from which they had come.

"John! Dear Lord, John!" Charmaine screamed.

John looked back. "Good God! Where is she?"

The twins only shrugged.

"Stay put. I'll be back."

He angled Phantom around them and set the steed on a fast trot, rounding the bend just as Charmaine cried out again. The mare was on her hind legs, front hooves pawing the air. "Stop pulling on the reins!" he shouted.

Charmaine was too petrified to hear him.

Pierre burst into belly-shaking laughter. John jumped off Phantom, lifted the boy from the saddle, and set him down a safe distance away. "Stay here."

He approached the mare, dodging the thrashing hooves. "Grab

her mane! For God's sake, Charmaine, let go of the reins and grab her mane!"

Their eyes connected, and Charmaine finally heard the command, but at the moment she released the leather strap, the crazed horse reared again. John winced as her hands came up short of the mane, clutching air instead. She sailed over the horse's rump, and her backside met the ground with a painful thump. There she sat, too stunned to move, her hair combs askew, the copious tendrils tousled and sagging in defeated glory. Unburdened, the mare loped over to the weeds that had instigated the unfortunate episode.

John swiftly knelt beside her. "Are you all right?"

The twinkle in his eyes and the smile on his lips belied the concern in his voice, and Charmaine's eyes narrowed on him as she brushed the tangled locks from her face. "It's not funny! I could have been hurt!"

"Then you are all right?"

"I think so," she answered, accepting the hand he extended to help her up. The loosened combs fell to the ground, and the abundant tresses tumbled over her shoulders in a riotous waterfall of curls. In growing displeasure, Charmaine stomped her foot. "This is entirely your doing, I'll have you know!"

"My doing?" John asked, placing a hand to his chest.

"Yes, your doing!" she accused. "Just look at my hair!"

"I'm looking," he replied wickedly, "and I like what I see."

"Oh, you would!"

"What is that supposed to mean?"

"Never mind. I'll not waste my breath explaining it to you. Why couldn't you leave me behind today? Why did you have to press me into this—this—"

"Adventure?" he offered.

"Stop ridiculing everything I say!"

"Stop blaming me for your mistakes," he retaliated. "It was your fault the mare threw you. I warned you this morning not to pull so fiercely on the reins, but did you listen? She might have upset you, but you panicked and yanked too hard on the bit. Now admit it, Charmaine, you confused the poor beast into throwing you. It was entirely your doing."

"My doing?" she raged. "I told you I didn't know how to ride, and still you insisted I join you, promising no harm would befall me! And the poor beast? What about me?"

He was chuckling before she had finished, and quite unexpectedly, her anger ebbed. Then she was laughing with him, her anxiety yielding to relief, returning Pierre's hug when he ran over to them and wrapped his arms around her legs.

"What am I to do with my hair?" she complained.

"Here," John replied, retrieving her combs. "These should keep it out of your face. A prim bun never belonged to the day in the first place."

"But it's too hot to leave down! I should have worn my bonnet, but I didn't think our *little* ride was going to turn into a full day's outing."

"You can borrow my cap," he offered, scratching vigorously behind his ear with a laugh. "The last time I looked it was nit free."

She clenched her jaw and refused to comment.

"Not to worry. It's cool where we are going, and I prefer you this way."

She reached for the combs, but he stepped forward with arms extended. "I'll do it, thank you," she said, snatching them away.

Once the locks were coiffed, she brushed the clinging twigs and moist leaves from her dress, relieved to find the garment was not soiled beyond repair. When she looked up, John was walking the gray mare toward her and Pierre. "Ready to try again?" he asked.

"You cannot be serious!"

"Quite."

"No, sir. I'm not getting back in that saddle, not for a million dollars!"

"Why not?"

"*Why not?* You saw what just happened! I value my life!"

"You have one of two choices, Miss Ryan. You can either get back on your own mount, or we can place Pierre in that seat and you can ride with me."

"Oh, goodie!" Pierre laughed. "I want my own horse!"

"And I have a third choice, sir. I'll walk."

"*Walk?*" John expostulated. "At that rate, we won't picnic until sunset!"

"I doubt that," she said, brushing past him and trekking up the trail.

John ran his hand through his hair, then scooped up Pierre and placed him in the mare's saddle. "Hold on tightly," he admonished as he grabbed Phantom's reins as well and lengthened his strides to catch up with the willful woman.

"How did you find this path, anyway?" she asked, clearly recovered.

"George and I uncovered it when we were boys," he replied. "We used to track through this area whenever we went hunting, and came upon it accidentally one day. Occasionally it's used by the bondsmen."

"Occasionally? Why only occasionally?"

John was about to explain the trail was too narrow to accommodate buckboards, but was suddenly inspired. "The men use it when they're in a hurry, and only when on horseback."

"But why?"

"Because of the wildlife," he replied.

"What kind of 'wildlife'? Certainly not dangerous wildlife?"

John didn't answer.

"It wouldn't be what you and George used to hunt as boys, would it?"

"Actually, yes," he conceded.

"Yes, what? They are dangerous creatures, or they're what you hunted?"

"Both. We trapped and killed a few rattlesnakes here."

"*Rattlesnakes?*" Her eyes shot to the ground and darted about. "Why come this way then?"

"There's nothing to worry about," he mollified. "We cleaned this area out long ago . . . haven't seen one in years, not since George shot his trophy."

"But if it's been cleaned out, why don't the bondsmen—"

"They're just a pack of ninnies," he cut in, "afraid of their own shadows and spreading tales about old man Lavar, who maintained he'd been bitten by one before he died. Robert Blackford claimed it wasn't a snake bite at all."

"But you said Dr. Blackford couldn't be trusted in his judgments."

"True. Still, if you are atop a horse you're safe, and if not, you're clad in boots. What are the chances of a snake biting through thick leather?"

"Probably none," she mumbled, noting John's boots next to her shoes and stockings. Suddenly, she wanted the protection of the lofty saddle. "I suppose I could give riding another try. It wouldn't be fair to impede our progress."

"Good," he said, smiling down at her.

They rounded the bend and reached the twins. "Did she fall?" Yvette asked.

"Yes, she fell. Just like you did the first time."

Yvette was miffed into silence.

With a soft chuckle, John helped Charmaine mount up. Amazingly, she replaced Pierre in the saddle with only a flash of white petticoats. He returned the lad to Phantom's back and led the stallion to the front of the procession.

"Is Mademoiselle Charmaine all right?" Jeannette asked him.

"She's fine. Her horse was just hungry."

They were on their way again, and this time, Charmaine kept her mind on task. After a while, she relaxed, taking in her surroundings: the cabbage and royal palm trees towering eighty feet above them, the sapodilla and calabash blooming in white and pale yellow flowers, the bearded figs with their thick trunks, sporting heavy growths of hanging roots, like ropes gone awry off the rigging of a ship, their interlaced branches harboring the tropical birds that hopped from limb to limb. The soft breezes intensified as they advanced, and soon the foliage began to thin. When the trail widened, John drew back to ride alongside her. Salt was heavy in the air, and they could hear waves thundering on the beach to their right.

Charmaine turned to ask him how long they would ride parallel with the shoreline when she caught sight of Pierre, who reclined against his chest, eyelids sagging. John's gaze followed hers. "He's quite a boy," he murmured, stroking Pierre's hair.

"Yes, he is," she whispered, touched by his gesture of affection.

The trees opened to sprawling sea grape shrubs, white sand, and aquamarine water as far as the eye could see. "Oh my!" she breathed, reveling in the buffeting gales that unfurled her long, wild hair.

"The perfect place for a picnic," John added, regarding her when she didn't immediately respond. "You're not displeased with the location, I hope."

"Displeased? Not at all! I love the ocean. Don't you?"

"That depends on where you are when you're looking at it," he replied thoughtfully, casting his gaze out to the water.

Charmaine studied him, but he said no more.

"Where to now?" Yvette called.

"Why don't you find a spot where we can have our picnic?" John suggested.

"All right," Yvette agreed enthusiastically, "follow us."

They continued down the parched beach, the horses' hooves throwing sand high in the air. Not far ahead was a small cape, the curved projection forming a charming, secluded inlet, a natural barrier against the open ocean. Jeannette pointed to an enormous silk cotton tree, its towering branches spread far over the sandy shore, an inviting haven from the blistering sun.

Once there, the girls jumped from their ponies and led them into the woods where they could graze in the protection of the shade. Charmaine sat indecisively in her seat, apprehensive of dismounting.

"The sooner you take courage, my Charm," John remarked, "the sooner I can hand Pierre over to you. I don't want to awaken him."

Realizing the ordeal would be over quickly if she just got on with it, Charmaine swung her leg over the saddle rim and descended to the ground, quite gracefully for an amateur. She took charge of Pierre, cradling his limp body to her breast while John led the horses into the woods.

When he returned, the twins helped him spread the blanket, and they settled in, delving into the basket that had been packed with a feast. Pierre slept while they ate, Charmaine and the twins on the blanket, John reclining a few feet away against the tree trunk. Few words were spoken until the twins had swallowed the last of their dessert. "Johnny," Jeannette queried, "why didn't you ever bring us here before? I know Mama would have loved this spot."

He didn't answer, and Charmaine looked up. *Would he tell the girl the truth: he loathed her mother? Or was he remorseful for having scorned Colette?*

"Yes," Yvette piped in, "why *didn't* you bring us here when you and Mama planned all those picnics together?"

The statement shook Charmaine, thundered in her ears.

"It was too far to walk," he replied, grabbing his cap and walking to the water's edge. There he stood, gazing out at the horizon.

"But we used to walk much farther plenty of other times!" Yvette called after him. He didn't respond, and she shrugged. "Oh well, come, Jeannette, let's go collect seashells." They raced down the beach, paying little mind to Charmaine's admonition they not stray too far, leaving her to study the man.

What is he thinking? Surely those thoughts could answer a score of questions. She attempted to dismiss the possibilities and began collecting the lunch plates. But her mind betrayed her: *Why didn't you bring us here when you and Mama used to plan all those picnics together? We used to walk much farther plenty of other times! My dearest John . . . John has hurt many people; even Colette suffered at his hands . . . He's a menace to certain members of this family . . . you'll not speak of him again! Nobody likes John, they either hate him or love him, and it's usually in that order . . .*

Dear God, where did it all lead? Hate or love? Or something else? She regarded him again. He hadn't moved. The man was many things, but a seducer of his father's wife? No, she couldn't believe that.

Colette would have loved this spot. As in a daydream, Charmaine's vision blurred, and the blue-green waters melded into the eyes of her dear, kind friend. Just one year ago today, Colette was defending John to her husband. What secrets had she taken to the grave? It was better—safer—not to know.

And the letter. Did Frederic know his wife had written to John a month before her demise? What telling words were contained within its pages? *It is not my intention to cause you greater pain . . .*

Yes, John had known pain. That was obvious. He had remained closeted in his chambers for days after he had learned of Colette's death, brooding in the oblivion of alcohol.

My God! Charmaine thought with quickened pulse. Colette and John. John and Colette. Intimate lovers? Never. Chaste lovers? Possibly. But how? Why? It made no sense and made perfect sense. She refused to believe it, certain her mind was playing tricks on her, yet the more she tried to suppress the unholy thoughts, the stronger they became. She closed her eyes in wild confusion, hoping to calm her raging mind. It did not. They opened to a sound at her feet. John had returned to the blanket.

"Tired?" he asked.

"A bit," she murmured as he settled next to her.

"Riding can be tiring," he said as he pulled his knees up and encircled them with his arms, his eyes trained on the water.

Because he did not perceive her profane thoughts, she felt at ease to study him in a new light. The breeze caressed them, mussing his wavy hair. The sun's rays glinted reddish-blond off the lighter strands, which curled about his ears, over his sideburns and white collar. The locks framed his profile: the wide brow, intense eyes, and clean-shaven cheeks. As he raised a hand to rake back the tousled strands, her gaze traveled to his flexed arm and the play of muscle against his shirtsleeve. Disconcerted, she breathed deeply against her thudding heart and the strange feeling building inside her. She looked at him as a woman looks at a man, perhaps in the manner in which Colette might have.

He leaned back on his elbows, stretching out his long legs and crossing them. Self-consciously, belatedly, she looked away, carrying with her that last glimpse of him—his hair windswept. She wanted to touch those locks, savor their texture between thumb and forefinger, to go further and run her hands through them. Oddly, she felt cheated at residing so close to the object of such wanton desire and unable to act on it. He was affecting her in a most perplexing way, and she was not pleased. *Imagine, wanting to stroke his hair! What am I thinking?*

Pierre stirred beside her, opening sleepy eyes. Dazed, he looked around, then settled his head in her lap, muttering, "Mama."

"He loves you, doesn't he?" John mused.

"Yes," she said, stroking the child's hair, "but he misses his mother."

"Does he?"

"Very much. Colette cherished the children. They were her life.

Although her health restrained her in that last year, she spent as much time with them as she possibly could, even if it was only to be in the same room as they, or hold Pierre on her lap. I know he misses that."

"And the twins?"

"The wound is healing, but the scars remain," she answered. "I'm sure you can appreciate the pain they've suffered. I know the feeling all too well myself."

"I never had a mother to lose," he replied dispassionately, "so I suppose I don't know what they're experiencing."

"Experience isn't the only teacher. Sympathy is easy, defeating their misery, another matter. Time and routine have seen them through the worst. They've accepted the fact their mother is gone."

"And what of you, Miss Ryan? Surely you've given them the love they've needed. Isn't that important for their recovery?"

"Yes, it's important, but I can never replace Colette."

"Perhaps you can. Perhaps you already have. They're quite fond of you, and fondness can grow into love. You could become as irreplaceable as their mother."

"I seriously doubt it. They turn to me because they have no other choice. But if Colette were here, I know to whom they would run." She met his quizzical gaze, then boldly said, "Colette was a fine lady, good and kind."

He didn't disagree, though a wry grin broke across his face. "And you are not?"

"I didn't say that." When his smile broadened, she backtracked, "I mean, I try to be a good Christian, but Colette . . . she was perfect."

"Nobody is perfect, Charmaine."

"Not even you?" she challenged, unable to quell the urge to best him.

His eyes only sparkled. "There's an exception to every rule."

She clicked her tongue and rolled her eyes. Pierre turned his face into the folds of her skirts, calling for his mother again.

"Does he do that often?"

She massaged the boy's back. "Only when he's sleeping. Sometimes I think he feels the loss more than either of his sisters."

"Surely memories of his mother have faded. He's so much younger."

"True, but Colette spent the most time with him."

"Why was that, do you think?"

"Pierre was content to play near her, whereas the twins were always running off, and she couldn't keep up with them."

He seemed displeased with the answer, compelling her to explain. "She would have liked to chase after the girls. In fact, she often complained of how her malady restricted her. That is why she insisted on a governess. She didn't want her infirmity to stifle them. She sought to make them happy, to see them run and play, to . . ."

"Go on," John pressed, "I'm listening."

"I'm afraid I'm talking too much."

"No, you're not talking too much," he said. "In fact, this is the first time you've really talked *to me*. I must admit, I'm enjoying the conversation."

"Circumstances never permitted me to do so, sir," she tersely replied, aware they now tread upon dangerous territory.

"Ah, but I kept the faith," he proceeded lightheartedly. "I knew, given time, I would break through your raging righteousness and reach the real Charmaine Ryan."

"Really?" she snapped, annoyed he presumed to know her so well, that he blamed her for their strained conversations.

"Yes, really," he smiled placidly. "Now, let us not destroy such a hard-won accomplishment. Finish what you were saying, Mademoiselle."

"And what was that?" she asked coolly.

"About the Mistress Colette, and why she favored Pierre over her daughters."

"Favored? That wasn't the word I used." *Why the misinterpretation?* "She loved the twins just as dearly."

"But, according to you, she spent more time with Pierre. Isn't that favoritism?"

"Not necessarily. I told you, the girls were more active than he. Beyond that, I think Colette knew she was dying and wanted to leave him with as many good memories as possible. I suppose she thought the girls would remember her because they were older. With Pierre, she wanted to be especially sure. Even to the end, when most days she was bedridden, she'd find the strength to come to the nursery before he fell asleep at night."

"Does he ask about her when he's awake?"

"I don't think he has to. I think she is with him always, and he happily accepts her presence."

John didn't respond, his eyes shadowed as he looked down at the sleeping boy, and Charmaine knew he'd fallen into his contemplative mood again.

They turned to the sound of laughter and the girls racing toward the blanket. Yvette reached them first. Out of breath, she greeted John by dropping a finely shaped seashell in his lap with the word, "Look!"

"A very nice discovery," he said, holding it up for inspection. "How far did you travel to find it?"

"Oh, not too far. A few miles or so."

"A few miles?" he queried, receiving a shrug.

"You know, Yvette," Charmaine interjected, "if you place the opening to your ear, you'll be able to hear the sound of waves crashing upon the shore."

"Now why would I do that when I'm standing right here and can hear them without some stupid old shell?"

John chuckled. "You were gone all that time and only collected one shell?"

Yvette turned a triumphant smile upon Jeannette. "See? I told you he'd ask that question!" She produced a badly battered chalice she had concealed in the folds of her frock. "This is the real treasure we found!" she bragged, handing him the tarnished item. "Isn't it magnificent?"

"Yes," he agreed as he studied it, the encrusted jewels sparkling in the sun. "Where did you find it?"

"Over by the reef. It was buried in the sand, but I saw something shining, so I decided to investigate. Do you think it's valuable?"

"Valuable? Why, this may be the Holy Grail itself!"

"John," Charmaine admonished, "don't blaspheme!"

"Blaspheme?" he objected. "Mentioning the grail isn't blasphemy."

"What is the grail?" Jeannette asked.

Charmaine explained it was the cup Christ had used at the Last Supper, expressing her doubts Yvette had found the genuine article.

"But is it valuable?" the girl pressed again.

"Let George have a look at it," John suggested with a chuckle. "He knows almost as much about religious artifacts as he does money. The two together should really interest him."

"Where do you suppose it came from, Johnny?" Yvette asked.

"Well, now, I'm not certain, but I have a good idea."

"Where?"

"It is probably a relic from the shipwreck that brought that other 'relic,' Father Benito, to our shores some fifteen years ago."

"You never told us about a shipwreck before!"

"That is because it wasn't something to brag about. If Paul and I had known whom we were dragging from the surf, we would have left him to drown. But we didn't find out he was a priest until it was too late."

Jeannette spoke before Charmaine could protest. "You saved his life?"

"Unfortunately, yes."

Again Charmaine was on the verge of a reprimand, but what good would it do? "What about the others?" she asked instead.

"There weren't any survivors, other than Benito."

His eyes grew distant as if he could see it all before him. "It was a terrible night, fog covered the entire island, and a fierce storm was rolling in. The water was rough, the coastline invisible, the lighthouses useless. The ship crashed into the reef, probably near where Yvette found this. The town's men signaled the alert and came to the house, demanding the aid of the bondsmen. Then Father was off, forbidding us to leave the grounds. But Paul, George, and I weren't about to miss all the excitement. What did we know of devastation and loss of life? So, we sneaked out of the compound and reached the shore before most of the men. George saw him first, floating in the surf. Paul dove in before we could stop him. I knew I'd have my head handed to me if he drowned, so I plunged in after him. We dragged the body out together, fearing we'd rescued nothing more than a corpse. We realized he was alive when he moaned. The tide washed many others to shore the next day, all dead. Little of the wreck was recovered, until this." He studied the chalice again and shook his head. "Benito remained on the island. Father offered him the post of chaplain, and when he recovered, he decided to stay. He wrote to his bishop in Rome and gained permission to minister to our sooty island souls."

"Humph!" Yvette snorted. "You should have let him drown."

"Yvette!" Charmaine scolded, appalled by the corrupt remark. She turned on John. "Do you see where your twisted gibes lead?"

"I see," he muttered, massaging his brow, "so let us drop the nasty subject."

Yvette snatched the chalice from him and put it in the picnic basket for safekeeping, declaring she would not return it to Father Benito. If he hadn't missed it in fifteen years, then it belonged to her.

"We saw a boy swimming!" Jeannette volunteered.

"Yes," Yvette nodded, "and I wanted to join him, but Jeannette said she would tattle on me if I went in the water."

"It's a good thing, too," Charmaine said. "Proper young ladies don't swim."

"That means it's fun," Yvette rejoined scornfully. "It's unfair that *proper* young ladies are never allowed to do anything that's fun."

"Would you really like to learn to swim, Yvette?" John asked.

"Yes! Oh yes!"

"Very well then, take off your shoes and stockings and get out of your dress, but leave on your petticoats, and I'll see what I can do."

"Do you really mean to teach me?" Yvette didn't wait for her brother's affirmation. In a matter of minutes, she was standing on the blanket, barefoot and clad only in her undergarments. "Well? Let's go!" she cried. With a jump, she was off and running.

"Yvette!" Charmaine gasped. The ruse had gone too far. "Yvette, come back here! You'll ruin your petticoats and—"

"Who cares?" she called back. "We're rich! Besides, I have a hundred other ones just like it in my armoire!" She was already knee-deep in the bubbling surf of the cove, squealing as the waves slapped against her legs. She took a step farther out, and Charmaine shifted uneasily and began to rise.

John stopped her. "Leave her be," he chided gently.

She looked up at him, and her eyes grew wide, for he had doffed his shirt and was now bending over to pull off his boots. "Are you serious about this?"

"Of course. Yvette will be fine. She has the good sense to wait for me."

The boots were tossed to the far side of the blanket. His socks followed, leaving him barefoot as well. Next came his belt, and to Charmaine's utter humiliation, he began working at his trouser buttons, as if he fully intended to peel them off right there, in broad daylight. "Sir!" she gasped, quickly averting her gaze, mortified by what seemed a diabolical chuckle.

"Come, Charmaine, take a look. I know you're dying to."

"I'm not!" she objected, looking to Jeannette, whose eyes were trained on him, a bewildered expression giving way to a wide smile. She pulled the girl down beside her, certain she'd die of shame. "I'll never forgive you for this!"

"For what?" he asked and, stepping before her, laughed the louder when she clamped her eyes closed. "Such modesty, even for a woman! What will you do, my Charm, when you have a husband?"

"Put your trousers back on!" she demanded. "Please!"

Crouching before her, he pried free the hands that cupped her eyes. Though they remained closed, he coaxed them open with the words, "I *have* them on."

She took in the cut-off breeches the field workers wore, and her temper flared. "I'm sure you're quite proud of yourself, tricking me like that!"

"Perhaps, but it wasn't planned. Once again, you've brought it all down upon yourself, my Charm. You concluded the worst without allowing me the chance to explain. Do you really consider me so low as to disrobe in front of my own sisters?"

"Oh yes, you had it planned," she returned, "or you wouldn't have been wearing those—those things beneath your trousers in the first place!"

"I was wearing them, yes, but not to embarrass you. I had hoped to enjoy a swim today. That's why I chose this particular spot for our picnic."

Defeated, she refused to say more.

"And you, Jeannie?" he asked. "Would you like to learn to swim, too?"

"I don't know if I should," she faltered, not wanting to cause her governess further distress. But she grew exuberant when Charmaine encouraged her to go.

"It is so warm!" Yvette shouted as they approached, standing waist deep in the surf. "And there are so many fish! Hundreds of them!"

Jeannette dashed ahead, but as the first wave lapped at her feet, she squealed and scurried toward the sand. Then, with arms raised, she danced toward her sister. John followed, and together they made their way farther out, until the girls were shoulder-deep. There they commenced a splashing fight, dousing each other gleefully. When Yvette noticed her brother's hair was still dry, she shouted: "Let's get Johnny!" and turned on him. But he dove into the next wave, resurfacing some feet away, drenched. "I'll show you!" she protested. With that, another battle ensued, the girls showering him with a salty deluge that pelted his face and stung his eyes.

"Careful, Yvette," he warned, "you're setting yourself up to get dunked!"

"Don't threaten me!" she jeered, splashing him harder, screeching when he dove for her, laughing triumphantly when she dodged him. But he continued to stalk her, and with his second lunge, she scrambled to shore, laboring against the strong undertow. "You can't catch me!" she teased, miffed when he ignored her and waded over to Jeannette instead. It wasn't long before she rejoined them.

John took them beyond the breaking waves where they could ride the undulating swells. Clinging to him, they squealed each time they were lifted and dropped, not truly swimming, but swimming all the same.

Pierre awoke to a hearty appetite and ate greedily. He gazed out at the water, and his face lit up. Standing, he pointed to his siblings. "Look!"

"Your sisters are learning to swim."

"Me, too!" he declared, pulling off his shoes and socks. He ran toward the water as fast as his little legs would carry him. No sooner had he reached the shoreline and he was fleeing the bubbling surf that chased him up the beach. When the water receded, he planted himself where dry sand met wet. There he stood, mesmerized by his sisters' antics.

Yvette continued to throw water into John's face, knowing he wouldn't dunk her out there. Charmaine laughed aloud as the man sputtered and objected. She waved merrily back at Jeannette, who had spotted them at the water's edge.

When they tired of their play, John began to teach them to swim. Yvette mastered the strokes with ease, but Jeannette remained timid, clutching John repeatedly. Later, the threesome headed toward the beach, emerging from the breakers. They were soaked from head to toe, a sight to behold with tangled hair and clinging garments.

"Mademoiselle Charmaine," Jeannette heaved, "you should have come swimming, too! It was wonderful!"

"And easy!" Yvette added.

"So I see," Charmaine said, looking from the excited twins to John. He was pushing back a mop of hair from his saturated face.

"Yvette," he called, pointing to the horizon, "I think you forgot something."

With a frown, she squinted out to the water. He snatched her and dragged her back into the churning waves, swiftly dunking her under. She came up sputtering, her eyes shooting daggers that stifled Jeannette's hearty guffaw. John laughed harder. "It's not funny!" she fumed.

"Just evening up the score. Next time, you won't splash me every second."

"You make it sound like a terrible sin!"

"Do I? Well, then, you've been absolved." He reached heavenward. "Repent and sin no more!"

"Who do you think you are anyway—*John the Baptist?*" With that, she sloshed to shore.

Charmaine looked at John, who seemed to have met his match; he had no retort for his precocious sister. He shook his head and laughed anew. Then Yvette was forgotten as he noticed her at the water's edge, his gaze as purposeful as his approach, his bare chest glistening in the blazing sun. She looked down at Pierre, who was squatting at her feet and scribbling with his finger in the wet sand. She picked him up and faced John again, quelling the urge to step back, somewhat fortified with the boy between them.

He smiled down at the lad. "What is that in your hand, Pierre? Some hidden treasure?" The boy giggled and shook his head. "Can we see it?" John probed, poking at the pudgy knuckles.

Pierre pulled his fist away, grazing Charmaine's cheek and spilling its contents into her windblown hair. To her horror, the "treasure" moved, scrambling to safety in her dark tresses.

"Get it out!" she shrieked, sending Pierre into a fit of laughter. She deposited him on the ground, her hands flying to her head, blindly searching for the tiny intruder, recoiling when she touched it. "Get it out!" she cried with each tug of her locks, imagining the cocoon it wove. "Please get it out!"

Now she had an audience. "What's wrong?" Yvette asked.

"Miss Ryan has just made a new friend, and he's building a nest in her hair."

"You're absolutely no help!"

"I didn't think I was permitted to touch your hair, or perhaps you've changed your mind."

"Just get it out!"

"Very well," he chuckled, "now that I have permission, let's see where our little friend has disappeared to . . ."

Her eyes riveted to the flex of muscle in his arm, and her stomach fluttered as he placed a palm against her temple and raked his fingers through her long hair. Those butterflies soared when his thumb caressed her cheek. "It's somewhere in the back!" she hissed, pulling away from his tormenting hand, unable to meet his eyes. He stepped behind her, working at the tangled strands on her neck, lifting and separating the thick curls, unafraid of what lay beneath.

"There it is!" Yvette directed. "See—the hair is moving!"

Charmaine groaned in misery, but in the next moment, the nasty incident was over. The twins screamed and jumped back as her unwanted "guest" toppled out of its knotted lair, hit the sand, and scrambled to the safety of the breaking waves. It too, had had enough.

"Just a tiny sand crab," John shrugged, looking from Charmaine to Yvette. "Nothing to be frightened of."

"I wasn't frightened!" Yvette objected vehemently.

"No? Then why did you jump so high?"

"I was playing it safe."

"And now, Miss Ryan is safe as well. Delivered from one black monster . . ." He let his words trail off, leaving her to draw her own conclusions. "I believe I should thank you, my Charm."

"Thank me? For what?"

She received a raffish leer for an answer as he lifted Pierre into his arms. "That was not a nice thing to do to your governess," he chided lightly.

"Yes, it was!" Pierre giggled.

"Aren't you going to say you're sorry?" John probed.

"No. It was funny."

"Well, then, if you're not going to apologize, you will have to be punished."

Shocked, Charmaine was momentarily anchored to the spot. John was already walking back to the blanket, where he set Pierre down. He couldn't be serious. He didn't seem angry. She rushed up the beach after them.

Yvette shook a finger at the boy. "You should have apologized while you had the chance, Pierre. Now you'll catch it!" She grinned crookedly at John, as if savoring thoughts of the boy's chastisement. "What will the treatment be?"

"The usual, of course."

Charmaine began to tremble as he bent toward the boy, intent upon carrying out his ambiguous threat. To her horror, Pierre only chortled and slapped his hand away.

"So . . . it's a battle you're after!" John declared, his voice bordering on the wicked. He caught Pierre in his grasp—easy prey.

"*No!*"

Charmaine's cry was muffled by John's proclamation: "Now I've got you!"

He sat squarely on the blanket, tucked the boy between tented legs, and began tickling him. Pierre's laughter intensified to a fevered pitch as he squirmed and writhed. But no sooner had he blocked one part of his body than another was exposed. "Stop it! Do it again!" the three-year-old cried over and over again, heaving and out of breath. He managed to roll beneath John's knees and crawl to safety. Exhausted, John did not pursue him.

"Now I get the punishment!" Jeannette exclaimed, stepping forward.

"Only those who've offended Miss Ryan get the punishment."

"Let's all tickle Johnny then!" Yvette suggested. "He's offended Mademoiselle Charmaine lots of times!"

The girls fell on him, pressing the battle. He met their onslaught with one of his own, pinning and tickling each in turn. Recovered, Pierre attempted to join in, but was unable to penetrate the melee. He devised his own plan of attack, scooping up sand and dumping it on John's head. When he delivered a second load, John tore away and stood up. "Good God!" he complained, raking his fingers through his matted hair. "My head feels like an ant hill."

Charmaine's happy laughter drew him around. "You find this amusing?" he asked, sand still clinging to the wet strands.

"You laughed when he put a sand crab in my hair!"

"True, but I also attempted to coax an apology out of him. What's your excuse for not intervening?"

"I have no excuse. I believe you've gotten exactly what you deserve." She threw him a mischievous look.

"That is a most offending statement if ever I've heard one," he mused. "Don't you agree, girls? I think Miss Ryan deserves the punishment."

"Oh, no!" Yvette reproved. "That's only fun for you!"

John missed Charmaine's blush as he regarded his sister in astonishment. "Fun for me?" he inquired tactlessly. "And how would you know that?"

"Because I've had experience."

"Experience?" John reiterated facetiously. "With whom? Joseph?"

"No, not with Joseph. Not with anybody. But I have eyes and ears. I know when things are happening."

"Oh really? And you've seen and heard these 'things' first-hand?"

"That's right," she nodded haughtily.

"When?"

"When we were alone in our rooms about a year ago—the week before Mademoiselle Charmaine came to live with us."

"Really? And what exactly happened?"

"Mama had just left us. She had one of those long appointments with Dr. Blackford. He kept coming to the house . . . at least once a week. And each time he left, Mama seemed worse. She kept saying he was helping her with his elixirs, but I didn't believe that. I knew she wasn't telling us the truth, and I was worried, so I decided to find out for myself. I told Jeannette to tell anybody who came to our room I had gone to the privy. That way I'd have time for my spy mission. First, I ran to the kitchen, and I got a glass from the cupboard—the one that picks up the sound best. Then I—"

"Yvette," John interrupted, "what are you talking about?"

"Let me finish!" she huffed. "Since it was too risky to listen from the hallway, especially with Auntie Agatha patrolling the house, I decided to use Paul's room. That spot would be perfect, because the wall of his bedchamber meets Mama's dressing room wall, and I figured Paul wouldn't be home since it was the middle of the afternoon. Well, was *I* wrong! Not only was he home, but he was *in* his room, and he wasn't alone, either. That rude maid Felicia was with him, and she was only wearing her chemise. At first I was surprised, so I just stood at the bedroom door and watched. She was laughing because he was tickling her. Then, he pulled her real close and bit her neck like a vampire."

Mortified, Charmaine suffered through the narrative, certain her burning cheeks branded her the fool, and John basked in the heat of her misery.

"Oh, it was disgusting!" Yvette continued. "And I told them so. I suppose I should have tiptoed out of the room, or better still, hid and watched, but I didn't think of that until much later."

John burst into uproarious laughter, imagining his brother's stunned surprise when he was caught red-handed in Felicia's buxom embrace, his rapacious appetite whetted, but not satiated.

"What's the matter?" Yvette demanded, sure he was laughing at her.

"Nothing, Yvette," he breathed, "just continue the story; I'd very much like to hear how Paul extricated himself from this one." He continued to snicker and shake his head, vivid images of the man's volatile temper coming to the fore.

"Well, I don't have to tell you how angry he was!" she elaborated, confirming John's thoughts. "In fact, I've never seen him so angry! First, he chased me around the room a couple of times—"

"Don't flower it up, Yvette. Just tell me what happened. That's all I want."

"All right. He did cuss something fierce . . . words I've never heard before, not even on the docks. I tried to remember them all, and even Joseph didn't know what some of them meant. Anyway, I knew I was in *real* trouble, and if I wanted to stay alive, I had better get out of that room. So, as he grabbed his shirt, I ran out and raced down the stairs. But he was behind me before I could hide. Was I glad when Auntie Agatha walked into the foyer with a tray of food!

I ducked behind her, and Paul stopped in his tracks when he realized I'd been rescued."

"Rescued?"

"Well, I'm not stupid," Yvette declared. "I knew Paul didn't want *her* to know what he was doing. He didn't want anybody to know, so before he could say a word, I just mentioned Felicia's name. Then he told Auntie I'd gotten into some 'mischief' in his room and he was taking me back to the nursery. Once we were alone, he gave me a hard shake and warned me never to tell anyone what I had seen. He even threatened me with a spanking. But I only glared at him and promised nothing. After all, what could he really do? I suppose I'm still safe, even though I've told you."

"Unbelievable," John muttered, laughing all over again. "You seem to have a knack for uncovering the inconceivable, Yvette, and your story couldn't have come at a better time."

"Why is that?"

"Miss Ryan and I were discussing a similar matter on our ride here this morning. Isn't that right, my Charm?" he insisted, humiliating her all the more. "That is about as concrete as evidence gets."

"What do you mean?"

"Never mind. Oh, what I would have paid to have seen his face."

"I could do it again," Yvette offered, "and you could wait outside his room. How much are you willing to pay?"

"No, dear sister, I'm afraid I'll have to decline."

"I'll give you a discount if you listen carefully for all the swear words and tell me what they mean."

"I think not," he said, as he walked around the blanket and retrieved his clothing. "Your vocabulary is diverse enough."

"Huh! You're just afraid he'll say words you don't know!"

"You are probably right, Yvette," he answered. "But I hope that was the last time you went into Paul's room to eavesdrop."

"Don't worry, the next time I used the back staircase that opens right into Mama's old bedroom. But Doctor Blackford didn't say anything interesting, so I never tried again."

Charmaine's utter shock gave way to acute disapproval. "Well, young.lady, I will keep a better eye on you in future."

Yvette looked at her askance, smiling when she received another soft chuckle from her older brother.

Ignoring him, Charmaine directed the twins to slip out of their wet undergarments. Yvette protested, begging to go back into the surf, but John responded with a peremptory "no," saying the sea was unusually rough, the cove unnaturally turbulent, and a storm was likely brewing. A second swimming lesson would have to wait for another day.

Charmaine turned from them and bent low to Pierre, who had been tugging incessantly at her skirts to gain her attention. "What is it, my little man?"

"I need to go potty!" he insisted.

She hadn't thought to ask him about such necessities and realized she, too, was in need of such an accommodation. But before she could usher him to the seclusion of the brush, John intervened. "Let me take him."

"No, it's all right. He needs to . . . relieve himself."

"And I have similar business to attend to. Please, let me take him."

Realizing John's absence would allow her to see to her own needs, she agreed, and he and Pierre disappeared into the woods.

The bedraggled girls wiggled out of their wet petticoats, giggling when they realized they'd be wearing very little beneath their dresses for the remainder of the afternoon. Charmaine slipped away, glad to find them working out the knots in their tangled hair when she returned.

John reappeared, fully dressed, with Pierre riding upon his

shoulders. The three-year-old laughed hysterically when the man broke into a trot, bouncing him higher. "Guess what, Mainie?" he said when John set him at her feet. "Johnny has a really big—"

John's hand clamped over Pierre's mouth, muffling the remark. Frowning, Charmaine looked up at the man, his reaction as baffling as his crimson face. Then she understood, and a mixture of discomfiture and amusement washed over her. She'd never seen John embarrassed before, and a part of her longed to laugh out loud, but when he hoisted Pierre high in his arms again and whispered in his ear, "I told you not to say that," she turned away.

For the next half-hour, Pierre squealed as the foamy waves trickled over his feet. Charmaine had taken off her shoes and stockings as well and stood in the shallow surf, enjoying the cool water lapping around her ankles. It was as if it were washing away the pain of the past, replacing it with warm memories. Her mother's presence was strong, not in sorrow, but in contentment. Once, when she was a child, they had visited an aging friend who resided near the ocean. During that month, she and her mother had spent hours on the beach, enjoying a tranquil respite from their harsh life.

Presently, she looked up to the azure sky. Thick clouds were moving in from the southeast. A gull circled high above the water, its wings outstretched, gliding effortlessly. A battering gale sent it careening toward the water in a screaming dive. The bird was inches from the surface when another gust catapulted it upward. It flapped its wings vigorously and reclaimed its lofty flight, soaring out to sea. So near disaster, a brush with death.

Death. Charmaine thought of her mother again, but now she dwelled on the memory of her demise, those miserable days when her mother lay unconscious before passing away. Death. She remembered Colette and those anxious days when everyone was praying and hoping for a miracle. Death. With growing unease, Charmaine feared it stalked her still, the gull a tenebrous warning it wasn't yet satisfied and would take charge of her life again.

"Charmaine?" John's gentle voice brought her around. "You were awfully far away. Richmond, perhaps?"

"Yes, Richmond," she nodded.

"It is difficult to forget the past," he said, as if he understood her deepest insecurities. Odd how he had read her mind. He was holding Pierre against his chest, and she found she liked the combination. Her mother's presence grew strong again, washing away her anxiety.

As they turned back to the blanket, she noticed the twins were missing. "Where are the girls?"

"They ran off into the woods. They promised to return shortly."

"The woods? *Dear Lord!* What of the rattlesnakes?"

"Snakes?" John asked, and then, "Good God! How could I have forgotten!" His hand went to his chest and his brow creased in a show of concern, yet he made no move to find them.

Dismayed, Charmaine dashed up the beach. John raced after her, wearing a wide grin now, finally catching up and grabbing her arm.

"How can you laugh? I've just this minute had a premonition!"

"Charmaine," he said when she tried to wrench free, "there are no snakes."

The struggle ceased. Still, he held her. "What?"

"There are no snakes, rattlers or otherwise. I fabricated the story to get you back on the mare."

She twisted free with an irascible snarl. "*You lied?* I can't believe it! I can't believe you would go to such lengths to get me to ride!"

He chuckled deeply, and his eyes took on a leering gleam. "Ah, Charmaine, you can't begin to imagine the lengths to which I've gone. And if they could get you to ride, it would be worth the retribution of a thousand lies."

"Oh, you crude, dirty-minded—"

Unexpected thunder muted her barrage of insults, and the

amusement faded from John's face. He had dismissed the episode, his eyes on the inky sky, leaving Charmaine to fume all the more. But the next rumbling report caught her attention, too. The gathering clouds had darkened considerably.

"Pack up the food while I fetch the horses," he directed as he turned toward the woods. "This storm is moving in rapidly. The sky was clear a half-hour ago."

"What about the girls?"

"They hear it, too," he called over his shoulder, "they'll be back shortly."

"But Yvette's not frightened by thunder!"

"I'll lay money down she's running faster than Jeannette when they come out of the woods."

Charmaine hurried back to Pierre, who continued to play contentedly in the sand. She dusted him off, carried him over to the blanket, and quickly slipped on his stockings and shoes. She did the same for herself, then gathered up the remnants of their picnic.

Just as predicted, the girls appeared, racing up the beach. Another shudder shook the heavy air. Yvette turned a worried eye to the sky. "I think it's going to be a bad one," she whispered.

John returned with all four animals, and they quickly mounted and headed back the way they had come. Although they took the same route, everything was silent and menacingly still. Not a leaf rustled, nor a branch bowed.

On the main road, the skies to the southeast were black, dense and churning. The winds picked up, buffeting them with gusts that caught at their hair and unfurled the horses' manes. Day was ahead of them, behind them, a vision of night. Thunder shook the air again, and the twins squealed in delight. The horses were agitated, flicking back their ears and neighing loudly. Pierre squeezed his eyes closed. In growing trepidation, Charmaine's regard shifted to John, whose attention was on the sky, often looking over his shoulder. Her apprehension heightened when he shook his head.

Two riders approached at full gallop, and in a matter of seconds, Paul and George were reining in their steeds. Paul leaned forward to speak to John, his eyes cutting away from Charmaine and her disheveled appearance, her windswept hair. "I'm glad you're on your way back. It's a hurricane, and by the look of it, a bad one."

"I just got in from town," George said, "the *Raven* laid anchor not two hours ago. Jonah Wilkinson outraced the storm by forty leagues or so. We had trouble mooring her. The ocean is very rough."

"George is going to the mill," Paul continued, "and I'm headed into town to batten down the smaller ships and secure the quay. Can you come along?"

Charmaine braced herself for John's response. "What of the house?"

"Travis and Gerald are seeing to it. I need your help more than they do."

"Very well," John replied.

Another shaft of lightning and the horses neighed again, pawing at the dirt, a crack of thunder and they shook their heads, prancing in place.

"What about the children and me?" Charmaine protested.

"You're to go back to the house," Paul directed.

"Just follow the road," John added gently.

"*What if the horses panic?*"

John read the fear in her eyes and turned to George. "Can you go with them before you head to the mill? That way I can help Paul."

George nodded and took Pierre from John's lap. Then they were off: John and Paul at a breakneck gallop for town; Charmaine, George, and the children at a quickened pace for home.

They reached the safety of the portico none too soon, pelted by pebbles and twigs hurled on high winds. Even the branches of the great oaks bent to nature's will, their boughs dipping close to the ground. At the far end of the colonnade, two stable-hands labored to nail the shutters closed.

Travis Thornfield greeted them in the foyer. He stood erect like some sentry guarding his post. His normally stoic face was set in lines of concern. "We have six men securing the windows," he said. "Once they're finished, the very heavens may break open, and we will be prepared for it."

"Good," George nodded.

"Is it truly a hurricane?" Yvette asked, eyes dilated with fearless excitement.

"By all outward signs, yes, it is a hurricane," George confirmed soberly.

"Oh, good!" she piped with pleasure. "The house is sure to rumble tonight, and Cookie will be telling her stories!" She recounted the superstitious tales and severe damage sustained during the last hurricane, which had hit Charmantes a year prior to Charmaine's arrival.

"Are such storms really that destructive?" Charmaine asked, disquieted by Yvette's disturbing description. "Surely this one won't cause injury?"

"Charmaine," George said bracingly, "they can be very bad, but not always. All we can do is wait and pray it doesn't hit us directly."

"But Paul—and John—they're still out there!"

"They have plenty of time to secure the island before the worst of it arrives. Remember, they were born and raised here. They know how to deal with a hurricane. Now, I have to get to the mill. I'll be back as soon as I can."

Despite George's reassurance, Charmaine remained worried. It was best to focus on other things, so she ushered the children upstairs for baths and fresh attire. The bedchamber was so dark she had to light the lamps.

She bathed Pierre first. He was very nervous and reached for her each time the wind howled or the thunder rumbled. "Let us talk about our day," she cajoled, certain if she could take his mind off the storm, he'd relax. "What was the best part of our picnic?"

"Ridin' on Johnny's horse," he said with a timid smile, allowing her to strip off his clothing. His gaze traveled up from the floor, his cheeks puffed up in the widest of grins. She smiled in return. Her ploy was working. "Now I know what that's called, Mainie," he declared, pointing to his crotch. "Johnny told me. It's a penis." Charmaine's smile vanished.

"What did he say?" Yvette asked.

"Nothing," Charmaine scolded. "He said nothing."

She quickly turned back to the boy. "That word is private, Pierre. You mustn't say it again."

"Why?"

"Because it is impolite to talk about. Do you understand?"

"What did he say?" Yvette persisted.

"He is not repeating it. Are you, Pierre?"

He obediently shook his head "no," and the matter was put to rest.

The girls had just finished their baths and were brushing out their wet hair when Travis Thornfield appeared at their door. "Your father would like to see you in his chambers," he told them.

Charmaine's face paled, but Jeannette hugged her with a happy smile. "Papa probably has a present for us." Charmaine wasn't so sure. She hadn't even thought of Frederic this morning and felt ashamed that, without a word, she had whisked his children away for the day. Last year, he had specifically set aside time for them. Memories of that first encounter still disturbed her, but that was no excuse for not bringing them to his chambers for a visit. Would he be angry they had spent the entire day with their older brother—that their governess had agreed to the excursion without his permission?

A short while later, they were sitting in the man's antechamber, and to Charmaine's chagrin, the girls immediately dove into a recounting of their most adventurous of birthdays. "We even learned to swim!" Yvette finished.

Frederic nodded, his eyes intense. "I gather you had a nice time then?"

"It was fun!" Pierre replied blithely. "I got to ride on a great big horse!"

Frederic smiled down at the boy who sat in his lap, and Charmaine breathed easier. It was the first sign he wasn't upset. "And you weren't frightened?"

"Oh no, Johnny was holdin' me tight."

"Johnny?"

"Uh-huh," Pierre nodded. "I love him, Papa," he went on in earnest, hugging the man to emphasize his simple declaration. "I'm glad he came home."

Frederic's eyes turned sad and distant.

Yvette spoke across his thoughts. "Those ponies are the best presents we've ever gotten!"

"Yes, I suppose they are," he replied. He smiled again, a mechanical smile by Charmaine's estimation, and she wondered over his sudden melancholy. "I've something for you as well, but I'm afraid it is nothing as grand as your ponies."

"What is it?" Jeannette asked.

"If you look over there in that basket," he answered, nodding toward a corner of the room, "you'll see."

The two girls quickly crossed the chamber, and finding the furry bundles snuggled together, they began to "ooh" and "aah" over them. Pierre quickly jumped from his father's lap and scampered over to his sisters. In the next moment, the kittens were lifted from the basket and tucked under each girl's arm. "Look, Pierre," Jeannette said as she sat on the floor, "a kitten."

"He's so soft!" Pierre observed once he'd stroked the marmalade fur.

The small animal began to purr, and Pierre's eyes grew wide in wonderment. "What's that noise?"

"He's purring," his sister explained. "It means he likes you."

"It means *she* likes you," her father corrected. "Millie says they are female."

Jeannette smiled brightly. "Sit down, Pierre, and I'll let you hold her."

He complied, and she placed the kitten in his lap. He giggled uncontrollably as the orange tabby circled once and twice, then jumped from his embrace. It was time to play, and Yvette's kitten also struggled to be free. In the next moment, the two balls of fur were scooting across the room, wiggling their bottoms and hunching their backs before pouncing upon each other. Then they were wrestling and tumbling, swiftly springing apart to begin the fray all over again, eliciting everyone's laughter. The children drew their happiness from the kittens, Charmaine and Frederic, from their carefree glee, the storm forgotten.

Yvette crossed to her father and threw an arm around his shoulders. "You're right, Papa, they're not as good as the ponies, but they are a lot better than the dolls you gave us last year."

Frederic gave her a fierce hug. "You are a wonder, Yvette."

She moved away, and Jeannette took her place. "I love them just as much as the ponies," she offered sincerely, bestowing a kiss. "Thank you, Papa."

Pierre said nothing. He was mesmerized by the feline's antics and giggled each time they darted from behind a chair and scurried across the floor.

They returned to the nursery, the kittens sound asleep in their basket. Pierre took heed; no sooner had he settled on his bed and his heavy eyes closed, oblivious to the howling hurricane.

With nothing to do, the girls insisted on resuming their treasure hunt. Charmaine agreed—Pierre slept blissfully—and so, they headed downstairs, the girls in search of their remaining gifts, Charmaine, a cup of tea.

As they reached the foyer, George dashed inside, drenched. "The mill's secured," he said with a shiver. "How are you faring?"

"Glad I'm not out there," Charmaine replied. "Is the storm very bad?"

"It's bad, but the worst is yet to come."

"Surely it can't be any worse than what we've already heard?"

"This is only the edge of it. It *will* get worse and last the whole night. I'm soaked and need a good hot cup of tea."

"I was just going to get a cup myself."

"Let me join you then, as soon as I change into dry clothing."

George returned just as she was pouring hot water from the teakettle Fatima had set on the dining room table.

"Still nervous?" he asked, taking the chair across from her.

"Yes. I hate these storms. They were never like this in Virginia. When I see how unaffected the twins are, I feel like a ninny. Will I ever get used to them?"

"No one gets used to them, Charmaine. I've lived here all my life, and even I get the jitters."

She smiled gratefully. "How long does it take to secure the harbor?"

"That depends. But if you're still worried about Paul, you needn't be. With such a lovely lady here to fret over him, he'll be eager to return safe and sound."

She bowed her head with his compliment.

"Besides," he went on, "John is there to lend a hand."

"Will he—lend a hand?" Charmaine asked dubiously.

"Of course, he will," George said, brow knitted. "Don't you believe me?"

She only shrugged, belatedly realizing she had offended him.

"That's hardly an answer, Charmaine."

"I'm sorry, but I've seen them together. You can't deny there's little love lost there. Surely you can understand my reservations."

George put his teacup down. "There has always been a rivalry between them. It goes back a long way, even to when we were boys."

"Yes, and John never misses an opportunity to make Paul angry."

"It works both ways," he replied gruffly.

"What do you mean?"

"Paul does his share of provoking, only it's harder to see."

"Don't tell me John has won you over to his side?" she rejoined.

"There are no sides, Charmaine. I've known them for as long as I can remember. They are brothers to me. I also know what motivates them." He read the confusion on her face, and expounded. "When we were growing up, they vied for their father's approval, but that approval always weighed in on Paul's side."

Charmaine was not swayed. "And I can understand why a father would favor a son who is well behaved over one who is bad mannered."

George shook his head. "Frederic was downright mean to John. So, imagine how John felt when he watched his father's adopted son claim that man's love, while day after day, week after week, year after year, he, the legitimate son, came up empty-handed. Perhaps then you can understand his cynicism."

Perturbed by the revelation, Charmaine had no rebuttal.

"Even so, I know John does not hate Paul for it, and I *know* he would come to Paul's aid if Paul were in jeopardy. And Paul would do the same for John. You might not believe this, but there was a time when they were close, all three of us, we were very close."

"So why the fighting now?"

"Most of it is not as serious as you think. You've seen enough of John to know he's a mischief-maker, and Paul is his favorite target because he takes everything so seriously, always rising to the bait. Most of their quibbling doesn't go any deeper than that."

The late afternoon wore on, and the family gathered in the dimly lit drawing room. Suddenly, there was a commotion in the foyer, a whistling whoosh and the heavy thud of the main door slamming shut against the elements. Charmaine and the twins raced to the archway, followed closely by George. There stood a badly beaten, but laughing, John, who was saturated from head to toe in an exact replica of the night he arrived home. The only thing missing was his cap.

"What happened?" Yvette demanded.

"Where is Paul?" Charmaine added.

The door banged open again, and Paul stumbled in, fighting to secure it behind him. He was equally battered, but was laughing as well.

"What happened?" Yvette echoed.

"Johnny tried to moor a dinghy on his own and took a little dive in the harbor instead!" Paul chortled. "Why you didn't wait for me, I'll never know."

"I did," John replied, his guffaws louder than his brother's, "in the water. It was worth staying under just to get you to jump in after me."

Paul grunted jovially. "I should have left you there, but I care too much."

"If you had really cared, you would have retrieved my cap," John objected facetiously. "I've lost it because of my tomfoolery."

"Well worth the swim, dear brother," Paul snickered, slapping John across the back, "well worth the swim."

"The second one I've had today, only this time I was fully clothed."

Paul stopped laughing, and the smile froze on his lips. "Funny, but I didn't know you were so fastidious about bathing, John. I always thought your tastes ran toward the tainted and soiled."

"Tastes can change," John quipped.

Paul didn't respond, his clenched jaw twitching, his hardened eyes on Charmaine. He stalked off, taking the stairs two at a time.

The assembly stood in awkward silence, flinching with the slamming of his chamber door.

John shrugged. "I suppose all good things must come to an end."

"Especially when you ruin them!" Charmaine blurted out. "You said that on purpose!"

"Actually, it was quite spontaneous, my Charm."

Furious now, she took a threatening step forward. "Oh! If you call me that—that—*stupid* name one more time, I'll—I'll—"

"You will what, *my Charm*?" John pressed, stressing the endearment as he, too, advanced.

"Oh, just leave me alone!" she cried, whirling on her heel and sidestepping George, who eagerly retreated, and the twins who stood their ground, snickering.

John pursued her up the stairs, entertained by her fiery temper. "You should be glad I call you 'my Charm,'" he proceeded to explain. "It's very individual, you see. Not at all like the standard 'y' or 'ie' endings I usually employ. Nothing so common as Paulie, or Auntie, or even Cookie."

Charmaine bit her tongue, determined to say nothing as she reached the crest of the staircase. Raising a hand, she purposefully pushed him aside. With her path cleared, she strode briskly toward her bedchamber door.

Still, he trekked after her. "I had considered an 'ie' ending," he mused, "but, I didn't think 'Charmainie' had quite the right ring to it. For Pierre, 'Charmainie' might be fine, but for *me*, well, it just wouldn't do. What do you think?"

She turned on him to deliver one last retort when their eyes locked. He stood there, soaked to the skin, yet he was smiling, his hands folded behind his back, as if he were the most respectable gentleman come to call on his lady. Unmindful of where her anger had fled, she only knew the absurdity of the situation and the ridiculous dilemma he wished to resolve.

"Well?" he asked. "Will it be 'my Charm' or 'Charmainie'?"

She answered with a genuine giggle.

"There now," he nodded, "you're not so angry after all."

He stepped closer, the flickering lamplight of the wall sconces dancing in his amber-brown eyes. His fingers raised to her cheek and brushed aside a stray lock of hair. Her stomach lurched at the contact and she broke away. His hand remained suspended momentarily, as if to lure her back.

"I—have to check Pierre," she said and headed toward the nursery.

Again John followed her. "He's all right, isn't he?"

"Yes," she whispered as she opened the door and tiptoed in. "He has been napping for nearly two hours now."

At the sound of her voice, Pierre sat up in bed and rubbed his bleary eyes.

"So, you're not asleep," she greeted affectionately, sitting beside him and giving him a hug. He yawned and shook his head. Charmaine looked up at John and found his admiring regard fixed on the boy.

The moment was broken by Yvette's loud entrance. "Cookie told me to inform you dinner will be served at the usual hour of seven."

Pots and dishes clattered in the kitchen, but for all the ruckus, dinner had yet to be served. Agatha pursed her lips and reserved comment, raising a winged brow in a show of impatience. Two chairs remained unoccupied. John was always late, but Charmaine fretted over Paul's unprecedented tardiness. Would he hold his brother's knavish remark about swimming against her?

"So, Miss Ryan," Agatha commented. "I've been told you took the children on a picnic today."

Charmaine regarded her warily. Though the query seemed benign, the woman never addressed her without a hidden agenda.

"Did you have a pleasant day?" she pursued.

"Yes, we did," Charmaine answered simply, hoping to end the discourse.

"And my nephew, John—he accompanied you?"

"He purchased ponies for the girls' birthday. The picnic was his idea."

"I see," Agatha replied. "So, how did you spend all those hours *alone?*"

"We weren't alone," Charmaine responded sharply, the insinuation clear. "We were minding three children."

"I'd hardly term them qualified chaperones, Miss Ryan. For all we know, you could have deposited them anywhere on the island and then . . ." She artfully let her words drop off.

Seething, Charmaine retaliated impetuously. "Oh dear, you've found us out. We dumped the children in the woods and passed the afternoon in one another's embrace. Does that clarify the day's events to your liking, Mrs. Duvoisin?"

The mistress gasped, her slackened jaw falling farther open in unadulterated revulsion. But the rest of the diners chortled, their glee led foremost by George.

Charmaine instantly regretted the sullied remark. *What was I thinking? Dear God, the ramifications!* She blushed profusely and quickly bowed her head. When the merriment subsided, she took courage to look at George, whose eyes applauded her. Just as she smiled in return, John entered the room, humming.

Though informally dressed, his attire was respectable once again, with finely tailored shirt and trousers that highlighted each masculine angle. His hair was wet, but neatly combed, curling deviously over his sideburns and collar. He threw Jeannette a wink as he took his seat.

Footsteps resounded in the hallway, and Paul walked into the room. Her heart skipped a beat with the handsome figure he cut. Like John, his hair was still wet and combed in place, save one glossy black lock that fell on his forehead. His jaw remained set, his brow creased. As he stepped up to the table, Charmaine admired the crisp dinner jacket, white shirt and black trousers he wore, the fabric catching against the well-toned muscles in his legs. She averted her gaze to John, certain he watched her, but he was staring up at Paul.

"Take your feet off my chair," Paul growled.

John abruptly sat up, snickering.

When Paul was seated, Agatha addressed her nephew. "I have been informed you spent the day with Miss Ryan."

"Informed?" John asked lightly. "To be informed, one must have an informant. Who would that be, Auntie dear?"

"Rose."

"Ah . . ." John nodded. "And I'm sure Rose also told you I was spending the day with the children, and their governess accompanied us to assist in their care. So, why are you insinuating I spent the day *only* with Miss Ryan?"

George's chuckle snagged his attention. "Did I say something funny?" he asked, receiving from his friend a shake of the head.

"I know why he's laughing," Yvette spoke up, her smug smile fading when she caught Charmaine's harsh glare.

George opened his mouth, but a bellowed "Ouch!" was all that came out. He reached under the table and rubbed the shin Charmaine had kicked.

John regarded her next. But she wore the same innocent expression he so often employed when making mischief. Something was definitely brewing here.

Pierre's small voice came from out of nowhere. "We went on a picnic, and Mainie said you dumped us in the woods—"

"—and then you spent the afternoon in each other's embrace," Yvette piped in, eager to be the one to divulge the juicy information.

John's eyes shot to his sister. "Mademoiselle Ryan said that?"

When he looked to Charmaine for confirmation, he caught Paul's steely eyes on him. The topic was too hot to drop, and he couldn't restrain himself. He leaned across the table and, to Charmaine's utter shame, clasped her hand much as a lover might. "I fancied our little tryst a secret, my Charm," he murmured, "something just between the two of us, a—"

"Steady, John," George interceded, ending the amorous pledge; Paul could be pushed just so far. "Charmaine was only engaging in a bit of humor. Surely she's allowed an innocent gibe now and then?"

"I'll gibe with her whenever she likes," John responded with a wicked chuckle, his eyes never leaving Charmaine's bowed head.

"And guess what Jawj?"

Pierre, having enjoyed his moment's attention, spoke enthusiastically. Grateful for the distraction, George regarded the boy. "What is it, Pierre?"

"Johnny has a *big* penis! And mine's gonna be that big someday, too!"

"Good Lord!" Agatha squawked. "Of all the scurrilous comments!"

Charmaine hid her face behind a trembling hand, wishing there were a hole nearby. Crawling into it would have been preferable to enduring Agatha's gasps of outrage, Paul's fists striking the table beside her, George's uproarious laughter, or Yvette's declaration: "So that's what Mademoiselle Charmaine told you not to talk about!" John's merry: "There's no substitute for a positive outlook," didn't help matters. There was nothing to do but remain mute and allow the humiliating hullabaloo to die down.

Dinner was served, but it was consumed in relative silence. Paul did not speak at all, and Charmaine dared not look his way. She prayed when he calmed down, he'd accept her remark as nothing more than a joke. As for Pierre, surely Paul could comprehend what had happened there. Still, his rigid form bespoke a man who was beyond angry. So, tonight, he, and not John, perpetrated a quiet misery.

As dessert was served, he pushed away from the table, declining the cup of coffee Felicia offered him. Charmaine's stomach twisted as she looked up at him, chilled by his curt manner. "I would have a word with you privately, Miss Ryan." When she moved to stand, he halted her. "Later."

She felt like a scolded child and lowered her gaze, avoiding eye contact with everyone, especially John.

Paul had been gone all of a minute when Fatima presented a huge cake to the twins. "Happy birthday Miss Yvette and Miss Jeannette. I made your favorite just for you." She placed it in front of the girls and began slicing it. "Oh no, you don't, Miss Yvette," she scolded, "Master John gets the first piece."

"John gets the first piece?" Charmaine reiterated in annoyance.

John leaned forward. "I have to taste everything that leaves Cookie's kitchen. Poison, you see."

The twins giggled, but Charmaine was not amused. "A clever excuse, but the girls should be served before you. It's their birthday." The twins giggled again, and she grew befuddled.

"Tomorrow is Johnny's birthday," Jeannette explained. "Whenever he comes home, we celebrate the two days together. Didn't you know that?"

"No, I didn't know," she replied, looking back to John. "Is tomorrow really your birthday?"

"Yes, tomorrow is really my birthday."

"Why didn't you tell me? We spent this whole day together, and you never said a thing."

"Why should I have?"

"Because, I would have wanted to know."

"Why? Were you planning on giving me a gift?" he quipped. "I know how eager you'd be to choose something special."

"I would have at least liked to wish you well," she answered feebly.

He didn't believe her, his visible skepticism aggravating the awkward moment. Self-conscious now, she babbled on. "I can't believe no one mentioned it in preparation for tomorrow."

"Preparation?" John asked. "What preparation?"

"To celebrate—as we do with everyone else in this household."

"Jeannette has already told you we combine the two days. I'm a big boy now, Miss Ryan, further celebration is not necessary."

For the first time that evening, he seemed disturbed, heightening her confusion. Unwisely, she did not let the matter rest. Had she looked to Rose or George, she would have bitten her tongue. "But a piece of cake is hardly a celebration."

"My birth is not a celebrated event in this house," he said in a low voice. "More important than marking the day I entered this world, it marks the date my mother passed from it. Therefore, my father has never permitted any type of festivity, birthday or no."

"But that's—that's ridiculous," Charmaine sputtered, stunned by his stolid declaration. "Your birthday was never celebrated?"

"No," he replied coldly. "To commemorate such a day would have been nothing less than blasphemy. You see, my father holds her memory *sacred*."

She was incredulous, her heart tied in a painful knot. She took in Rose's bowed head and George's grim face. Only Agatha remained indifferent, her shoulders thrown back, chin jutting in the air.

As everyone began to eat, Charmaine studied John again. He seemed to have dismissed the conversation. Or was he concealing his anguish behind a mask of apathy?

Charmaine preceded Paul into the study. He closed the door, crossed his arms and legs, and leaned one shoulder into the panel as if guarding against possible escape. She had dreaded this confrontation as she waited in the children's nursery after dinner. Now she silently cursed John. He could have denied the fabricated encounter, doused the fire, but no, everything was a joke to him, and pushing the sticky situation to the limit had been so wickedly pleasant, he'd banked it instead.

Paul's face remained stern, like a father about to discipline a disobedient child. Apprehension was now a tangible thing, a demon that somersaulted inside her belly and made her ill. The lengthening silence told her she was already condemned. Then he spoke. "I never thought I'd be forced to this, but your conduct, the example you've set for the children, leaves me no other choice."

She was cut to the quick and could not summon the anger needed to refute his claim. Would he dismiss her? At this moment, she didn't care, for nothing, not even the loss of her position, could cause her greater distress than the censor in his eyes and the rebuke in his voice.

"Have you nothing to say?" he demanded as he pushed away from the door. "Have you no defense?"

"You leave me none!" she choked out.

"I leave you none? You blame me? I wasn't the one who acted improperly today, traipsing about the island with a man renowned for his debauchery. Your behavior was at best depraved!"

"Depraved? It was an innocent birthday picnic!"

"Come, Mademoiselle," he snorted in vexation, "don't pretend you don't understand. You continue to ignore my warnings and allow John to use you, in front of the children—*and*—by every indication, have very much enjoyed it."

"How can you say that?" she objected. "You know I've tried to avoid him!"

"Forgive me if I no longer believe it. I'm not a fool. I've seen many a woman play your little game. But your slip of the tongue? *That* was a major blunder."

"A slip, yes!" she pleaded through tightened throat. "But you can't possibly believe what I said actually occurred today! I swear—"

"Miss Ryan," he interrupted, "you spent the entire day in John's company."

"With the children ever present!"

"And—" he held up a hand to silence her "—did not seem to be avoiding him."

"I had no choice! He insisted the children were my responsibility— that I must accompany them."

"Exactly. He used you—with your consent. You even let your hair down for him!" he declared childishly, his lips twisted in rueful triumph. "Don't think I didn't notice that bit of incriminating evidence when I met you on the road this afternoon. You needn't deny it, Charmaine, for I know you would never have said what you said this evening if you didn't feel comfortable with my brother, *very* comfortable."

"That is not true!"

A shriek penetrated the closed doors of the nursery. When no one answered his knock, John went in. Pierre was playing with the kittens in the middle of the floor, but Jeannette was in the far corner of the room, cowering, while Yvette dangled something above her head.

"Keep it away!"

"Yvette!"

The twins turned toward John's voice, and Yvette rapidly tucked her hand behind her back. "What have you got there, Yvette?" he demanded as he advanced on the girl, his eyes trained on her reddened face.

"It's only a spider," she answered, presenting the creature that wriggled lamely against a trapped leg.

"Throw it down!"

With a click of the tongue, Yvette complied.

John looked about the room. "Where is Mademoiselle Ryan?"

"Paul called her away a little while ago," Jeannette responded.

"To take her to his dungeon, no doubt," John contemplated aloud.

"Dungeon?" Jeannette queried. "Does he truly have a dungeon?"

"No, not literally, Jeannie. But when Paul gets his dander up, being cornered by him is tantamount to torture. Tonight we must act as Miss Ryan's champion."

"Champion?" Yvette asked suspiciously.

"We must rescue her from his clutches," he explained. "The question is, who would like to help me with this chivalrous endeavor?"

"I would!" Yvette volunteered excitedly. "How much do I get paid?"

"Paid? Since when do I have to pay you to help me?"

"Oh, all right, I'll help you for free."

Charmaine was near tears, certain the worst was yet to come—at any moment Paul would mention Pierre. "I cannot believe you are saying this to me!"

"Do you deny he went swimming?"

"He took the twins into the water, and they were all clothed!"

Paul snorted. "I used to believe you were the epitome of decency."

"And now you don't?" Charmaine queried in a tiny voice.

"Now I think you were playing me for an idiot! All these months I've respected your wishes, treated you as a gentleman should, have waited patiently in deference to your *innocence*. I was taken in by your professed virtue, until today. Should I have acted differently? Would you have preferred a direct attack? Is that how my brother has succeeded where I have failed?"

"What—what are you saying?"

"Don't you know? Damn it, Charmaine, I want you—have wanted you from the start. And damn you for preferring to spend the day in John's embrace!"

"But I told you that didn't happen! I was angry with Agatha.

She had passed innuendoes at the table, and I lashed out at her sarcastically without thinking. I swear, there is nothing between John and me! Please believe me!"

It was too much! She burst into tears.

"Damn it," he swore under his breath, his anger flagging, "don't cry. God, how I hate it when you cry." He pulled a freshly laundered handkerchief from his dinner jacket and pressed it into her hand, contrite.

Even with his change of mood, Charmaine could not stop crying.

His remorse increased. "He's done it again, hasn't he?"

"What has he done?" she heaved.

"Connived and twisted an innocent situation to his advantage. He knew his remarks would lead me to believe the worst—send me on this rampage. He counted on it. I suppose I'm no better than he." He drove his fingers through his hair. "I've asked for your forgiveness before. I do so again, though I would understand why you might not find it in your heart to pardon me."

His voice was sincere, his eyes just as earnest, and, as he grasped her shoulders, the electrified atmosphere swiftly changed.

Without warning, the door swung open, and Yvette crossed the threshold. "Mademoiselle Charmaine?" she queried in an unusually meek voice.

"Damn!" Paul swore again, oblivious to his sister's apparent distress.

Charmaine ignored the man's rekindled temper. "What is wrong, Yvette?"

"Well . . ." she began reluctantly as she fiddled with her fingers.

"Well and what is it?" Paul barked. "Let's have it out and over with!"

"Pierre had an accident!"

"An accident?" Charmaine gasped, racing halfway across the room before the girl spoke again.

"In his knickers."

"Jesus Christ!" Paul sneered. "And did you think this 'accident' warranted an interruption, young lady?"

"If you were in our room you'd think so," she rejoined. "It smells something terrible up there!"

"Then you'll just have to endure the stench until your governess and I are finished. Now, return to your chambers and do not leave them again."

"But it's awfully messy up there," Yvette complained. "Jeannette tried to change Pierre's pants, but he only giggled and pulled away from her and . . . and . . . he ran into your dressing room. He even locked the door and refuses to come out!" she added, as if on an afterthought.

"My room! What in the name of God is he doing in there?"

"Hiding I suppose."

"You suppose? *You suppose?* You have two minutes—two minutes to get him the hell out of there. Do you hear me, young lady?"

"But—"

"No buts!" he shouted. "Just do it!"

"Paul—" Charmaine interposed "—I've left them unattended for far too long. I really should return to the nursery."

"No! John is problem enough. I'll not have the pestering of a passel of brats continually trespass against my time with you."

He faced Yvette. "Go back up those stairs and get your brother out of my chambers immediately—soiled knickers and all!"

Confident she had presented a convincing act worthy of John's praise, Yvette strutted from the volatile room. Beyond the doorway, she met him. He was fighting the urge to laugh aloud, biting down hard on a white-knuckled fist.

"You had better make it good," she warned in a whisper. "He's fit to be tied."

John subdued a last chuckle, wiped the moisture from his eyes, and rapped on the doorframe. "May I come in?" he asked with dramatic courteousness.

"What do you want?" Paul growled.

Charmaine stepped forward. "I shall leave the two of you to speak privately. I must see to Pierre."

John agreed, clearly entertained. "Having just now spoken to Yvette in the hallway, I would say he is in dire need of Miss Ryan. Yvette is in quite a dither."

Paul's scowl blackened, his rancor proportionate to his brother's delight, and he fired a barrage of French expletives.

"Watch your tongue, dear boy," John warned as if shocked. "What will Miss Ryan think, since she doesn't know the language? Why, it's like talking behind her back."

"That's right, John, you just keep it up!" Paul sneered, teeth bared.

"I fully intend to."

"You lewd, despicable—"

"How despicable must I be before you storm from the room again?"

"So—you want me to leave? Is that it?"

"I want you to *leave* Miss Ryan alone," John responded. "We all know why you've cornered her this evening, demanding you speak with her privately. I'd call it a brow-beating, and I decided to put an end to it."

"Since when have you become her paladin?"

"Let us just say I've grown fond of her," John answered.

"Let's not. Let us get to the real point, John."

"The point is: you are jealous," John replied, his voice high with merriment. "So there is no point in trying to uncover your point. Get the point?"

"Fine, John, just fine!" Paul threw up his hands and strode to the door.

"Where are you going?" Charmaine called after him, her turmoil resurrected. Everything she had believed to be reconciled was once again in the balance.

"Out!" he blazed. "To get some air!"

"But Paulie, there's a hurricane about!"

"Aye, and its company is preferable to yours!" With that, he was gone.

Charmaine turned to John. "He wouldn't really go out there, would he?"

"I wish he would," he replied flatly.

Her perturbation spiraled into fury, his cruelty solidifying every misery he'd caused her that day. "Oh, how I despise you!"

"Someday that will be different."

The statement seemed a promise, and she balled her fists in outrage.

He stepped in close. "Do you realize how dark your eyes become when you are angry? How the tip of your nose wiggles when you rant and rave?" He placed a forefinger on it.

She tried to swat it away, but his fingers deftly encircled her wrist, lowering and then pinning it to the small of her back. He drew her against him until their bodies met in the most agonizing of places. She pushed futilely against his chest with her free hand, turned her face aside, but he grasped her hair at the base of her neck, entwining it round his menacing fingers. Ever so slowly, he pulled her head back, dashing any hope of escape. Insidiously, he lowered his lips to hers until they touched—a gentle, teasing caress—his embrace like iron, demanding, his kiss tender, pleading. His mouth moved on to the hollow of her neck, and she could feel an intake of breath as if he were savoring her scent. She renewed her efforts to break free, stumbling back a step when he decided to release her.

"As delectable as I had imagined," he murmured.

The sentiment was not reciprocated. Charmaine's hand lashed

out, but for all her swiftness, John caught her wrist again. "You weren't going to slap me, were you, my Charm? Not a very kind gift to bestow on the eve of my birthday."

Twisting away, she glared at him defiantly. "Don't ever try that again!"

"Saving yourself only for Paul, are you?"

"That's right!" she retaliated, and she rubbed her forearm viciously across her mouth, proof of her revulsion. Unmoved, his smile broadened. She gritted her teeth and marched to the doorway.

"Where are you off to, my Charm?"

"To see to the children. You've detained me from my duties long enough!"

"Duty?" he called after her. "There is none."

She came to an abrupt halt and eyed him suspiciously over her shoulder. "What do you mean, 'there is none'?"

"Duty," he reiterated. "There is no *duty*—or should I say, doo-doo? The story about Pierre was a little ruse."

"A ruse?" she asked in stupefaction.

"Yes, a ruse. Concocted to rescue you from my furious brother."

"Saved from his grasp only to fall into yours," she threw back at him.

"A brilliant observation, my Charm," he commented rakishly. "But wasn't it worth it? After all, now you have a basis for comparison."

After a brief lull, the tempest raged again. Charmaine remained in the nursery long after she tucked the children in for the night, but when they refused to settle down, she withdrew to her own room, taking Pierre with her. At the girls' insistence, she left the door open, and slowly, their chattering subsided.

Pierre was asleep in no time. Unfortunately, the arms of Morpheus evaded her. The house moaned and creaked with each ferocious gale, a mimicking reminder of all that had happened that day. Try as she might, she could not get John out of her mind: his taunting, the awkward attraction, his kiss! Her pulse quickened as she recalled his hard body pressed against hers, his lips—not displeasing—a tender caress. She had made certain he didn't know how he had affected her. At least he could not say she'd enjoyed it.

She chided herself for her desire to uncover the soul of the man, to figure out what made him tick. She thought about his quarrel with Paul and wondered if the whole of his waking hours were spent trapping and tormenting his opponents. But he had other sides, too. She had never known a person to display such an array of dispositions. Hate—love, and everything in between.

My birth is not a celebrated event in this house . . . Had Frederic truly spurned him? What happened to this family so long ago? To the adult brothers? *They were close once . . . very close . . .* And where did Colette fit in? *The mistress Colette was a very different woman than the one you have made her out to be . . . She should never have become Mrs. Frederic Duvoisin . . .*

Yes, the hatred was there, manifested in moments of apathy, bitterness, and anger. But John loved as well. This morning, Charmaine had denied his capacity for love, but she was losing stock in that axiom. He loved his younger siblings. At first she thought he sought them out to infuriate her, but she didn't believe that anymore. *They need somebody to love them.* He'd spoken those words earnestly.

She wrapped an arm around Pierre.

For all the love he'd been denied, he hadn't begrudged his sisters any. He had spent the entire day making their birthday special: from the treasure hunt, to the ponies, to his undivided attention. No wonder they loved him so much.

It seemed unfair that a piece of cake presented by the cook would be the only acknowledgment of his birthday. *They ought to reciprocate—show they love him, too.* She quickly formulated a plan, and thus reconciled, cuddled closer to Pierre.

The clock tolled eleven, and John rose from the desk in the study where he'd been reading through documents Stuart Simons, his production manager in Virginia, had forwarded to him. In the hallway, he met Paul, who glared at him. Neither spoke as they strode toward the staircase, reaching it at the same time.

"After you, by all means," John invited, stepping back.

As Paul ascended the three steps to the landing, John's voice halted him. "Oh, Paul, I think you dropped this in the study earlier," and he extended a crumpled handkerchief embroidered with the initials PJD to his brother, dangling it between forefinger and thumb. Paul ripped the linen from John and shoved it into his pocket. His eyes were smoldering, but he refused to speak.

"Don't make her cry too often, Paulie. You wouldn't want to lose a gem like Charmaine."

"I don't intend to."

John's smirk infuriated Paul more than his words. "And not even your manipulation of Pierre will serve your purpose to the contrary," he added.

John's face turned turbulent for only a moment, then he was chuckling. "What's the matter, Paul? Afraid you don't *measure* up?"

"Just stay away from her," Paul sneered, "or I'll be forced to—"

"To what, Paul, inform Father his bad boy son has turned an eye upon the governess? That can hardly hold a candle to my other, more serious, offenses."

"There are other ways to deal with you, brother," Paul enjoined, "and let that be my warning to you."

John only yawned and walked past him, mounting the north staircase. Paul ascended the opposite flight, and had just placed his hand to the doorknob when John's voice cut across the stillness. "Step lightly in there. There was a terrible stench coming from beneath that door an hour ago." John chuckled again and entered his bedchamber.

It reeked of cheap perfume. Felicia reclined in his bed, an inviting smile on her lips, a blanket clasped to her bosom. She sat up, lifting her hands to the back of her neck, removing hairpins, the coverlet dropping to her waist, revealing generous breasts that were quickly veiled beneath the black mane she had loosed.

Without a word, John stepped closer, his eyes never leaving her. She shook her head, and the straight tresses scattered wildly, offering another tantalizing glimpse of her wares. When she spoke, her voice was husky. "Good evening, Master John."

He inhaled and watched as she artfully raised her hands to the base of her neck and pulled her hair up and over the pillow, exposing everything to his view. He moved closer still. "Aren't you in the wrong room, Felicia?" he demanded as he tried to ignore her seductive display. He concentrated instead on holding his anger in check, anger at himself that he was tempted to take advantage of the maid's invitation. In his younger days, he wouldn't have thought twice about it. But then, life had taught him some hard lessons, so perhaps he was learning from his mistakes.

"I was frightened by the storm," she pouted with a giggle. "I thought you would protect me."

Her reply did not soften his stern visage. Instead, his scowl deepened. He scanned the room for her clothing, spotting the garments strewn over the far chair. In three strides, he was across the chamber to retrieve them. She jumped when he flung the articles at her. "I am sorry to disappoint you, my dear," he said in a low, threatening voice, "but I'm in no mood to entertain a frightened housemaid."

"Then allow me to entertain you," she purred.

"No, Felicia. I don't settle for cheap entertainment. But Paul's room is just a short walk away. Perhaps he'd be interested. A word of warning, though: Once he's tired of a woman, he rarely invites her back to his bed."

She was stung by the truth of his words and fell mute.

"Now, I'm leaving this room for five minutes. When I return, you'd better be gone. Otherwise, I'll be forced to evict you, which might rouse the entire house. I doubt even you could bear such humiliation."

The nursery was peaceful, punctuated only by the sound of wind, rain, and deep breathing. John stepped closer to the beds and looked down at his sisters. Next, he turned an eye toward Pierre's bed, but the soft lamplight did not penetrate that quarter of the room. He approached it carefully, and with his palm flat, he brushed over the thin coverlet, searching for a limb, a shoulder, or a tousled head. His hand came away clean. He scanned the mattress again, spanning its full length. It was empty. Alarmed, he turned back to the twins. Perhaps Pierre had settled in with one of them. But his initial impression of the sleeping arrangement was correct; his sisters slept alone.

It occurred to him Pierre was with Charmaine. He stepped through the open doorway, relieved to discern two forms in the four-poster bed, the flickering lamplight dancing over them.

Pierre was sleeping in the bend of Charmaine's body, his back pressed against her bosom and belly. Like his sisters, his breathing verged on a snore, his mouth agape in total relaxation. Charmaine held him fast, her right arm encircling his waist possessively. Her face was expressionless, her locks, usually plaited into obedience were loose and curling over her pillow and shoulders.

She was pretty, more so than the first night he had laid eyes on her, certainly more desirable. John shook his head, now filled with the lovely vision. *Ah, my Charm*, he thought, *if only you had surprised me in my bedchamber tonight. I would not have evicted you.* He studied her face: so innocent. The temptation to exchange places with the boy, to lose himself in the young woman's inviting embrace, was strong. But he wouldn't make that mistake either. Charmaine Ryan was the kind of girl a man married if he took her to his bed. But it was pleasant to dream, and fantasies didn't hurt anyone, so long as they remained fantasies.

As if she heard his thoughts, she sighed in her sleep.

Realizing just how closely he stood over them, John quietly withdrew. When he returned to his chamber, the only vestige of Felicia's presence was perfume in the air and the rumpled sheets she'd thrown on the floor.

From the moment Paul settled his weary body on the bed, he knew slumber would evade him. Tomorrow would demand more of his time in the wake of the storm, and he'd be a fool not to get some sleep tonight. But, he was haunted by a young woman's face: large dark eyes imploring his trust, trembling lips begging to be kissed, long wild tresses swirling about him. Yes, Charmaine Ryan was a temptress, an innocent, unknowing temptress. He'd been an oaf thinking she was anything else, yet she made him so damned angry when she permitted John that sweet glimpse of her vulnerability. John would only use her, hurt her.

He punched his pillow and turned onto his side. Why did it all matter so very much? Why did he lose sleep over it? He'd never lost sleep over any woman before, but then, the others had spent their nights beside him, and he had known exactly where he stood. Charmaine was different, so very different.

Odd, but in her innocence, she was more woman than those with years of experience, a woman he desperately wanted. Their aborted encounters had become increasingly painful, and though he admitted to lusting for her, he also knew she meant more to him than the shallow housemaids whom he had previously used at leisure. Charmaine was far from shallow. She was intelligent, vivacious, and capable of reciprocating any man's passion as long as he loved her.

He tossed in the bed, uncomfortable with the word. *Love* . . . It had always been absent from his romantic vocabulary, a word he avoided to keep his life on an even keel, less complex. He'd seen the games a woman could play with a man's head, the lasting scars she could leave on a heart laid bare, and he wasn't eager to step into that role. Better to keep the upper hand, sample the fruit and move on.

But would a taste of Charmaine be enough? Did he want it to be enough? Where once he believed a simple conquest would vanquish his need for her, now he was uncertain, acknowledging he would not tire of her quickly. In fact, he knew she would please him more than any of the others who had gone before. Was this then love? Somewhere deep inside, he acknowledged that possibility. But he had never been in love before; so how could he know for certain?

Then there was his brother to consider. Charmaine had become exceedingly enticing once he had to compete for her attention. He would have seduced her the night John returned if they hadn't been interrupted. And so the game had begun. He'd lost his temper thrice this night on John's account. He would not allow it to happen again.

He was confident Charmaine could not be attracted to the likes of John, no matter how well his brother played his hand. Sooner or later, John's pranks would push her away, and John would be forced to throw in his hand. Yes, John would definitely lose; he always did. But if he hadn't learned who would take all, Paul would oblige him with one last turn of the card. It was a game in which they had engaged many times, ever since childhood, and John had never claimed the winning hand. All Paul needed to do was sit back, enjoy the spectacle his brother would make of himself, and wait for Charmaine to come running back to him. And when she did, the companionship he would offer would not require a commitment. Yes, John would unwittingly resolve all, including this gnawing fear of love and entrapment.

Chapter 5

Friday, September 29, 1837

CHARMAINE'S eyes fluttered open. The bedside lamp cast a glow around the nursery, but it took a full minute to realize where she was and why she had spent a part of the night in Pierre's bed. Close to three in the morning, a branch from the oak tree had crashed through the shuttered French doors of her bedchamber, rousing the entire house. Within minutes, a crowd had congregated in her room: the children, Paul, John, and George were all there, discussing what to do. Even the servants loitered in the hallway. Agatha appeared and took charge.

John grimaced. "Auntie, why don't you leave?"

"Leave?"

"Yes, leave. This bedchamber—now. The house—tomorrow. Charmantes—forever."

"That's it!" she shrieked. Pursing her lips, she flounced from the room.

Charmaine stifled a giggle and withdrew to the nursery, settling into bed with Pierre. She drifted off to sleep to the sounds of Paul and John removing the large branch, their discourse congenial, brotherly even.

Now, the storm was gone, and all was peaceful, slivers of morning light springing through the slats of the shuttered French doors. She snuggled deeper under the covers and closed her eyes, content. It was too early to rise. The girls were still asleep and Pierre . . .

She bolted upright in the bed. Pierre was not there, and the hallway door stood ajar. She flew into the corridor, pulling on her robe as she went. Everything was shrouded in darkness, save the same broken rays streaming through the boarded-up staircase windows overlooking the gardens. Another shaft of light poured from the slight crack at John's dressing room door. Charmaine moved toward it. A youthful giggle confirmed her suspicions.

"Pierre, are you in there?" she whispered.

A moment's pause, and the door opened, revealing a magical elf. Pierre beamed up at her, sporting a white beard concocted of shaving lather.

"Oh, Pierre! What have you gotten into?"

When she bent over to pick him up, he kissed her, and half of his moustache came away on her cheek, branding her a conspirator. The door opened entirely, and Charmaine's eyes swept upward—from stocking feet to trousers, bare chest to manly face. John was laughing down at her, his own face blanketed in white.

"Is there something you desire, my Charm?" he asked.

She straightened up quickly. "I was looking for Pierre."

"He found his way into my room, so we were using the time wisely. I'm teaching him how to shave."

"Isn't he a bit young for that?"

"You can never learn too soon." He stepped in front of the washstand, took up the straight razor, and caught her eye in the mirror. "It's a tedious chore."

Pierre scurried after him, perching on a chair set to one side of the basin, absorbed with the first stroke of the razor.

"Would you return him to the nursery when you've finished?"

"Certainly," John replied, throwing a wink to the boy.

Five minutes later, Charmaine returned to the doorway. Now John was entertaining his twin sisters as well; they weren't about to miss all the fun.

"But I want to learn, too!" Yvette insisted.

"Girls don't shave," came the answer, and then: "Welcome back, Miss Ryan. I suppose you'll be demanding a lesson as well?"

"Not in shaving, thank you."

He chuckled, mumbling there was hope for him yet.

She comprehended his meaning when his eyes traveled to the bed, and her cheeks grew warm.

"Why do you shave anyway, Johnny?" Jeannette inquired.

"Because he doesn't wanna grow a beard," Pierre answered.

"Exactly," John nodded as he cocked his head to one side and drew the razor across the remaining strip of foam, his voice distorted when he spoke. "I like my face nice and smooth for the ladies I kiss."

"You kiss ladies?" Jeannette asked, astounded.

"Once in a while—if I'm lucky."

"You like kissing them?" Yvette questioned, equally incredulous. "Do you kiss them on the lips like Paulie does?"

"On occasion," he replied, setting the razor aside and wiping his face clean.

"When was the last time?" she interrogated.

Charmaine's eyes met John's in the looking glass and her blush deepened.

"Yvette," he admonished mildly, "that is not a proper inquiry to place to any man, even your brother."

"Just answer the question. When was the last time?"

"Hmm . . . let me think . . ."

"It's disgusting!" Yvette gagged. "I'll never allow a boy to do that to me! All that spit! Yuk!"

John finished drying his hands, then faced them. "Thank you, Yvette."

"For what?"

"For clearing something up for me. You see, one lady I kissed quite recently did not seem to enjoy it at all and responded to my gesture of affection by wiping away my 'spit' with the back of her hand. I suppose she must feel the same way you do. It's certainly an explanation to keep in mind. Then again," he pondered offhandedly, "it could be she prefers a bristly face to a clean-shaven one."

Agatha did not pass a pleasant night. John's newest affront rifled through her mind relentlessly, inducing a maddening headache. Why was life so complicated, hazardous? Why did it constantly throw stumbling blocks in her path? Well, she'd not stumble, had no intention of stumbling. By the crack of dawn, she was composed. She knew exactly how to proceed.

She entered her husband's dressing room just as Paul arrived. Camouflaging her delight, she quickly augmented her strategy and spoke decisively. "I don't want to add fuel to an already blazing fire, Frederic, but this condition extends far beyond John's insults. You've asked me to swallow my pride, even in front of the servants, and, for you, I have, enduring his relentless ridicule. However, I guarantee his abominable behavior is only a prelude of what is yet to come." She paused, her voice waxing with concern. "Last night, I discovered his motives, why he has returned to Charmantes after all these years."

Frederic's pulse quickened. "What are they, Agatha?"

"Isn't it obvious? He's uncovered the plans for Paul's Christmastide gala and is determined to undermine the event. Stephen Westphal has mentioned a number of things he's already done to hinder the endeavor. He wants Paul to fail."

Frederic said nothing, in fact, he seemed relieved, and Agatha bristled, frustration riding high in her voice. "I warn you now, Frederic. I refuse to be humiliated in front of your prestigious Richmond associates and their wives. If John is allowed to remain on Charmantes—if you permit him to play his little games at Paul's expense—then I will remove myself from the planning of those festivities."

She sent beseeching eyes to Paul. "I'm sorry, but I won't participate in the spectacle I am certain your brother intends to manufacture. We will become the laughingstock of influential Southern society."

"Agatha," Frederic attempted to appease, "I hardly think John has any intention of manufacturing—"

"On the contrary," Paul cut in, his eyes stormy. "Agatha is right, Father. We all know what John is like. If he remains on Charmantes, he *will* wreak havoc on this event. He already has."

"How?"

"When the *Raven* laid anchor yesterday, she carried disturbing documents from Edward Richecourt. I was out to the harbor at dawn and received these." He flashed the folio he had been holding. "They're the reason why I'm here this morning. John definitely knows of our plans, learned all about them as early as last February. He's questioned the directives I left with Richecourt in January. Thanks to him, important papers have been delayed and will not reach New York until Richecourt receives word from you overriding John's power of attorney."

"The *Raven*?" Frederic asked. "How long will she remain in port?"

Paul was confounded. He'd noted the man's intense eyes and thought they reflected anger over John's interference. Why then this inquiry about the *Raven*? "A few days," he answered with a frown. "Why?"

Frederic shook his head, his gaze fixed on the far wall. "No reason . . . I'd like to speak with Jonah Wilkinson before he sets sail."

Again, Paul puzzled over his father's reaction, the peculiar request, and was quickly becoming annoyed with his parent's disinterest in the more important matter at hand. "Can we get back to the subject of John?"

"Yes," the elder murmured, his mind feverishly working. Last night, he had debated his choices and struggled with a decision, frustrated to conclude it lacked direction. The *Raven* pointed the way, provided the rudder. Frederic rubbed his brow, detesting this course of action, his thoughts sinking like deadweight on his chest. If only John and he could speak civilly, but that option was closed to them; John would only accuse him of scheming—exactly what he was forced to do.

"Father?" Paul pressed, shattering Frederic's perplexing thoughts.

"Yes . . . John," his sire acknowledged, regarding Paul once again. "I have good reason to believe he will be leaving before week's end."

Though stunned by the prediction, Agatha and Paul remained doubtful.

"If it pleases you," Frederic continued, his eyes traveling to Agatha, "I will speak to John tonight at dinner."

"At dinner?" she asked. "You'll be taking dinner with the family?"

"Am I not allowed to dine at my own table?"

"Of course you are. It's just—"

Perturbed, Paul didn't allow her to finish. "You realize what day it is?"

"Yes," Frederic said, his voice dispassionate, chilling in its emptiness.

Charmaine and the children sat down to a late breakfast. The house had been an exciting place all morning as the barricades from the storm were pulled down, restoring the manor to its palatial glory. John was at the table, sipping the last of his coffee, and leaned back in his chair as the foursome took their seats. Paul was right behind them.

"Have you been abroad to survey the damage?" John asked amiably.

"Hours ago," his brother replied just as congenially. "We were fortunate. The storm didn't strike us directly. Some of the fishing boats are in need of repair, but we didn't lose the *Raven*."

"Good. And the mill?"

"Minimal damage, the only casualty the sugarcane, which will require a few days' salvage work, but if we get on it quickly, it shouldn't be a total loss."

Astounded, Charmaine listened as Paul and John exchanged ideas. They conversed like brothers. *There was a time when they were close—very close.*

The conversation turned to the news of the day. The *Raven* carried various periodicals from England. King William was dead, and the new monarch, his young niece, had ascended the throne. What effect would Queen Victoria's reign have on Duvoisin commerce?

George emerged from the kitchen. Charmaine had hoped to catch him this morning, but when she realized he was only passing through the room, she slipped from her chair and called after him. "George, may I speak with you?"

"Certainly," he smiled, surprised when she boldly took his arm and led him toward the hallway where they could converse privately.

Paul's regard followed the departing couple. He looked at John, but received only a shrug. By the time Charmaine returned, John and he were talking with Pierre.

"And how did you like sharing your bed last night?" Paul asked.

"I wuved it!" the three-year-old replied emphatically. "It was nice and warm when Mainie cuddled me."

"And did you cuddle Mademoiselle Ryan, too?"

"Uh-huh."

"Now, there's a boy who knows how to treat a lady," John interjected for his brother's benefit.

Paul ignored the remark. "Wasn't it a bit crowded, Pierre?"

"Nope," the lad replied, shaking his head twice and crossing his hands over his protruding abdomen. "And the next time there's a huwacane, I'm gonna stay with Mainie in *her* bed. And I'm gonna puh-tect her, too, 'cause I'm not a'scared of no stupid branch."

"But what if we don't have any more hurricanes?" John asked, treating the boy's proclamation quite seriously.

"I can still sleep with her—if I'm very good. Wight Mainie?"

Charmaine nodded quickly, aware of John's laughing eyes on her, certain of what he would say next.

"And if *I'm* very good?"

Pierre supplied the answer. "You can sleep with us, too!"

Charmaine was shocked when Paul chortled, his hearty guffaws eliciting contagious giggles from Pierre, who was quite proud of himself.

John, however, held silent, his chin perched on a fist, a faint smile tweaking his lips, and tender eyes caressing the boy, as if the sight of the child's uninhibited joy was enough to sustain him for the day.

Pierre and Yvette watched the reparations under way. The huge branch had been pushed out of Charmaine's room and onto the veranda last night, the glass removed this morning. Soon, Charmaine joined them, and the three stepped back as John and Joseph detached the splintered shutters and doorframes. Panels from one of the guestrooms awaited installation.

Wiping his brow with his forearm, John turned to the thick tree limb, lifting it as high as the balustrade. Joseph struggled to do the same with his end, but failed. On the third attempt, the branch splintered, falling on John's foot. "Damn!" came the muttered oath, born of frustration rather than pain. Again he blotted his brow dry and turned to Joseph.

"I'm sorry, sir!" the lad blurted out. "I didn't mean to—"

"It wasn't your fault," John ceded, though his voice was rough and his scowl black. "I need a more able-bodied assistant. Where is your father?"

"He's busy with the stable-hands pulling the shutters off the windows. But I'm willing to try again, sir."

"Try again?" John echoed incredulously. "Try again to break my foot?"

"No, sir. I'll be extremely careful, sir."

"I'll help, Johnny!" Yvette volunteered. "And I won't break your foot!"

John sent his eyes heavenward. "You think you can lift something Joseph can't hoist above his knees?"

He missed Yvette's determined nod as he faced the servant boy. "Go downstairs and find my brother. I believe Auntie is gnawing his ear in the study. He should appreciate the interruption."

"But—"

John took a step toward the argumentative youth.

"Yes, sir!" the boy agreed. "Right away, sir!"

He dashed from the room, nearly colliding with Jeannette, who was rushing through the doorway.

"George is back!" she cried, disappearing into the nursery with her sister.

Charmaine and Pierre quickly followed, piquing John's curiosity. "I've never received that much attention," he grumbled. They exited the French doors adjacent to him and leaned excitedly over the balustrade.

George was still at the stable, retrieving a wrapped package from his saddlebag. He threw it under one arm before heading to the house.

"George!" Yvette called as he approached. "We're up here!"

John frowned, befuddled. The girl had never behaved like this toward George before, waving vigorously to be sure he saw her. And Charmaine. She had pulled George aside just this morning. Something was definitely brewing here.

He smiled down at his friend. "Good afternoon, Georgie."

"John," he nodded before turning to Charmaine, the package he carried now raised. "I was able to locate the item you requested."

"Thank you, George," she replied sweetly, "I owe you a favor."

"It was my pleasure. Do you think you can catch it?"

With her nod, he tossed it up, and Yvette quickly snatched it.

"Don't rip it open here," Charmaine ordered, her eyes meeting John's.

"What was that all about?" he inquired when George disappeared below.

Charmaine basked in the moment. "Aren't the employees entitled to a bit of privacy, sir?" she asked coquettishly.

Without waiting for a reply, she grasped Jeannette and Pierre's hands and stepped back into the house. Yvette smiled up at him smugly, then waved the mysterious parcel in front of him, spun on her heel, and joined her siblings.

Paul arrived, and the branch was hoisted over the banister. Joseph appeared below and was told to remove it from the drive.

"That should take him the better part of a week," John sniggered.

"Do you need me for anything else?" Paul asked as Charmaine and the children entered the partially restored room.

"No, that should do it."

"What about those?" Paul gestured toward the doors that needed to be installed.

"I can manage. Why don't you hurry off before Auntie corners you again?"

Paul's countenance sobered. "John," he started cautiously, "Agatha resents what you said to her last night. She's finally made good her threat. She went to Father this morning and complained about it."

"I don't care," John snorted and, as if to emphasize his indifference, turned his attention to the new glass panels.

"You should care," Paul contended.

"And why is that? What is her charge—defamation of character? Auntie doesn't need me to do that. She does it well enough on her own."

"John . . ."

Paul's faltering appeal seemed to reach the man, for he looked up from his work.

"Father plans to dine with us tonight and has promised Agatha he would speak to you."

"Isn't *that* nice," John sneered, cocking his head to one side and folding his arms over his chest. "Thank you for warning me. I'm just *quaking* in my boots."

"It's not a warning, John, it's just . . ."

"Just what, Paul? Just what?"

"Nothing," Paul replied with a shake of his head, "it's nothing."

"Just what, Paul?" John shouted as his brother left the room, waiting a moment longer as if Paul might return. Then he set the French doors in place, muttering "Just what?" one last time.

Charmaine reflected upon Paul's entreaty. Had it been meant as a warning? But to what end? A curbing of John's tongue? Or his abstention from the evening meal? This seemed more logical, and her musings found voice.

"Will you be joining us for dinner?"

"Why wouldn't I?" John asked gruffly.

"I thought—"

"It doesn't matter what you thought, Miss Ryan," he cut in. Then his voice grew heavy with sarcasm. "This is my home, too, and much as some people wish it weren't so, I'm a member of this *great* family. I have every right to take a seat at the dinner table tonight, one I fully intend to exercise."

Charmaine toyed with the ribbon that decorated the present in her lap. The children had been so excited when she told them about her idea this morning, accepting her recommendation they wait until dinner to offer their gift to John. They'd watched the clock all day long, their ebullience near bursting. She couldn't disappoint them now. Nevertheless, she feared the possible outcome of celebrating John's birthday; she was flouting Frederic Duvoisin's prohibition of the event. Was she mad? She'd never seen the two men in the same room together, save that chilling encounter after Pierre's spanking. And now, here she was stirring up a hornet's nest.

They entered the dining room to find Frederic already there, seated at the foot of the table, and not the head. That chair remained vacant, and with growing anxiety, Charmaine questioned the master's intent. If John did dine with them as he vowed he would, then he and his father would be facing each other, setting the stage for what could well become an out-and-out confrontation.

Agatha sat regally to Frederic's left, her hands folded demurely in her lap, a soft smile planted upon her lips. She'd mastered the deceptive portrayal of beneficent mistress—statuesque, beautiful in fact.

"Good evening, Papa," Jeannette greeted blithely, pausing to kiss his cheek as she circled round his end of the table.

"Good evening, princess. How are you tonight?"

"Very well, thank you," she responded as she settled into the chair next to her sister. "How are you?"

"I'm feeling quite fit," he said, his eyes traveling to his other daughter and the parcel she clutched. "What have you there, Yvette?"

"A present," she remarked flippantly, "for Johnny. It's his birthday, you know."

Charmaine inhaled, but was confounded by his benign reply. "Yes, I know."

Then his eyes were on her, and he nodded. "Miss Ryan."

"Good evening, sir," she breathed, quickly turning her attention to Pierre.

The greetings were exhausted and the room fell silent, an uneasy calm in which the seconds gathered into minutes. Charmaine was relieved when Paul's voice resounded in the hallway and he entered the dining room with Rose. He helped her with her chair, then took his own seat next to Charmaine. "Good evening, everyone," he said, and in particular, "Father."

Felicia and Anna appeared and glided around the table, pouring beverages from wine carafes and water pitchers. They exited and returned, bearing abundant trays of succulent meats, fresh green vegetables, fluffy white potatoes, and bread. This spread rivaled any meal Charmaine had partaken of in the manor. Clearly, Fatima had spared nothing when she learned the master of the house would be dining at the table this evening.

When everyone had been served, Frederic struck up a conversation with Paul. "Did you uncover any other storm damage this afternoon?"

"Not really, sir," Paul replied, his respectful response affecting Charmaine in an odd way, having never heard him address his father before. "Our efforts to secure the important areas paid off."

"Good," Frederic nodded. "I can always depend on you."

"Sir?"

Frederic didn't elaborate. "Espoir," he said instead, "any word from there?"

"No. But we secured the harbor in anticipation of hurricane season. The house is well built, and I imagine the burgeoning sugarcane is fine. Most of the plants are small, so I'm not overly concerned. I'll find out on Monday."

"Would you like some company?"

"Father?"

"I'd like to see the progress you've made firsthand."

Paul sat in awe of the statement, as did everyone else at the table. Even Agatha's expression betrayed astonishment. "You want to come with me?"

"Of course I do. Do you object?"

"No, sir. It's just—I didn't think you were ready for such an excursion."

"A few miles at sea aboard a sound ship is hardly an excursion. I'll be fine."

Frederic spoke to his wife. "What about you, Agatha? Would you like to join us on Monday?"

"Yes," the woman eagerly agreed.

"Then it's settled," Frederic concluded, raising his wineglass in a toast. "To Monday and Espoir."

"To Espoir," Paul concurred, warming to the inconceivable idea as he, too, raised a glass.

The cheers died down and varied conversations sprang up among those sitting near one another. More than once, Charmaine's eyes traveled to the vacant chair at the head of the table. Obviously, John had decided to stay away, and though she was certain his decision was for the best, inexplicably, her heart was heavy. She turned back to her plate when voices carried from the main foyer. The table fell silent as all eyes turned to the delinquent intruders. John and George didn't seem to notice as they casually took their seats, talking still.

Frederic laid down his fork and considered John across the table. There was no point in dallying. He'd best initiate the second stage of his plan. His family could not go on this way. It was time his son made a choice. "You're late," he reproved flatly and, after a moment's pause, added, "dinner is served at seven."

John leaned back in his chair, and Charmaine was certain she read sadness in his eyes. But they quickly turned turbulent, a shield erected for battle.

"Sir," George began, "it's my fault we're late. I asked John to help me in the tobacco fields—"

"Don't make excuses for me, George. No matter what you have to say, my father will choose to believe the worst. Isn't that correct, *sir?*"

The sneered title stood in stark contrast to Paul's respectful address.

"My judgment could never rival the Almighty's," Frederic rejoined.

Unnerved, Charmaine's pulse accelerated. Yet, John was smiling. She scanned the table. They all stared at their plates, save Agatha, whose satisfied eyes sparkled. Charmaine looked askance at Paul. His brow tipped upward, acknowledging her silent appeal. So this was how father and son behaved toward one another, the hostility that hardened their hearts.

John's regard remained fixed on Frederic. Finally he stood, grabbed George's plate, and piled it high with all the food within his reach. He placed the heaping dish before his friend, receiving a nod of appreciation. Then he served himself, sat down, and began to eat. After a few hearty mouthfuls, clearly a deliberate tactic to prove his appetite had not been affected, he spoke.

"How are those kittens of yours, Jeannie?"

"They're fine," the surprised girl replied, not daring to expound.

Yvette was not intimidated. "Smudge slept in Jeannette's bed last night."

"Is that the orange one?" he asked, seemingly oblivious to his sire's glare.

"No, that's Orange." When John snickered, she added, "Pierre named her."

"Well, Orange woke me up this morning by walking all over my face."

The children giggled, but Agatha clicked her tongue in disapproval. "The kittens are sweet, Jeannette," she said, "but they should sleep in their own bed, not yours."

The twins' faces dropped, but not John's.

"So, Father," he goaded scathingly, "how is married life after being a bachelor for so very long? Is my dear aunt the perfect wife or does my good mother still claim that special place in your heart?"

Frederic responded impulsively. "Elizabeth's goodness has never been reflected in you."

"Ah, Father, if not my mother, then whom *do* I take after?"

"Good question," Frederic volleyed. "Since the day you were born, you've brought nothing but pain and sorrow to this household."

"Since the day I was born?" John retaliated softly, pensively, the query's message brutally clear.

Frederic winced. *Damn! Why did I say that? Damn!* The wounds would never heal. Their only hope: stay out of each other's way. Tonight's stratagem would see it to that end. It is for the best, he resolved.

Charmaine toyed with her food, wishing only to leave the table. This dinner was all too reminiscent of those she'd partaken of as a girl. Why would a father say such a thing to his son? And why did John deliberately provoke the man?

The minutes ticked by, and the meal labored on. Out of the corner of her eye, she saw John return his knife and fork to his plate. He sat for a moment with head bowed, and then, abruptly, pushed back from the table. He would not be staying for dessert, and in premature relief, Charmaine sighed. They would give him his gift later, at a safer time.

Yvette was not of the same mind and called out as he stood. "Johnny, wait!" She jumped up and hastened around the table, offering him the wrapped package. "Happy Birthday."

Dumbfounded, John made no move to take the gift, so she placed it before him, waiting patiently as he fingered the ribbon that held the wrapping in place.

"You're the best brother in the whole world," she declared adamantly, "and we love you!"

He swallowed hard and released the ties. The paper fell away, revealing a leather cap. He sat back down and leaned his forehead into his hand. "Thank you," he choked·out.

"Don't you like it?" Pierre's voice carried across the table.

John lifted his head and opened his mouth to speak, but Frederic's command cut him off. "Pierre, come to me."

The boy looked back and forth between the two men before choosing. His gaze rose above Frederic's right shoulder. Smiling, he scrambled from his chair and climbed into the man's lap, wrapping his arms around Frederic's neck.

"I love you, son," Frederic murmured heavily. The words were sincere, and though they were spoken to Pierre, Frederic's eyes were on John, leaving Charmaine to wonder for whom they were meant.

"I love you, Papa," the lad declared brightly.

Wood scraped against wood, and John's chair crashed to the floor. He loomed over the table, palms planted on either side of his plate, face contorted and flushed, eyes glassy with tears. "I hate you!" he cried out, the air rushing from his lungs as if he had sustained a violent blow. He grabbed the cap and fled the room.

Charmaine slowly faced Frederic. She found him stroking Pierre's hair, a·twisted smile marking his drawn face, though his eyes were dark with sorrow.

The nursery offered little refuge from the pathetic episode. Charmaine remained numb and, much like the children who sat lethargically in the playroom beyond, was unable to concentrate on any task. Her mind raced on, one thought dominating all the others: hatred, definitely hatred. It was an emotion she knew well, for hatred had been her close companion those tender years when she was growing up. But she'd always kept it inside: a silent, bitter devotion. Not so John.

And what of Frederic? His disdain was just as apparent, just as nauseating. Charmaine was revolted by the polar extremes she'd witnessed: the healthy accolades he'd bestowed upon Paul and the dark slander he'd hurled at John, all in front of his impressionable young daughters. It didn't make sense. Why didn't he just banish John from Charmantes? And why did John, for all his proclaimed hatred, remain? Didn't she know? *No, you don't.*

She jumped with a knock on the door, surprised to find John standing there. "I'd like to speak with you," he said softly. "May I come in?"

She hesitated. He was the last person she had expected to see. "Of course."

He stepped into the room. "I apologize for my behavior this evening. I didn't intend—"

"You needn't apologize to me," she interrupted, uncomfortable with his strained words, relieved when Yvette appeared in the playroom doorway, smiling for the first time since dinner.

"Did you try on your cap?" she asked, walking over to him. "Does it fit?"

"It's perfect. In fact, that is the reason I'm here. I came to say thank you. Though it may have seemed I didn't appreciate it, I do, and I shall wear it as proudly as I did the last one."

"Really?

"Truly," he replied, nodding to Jeannette and Pierre as they, too, entered the bedroom. "Actually, I like it better than the one I lost."

"Why did you tell Father you hate him?" she abruptly asked.

John's eyes dropped to the floor. "It's a long story. It took twenty-nine years to live, and it would take almost as much time to explain."

"Well, if you hate him, then so do I!"

"No, Yvette!" he objected, falling on one knee before her. He took hold of her shoulders and looked her straight in the eye. "You mustn't hate somebody just because someone else does. Hatred is a terrible thing. It destroys lives."

"Then why do *you* hate him?"

"I shouldn't have said what I said tonight. I said it because I was angry, but I shouldn't have said it."

"Why were you angry?"

"You are too young to understand," he tried to reason. "But Father loves you, and it would hurt him to hear you say you hate him."

"Didn't you hurt him?"

"I don't know. But *you* wouldn't want to hurt him, would you?"

He patted her head when she said "no," then stood and whispered a few last words to Charmaine. "I thank you also, Miss Ryan."

"For what?"

"For attempting to make my birthday a special occasion."

Saturday, September 30, 1837

The house was painfully quiet for a Saturday afternoon. It seemed everyone had taken heed of the past night's persecution and had either fled the house or tucked themselves in some remote quarter. Paul was gone at the crack of dawn. The mistress, usually a late riser, followed shortly afterward, leaving by carriage at the unheard hour of seven. And finally, Rose and George departed for town, taking the twins with them. Charmaine had decided to remain behind with Pierre. Now, hours later, she wondered why she hadn't joined them, for the desolate manor feasted upon her melancholy heart. Even Pierre's innocent smile could not lift her downtrodden spirit.

He must have comprehended her somber state, for he gave her a hug and jumped from her lap, dismissing the alphabet book they had been reciting. Presently, he was playing with his blocks, constructing a simple structure.

Charmaine's eyes left him and traveled across the room, settling on the large painting that hung above the fireplace. Funny, of all the times she'd sat in this elegant parlor, she never once studied the portrait. Now she did, with startling clarity: a man and two boys, that's all it had been before. Today it was Frederic, embracing his adopted son, Paul, while his legitimate son, John, stood off to one side, dejected and alone. Her mind wandered far afield, and George's words rang in her ears: *They vied for their father's approval, but that approval always weighed in on Paul's side . . . Frederic was downright mean to John. So, imagine how John felt when he watched his father's adopted son claim that man's love, while he, the legitimate son, came up empty-handed . . .* Her dismal mood plummeted further. Was the portrait displayed just to smite John?

Pierre's tower clattered to the floor. Charmaine watched as he clambered under chairs to retrieve the scattered blocks, building it once again. As it grew taller, it inevitably swayed and crumbled. But the three-year-old was not defeated, and she watched with wonder as the edifice was erected a third and fourth time.

Could John's life be so easily reassembled? Charmaine frowned, greatly disturbed with the comparison. Why had she thought of him in those terms? Why had she thought of him at all? More important, when had she *not* been thinking of him? She was uncomfortable with the realization he had been foremost in her mind for two full days.

Of all the people who had run away this morning, only he and Frederic remained behind. How were they faring? She shuddered again with the memory of the fierce hatred she had witnessed and the conclusions she'd drawn. What if the children became pawns in their despicable game of animosity? Dear God, she'd be in the middle of it. How was she to handle it? There were no answers, but if she were to know any peace today, she had to cleanse her mind of such questions and move forward. With that resolution, she stood.

"Pierre?" she called, setting the primer aside on the table. He looked up. "I have to go upstairs for just a minute."

"Why?"

"I want to write a letter to my friends in Virginia, but I need some paper to do that and it's up in my room. Can I leave you here all by yourself?"

"Uh-huh," he nodded.

"And you'll play nicely with your blocks? You won't wander off?"

"No, Mainie. I'll stay wight here and wait for you."

She winked at him, her heart brimming with love. "I'll be right back."

He attempted to return the gesture, but both eyes blinked at the same time. He tried again, succeeding only when he held one eyelid open with his fingers.

Charmaine laughed heartily.

John leaned his shoulder into the doorframe that connected the study to the drawing room. He had been drawn away from the desk where he'd been reading by the sound of happy laughter, and now he considered the small boy who was singing softly to himself while crawling about on hands and knees, gathering his blocks. A quick scan of the room confirmed they were alone, and he savored the moment that permitted him to watch Pierre inconspicuously. This time belonged to him. He stepped forward. "Good morning!"

Pierre immediately turned around. "Whatcha doin' here?"

"I was about to ask you the same thing."

Pierre pointed to his blocks. "I'm buildin' a house."

"A house, is it? And when you're finished, who's going to live in it?"

"Me and Mainie and Jeannie and Yvie and . . . you!"

"I'd like that," John said, and looking about the room again, he asked, "Where is Mainie, anyway? I thought I heard her laughing."

"She was. But now she went upstairs. She tol' me to wait wight here and she'll be wight back. Then she's gonna make me do the albabet again."

"The albabet, eh?"

"Al-*fa*-bet!" Pierre corrected, annoyed with John's mispronunciation.

John's eyes twinkled. "So you *can* say it properly."

"Yep! Do ya wanna hear it? I can say it real good now and I don' even make no more mistakes."

John listened, nodding his approval when the boy had finished.

Pierre pushed up from the floor and walked over to him. "Do ya know what letter I like the bestest?" he asked.

"No, what letter is that?"

"M."

"M?" John queried. "Why M?"

" 'Cause the two peoples that I love bestest in the whole world start with that letter. Jeannie tol' me so."

John was bewildered. "Really? And who are they?"

"Mainie and Mama, silly."

"Of course."

Pierre grew serious. "Do you know my Mama? She's very boo-ti-ful."

"So I've heard," the man mumbled.

Pierre tugged on his hand. "I'll show you her."

John's face went white; he followed the boy nonetheless.

Their pilgrimage ended at the landing of the north and south wing staircase, there where the portrait of Colette Duvoisin hung—reserved beauty, breathtaking in her unadorned loveliness. Cast in shades of blue, she could have been the Blessed Mother; her eyes radiated compassion born from her own burden of pain.

"Lif' me up!" Pierre demanded, yanking the harder on John's shirt when he didn't respond. "Lif' me up higher!"

John complied and stepped closer to the huge painting. They were directly beneath it now and had to crane their necks to look at the lifelike image.

"That's my Mama," Pierre whispered as if he might awaken her. "Isn't she boo-ti-ful?"

"Yes," John whispered in kind. "She's very beautiful."

Following the man's example, Pierre stretched out a tentative finger and caressed the ivory hands folded on the woman's lap. At the contact, his brow creased in displeasure. The texture of the canvas destroyed the artist's illusion, for it mocked the splashes of color that had so vividly captured the essence of his mother. "She's not alive no more," he said, his candid regard on John now.

"No," John muttered, the words catching in his throat, "she's no longer alive."

Pierre tilted his head to one side, studying John's glassy eyes. "Why are you cryin'?"

"I suppose I . . . miss her," John answered softly.

"Do you love her?"

"Yes."

"How much?"

"As much as you." John gulped down his pain, grasped the boy tightly to him, and buried his lips in his soft hair, taking succor from the embrace.

By the time Charmaine reached the landing, his emotions were in check.

"Good morning, Miss Ryan," he greeted. "Pierre and I were just keeping each other company."

She was pleased to see a smile on his lips, if not in his eyes. "I'm sorry I left him unattended. I only went upstairs to—"

"No need to apologize. We were enjoying our chat, weren't we, Pierre?"

The boy nodded, but was ready to return to his blocks. John set him on his feet and watched him race back to the parlor. He faced Charmaine, waiting for her to reach the landing. Together, they rejoined Pierre, who had resumed his construction of houses and towers. John took a chair close to him.

Charmaine set the stationery aside and sat opposite the man. He seemed intensely interested in the newest structure being erected until he looked up and their eyes locked. She spoke rashly. "Are you . . . well?"

He puzzled a moment. "If you are asking if I've recovered from last night's ordeal," he commented blandly, "I'll survive. There are no visible scars."

"Only concealed ones?"

Again a befuddled frown, and then, a twisted smile. "Why, Miss Ryan, could it be you are coming to understand me?"

"No," she replied, shaking her head. "I'll never pride myself of that."

"Ah," he breathed, "but you are trying."

"I didn't mean to pry," she apologized, uncomfortable with the sardonic smile that now danced in his eyes.

"I don't believe you did. In any case, I don't fault your curiosity." He leaned back in his chair, lending his full attention. "We've spent the better part of two months together, and you've seen most sides of me, many of them ugly. I think it only natural to contemplate my motives."

He paused for a moment, and Charmaine wondered if he were waiting for her to comment. When she didn't, he pressed on, arms folded across his chest. "I'd very much like to hear your assessment—your *honest* assessment of me."

She was flabbergasted. *Is he serious?* "I'm afraid I couldn't!"

"Why not?"

"Because— because—I just couldn't."

"I guarantee you've seen the worst of my temper, if that is your concern. And remember, you did survive." He chuckled. "Come now, I *know* you've waited for this moment—the moment of truth, so to speak—when you could tell me exactly what you think of me, and force me to listen."

"You are wrong!"

"Am I?" he asked dubiously, her flushed face at odds with her assertion. "Well, no matter. I'd still like to hear your evaluation. What if I promised to remain passive and keep a level head? Better yet," he added on an afterthought, "if you pledge honesty, we'll shake on it, and I shall be honest with you. I'm certain there is some family secret you would like to inquire about, something concerning Paul, perhaps? If I can, I will answer any question you place to me."

Charmaine's eyes widened. He had whetted her appetite and knew it.

"Is it a bargain?"

Suddenly, he was towering over her, and unsettled, she quickly came to her own feet. She was uncertain of his intentions until he extended his hand. Slowly, she placed her cool palm in his warm one, her eyes fixed upon the union. She met his gaze, losing herself in the caramel-colored eyes.

"It's a pact, then," he murmured, holding it a moment longer than necessary. "To truthfulness and honesty."

"And you'll answer my questions?"

"As soon as you reveal the real me," he replied with a crooked smile.

She didn't know where to begin . . . Then she did. Hadn't conjecture mercilessly plagued her these past two days? "I think you are a man with a past," she began cautiously, watching for the first sign of discontentment. "Something has either hurt you or left you disenchanted. Hence, you hide behind a shield of sharp gibes and joviality. Life has dealt you a heavy blow, and you intend to repay it in kind. It is easier to be cruel than to forgive, to laugh than to cry."

"On the contrary, my Charm. Most times it is easier to cry than to laugh. Laughter is a hard-won, diligent effort. It must be refined day in and day out to bar despair and ruin. Only then can one subsist—"

"Did you love her?" she whispered, too late regretting her blunder. Already his eyes had hardened. "I'm sorry. I shouldn't have asked—"

"Don't apologize," he snapped. "I shook on our pact." He chuckled hollowly. "That particular question, however, is becoming quite tiresome. Pierre asked the very same one not ten minutes ago."

"And your answer?"

"What do you think I said to a boy inquiring about his deceased mother?" he replied caustically. "Of course I loved her. She was, after all, my 'stepmother.' "

He closed the conversation as swiftly as he turned his back on her. *So much for honesty*. But even in the lie, she glimpsed the truth.

Paul bathed quickly; Stephen Westphal was due within the hour. Much as he'd have liked to postpone the meeting, the banker had flagged him down in town, maintaining his proposal could wait no longer. It was time to bring Espoir's construction phase to a close and her commercial phase to a beginning. With the first ship arriving any day now, Paul needed to cement ocean routes, buyers, and sellers. To that end, Westphal had worked tirelessly for him, his Stateside business connections invaluable, thus the reason for this evening's meeting.

Paul entered the drawing room. It might as well have been deserted, for John stood solemnly at the far end, studying something through the French doors, while the banker fiddled with the starched collar that pinched his reddened neck. "Good evening, Stephen," he greeted.

The man's regard bespoke undying gratitude, as if he'd just been raised from the depths of hell. "Paul," he returned, jumping to his feet, arm extended for a hearty handshake, "I didn't realize how early I was."

Paul moved to the liquor cabinet. "I apologize for keeping you waiting. I was delayed at the cane fields. We're still cleaning up after Thursday's storm."

"Of course, of course," Stephen nodded.

"May I pour you a brandy?" Paul inquired over his shoulder, his eyes going fleetingly to his brother, who already held a glass.

"That would be wonderful," Stephen answered, "if it isn't any trouble."

Paul considered John again. "Couldn't you offer our guest a drink, John?" he inquired sharply.

John turned. "It's not mine to offer. Not yet, anyway."

Paul's eyes narrowed. Obviously, the two men had exchanged words; the question was, what had John said? Agatha's assertions played heavily in Paul's mind. John's behavior toward Westphal could be a preview of what was yet to come, disaster right around the corner if potential investors and business partners were led to believe his brother was undermining him.

Agatha entered the room and showered the banker with exaggerated salutations. "Stephen, it's been too long! How nice to have you as our guest!"

"Agatha, I assure you, the pleasure is all mine."

John winced, muttering, "He's easy to please."

Paul fought the mounting tension. Much as he'd like to tell John to run off and play with the children, a vulgar retort came to mind, and he knew his brother was not above voicing it.

"Will Frederic be joining us?" Stephen asked.

"I'm afraid not," Agatha stated. "He asked me to extend his apologies."

"I'm sorry he cannot be with us." The banker's eyes shifted to John. "Your nephew mentioned a family gathering the other night. Might I presume Frederic's health has taken a turn for the better?"

"In fact, it has," Paul interjected charily. "This Christmastide conference was his idea. He's assisted in every aspect of its preparation, his advice and know-how as invaluable as the funds he's supplied. None of us would be where we are today if it weren't for him, now would we?"

"I'll drink to that," John mordantly agreed, raising his brandy glass.

Paul cast him a murderous glare before suggesting they sit down. "Dinner will not be ready until seven, so we have a bit of time to get started."

Agatha settled into an armchair, but Stephen moved to the desk, unfastened the straps of a leather portfolio, and withdrew some papers. "First, the invitation list," he said, handing it over to Paul. "Those are the men you should invite: farmers, investors, and brokers. The farmers will provide the cargo, and of course, the investors will be critical as the business expands, but it will be the brokers who bid on your cargo space. If you're to commission additional ships as you've indicated, these men, especially the wealthier farmers, could certainly provide the finances. That would, of course, be contingent upon your success. Most would be interested in a long-term return, say, over a five-year period."

Paul looked over the names, his eyes gleaming with pleasure. If only half these men came in December and a mere quarter invested, the cornerstones of financial success would be laid, and he, Paul Duvoisin, the illegitimate son of the renowned tycoon, Frederic Duvoisin, would be on his way.

"I recommend Williamson, Brockton, Carroll, and Farley," Westphal was saying. "They own some of the largest and most lucrative plantations in the South, and are always seeking alternate carriers. Every year their harvests increase, so I suggest you approach them directly. They usually deal with Hiram Gimble. His brokerage is well known, his success due to his bidding clout. If these farmers gain a vested interest in your shipping line, then I'm certain it would affect how they negotiate with Mr. Gimble, bringing their influence to bear, so to speak."

Paul embraced the clever proposal, reveling in the excitement of making his first business deal, the delectable fruits of years of labor.

"These men will indeed be invited, including Mr. Gimble!" Agatha chimed in, her face alight in voracious anticipation, as if the strategies being discussed couldn't be executed quickly enough.

Paul concurred. "But once I've finalized this list, we'll need to meet again and discuss these men in greater detail. Some of the names I know well, but the ones you've just mentioned I've only heard in passing."

"They're all cotton farmers."

Paul faced his brother, who had spoken from the settee where he now reclined. "You say that as if it's a problem, John."

"In the short run, no. Potentially, yes."

Paul weighed the remark. "Do you care to expound, or must I pay you, like you do Yvette, for more information?"

"You're paying Stephen," John returned glibly. "Perhaps he can tell you."

Stephen bristled in unmasked aggravation, his hand going to his waist. "If you're trying to trivialize my knowledge, John, I am the first to admit I am not an expert in farming. I *am* a banker, however, and common sense dictates the men with the largest bank accounts know the most about commerce."

John considered Westphal's monologue for a moment, head cocked, legs extended and crossed, one hand clasped over the other in his lap. "No wonder you doubt my observation. I don't bank with your establishment."

"This conversation is ridiculous!" Agatha expostulated. "Why do you listen to him, Paul? He's trying to distract you. No, worse—undermine you! I don't trust him! You should make him leave!"

Paul ignored her. Much as he hated to admit it, he was curious. "What is your point, John?"

Agatha jumped up. "Paul!"

"Auntie," John cut in coolly, "sit!"

Paul did not intercede. Furious, Agatha bit her tongue and sank back into her chair. Then, realizing she was obeying the command much as a dog would its master, she straightened, pretending at grooming her skirts.

"I concede all the men you mentioned are well-established cotton farmers," John proceeded. "But is cotton the only product you want to ship? Cotton isn't in demand this year. In fact, prices are quite low. Next year, that might change. But the risk always remains high when you place all your coins on one bet."

Westphal took further offense. "Cotton is more than fifty percent of the market. In addition, Williamson, Brockton, Carroll, and Farley afford cargo contacts from regions other than Virginia. Should blight damage the tobacco harvest—or a hurricane, even—Paul would have a second crop to fall back on. Even so, he wouldn't be dealing in cotton alone. The other farmers on that list harvest tobacco, and his Caribbean contacts would be supplying sugar."

The man smiled smugly, and John knew he had devised his reasoning as he spoke. "Ingenious."

Paul frowned. "What else, John? There's something else."

"There are rumblings of a war. It may not happen next year, it may not happen in ten years. But do you really want to take that chance? Throw all your money and hard work into Southern commodities alone?"

"Don't tell me you're preoccupied with this war talk, too? I can't believe this explosion is just around the corner as so many claim."

John shrugged derisively. "I'm surprised you're so indifferent about it. Now, I know all of this speculation is coming from nasty-no-good John, but isn't it just common sense to have all the facts before making a decision? This slave business will not go on forever. The Negroes have had enough of it. Nat Turner proved that in '31. Perhaps invention will beat confrontation to the finish line, but a war almost happened last year. What are you going to do if all of your ports of call are blockaded? Remember, you'll be labeled the Southern sympathizer, so your standard won't be welcome in New York or Boston. Then what are you going to ship, and to where are you going to ship it?" He sighed and shrugged again. "Just a little insight from someone who's been on the mainland for ten years now and knows what the talk is from day to day, in the North as well as the South."

Paul settled into the desk chair, eyes trained on his brother. John's rationale made a great deal of sense, but could he trust the source? John would enjoy seeing him fail at this costly undertaking. "If what you say is true, surely it doesn't bode well for you, either. After all, you're a tobacco farmer and a Southern shipper. So, what are you doing about it, John?"

"Come now, Paul, you've bucked and complained over the changes I've instituted over the last few years. Anything else shall remain unspoken, all in the spirit of fair play."

"What are you driving at, John?"

"I was not privy to any of the plans you were making here and on Espoir before I came home in August. In fact, there was a concerted effort to keep it all a secret from me."

John looked pointedly at Stephen Westphal, who squirmed in his seat for the second time that evening. "What I did find out, I had to coerce out of father's solicitous solicitor, Mr. Richecourt. What I don't understand is: *why?* But, since you felt it necessary to leave me out of the equation, two can play at that game. I've been quite generous in giving you this bit of advice."

Paul rolled his eyes, unmoved. "You know very well why I prefer to leave you out. You've alienated all of influential Richmond with your sharp tongue, and when it's not that, it's your rebellious behavior. You released all of your slaves, without Father's permission, when the rest of the South has been struggling to preserve its right to keep them. And you're telling me about good business decisions? Does it make sense to throw away free labor? And don't sermonize about slave degradation. They can be treated civilly and still be slaves. And what about the people you associate with? They're barely fit to walk the face of the earth, let alone move in the circles of proper society. Edgar Allan Poe. Really! Then you wonder why I don't want you involved in this?"

John leaned forward, placed his empty glass on the table, and smiled. "Nevermore." He stood and strode to the open doorway, turning back as he reached it. "Go ahead and listen to Mr. Westphal, Paul. I'm sure he knows much more about all this than I do. I'll see if dinner is ready."

Paul stared at the vacant archway, then faced the banker. "I'm sorry for that disruption. If you don't mind my asking, Stephen, what did my brother say to you before I arrived? I hope he wasn't insulting."

"It was nothing," Stephen countered with a gracious wave of his hand.

"Nothing?" Paul probed, unconvinced. "Was there some sort of dispute?"

"It was my own fault. Let us not speak of it."

"No, Stephen. You should tell me," Paul insisted, determined to get the details of a discussion that could have serious repercussions on his interests. "I'll take the matter up with my father, if need be. John has no right to insult a guest."

"No need to upset your father, Paul. For some reason John assumed Frederic had invited me to the house. He sarcastically lamented my daughter wouldn't be interested in him once his name was removed from the will."

Agatha jumped in. "You must take these remarks from whence

they come, Stephen. I've learned to ignore anything my nephew has to say. But speaking of Anne, you must supply her address. She must attend our affair this winter. After all, what will the event be without a sophisticated, cultured young woman to grace its festivities?"

Stephen lit up with the suggestion.

Paul, in turn, considered the invitation, appreciating the prospect of Anne London's presence on Charmantes. For all of his brother's assertions to the contrary, John must have encouraged the Richmond widow at some point, thus fanning her forwardness. He pondered the panorama ahead. If John had succumbed to Anne's charms once, he could be vulnerable again, and how would the naïve Miss Ryan feel about him then? It was just the insurance Paul needed, should John remain on Charmantes.

"What about John?" Stephen questioned worriedly, as if reading Paul's thoughts. "I don't think he'll be pleased—"

"It is not *his* invitation," Paul cut in smugly, "it's mine."

Stephen brightened again. No doubt his daughter would be pleased to meet Frederic's other handsome, soon-to-be-wealthy, bachelor son.

Sunday, October 1, 1837

Charmaine finished changing out of her Sunday dress and into her everyday apparel. The girls shouted to her from the other side of the closed door. "We're done! Now may we go down to the stable to see our ponies and the kittens?"

"Yes, but be careful!" Charmaine called to them. "And don't go near any other horses except Angel and Spook!"

"We won't," came the reply.

"And be back in a half-hour for breakfast!"

No answer . . . they were already gone. Charmaine shook her head, grateful they remained happy amid the undercurrents of pain that plagued the house.

Just this morning John had convinced them to move the kittens to a more sensible home: the barn. "You can make a nice bed for them there, and they will keep your ponies calm and happy." When Yvette appeared unconvinced, John insisted she ask Paul and George if she didn't believe him. "Cats are good animals to have around horses. And I'll get a better night's sleep," he added. Apparently, three nights of kitten paws across his face was enough. Now the girls had three reasons to visit the stable: the foal, their ponies, and the felines.

Charmaine entered the nursery moments later and found John reclining on the floor alongside Pierre. They were sailing the boy's model ships across the floor. She paused in the doorway, enjoying the endearing scene. "Are you hungry, Pierre?" she asked. "Time for breakfast."

John looked up. "Hungry?" he queried, noting the late hour. "I'd be famished. I hope Holy Mass was worth the fast."

"It was," Charmaine declared, offended by the irreverent tone of his voice.

John chuckled. "Have Benito's homilies become inspirational?"

She refused to answer, to lie. The priest's fire and brimstone sermons had grown worse, making Sunday Mass nothing more than an obligation.

John's chuckle intensified sagaciously. "I guess some things never change. How can you abide his sanctimonious airs?"

"He is a priest!" Charmaine objected.

"Not by my estimation. Do the words compassion and kindness ever enter into his vocabulary? Better yet, has he ever exemplified them?"

Charmaine bit her tongue. Though John's words rang true, she felt he ridiculed her religious beliefs more than he mocked the island priest.

"I can see you are angry with me," he said. "I'm not faulting all priests. A good friend of mine is a priest, a kind and compassionate man, who could teach our Father Benito a thing or two. Though, I daresay, he is beyond redemption."

"Who?" she retaliated, "Father Benito or your friend?"

Before he could respond, Paul entered the nursery. He took in John's prone form and the deep frown that creased Charmaine's brow.

"Is he annoying you, Charmaine?"

"No," she answered, throwing John one last disdainful look, "not really."

"We were just discussing Father Benito," John supplied mildly. "What would you call him, Paul: good priest or bad?"

Paul grunted, refusing to side with his brother. "I don't have time for this, John. I need to discuss something with you."

"And what would that be?"

"Privately," Paul replied. "I'd like to speak with you privately."

John mumbled something under his breath, but stood and followed his brother into the hallway.

When they were closeted in the study, John flopped into the sofa.

"We will be leaving first thing in the morning," Paul began.

"We?" John puzzled aloud.

"Father, Agatha, and I, as well as a number of the servants."

"What are you talking about?" John asked, completely baffled now.

"We discussed it at the table the other night. Father wants to see my progress on Espoir. We shall be gone for the week."

John's brow gathered, his mind working. "I don't remember that."

Paul rubbed the back of his neck. "Maybe we talked about it before you came in. At any rate, we'll be traveling there first thing tomorrow, and I'd like to know Charmantes is running smoothly while I'm gone. My biggest concern is the sugarcane. Two fields were salvaged from the storm, but the pressing will take all the manpower we've got if we're to minimize the loss. George said he'd oversee all that, but he could use a hand loading the *Raven* once the casks are filled."

"The *Raven*?" John queried, his interest further piqued. "She should have been on her way to Richmond by now."

"She would have been, if not for the storm. Now I need her to transport the sugar extract." Paul paused a moment, but when John did not respond, he asked, "Can I count on your help?"

An eerie silence pervaded the room. John's gaze was fixed on the book-lined wall far across the study, and Paul knew his brother had dismissed the query. He wondered if John had heard him at all.

Paul changed the subject. "There is another thing. I'd like your word, as a gentleman, that you'll not bother Charmaine while I'm away." Again, his brother didn't answer. "John," Paul snapped impatiently, "are you listening to me?"

John's eyes focused on him. "Don't worry, Paul, don't worry about a thing."

Chapter 6

Monday, October 2, 1837

Chaotic commotion gripped the front lawns. A throng of servants, house staff and grooms alike, ran helter-skelter between manor and paddock. Frederic Duvoisin intended to travel abroad this day, and his employees zealously embraced this extraordinary event. Two horses were led from the stable and harnessed to the spanking new brougham, manufactured in Britain, ordered by Paul during his visit there last winter, and shipped to Charmantes only a month ago. The meticulously groomed animals pranced nervously against the bit as the final straps were secured. It took not one, but two footmen to hold them steady when they pulled up to the portico. Still, their skittishness did not deter Travis Thornfield; he hoisted another trunk into the carriage.

Standing out of harm's way, Charmaine and the children watched in wonder. Then the moment was upon them, and the front doors opened for the last time.

Frederic limped out of the house, his ebony cane striking sharply against the stone terrace. He stumbled only once, misjudging the first step, but he quickly righted himself, shooing away his fawning wife when she rushed forward to assist him. "Leave me some pride!" he snarled, the scolding nearly inaudible.

As Agatha backed away, Frederic's stormy gaze followed. Realizing his attention had been arrested, she turned to find the children and their governess loitering at the drawing room casement. "Have you nothing better to do, Miss Ryan, than to gawk at my husband? Surely, the girls have lessons. Or is this frivolous wasting of time a prelude of the week to come when I shan't be here to monitor your shabby supervision of them?"

"That is enough, Agatha," Frederic reprimanded, his words tight. "Miss Ryan is diligent in her care of the children."

"I fear you have been misinformed," Agatha protested, attempting to save face among the many servants who stared at her.

Frederic's ire was rising, but he concealed it beneath honey-coated words. "Have I? By whom? At least Miss Ryan loves my children."

Insulted, Agatha lifted her chin, descended the three steps of the porch, and ensconced herself in the carriage.

Charmaine cheered inwardly, grateful her utter shock forestalled a chuckle. The man was moving toward her, and she quickly composed herself. "Miss Ryan, I would like to say goodbye to my children. Do you have a kiss for me, Pierre?"

"What for?" the boy asked.

"To remember you by."

Frederic stooped over, and the lad kissed his cheek, but before Pierre could pull away, the man's unencumbered arm wrapped around his shoulders and squeezed him fiercely. After a prolonged moment, Frederic straightened up, aware of Charmaine's eyes on him. "One never knows when the last day might be," he offered.

"The last day? But you mustn't say—"

"Yes, I must," he corrected. "I'm pleased with your service to this family, Miss Ryan. My wife, Colette, was correct about you. You have been a wonderful mother to our children. Therefore, remember, I'll not hold you responsible for any circumstances beyond your control."

"Sir?"

"Just remember, Charmaine Ryan. When you become upset, remember." He nodded rigidly, stifling her reply, then turned away, never once requesting a kiss from either of his daughters.

As the brougham passed through the front gates, Charmaine noticed John standing in the shadows of the maimed oak. She couldn't read his expression, but his hand raked agitatedly through his tousled hair. Then he abruptly marched off.

Exhaling, she ushered the children into the house and, allowing for the favorable occasion, permitted them to run off and explore the unguarded homestead. Few had remained behind. The Thornfields boarded a smaller carriage and followed the family coupe to town. Felicia and Anna were already there. Charmaine could only wonder over Paul's whereabouts. He'd left very early, and she doubted she would see him before the ship departed.

So consuming were her thoughts, she walked headlong into George, who was charging across the foyer. Excusing herself, she looked down at the baggage he carried and was horrified to learn he was deserting her as well.

"It was all discussed last night at dinner," he said. "We have to press every stalk of cane we can. Time is of the essence, and I can get a lot more accomplished if I just camp out with the men. Frederic has promised me a bonus if the entire crop is processed before he returns."

Charmaine's trepidation spiraled, and George regarded her bemusedly. "Why should my absence from the house upset you, anyway?"

"I'll be here all alone tonight."

"Alone? You won't be alone. John is still here."

"Exactly. John and only John."

With the dawn of comprehension, George burst out laughing.

"It isn't funny!"

"Oh, but it is!" he wheezed.

"How can you say that? Don't you see, I won't feel safe knowing John is prowling about, worrying that at any moment he could—"

"Could what?" he prompted, noting Charmaine's flushed cheeks, a condition that fed his jocularity.

"I thought you were my friend!" she threw back.

"I am," he avowed, his laughter sobering to a chuckle. "Don't be angry, and don't fret over John. He's the last person you need fear."

"That is easy for you to say."

"Easy because it's true." He was laughing again, a hearty laugh that followed him out of the house, across the lawns, and into the stable.

Agatha studied her husband as intently as he studied the foliage that sped past them. He had scarcely glanced her way since falling into the cushioned seat opposite her. But that mattered very little, as little as his truculent remarks in front of the servants. He didn't mean what he said, hadn't realized how cruel he sounded. His comportment was always sharp, spawned by his handicap and, therefore, easily forgiven. If he were harsh, she would remember they were finally married—that she was his wife, a title that soothed any injury. If the present with its many obstacles was at times difficult to swallow, the promise of tomorrow lighted such days with a shimmering ray of hope. The future was hers, secured by the title of Mrs. Frederic Duvoisin, a title that guaranteed her time to win back his love. Hadn't she waited her entire life, spent every waking hour planning to attain what was hers at long last? She was his wife. Though Robert had scoffed at her purpose, attempted to expunge it, she refused to admit defeat, never permitted the word to whisper through her mind. How could she, when her sole desire was Frederic and only Frederic?

From his first kiss, she knew she could never be satisfied with another, never be whole without him. Dear God, how she loved him. After all these years, she was still in awe of her intense yearning, drawn to him like a moth to a flame. He might be her undoing, but she'd gladly lay down her life if just once he whispered the three words she longed to hear. Then she'd know that no matter what she had done in the name of love, it could not be considered wrong.

Frederic . . . he was handsome still. For all his three score and two years, he could still set her heart to hammering, her limbs quivering, her mind reveling in the memory of wanton passion. Since their marriage, they had shared a few moments of intimacy. For the past two months, however, he had brushed her aside. She pined for his touch of years gone by, before the seizure had sapped his virility. Could it ever be the same again? Dare she hope? With a half-smile, she promised herself she'd do more than that. Thirty years ago, she had been but a novice at the game of love. If only she could have had the experience then that she had now. Frederic would never have dismissed her so easily, would never have been distracted by the wiles of a sister five years her junior.

Elizabeth . . . the fountainhead of her pain, the ruination of her life. Elizabeth . . . eager to snatch away what didn't belong to her. Elizabeth . . . married to Frederic with the change of a season. Elizabeth . . . snickering at her conniving conquest, leaving Britain without a backward glance, without a care for her desperate sister. But, the Almighty had dealt a severe punishment. For all the newlyweds' so-called love, Elizabeth had not survived, a sign their love was not love at all.

Frederic . . . Once again she studied him across the carriage, longed to squeeze alongside him. She'd brush back the lock of hair that had fallen onto his stern brow and caress away his dark scowl. He'd seen so much sorrow, endured so much pain. First Elizabeth, and now John. Like mother, like son. How she longed to set it right for him. But in his bitterness, he overlooked the one person who loved him more fiercely than the sum of all those he claimed to cherish: not his adoring Elizabeth, nor his youthful Colette, not his simpering Pierre, nor his pampered daughters, not even Paul loved him as surely as she did. Someday very soon, he'd see that. He'd realize how blind he'd been, how very wrong to allow John to ridicule her, how convoluted to place obligation and the mores of society first when distributing his wealth. Someday, he'd turn to her as a husband turns to a wife and she would be there for him.

Frederic leaned back into the soft cushions and feigned sleep, contemplating his wife beneath hooded eyes. In a rush, the past spilled into the brougham. It was the year 1807. He was thirty-two, a wealthy bachelor in the prime of his life. She was twenty-two, young and beautiful, very beautiful. But his eyes weren't on her as the carriage sped to Charmantes' harbor. His eyes had found Elizabeth, head slightly bowed, hands folded demurely in her lap, cheeks slightly flushed from their brief exchange in the stable.

Audaciously she had asked, "Are you in love with my sister, Mr. Duvoisin?"

He responded to her intrepid, yet curious, query with one of his own. "What has love to do with a sound business decision?"

She should have been offended; yet, he read something quite different in her brown eyes. It intrigued him.

"But my sister loves you, doesn't she?"

Irritated now, he frowned. "How old are you, Elizabeth?"

"I've just turned seventeen."

"All but grown up," he remarked derisively.

Moments later, she dared not meet his gaze, her manner suddenly diffident. But that did not deter him from feasting his eyes upon her as he had done for the better part of two weeks: not half so beautiful as her older sister, but lovely, animated, and captivating. He had misread her inquiries, thinking it a puerile interrogation born of concern for her sister. He'd grossly underestimated the power she would wield over him and, even today, thanked the Good

Lord he had. That had been the spring of his love. God, how she had haunted him since. The attraction to Colette had been the same, but then, they were alike in so many ways. He recalled the stable; even their private encounters had been similar, uncanny.

Sadly, only Agatha occupied the bench across from him today. At times such as these, he was guilt-ridden. He had probably ruined her life as surely as he had his own. Paul was right: He should never have married her. He prayed his present purpose ended more favorably than their courtship had. He would offer the two in atonement for his many sins.

"But *you'll* be there!" John appealed earnestly. "I want you to come. I'm begging you to come!"

"I'm sorry, John, I can't. That's not what Colette wanted. Beyond that, you haven't even considered Yvette and Jeannette. They'd be crushed."

"Nan—"

"John—I can't. I just can't."

Rose turned away slowly, her heart fraught with despair.

Charmaine froze in the archway. "I'm sorry. I didn't mean to—"

John wheeled round, his face contorted, anguished, like the morning he'd learned of Colette's death. He swiftly masked the emotion and forced a sheepish smile. "Come in, Miss Ryan. Rose and I are finished."

The remainder of the day passed on the same eerie note, escalating Charmaine's initial anxieties. Not even Yvette's exclamations of: "We have the run of the house!" and "No Auntie Agatha to scold us!" or "Just Johnny and us for a whole week!" could quell her misgivings.

Just Johnny and us . . . Therein lay the rub. Charmaine didn't need a week of "just Johnny and us"—didn't want one night of it. Johnny's behavior was peculiar, as were the others'. At dinner, Fatima

Henderson insisted he take extra helpings, as if his meals to come would be sparse. And Rose had taken supper in her room, leaving Charmaine and the children alone with him at the table. He had studied her keenly, a scrutiny that bordered on an assessment, as if he were weighing her worth. Extremely uncomfortable, she had eaten quickly and retreated with the children to the nursery.

Now it was ten o'clock, and they were long asleep. Determined to remain wide-awake until John retired as well, Charmaine needed a book. When she reached the foyer, she hesitated. Did she really want to intrude on the man?

John had closeted himself in the study after dinner, relentlessly pacing. Evidently, it hadn't lessened his turmoil; he was marching still. She'd be a fool to walk into the lion's den. She returned to her room.

The night was a precipice of indecision, punctuated by malicious moments of desperation. Seconds turned into weary minutes, minutes accumulated into plodding hours, and the hours begged for dawn. The great clock struck twice in the foyer. As the tolls diminished, the walls grappled for the reverberating sound and, in the end, surrendered to the void.

John lay abed, listening to his amplified breathing. For the first time in many minutes, his mind was blank. Too long had he deliberated his present crucible, weighing each option, rejecting those that suited him best, realizing—even from the onset of this miserable day—he could not wrest what he had never claimed, for in so doing, he would forfeit the precious, meager contentment he had been rewarded these past weeks.

His happiness depended on that of another. And since no one would conspire with him, he would be wise to surrender to the hopelessness of it all, his inability to proceed in any direction save the one thus far charted. Float with the tide . . . the course destined to govern his life.

God, how he hated this prison that had shackled him for so many years! He could not advance, he could not retreat, he could only remember and curse heaven for the hard hand dealt him, the hand he had chosen to pick up and play. And yet, something had to be done. If nothing else, he'd be damned if he'd pass another three hours in his rumpled bed, tossing and turning in exhausted turmoil.

He threw aside the linens and jumped up. But as he started pacing again, piercing memories took hold. He had devoutly embraced those recollections, hoping the future would set them free. The future had never come; the past had never died. It was time the two met and were buried, peacefully. Perhaps there was a chance for that, if only he could evoke his passion and release his despair. Suddenly, he knew where to turn. He pulled on his robe and, unmindful of those he might disturb, slammed the door as he left his room.

Charmaine bolted from a fitful slumber, feverishly tracking the tread of heavy footsteps diminishing in the corridor beyond. She knew who was stalking the house at this late hour. She strained to detect the returning steps of her predator, certain they would be menacingly soft, perhaps imperceptible. Even though she'd locked her door, she feared access from the veranda or the unused dressing room, or even the nursery. Seconds gave way to minutes and, as her racing heart lulled, so too did her breathing. Nothing—no sinister sound of danger. Had the man left the house or merely his chambers? Was he once again pacing in the study, perhaps plotting his assault of the vulnerable governess? John wasn't like that, she reasoned. He'd never given her reason to believe him capable of rape. After all, she'd been just as defenseless the night of his arrival. Still, that first night had not offered the same unencumbered opportunity. Tonight, there was no Paul, no servants, no one to come to her aid should she scream. Rape . . . She shuddered. But wouldn't he have accosted her sooner? The night was half spent and, save the fact he could not sleep, would be no different than any other.

Then it came: an abandoned melody. *Am I dreaming?* She canted her head, but could only capture wisps of the blossoming sonata. Instantly, she was out of bed. She wasn't dreaming! Someone was mastering the incredible score, calling her to come and listen. She rushed out of the barricaded room, pulling on her robe as she went, following the music that floated up to her on silken wings. If only Colette were here . . .

She found herself standing barefoot in the drawing room doorway without memory of her descent. John was seated at the piano, his back to her, head slightly bowed. At first, his hands caressed the keys, coaxing from the instrument a heart-wrenching loneliness, a fervent yearning. Abruptly, his irate fingers struck out, evoking a tidal wave of passion. Her eyes were drawn to the candelabrum, mesmerized by the flickering flames that danced wildly to the amplifying rhapsody, the man's movements displacing the air nearest them. She felt akin to the wick, scorched and devoured, spent in the wake of such power and majesty, yet transformed and at peace, like the hot wax that wept onto the piano's ebony surface.

As the climax broke, John faltered. A jarring dissonance echoed off the walls, and he pulled away as if cauterized. Then, his hands came crashing down again, as if he could pound his mistake from existence. The keys locked, and a deliberate, brutal cacophony seized the air.

Charmaine grimaced, aching for the loveliness that had been annihilated.

Slowly, the punishment ebbed. Laying both arms across the keyboard, John buried his face there, weathering the constricting thud of his battered heart. He'd hoped to exorcise his demonic desolation, not conjure it. He inhaled deeply, then shuddered as he released the pent-up breath, unaware of the young woman who stood in the shadows, observing him in this new light.

Much later, Charmaine would wonder why she hadn't escaped back to her room. "Don't stop," she implored, stepping into the parlor.

John turned and scowled. Tonight he needed to be alone.

"What I mean is—you play very well."

John grunted. "The one thing I'm able to do right."

"Except for the last few measures."

"Except that," he agreed, his voice hard.

She took no offense. He seemed to be chastising himself. "Even so, one mistake shouldn't cause you to dismiss the piece entirely. After all, look how well you've played most of it. Mrs. Harrington used to always say—"

"Isn't it a bit late for you to be up, Mademoiselle?" he cut in brusquely.

Charmaine faltered. "I was awakened by the music."

"My apologies."

"No need to apologize. I happen to love that particular piece."

"Do you?" he mocked. "I've never heard you play it."

"I don't do it justice. Colette used to encourage me, but after she died, I was forbidden to—"

"Forbidden?" he demanded, his vexation giving way to full-fired wrath. "Who forbade it?"

The truth had stood just behind a doorway, awaiting the portal to be thrown open, and comprehension, with all its answers, came crashing down upon Charmaine. *Forbidden* . . . the word that unlocked so many doors and shed light on so many questions. Playing the music—forbidden. Mentioning John's name—forbidden. Writing to him—forbidden. John seeking out the children—forbidden. Bearing more children—forbidden. John and Colette—*forbidden!* Everything Charmaine had surmised was true! Had to be true! Pray God it wasn't true!

"I—shouldn't have come down here," she stumbled aloud.

But before she could reach the archway, John caught her arm

from behind. "Not so quickly!" he ordered, pulling her around to face him. "You haven't answered my question."

She didn't flinch, neither did she pull away. Her melancholy eyes lifted to his, dousing his fiery reaction. "Please . . . don't go," he whispered, releasing her arm. "It was my father, wasn't it? He was the one who wouldn't allow you to play the piece, wasn't he?"

"Yes," she conceded. "I'm sorry."

"Why? Why should you be sorry?"

"I don't want to make matters worse between you and your father."

He snorted in disgust. "Colette used to say the very same thing, but you have less control over this miserable situation than she did, and she had precious little then. As I've said before, it took twenty-nine years to live. Nothing can worsen what is already the most deplorable of relationships between a father and son."

"Even so, it must pain you, though you deny it."

"I deny nothing, save the fact neither you nor Colette are to blame."

"But I am responsible for mentioning it. It doesn't please me to know I've hurt you."

The statement seemed to confound him. "Why would you harbor any compassion for me?"

"I don't know," she answered truthfully. "Perhaps it's because I'm beginning to comprehend your past. I'm not certain what happened here years ago, but I think it transcends your childhood and . . ." She hesitated, reticent.

"And?" he probed.

"I think I've grown to like you, in some ways, even respect you. In either case, I don't think you deserve to be hurt."

"No one deserves to be hurt, Charmaine, least of all an innocent child."

At first she thought he spoke of himself and his father, but his eyes betrayed no sign of self-pity or resentment. He appeared instead to be at peace, as if he finally understood something that had eluded him for hours. When he spoke again, she was completely baffled. "Would you like to hear the entire piece?"

With her affirmation, he returned to the piano, and she followed. He sat, rested his fingers on the keys, and contemplated the first flourishing stroke.

The initial measures were soft, poignant. Then the room exploded with sound. Not once did his fingers falter, rather they bent to his will, summoning from the instrument a fine-tuned cadence, an unfathomable longing that swelled and ebbed like the tides of a tempestuous sea. Without warning, the last strains cried out, heralding the final chord.

Doleful, yet satiated, Charmaine could not speak, sighing deeply instead.

"You seem displeased, my Charm."

It was a moment before she realized John had spoken.

"Displeased?" she queried. "No, I'm not displeased, just sad it is over."

"I shall play it again whenever you wish," he promised with a lopsided smile, "that is, if you can abide this particular rendition."

"Oh yes, I can!" she answered fiercely. "The last measures are extremely difficult. I'm certain the composer would be satisfied with your conclusion."

"It was the only one open to me."

Before she could reflect upon the bizarre remark, he approached her.

"I'd like to apologize for my behavior today," he said, standing only a breath away. "I know it must have been unnerving."

Charmaine inhaled slowly. "I feel quite safe at present."

He chuckled softly, just now savoring the femininity before him, a vision imbued with the tantalizing fragrance of purity, an invasion of the senses. At this moment, she was more desirable than ever before. "Perhaps you shouldn't."

Suddenly, she was in his arms, and his mouth captured hers. He kissed her thoroughly, stealing her breath away, his lips playing a seductive, coveting game, soft one moment, intense the next. She did not resist, nor did she respond, rather she caught hold of him and drew strength from his solid form. Her heart soared and every nerve in her body, down to the tips of her fingers, tingled. Her legs turned liquid, and she clung more tightly to him, submitting completely to his will. She was certain the moment lasted an eternity, yet it was only a moment, she told herself, one unexpected moment. Later, she would argue: if she had been forewarned, she would have fought off his advance—successfully. For now, she permitted John his embrace, her eyes closed to reason and reality, her senses open to the sweet sensations this man stirred inside her: his warm palm on her cheek, his sinewy arm cradling her head, his hard chest pressed to her breasts. He traced kisses along her jaw until his face burrowed deep in the hollow between her neck and hair, where his lips nuzzled the ivory column and his tongue caressed an aching earlobe. She was paralyzed by his magnetism, her agony most manifest when his head lifted and his arms fell away. She swayed on unsteady legs and could hear her heart pounding in her ears.

"We had best leave it there," he whispered raggedly.

He, too, was bereft and studied her for one hopeful moment. When she said nothing, he smiled. She was an innocent, completely unaware of the effect she had on him, the blood that thundered in his veins and quickened in his loins. She certainly didn't deserve to get mixed up with someone like him.

"Dawn is only a few hours away," he continued determinedly, "and we both need some sleep. It shouldn't be too difficult to find that golden slumber now."

She disagreed, but wisely held her tongue as he lit a candle and snuffed the candelabrum. When he grasped her elbow, she began to speak, but he put a finger to her lips. "No need for words, my Charm. They'd only mar the moment and spoil the calm." She took heed.

They walked through the foyer and ascended the staircase, a climb that seemed endless in the shadowy darkness. As they neared the crest, her apprehension mounted, and she drew her robe more tightly around her.

"Cold?" he asked, misreading the action. "Not to worry. You'll soon be warm beneath the covers."

She was reassured he hadn't mentioned joining her there. Still, she mistrusted herself and looked up at him slowly when they reached her door. His regard was intense, an unusual warmth in the amber-brown orbs. He leaned forward and placed a fatherly kiss on her forehead. "Thank you," he said, looping a stray lock behind her ear.

"For what?"

"For the past few moments—for tonight. It wasn't the resolution I'd expected to reach at the onset of this day, but it's not one I scorn. You've given me something precious just now, something I couldn't have given myself."

"What's that?" she asked, intrigued.

"Hope—in the future. I'll float with the tide, not against it, and perhaps someday, it *will* right itself. Goodnight, my Charm."

He walked away, but Charmaine stared after him until the light from his candle died with the closing of his chamber door. Certain she would not sleep even if he did, she heaved a perplexed sigh and went into her own room. But as she nestled into bed, the rhapsody resounded in her head, and she felt John's strong arms enfolding her in a cocoon of contentment.

Tuesday, October 3, 1837

Much as she longed to shirk her duties, Charmaine could only groan at the light, yet insistent, knock on her bedchamber door. "Come in," she beckoned as she stood and retrieved her discarded robe.

Mrs. Faraday pushed into the room carrying fresh bed linens. Bleary-eyed, Charmaine watched as, without a word, the woman bustled about the chamber, drawing a drape here, extinguishing a lamp there. She turned to the bed.

"That won't be necessary, Mrs. Faraday. As I've told you before, I'm capable of making my own bed."

"Be that as it may," the older woman commented sharply, "today is Tuesday, wash day. The mattress must be stripped and fresh linens spread."

"And I'm capable of doing that as well."

"If you were capable, Miss Ryan, it would have been done already. I cannot afford to have my schedule upset by someone who sleeps the day away. As it is, I'm short staffed."

Charmaine frowned. "What time is it?"

"Nearly eleven."

"But it can't be! The children would have awakened me!"

"It is, and they would have had Master John not interceded on your behalf." She clicked her tongue in evident disgust, tearing the sheets from the bed without a glance in Charmaine's direction. "Why the master of the house would take it upon himself to mind three children when his father is paying a governess to do so is beyond my comprehension. I'd say it's a trifle queer she's in bed, regaining her— how did he put it?—needed sleep, when he's up and about, full of vim and vigor. Very queer indeed, if you ask me."

Charmaine groaned inwardly, certain her crimson cheeks condemned her. "I didn't ask you. I'm sorry you've misconstrued a kindness for something lewd."

Mrs. Faraday scoffed. "Miss Ryan, I'm no simpleton. That remark you made at the dinner table has the whole house talking. I thought you were attempting to make Master Paul jealous at the time, but now—well, now I don't know."

Humiliation yielded to outrage. "Mrs. Faraday! You may pick up your linens and kindly leave my room!"

The woman was silenced. She pursed her lips and bundled the sheets.

"And the next time I'm sleeping," Charmaine added, "do not disturb me! I'm not being paid to endure your verbal abuse."

The door thundered shut, but Charmaine remained planted in the center of the room, fists balled at her sides, teeth clenched in unspent fury. She was proud of her mettle, yet, still so very angry. The audacity of the woman! At this moment, Charmaine was certain she was worse than Agatha.

Slowly her ire ebbed. As she turned to make her bed and get dressed, John seeped into her thoughts, reviving those exquisite feelings of the night before. She had slept peacefully; nevertheless, she knew, without specific recollection, John had occupied all of her dreams. How would he greet her this morning? How would she greet him? Unlike the first time he had kissed her, she could not hide behind a façade of injured pride or pretended disgust. She had enjoyed his embrace completely, and her pulse raced with the memory. She prayed he'd heed his own declaration and keep silent about the intimate encounter. But knowing John as she did, she feared he would not.

"Anything?"

"Anything within reason," John answered, his gaze fixed on Yvette across the dining room table. They were eating lunch!

Pierre spotted Charmaine first and scrambled from John's lap. "Mainie's here!" he announced, grasping her hand and drawing her into the room. "Come . . . you hafta help us plan the week!"

"What week?" she asked, avoiding eye contact with John.

"This week, silly," he giggled. As she sat down, he climbed into his own chair and gave John his full attention. "All right," he said most maturely, elbows propped and chin cradled in his hands, "we're ready now."

"As I was saying to the children, Miss Ryan, the week belongs to them."

She looked directly at John in spite of herself, surprised to find his smile assuasive rather than sardonic, and her heart skipped a beat.

He turned back to the twins. "Your wish is my command," he continued. "We'll spend the next four days in any manner you'd like. And, to be fair, I'll give each of you a day of your own. We'll begin with Pierre. Today will be his day. Tomorrow, Jeannette may decide what we'll do. Thursday will belong to Yvette, and Friday will be Mademoiselle Charmaine's. How does that sound?"

"Why do I have to wait until Thursday?" Yvette objected.

"I thought you would like time to plan the best possible excursion."

"Oh," his sister pondered aloud, quickly warming to the idea. "Yes, I suppose I would, and I promise it will be something extra special, something no one else would ever dream of."

"I'm certain," he said. "So, Pierre, what should we do today?"

"I want Fi-day," the boy insisted. "I need more time, too!"

John chuckled. "I suppose that can be arranged, if Mainie doesn't mind exchanging days with you."

He looked at Charmaine, and she quickly consented, realizing too late she would have to contrive some fabulous plan for the afternoon. *But what?*

John folded his arms across his chest and, with an exaggerated yawn, propped his boots atop the tablecloth. He pushed back, and balanced the chair on two legs.

"Johnny!" Jeannette scolded, "Cookie is going to tan your backside if she comes in here!" Yvette and Pierre giggled.

"I said anything," he replied, ignoring his sister's reprimand as he rocked the chair to-and-fro. "Miss Ryan, we are awaiting your pleasure."

"It would please me to see you sitting properly in that chair. You are teaching the children terrible things, and if you're not careful, you'll topple over and injure your back."

As if on cue, the chair wobbled precariously, then fell away from the table entirely, spilling John on the floor. The children screeched, but Charmaine flew to his side, worry creasing her brow. "Are you all right?"

"I think I've fractured my spine!" he groaned, his face a mask of pain.

"I knew it!" she gasped, crouching closer and looping an arm around his shoulders. "Do you think you can get up?"

"I—I don't know."

"Please try," she coaxed, so focused on assisting him she was unprepared for his swift movement that stole a kiss. *Tricked!* John was laughing up at her, and her cheeks burned red from the momentary contact.

"Johnny kissed Mademoiselle Charmaine!" Jeannette squealed in delight.

"On the lips!" Yvette gagged.

Charmaine shot to her feet. "Ssh! Do you want the entire house to hear?"

"What's going on in here?" Fatima Henderson demanded as she barreled into the dining room, her thick girth heaving. "What are you up to Master John?"

"Nothing, Cookie," he reassured as he slowly stood and righted the chair. "I took a little spill, but I'm fine."

Unconvinced, she cocked her head. "Master John, I don't know what mischief you're calculating in that handsome head of yours, but I say it's about time you went about your business for the day. Didn't Master Paul ask you to do some work for him?"

"He asked, but I didn't answer."

The children laughed, but Fatima sucked in her cheeks.

"Later," he promised, "I'll do some work later. Right now I'm waiting for Miss Ryan—"

"Miss Charmaine ain't your concern. She hasn't even eaten yet, and already you're in here harrassing her."

"Harassing? Me? I assure you that was not my intent. As soon as she tells us how we are to spend the day, she may eat in peace."

"A swing," Charmaine replied, drawing all eyes to her.

"What?" John queried, confounded.

"A swing," she repeated. "I would like you to construct a swing for the day's enjoyment."

"A swing?"

"Yes, a swing. S-W-I-N-G," she repeated for a third time, smiling as she imagined John high in the branches of one of the oak trees, where she'd be safe from his capers.

"You spell quite well," he complimented with a twisted grin. "Still, I don't see much fun—"

"Are you saying you won't do it?"

"No, I didn't say that. It's just, I don't think—"

"That you can't do it?" she pressed.

"I didn't say that, either," he argued, his amusement fading. Damn, she was playing the game too well.

"What then?" she asked with arms folded across her bosom, eliciting a chuckle from Fatima Henderson as she returned to her kitchen.

"If you'd let me finish, I was going to ask: where would we hang it?"

"From one of the oak trees nearest the front portico. Yes, that should do nicely . . . A capital way to spend the day."

John only snorted. "Actually I think it's rather—"

"It doesn't matter what you think, does it? You said the day was mine and I could spend it in any manner I wished. That was what you said, wasn't it?"

"Yes, that was what I said."

"In that case, why don't you locate the materials you will need: a nice smooth board and a good length of rope. When I've finished eating, the children and I will join you."

Yvette clicked her tongue. "But I've already eaten. I want to go with Johnny!"

"Me, too!" Pierre chimed in. "I wanna build me a swing!"

"See," Charmaine pointed out, "they like the idea."

"So they do," John replied debonairly, "so a swing we shall build."

He winked at Pierre as if the idea had been his all along, then took the children with him.

An hour later, the swing was suspended, a feat less difficult than Charmaine had at first imagined, especially with the aid of the stable-hands. Presently, she sat on the terrace and watched the children as they took turns on it. Yvette quickly mastered the rudiments of pumping the board to dizzying heights, squealing each time she plummeted toward the earth. Next, it was Jeannette's turn and finally Pierre's. The latter had to be pushed gently, a chore Jeannette eagerly assumed once Yvette plopped in the grass some feet away.

"Well, my Charm, you have your swing," John said as he climbed the steps of the colonnade and sat next to her. "Aren't you going to at least try it?"

"Later," she answered, "when the children have tired of their play."

He considered her, his eyes eventually resting on her lips, a point of interest that caused her to shiver. "I thank you for this favor," she said, hoping to distract him, relieved when his regard lifted to her eyes. "I would ask another."

"And what would that be?"

"Refrain from displays of affection toward me," she replied.

"Displays of affection? If you're speaking about my passionate kiss this morning—"

"Exactly," she interjected, not allowing him to finish.

"I'd hardly call such an overture passion, my Charm. I assure you, it was completely innocent."

"Innocent to you, perhaps," she argued, fighting hard to retain her poise, "but what do children know of innocence and passion? To them, the two are one and the same."

"And to you, Charmaine?"

She'd lost the battle, and she felt her face grow warm. She couldn't answer; neither could she look his way.

"Very well, my Charm. I do not want to spoil our week together, so you need not fear any further overtures from me, passionate or otherwise."

"Thank you," she whispered, studying the hands in her lap.

"And I'll speak to Mrs. Faraday as well, if you'd like."

Stunned, her eyes flew to his face. "How did you know—"

"I didn't. Not for certain, anyway. But the look she gave me this morning when I insisted you not be disturbed . . . let us say, I realized my mistake. Don't worry, Charmaine, she won't be telling Paul. And even if she does, it could work in your favor."

Charmaine's shame turned to anger, but she bit her tongue when she noted the deviltry in his eyes, that familiar expression that meant he was teasing her.

"You know," he goaded when she refused to retaliate, "a bit of jealousy could work wonders at bringing my brother around."

"Bringing him around?"

"To the altar, Charmaine. That *is* your deepest desire, is it not?"

Holding silent, she stared out across the lawns. John allowed the minutes to accumulate, and Charmaine knew he studied her. Then, he dropped the subject altogether. "So, what are we going to do for the remainder of the day?" he asked. "It's still early. Perhaps a visit into town?"

"You could play the piano for me—and the children."

His smile broadened as if he'd extracted a confession from her. He waved off the idea. "You play for them every day, surely there's something else—"

"Not nearly as well as you do. After last night, I understand why you . . ."

"Why I what? Why I inferred your musical ability was lacking?" She didn't answer.

"You play very well, Charmaine, and I enjoy hearing the children sing along when you sit at the piano. I was an ogre those first few days home, especially to you. I misjudged you. George tried to tell me I was wrong, so did Paul, but I guess because I was hearing it from my brother, I refused to believe it."

"Why?" she asked. "Why do you mistrust each other? Why are you constantly at odds?"

"There are a number of reasons. Most of them revolve around my father."

"Are you angry with your father for giving Paul an island?"

"No, I'm not angry. At least, I don't think I am."

She frowned at his curious reply. "Is it the enthusiasm he's given Paul's endeavor? I imagine you must have your own accomplishments in Virginia that deserve recognition."

"If my father knew of my accomplishments in Virginia, he'd probably put Paul in charge there, too."

She digested the sardonic statement. "Still, it means a lot for a parent to show an interest in an offspring's undertakings. I know how it feels to be unappreciated, to be scorned."

"You were scorned?"

"Yes, by my father I was."

"Well, then, my Charm, it seems we have something in common." He was quiet for a while and then asked, "What happened to your mother?"

Charmaine inhaled. Even after two years, the memory was painful. Strangely, she didn't feel she had to hide the truth from him any longer. She could tell him about it, and he would understand.

"My father, he was drunk and angry. He brutally beat my mother, and she died of the injuries he inflicted. He disappeared, and nobody has seen him since." Tears sprang to her eyes without warning. "It was my fault," she choked out, turning her face aside.

"Your fault?"

"I was hiding my wages from him. He was a lazy good-for-nothing, who rarely worked. When he did, the money was spent on spirits. Most times he relied on my mother to tarry. When I found employment with the Harringtons, he felt he was entitled to my earnings as well. Then one night, when he was good and drunk, he came to their house hoping to collect my wages. When he didn't find me there, he went after my mother instead, assuming we were conspiring to hide my salary. He'd never have touched her if I had given him the money."

"No, Charmaine, it wasn't your fault," he refuted in disgust. "There is no excuse for a man to beat a woman. I've known men like him. If it weren't about money, it would have been about something else. You shouldn't blame yourself."

She was comforted by his sincerity. She'd never told anyone she held herself responsible for her mother's death. She wondered why it had been so easy to tell John, why his reaction relieved her burden of guilt.

"What is your father's name?"

"His name? Why do you ask?"

John shrugged. "Just curious, I guess."

"John Ryan."

A sudden, perspicacious grin broke across his lips. "John, eh?"

Uncomfortable that he'd be examining her soul next, Charmaine redirected the conversation. "Your father has scorned you as well, hasn't he?"

The smile vanished. "You were at dinner the other night, Charmaine. You tell me? It is just another reason why Paul and I don't get along."

Understanding dawned. "So that is why you're not interested in Duvoisin business. Without your father's love and acceptance, you have little desire to promote his enterprises." When he didn't respond, she continued. "Paul has your father's love but longs for legitimacy, while you long for your father's love and care little about your legitimacy."

"No," John bit out, amazed, yet annoyed with her astute assessment. "Paul longs for it all, but he won't get it! You see, my father enjoys having him dangle as well."

"Dangle?"

"You wouldn't understand, Charmaine. Frederic Duvoisin is the master of manipulation, the consummate puppeteer."

She was saddened by his summation. "I've found your father to be forthright."

"That proves how very naïve you are," he scoffed sourly. She bristled at the insult, but John was just as vexed. "I don't want to ruin my day with talk of my father. If we're going to continue our little heart-to-heart, let's restrict it to Paul. Anything you'd like to know about him?"

He was right; Paul was a far more interesting topic. But she was also wary of the insights John might offer. There was one question that seemed benign. "Who is older, you or Paul?"

John's brow lifted, and his eyes darted around, mischievous again. He leaned in close and whispered as if the mansion had ears. "Well, now, my Charm, that's the big family secret. No one knows for sure. Some say the baby—that would be Paul—was brought to my father in the middle of the night before I was born, from origins unknown." He straightened up and answered directly. "I don't put credence in that, though. I've often wondered how my mother accepted Paul's arrival, if she had to accept it at all. It seems more logical Paul was born after she died, then my father's philandering wouldn't have mattered. Either way, he was a busy man, sowing his wild oats, so to speak."

"And Paul's mother?"

John shrugged. "Dead, according to my father. But my father never doubted Paul is his son, bastard though he be."

Charmaine winced, stung by the harsh words.

"Come now, my Charm," he cajoled, "Paul has accepted what he is. There's no need to pity him. There's many a man who would gladly trade places and take the title of bastard if it would secure him a share of the Duvoisin fortune. I know George would." He chuckled softly, ignoring her frown.

Pierre bounded over to them. "This time I go very high!" he declared, tugging on John's hand and coaxing him up and out of the chair.

Charmaine stood as well and meandered across the lawns to the girls. They were at the paddock now, petting the two-month-old colt, Sultan.

"May we bring the ponies out?" they called.

Thursday, October 5, 1837

"Again, I do not approve," Charmaine feebly protested from where she sat in the swaying brougham. The twins had petitioned to ride atop the conveyance on either side of the driver, and their governess found herself closeted in the plush carriage with John and Pierre.

"There's no reason to be dismayed, my Charm," John replied.

"Why couldn't she have been satisfied with a day similar to the one we passed yesterday? The ride was lovely, the picnic pleasant, even the rain didn't spoil our time, and—"

"—Yvette will never be content in the shadow of repetition," he finished for her. "She's not Jeannette, and the only similarity that will ever exist between them is their looks. You should know that by now, Charmaine. Besides, I find her choice a singular idea."

"Singular, indeed," she mumbled. "And what will your father say when he finds you've escorted your sisters to Dulcie's? I know—" she held up a hand to ward off his answer "—you don't care!"

"I wasn't going to say it quite like that, but in a manner of speaking, yes."

"You can afford to be incorrigible, but what about me? I'm

responsible for their welfare. I'll rue the day I compromised my morals for this little escapade."

"And what morals could possibly be in the balance if we visit a saloon? I guarantee only Dulcie will accost us."

"A saloon?" Charmaine scoffed. "Aren't you being a bit generous? It's a gambling establishment, not to mention—"

"Yes?" he probed with brow raised.

She could not speak what thundered in her mind. She recalled Felicia's tales of the barmaids who cavorted with the seamen in the bedrooms above the common room.

"Don't fret, Charmaine," John proceeded knavishly, "Dulcie's can't be completely condemned if my brother patronizes it."

"Paul is a grown man! Not a child!"

"Exactly! And as such, is more susceptible to the evils of a brothel than any child could ever fear to be."

Charmaine's cheeks flamed red with the declaration. "You think you have all the answers, don't you?" she squeaked out.

"As a rule," he replied proudly, "and if you pay close attention, you may recall them should anyone confront you on the matter."

Her eyes narrowed, bolstering his lighthearted mood. "Don't be angry with me. We've enjoyed two splendid days with the children. Today can be just as wonderful if only you'd make it so. And, if anything should go wrong at Dulcie's, I promise to intervene and assume full blame. Isn't that right, Pierre?"

"Yep," the lad chirped.

"I still don't approve," Charmaine reiterated.

Remember, I'll not hold you responsible for any circumstances beyond your control. When you become upset, just remember.

Charmaine sighed. She certainly couldn't issue orders to Frederic's son, Yvette's excursion was definitely beyond her control, and she was quite upset. Did this then annul her responsibility? She hoped so. With that thought, she leaned back into the cushions and attempted to enjoy the scenery.

John was correct; there was nothing to fear. When they left the bright boardwalk and slipped into the saloon, Dulcie was expecting them. She ushered them to a prepared table where she set lemonade before them, followed by a delicious meal. They were treated regally and, to Yvette's chagrin, did not behold the true workings of the quiet tavern. Few were about, and not a single gaming table was being used.

John explained the rules of one card game he called "poker," informing them George had concocted it from a few European games they had played at university. The twins remained skeptical, certain their brother was telling another tall tale. But he maintained that every Friday night was "poker" night at Dulcie's, and for their benefit, suggested they play a hand. Demonstrating the stakes usually bid, he threw an imaginary coin into the center of the table and dealt them each five cards. Uncharacteristically, Jeannette caught on more quickly than Yvette and pretended to rake in the kitty four out of five times, but since the pot was imaginary, even she grew bored.

"I wonder what is upstairs," the kind-hearted twin sweetly mused. "I would really like to see."

John's eyes narrowed suspiciously. "What game is this—*Yvette?*" he inquired pointedly of Jeannette.

She shrugged.

"Have you done this before?" he demanded, no longer duped.

"Done what before?" came the innocent question.

Charmaine was baffled, her eyes drawn to Yvette who now stepped forward, an unusual expression on her face.

"I'm Jeannette, Johnny," she said, leaving her accomplice, who'd given one of her braids a fierce yank, scowling. "And only a couple of times."

Charmaine stood amazed and vexed by the clever deception.

The real Yvette stomped her foot, annoyed nothing was going as planned, unmoved by her governess's look of disapproval. "I still want to see upstairs," she insisted. Her petition ended there, however. John's scowl had deepened, his refusal firm and nonnegotiable. She'd have to devise another scheme to satisfy her curiosity.

They departed the saloon to amble along the boardwalk, which took them directly to the harbor and the *Raven*. Pierre and the girls begged to go aboard, and Charmaine was happy to comply. She wondered if she'd see Captain Wilkinson. What would he think when he found her walking the ship's deck on John's arm? Maybe he wouldn't remember her at all.

It was an odd feeling ascending the gangway. Not since the day the Harringtons had embarked for Virginia had she done so—a full year ago! She marveled over all that had happened in that time, how she herself had changed.

The vessel sat dormant. According to John, she awaited the salvaged sugarcane harvest before setting sail for New York. With little to do, Jonah Wilkinson had abandoned her, leaving an abbreviated crew to holystone and caulk the decks, tar the masts, and mend the frayed canvases.

Yvette and Jeannette sidestepped them, scurrying across the ship's waist, leaning over the starboard wall, attempting to swat the shrouds or catch a swooping seagull. They climbed atop the forecastle deck, surveying their surroundings from that lofty summit.

John and Charmaine meandered leisurely, starting at the prow, stopping when they spotted something of interest to point out to Pierre, John a wealth of information, the sailors nodding respectfully to him, he reciprocating. When they reached the quarterdeck, he dragged an empty crate over to the helm and stood the lad behind the huge wooden wheel. Charmaine leaned back against the rail and watched as he demonstrated how to grip the wooden spikes and steer the vessel, his eyes alive, indicating that, for all his repudiation of his heritage, he was proud to be a Duvoisin.

"My turn!" the boy demanded, instantly immersed in the imaginary task, supplying the sounds of lapping water against the hull as he guided the bark out of the harbor.

John patted his back, then stepped away and joined Charmaine. She smiled up at him, charmed by his attachment to the lad. "What are you laughing at?"

"You," she answered. "I think you'll make a good husband someday."

It was his turn to smile. "Why do you say that?"

Embarrassed, she quickly backtracked. "What I meant to say was 'father.' You'll make a good father."

His expression sobered. "I fear that avenue is closed to me."

"But you're so good with children," she countered mindlessly, unnerved by his abrupt change of mood. "You should have many of your own."

"Have you forgotten I'm a bad influence?"

"I was wrong about that. You've showered Pierre and the girls with more love and affection than I thought possible of any man."

He forced a smile, but didn't answer.

"I'm sorry . . ." she murmured. "I've offended you."

"No, my Charm. I appreciate your accolades, but you are mistaken. I'd be a poor substitute for a father." When she opened her mouth to object, he rushed on. "Fortunately, I do have Pierre and my sisters."

"They will miss you when you leave," she said, startled by her sudden heaviness of heart.

"They won't have to," he replied, turning away from her and gazing out across the peninsula. "I plan on staying around for a while. I didn't realize how lonely my homes in Virginia and New York were until I ventured back here."

"Really?"

"Unless my father permits me to take the children to Richmond for a visit."

"Do you plan to ask him?"

He faced her, his eyes intense. "Would you come with us if I did? If my father gave his consent? They would need to have you there, especially Pierre. And you'd be able to visit your friends."

His voice held a note of expectancy—excitement—as if his happiness depended on the case he now set before her. Then, like quicksilver, he chuckled disparagingly, brushing the fanciful thought aside. "Not to worry, Charmaine. We won't be traveling anywhere together. I know what my father's answer would be, so why bother to ask?"

Charmaine held silent. Sadly, she knew he was right.

They left the *Raven* shortly thereafter and strolled along the town's main thoroughfare. Charmaine felt many eyes upon them and was proud to have John as her escort. Not so long ago, she would have recoiled from such attention, scorned any conclusions drawn by the islanders. But today was different. John was not the man she had so sharply misjudged him to be, and for the first time, she acknowledged her gladness for having come to know him.

Friday, October 6, 1837

Children's laughter wafted off the lake, much like the afternoon breeze that caught at Charmaine's hair and loosed strands from the bun tucked beneath her bonnet. They settled as stray ringlets, framing her pretty face. Still, she was unaware of the picture she painted, sitting on the blanket John had chivalrously spread for her. Her eyes were on the man who, with his back to her, sat some hundred feet away in the small dinghy he had purchased for Pierre a few weeks ago. With the lad in his lap and his sisters seated across from him, he continued to paddle out to the lake's center, pretending all the while Pierre was propelling the vessel. Charmaine's smile widened as they glided to a stop and John bent over, retrieving the fishing rods he had carelessly thrown in the bottom of the small craft. Few complete sentences reached her ears, but the manner in which he worked at the rods led her to believe the worst: the lines were dreadfully tangled. Well, she had warned him, but the children had been so excited he hadn't listened. Now he was paying the piper, for already Yvette was tugging at her pole and Pierre, his. A lighthearted laugh escaped her lips. It was swallowed when the fishing boat swayed precariously. John stilled the motion with outstretched arms and shook a finger at Yvette. Charmaine smiled again, glad she had had the good sense not to further encumber the crowded boat. She was safe where she sat. At last, the lines were cast. As their activity lulled, she studied her surroundings once again.

They were nestled within a forest, an idyllic clearing that ran along the perimeter of a central reservoir, which, according to John, was dug from a small pond by his grandfather and fifty laborers over seventy years ago. She had been astonished when they had walked not fifty yards, entered the line of thick pine trees from the grounds at the rear of the manor and, in less than ten minutes, practically stumbled upon the pristine freshwater lake. Only a small bungalow and dock marred nature's untamed beauty. All else remained unspoiled.

Charmaine breathed deeply, contented. Presently, a pair of flamingos meandered to the water's edge and waded along the bank. This beautiful glade, just beyond the mansion . . . She thought of the twins' birthday picnic on the beach and that first picnic on the bluffs. Because of John, she'd experienced firsthand the majesty of Charmantes. John. Again, her eyes were drawn to the man. How many times during their week together had this happened? It was an unsettling question, and she marveled at the great distance they had traveled in two short months. She could not know the journey had just begun.

It was late, yet a brilliant half-moon illuminated Charmantes' cove. The *Falcon* reduced sail and drifted into the harbor. As she was moored, Frederic stood stoically at the rail. The *Raven* was gone, and a foreign ship was berthed in her place, a fact that should have pleased him. His torment would haunt him for the rest of his days. However, what was done was done, and what he had set out to accomplish this week had been accomplished. Downtrodden, he wondered if he'd ever see his son again. He swallowed against the thick lump lodged in his throat, impeding speech.

"Father, we'll be going ashore now."

Frederic averted his gaze. "By all means," he coughed, "lead the way."

A half-hour passed before a conveyance was obtained from the livery and the luggage hoisted into it. In that time, Frederic surveyed the new merchantman.

"The *Wanderlust*," Paul breathed with pride, slapping her hull. "The first of the new fleet. One-hundred-fifty feet of the finest white oak the States have to offer. I shall meet with her captain in the morning. Would you like to accompany me—look her over?"

Frederic said nothing, and Paul stood bewildered when his father turned and limped down the pier. The man had shown great interest over the past five days, his enthusiasm ever expanding, and now this. Clearly, he was exhausted.

After Agatha and the servants were settled inside the landau, Frederic declined the seat saved him. "You go ahead. The carriage is far too crowded. I'll await its return at Dulcie's."

"Dulcie's?" Agatha objected. "That place is nothing more than a—"

"Agatha, I'm acquainted with the establishments that operate on Charmantes. Paul and I will wait at Dulcie's."

The vehicle pulled away, and Frederic faced his blatantly confused son. "Don't tell me you're concerned about the trouble I could get into there?"

Paul laughed. "No, sir. But the past five days were long and strenuous. You must be tired and—"

"Before all that, I'm the master of this island," his sire interrupted. "I'd like to find out what has happened while we were away. What better way than to visit the tavern where the gossip is high and everything known?"

Bawdy music spilled into the street just outside Dulcie's, a syncopated rhythm livened by the boisterous laughter of men and women alike: the shout of a longshoreman, the squeal of a doxy, the snap of the spinning wheels, which drew huddles at the gaming tables.

George Richards strode into the raucous common room looking forward to a stiff drink. The week's work had been grueling: first the sugarcane harvest, then the loading of the *Raven*. The vessel hadn't embarked until late that afternoon, and then he'd helped secure the new ship that pulled into port just behind her. After that, he'd traveled to the mill, relieved to find it running smoothly. Still, George would be glad when Paul returned. Managing Charmantes was too much for one man, and though John was there, he had been no help whatsoever, informing George at the onset of the week his father's work was Paul's work, not his. Therefore, everything had fallen into George's lap, and tonight, he was bone-weary and spent.

He sat at the bar and swiveled around on his stool. He watched as one surly sailor coaxed a barmaid into his embrace, only to find her less than willing when he didn't hand over the coin he jangled. Though the man's grip tightened, the buxom wench pushed hard on his chest, sending his chair tumbling to the floor. She rubbed her hands together and turned a proud nose upon his compatriots. "You don't pay, you don't get no service." She sauntered toward another, more promising table, a mound of cold cash just now doubled at its center. George smiled as the strumpet leaned heavily into the shoulder of the man dealing the next hand. He shooed her aside with a slash of his arm, a sure sign he was losing. Indifferent, she moved around the table. George's eyes followed as he raised a frothing tankard of ale to his lips. He took a long draw off the top, but spewed it down his shirtfront, choking.

There, sitting in the circle of the gaming table, her back to the door and five cards clasped firmly to her chest, was Yvette Duvoisin, disguised as a guttersnipe, her mcek sister, similarly garbed, standing directly behind her and sorely out of place.

He jumped to his feet and was at the table in the bat of an eye. "What in blazes are you doing here, Yvette?" he roared.

Alarmed for only a moment, she quickly recovered and raised her chin in defiance. "Playing poker. Five-card draw, to be precise. Isn't that what you call it?" and she turned back to the men for affirmation.

They nodded with a grumble, awaiting her bid.

"I'll raise it ten," she announced, fingering a stack of coins before pushing it into the pot.

George grabbed her by the arm and yanked her to her feet. "The game is over! Throw in your hand, we're going home!"

"No, I won't!" she protested, wrenching free. "I'm not leaving until the pot is broken. I have over ten dollars in there!"

But for all her recalcitrant bravado, she stumbled backward, cards still clasped to her chest, her resistance wavering under George's uncommon fury.

"Wait a minute, bud," one of the gamblers objected, anticipating the outcome of the showdown, "no need to rush the little lady. She ain't your kin is she?"

"He's only a friend," Yvette swiftly answered. "He can't order me around."

"Well, then," another bolstered. "Why don't you leave our little missy alone? She's doin' a fine job takin' care of her herself. Won a hefty sum of our money, she has, and we'd appreciate the chance to win it back."

George turned on the men in disbelief. Evidently, they were

new to Charmantes, off the maiden ship that had docked that afternoon and ignorant of Yvette's identity. Her ragamuffin apparel didn't
help. Still, she was a mere child. "Have the lot of you gone mad?" he
exclaimed. "She's a nine-year-old girl—"

"Hold it right there, fella!" the dealer warned. "She came in here
with a hefty purse and demanded we let her play. Anyone can game
if he has the money to lose, them's the rules of any reputable gam-
blin' house. At first, we thought we'd humor her. But she's won a few
hands, and now it's become serious. So why don't you leave us be?"

"You can go to—"

"George!" Yvette cut in. "One more hand—just let me play one
more hand, then Jeannette and I will go home. I promise."

George eyed her suspiciously, still simmering. But reason cautioned him a level head. Her consorts were less than friendly, especially in the face of their losses, and the last thing he needed was an
out-and-out brawl. He was, however, going to wring John's neck.
When the man had ridden over to the bondsmen's keep and bragged
about his weeklong escapades, George had been dismayed and
warned him his visit to Dulcie's would come back to haunt him.
John had only mocked him for sounding like Charmaine. But of
course, the instigator of this unfolding calamity was at home, while
he, George, his so-called friend, was dealing with the consequences.
And where in God's name was Dulcie? Did no one know who the
twins were?

"One hand—that's all you're getting—one hand!" he relented.
Whirling on his heel, he strode back to the bar and the drink he
desperately needed. It would be a miracle if he escorted her home
without a scandal. "Whisky—straight," he ordered after downing
the ale in one gulp, "and make it a double."

Again he pivoted on the stool and observed the ludicrous scene.
Jeannette was bending to her sister's ear, probably whispering some
urgent plea they leave the saloon. Yvette, in turn, shook her head
once and proceeded to fold two cards from her initial hand of five.

Three of a kind, George surmised as he watched her draw two more from the dealer.

A gush of cool night air, refreshing in the malodorous, smoke-filled tavern, heralded the arrival of newcomers. Snared by the hush that fell over the large room, George turned an eye to the entryway. There, on the threshold of Dulcie's saloon, stood her benefactor, Frederic Duvoisin.

Panic-stricken, George reached the door in three enormous strides. Frederic and Paul lingered there, surveying the establishment and its occupants, who slowly turned back to their vices. "Frederic—ah hum—Paul," he coughed, thanking heaven itself when they gave him their undivided attention. "I didn't expect you back so soon."

"Didn't you?" Paul queried with a frown. "I said the end of the week."

"So you did, so you did," George laughed falsely, taking hold of Paul's elbow and firmly pulling him round. "I suppose I've just been so busy I didn't realize what day of the week it was. Friday night already, my, my!"

"George, is something wrong?" Paul interrupted, looking down at his arm.

"Wrong? No, nothing's wrong," he replied with another hollow chuckle. "Why would you think that?"

"You seem harried, and you're pulling on my arm."

"So I am," he responded, releasing the limb as if burned. He mustn't be conspicuous. "Actually," he said, inspired, "there was a bit of a problem while you and your father were away. But I need a breath of fresh air. It's so hot in here. Why don't we go outside?"

Frederic observed George with a mixture of satisfaction and regret. "If you have something to tell us, George, I prefer to hear it now, where I stand."

"Sir?" George gulped, by all signs a man with something to hide. Suddenly, a piercing screech rent the air. George cringed and cursed under his breath. "You've cheated!" Yvette cried, jumping to her feet and throwing a branding finger at the dealer. "You drew the third ace from your sleeve!"

"Prove it!" the man retorted with a wicked chuckle.

"There!" she spat, tossing the same card on the table. "I was holding the ace of spades in the hopes of drawing a higher pair!"

The sailors shot to their feet, chairs clattering to the floor. Yvette was certain they were going to devour her, but one look at their faces and the cards they'd cast aside, and she realized she held the winning hand. She'd uncovered the dealer's underhandedness, and now, with George beside her, she could claim her winnings and go home, just as soon as the snake who had raked in the pot pushed it back in her direction. "All of those coins are mine!" she proclaimed flippantly. "And those, too! Tell them, George!"

From nowhere, a black cane struck the table, jolting it like the crack of a whip against the flank of a horse, leveling stacks of gold and silver coins and sending them tinkling to the floor. Others rolled in indecisive circles before toppling to rest. Her mind a blur for only an instant, Yvette recognized the familiar staff, stole a side-long glance at the broad hand that clutched it, thick veins protruding against taut skin. Murmurs went up around her: "Frederic Duvoisin."

Ever so slowly, she faced her father and fought the urge to cower, looking up into his livid features, braving the clenched jaw—there, where a muscle twitched fiercely—the turbulent eyes, and the sharply creased brow. Worse still was his rabid silence, and she dreaded his leashed wrath. Never before had she seen this side of his ferocious temper. Now, here she was, the object of it.

"Sir?" she gulped with colossal courage.

"What are you doing here, daughter—and in those clothes?"

The query was menacingly soft, yet devastating. Out of the corner of her eye, she took in the ashen complexions of her fellow gamblers.

"Mr. Duvoisin," one man dared to interrupt, "we thought she was a street waif. We had no idea she was your—"

"Silence!" Frederic thundered, striking the table again. "You indulge in gaming with a child—a girl, no less—and then you attempt to extricate yourself by pleading ignorance? By God, man, you tread upon perilous ground! And you, young lady!" he growled, sweeping the table clear of its booty and leveling his gaze once again on his wayward daughter. "You will wait for me outside!"

Yvette bobbed her head, then dashed around him and through the doors.

As if seeing Jeannette for the first time, Frederic's visage softened. "Go," he indicated with a jerk of his head. She nodded woefully, then departed the tavern exceedingly slower than her sister, her head bowed in contrition rather than fear.

Yvette was halfway down the street when her sister called after her, but she didn't stop running until she reached the livery. "Yvette!" Jeannette scolded once she'd caught up. "Father said to wait for him outside Dulcie's!"

"I know what he said," Yvette heaved, rubbing the pain in her side, turning to the bleary-eyed man who stepped out of the building. "Martin, I want my pony now," she ordered, "and my sister's as well."

Grumbling, the farrier disappeared into the livery.

"If you know," Jeannette rejoined, "then why didn't you do as he said? You're only going to make matters worse this way!"

"*Worse?* Jeannette, how could it be any worse? I probably won't be alive tomorrow morning. But I'm not going to die without a fight!"

"How, by running away?"

"Yes! Don't you see? Down there—" and she pointed to the vacant street just outside the saloon "—I'd be murdered on the spot! But at home, I can hide behind Johnny or Charmaine!"

"Yvette, you can't! You know how terrible things are between Father and Johnny, and if you get Mademoiselle Charmaine involved, Father might dismiss her! Please—"

"And what about me?" Yvette demanded. "I'm your sister! Don't I count? Do you want to see me killed? How would you feel then?"

"Yvette, I don't think Father is going to—"

"Oh dear, oh dear!" Yvette fretted, ignoring her sister altogether as she began to wring her hands. "Where is that man? If he doesn't come back soon, I'll be done for before I even have a chance to run away!"

Endeared to be home, Agatha issued a spate of orders from the foyer, then watched as each servant hastened to follow her directives. Her satisfaction was short-lived, however. John, paper in hand, stood in the study archway.

"Well," he said with a tight smile, his shoulder propped against the doorframe, "you're back."

"Yes," she said proudly, "in *my* home."

"Tell me, Auntie, has my father accompanied you tonight, or did he have his fill of you this week and decide to remain on Espoir instead?"

"It's not like that between your father and me," she refuted with dignity. "He loves me. And yes, he has returned, by my side."

"Really? Oh well, I knew heaven couldn't last forever, but I *was* hoping to avoid hell. Where is he, anyway?"

"I have no intention of playing your little game," she replied haughtily. "The week we spent on Paul's island was too marvelous, and not even you can spoil its lasting pleasure. Goodnight."

She'd just reached the landing when shrieks echoed from the front lawns, followed by thundering footsteps on the portico. The oak door was attacked, and Yvette stormed into the house as if demons chased her, Jeannette right on her heels. "Johnny! Charmaine!"

she cried. "Help! Please help me!" She spotted John and threw herself into his outstretched arms, sobbing mercilessly, "Oh no! He's
right behind me!"

"What the devil's going on?" John demanded, attempting to
peel her free.

But she offered no explanation, clinging to him fiercely, her face
buried in his shirtfront, moaning the incantation: "Oh, Johnny!"
over and over again.

This is not a farce, he finally realized. Dismayed now, he looked
to Jeannette for an answer. "What's happened? Why are you up and
out of the house at this late hour? And why are you dressed like this?
Where is Charmaine?"

"Here!" she called from above, belting her robe as she hurried
down the stairs. "The cries awoke me." She took one look at the tat-
tered twins and her worry increased. "What is going on?"

"That's what I'm trying to sort out," he said in growing vexation. "*Yvette?*"

Still the girl whined. "You must save me! He's going to kill me,
I know he is! At the very least, he'll beat me, whip me!"

"Who—who's going to—?"

Frederic stepped across the threshold, and all went silent. Yvette
choked back her tears, sniffling pitifully. She sidled behind her pro-
tector, her beseeching eyes lifting to Paul and George, who had
drawn up alongside her father.

"I told you to wait for me outside Dulcie's," Frederic growled.

"Dulcie's?" John queried in compounded shock. "She was at
Dulcie's?"

Frederic's regard, which had been riveted on his delinquent
daughter, shot to John, and his rage flared, spawning the words:
"*Why are you still here?*"

The inquiry took everyone by surprise, save John, who smiled
belligerently.

Checked, Frederic hurled his fury at an easier target: his trembling daughter. "You have much to answer for this night, young lady. Come here!"

"No!" she retaliated. But when he took one scraping step toward her, she fled the safety of her brother, skirted past Jeannette and Agatha, and raced up the staircase, hiding behind Charmaine. "Don't let him touch me!"

"Miss Ryan, bring her down here!" Frederic demanded.

John had had enough. "Take her back to her room, Charmaine."

"Miss Ryan, stay!" came the master's command, his eyes trained on her and not the son who was attempting to usurp his authority. "I hold you responsible. Bring Yvette to me—now!"

"Charmaine—" this time Paul stepped forward "—do as John says and take Yvette to the nursery."

"Damn it!" Frederic bellowed. "This is my house! She will do as I say! Get out—all of you! This is between my daughter, her governess, and me!"

"That's right, Father, you crack your whip!" John fired back virulently. "But don't expect me to cower before you!"

The man wheeled around, his cane slicing up and over his shoulder. John didn't move, his sardonic semblance piercing Frederic's heart and staving his intent. Nauseated, he lowered the cane slowly. "Get out of my sight," he croaked. "You pretend at being a man, but don't have the backbone to claim what is yours."

The declaration wiped clean John's inveigling smile, and his face paled as if he had suffered a debilitating blow. He bowed his head and exited the house, deserting them all. To Charmaine's horror, Frederic turned on her.

Mercifully, George stepped forward. "Sir, as I said in the carriage, this little calamity cannot be blamed on Miss Ryan. Certainly, she was asleep when—"

"Mr. Richards," Frederic cut in, "I have no intention of discussing this matter any further with you. I've yet to discern how you are involved; however, I do know you were at Dulcie's while my daughter tried her hand at a game of cards, and, by every outward sign, meant to divert my attention from her. Now, don't press your luck. Excuse yourself from this inquisition."

"Father—"

"And the same goes for you!"

"No!" Paul rejoined heatedly. "The same does not go for me! Now, I realize Yvette's behavior was unruly, and she should be punished. But your anger exceeds the bounds of rational thinking when you turn on Miss Ryan and hold her responsible. She couldn't have known about this. Or George and accuse him of conspiring with Yvette, Surely he was only trying to protect her!"

Paul's reasoning took hold, and Frederic's ire flagged.

The terrible ordeal ended when Jeannette valiantly stepped forward. "Paul is right, Father," she whispered. "Yvette and I waited until Mademoiselle Charmaine was asleep. Then we dressed in the clothes Yvette borrowed from the stable and slipped from the house. We knew we were doing wrong, but we didn't think we'd be caught, especially in our disguises. We just wanted to see what Dulcie's was really like, at night. When George saw us there, he was very angry, but Yvette had a good hand. She promised to leave after she'd played it out."

Charmaine held her breath, relieved when Frederic's response held a note of empathy. "And your sister couldn't tell me this? It was her idea, wasn't it?"

"Yes, sir."

"Then why you? Is she such a coward she cannot assume responsibility for her own actions, speak for herself?"

"She was afraid you would kill her," Jeannette answered simply. "But I didn't think you would. I suppose that's why I wasn't afraid to tell you the truth."

Frederic absorbed the statement with a mixture of surprise and regret. He looked up at Yvette, just now realizing the effect his naked wrath had on the rebellious nine-year-old. It was not the first time he had humbled someone to such quaking depths, and he was unhappy to realize he had not changed.

"I will speak with you tomorrow—the two of you," he said. "You needn't fear death, but you will be punished for your bad behavior."

He spoke to Charmaine. "Take them back to their rooms and make certain they remain there until I call for them."

"Yes, sir," she said. Beckoning to Jeannette, she turned Yvette around, and they proceeded up the staircase.

"I'm sorry, Father," Jeannette offered. "Truly I am."

But he did not seem to hear as he labored toward the study, his hesitant gait mocking the swiftness with which he had stormed the house minutes earlier.

"Oh, Mademoiselle Charmaine, what have I done?" Yvette moaned from Charmaine's bed, her head buried in the safety of her governess's lap. "I've been so naughty, and now everyone I love has been hurt!"

"There, now," Charmaine soothed, stroking the girl's blond head. She'd never seen Yvette so repentant and was deeply moved. "It's not quite so terrible as you imagine it to be."

"Yes, yes it is! First Johnny. I didn't mean to get him into trouble, but I did. Jeannette warned me it would be so, but I refused to listen. And then you. She warned me about that, too. But I didn't think Father would rant and rave at you like that! Even Paul and George. Oh, George will never forgive me! He didn't deserve any of Father's anger. He was only trying to protect me, and now he might lose his job. And Jeannette. She should hate me for all the trouble I've gotten her into."

"I don't hate you, Yvette," her sister reassured. "Really, I don't."

"You should," Yvette argued, slowly lifting her head. "Tomorrow you will be punished, too, and it's all my fault! Everything!"

Again she was sobbing. "I don't know why I do the horrid things I do! I don't even know why I think of them! Oh, why did I have to go to Dulcie's tonight? Why couldn't it have been last night when Father was still on Espoir?"

"Because you said there would be more action on a Friday night," Jeannette reminded her. "You wanted to play poker, remember?"

Charmaine was shocked. Yvette wasn't contrite over her intractable behavior, just sorry she'd been caught.

"And I was winning!" she wailed. "I'd more than tripled my money!"

"But that's good," Jeannette encouraged.

"Good?" Yvette exclaimed. "How can you say that? I ran out and left it all behind! Almost eighty dollars! One hundred, if you count the last pot! And those greedy, stinkin', cheatin', no-good lot of dirty swindlin' seamen probably shoved it all into their filthy pockets when Father left! We're out twenty dollars!"

George found John in the stable brushing Phantom's flank to a brilliant luster, as if the chore could draw out all of the poison that festered in the wound his father had so deftly reopened.

"Isn't it a bit late to be currying your horse?" George queried lightly.

"It's a bit late for a lot of things, George," the man bitterly replied. "I'm a fool, one damned fool."

"No, John, you're not. You did what was best. Don't allow your father to lead you to believe otherwise. You did what was best."

"Did I?"

"You know you did," George finished. "This is Yvette's night for mischief, not yours. No sense in acting the spoiled boy just because she's stolen center stage from you."

The remark brought a smile to John's eyes, and he laughed with his friend in spite of himself.

"Look!" George weighed a hefty purse in his hand before tossing it over.

"What is this?"

"Count it," George directed, watching John rake his fingers through the contents. "There's over a hundred dollars there. More than eighty-five in winnings by my estimation."

"Winnings?" John questioned bemusedly.

"Yvette's winnings. According to the men she was playing poker with, she took a seat at the table with a purse of twenty dollars. She won the rest."

"Won?" John asked incredulously. "Are you saying she won this off a surly lot of seamen?"

"Fair and square," George replied, "though I'm certain her manner of play was at best baffling. On more than one turn of the card, she held a high ace, hoping to draw a second pair. But the men misread the three cards she kept as beginner's luck, assuming she'd been dealt three of a kind. If your father hadn't stormed the table, it would have been downright entertaining."

"And how did you come to be there, Georgie?"

"Just stopped in for a drink," his friend answered. "But I don't mind telling you, I nearly crapped my pants when Paul and your father walked in."

"I'm sure you did," John agreed, a deep laugh erupting. "So, tell me more. From the beginning, if you don't mind."

"Not at all," George chuckled, and he launched into the entire story.

Chapter 7

Saturday, October 7, 1837

SPENT of curses, Frederic found the morning less to his liking than the night before. Cloistered in his private chambers, he could spare others his miserable disposition. But for himself, his refuge was nothing more than a prison, an incarceration of the mind, plagued by the memory of the life he had lived, the many opportunities he had wasted, the schemes he had forged in their stead. Another plan had failed. When would he learn he could not bend destiny? The Almighty was determined to prolong the agony of his failure: failure as a father, failure as a husband.

Voices floated up from the gardens, drawing him to the French doors. John was there, squatting and settling Pierre on one knee, his arm encircling the child's small shoulders. "Now, let me see," he said, taking hold of the boy's hand and turning it over for inspection. "Where is this terrible splinter Mainie can't see?"

"There!" Pierre pointed out. Charmaine moved behind John, watching from over his shoulder.

"Not a very big one," John commented softly, pulling the palm nearer his face, "but there all the same. They say the smaller ones hurt the most."

Pierre looked up at his governess, and John's gaze followed, the sun catching in his hair. He was talking to the lad again, the love in his voice disarming. "You won't cry when I take this out, will you?"

Pierre shook his head, and John stood, hoisting him into his arms. The sun glinted again, playing a color game with the reddish tints in the brown-blond hair, Elizabeth's hair.

The boy was a man already. Only yesterday, Frederic thought he had so much time. Suddenly, a distant memory transported him back to a time when John was a similar age to Pierre suffering his splinter. The ship pitched and plunged through the roiling waves. Bursts of thunder exploded, an untamed beast bearing down on them. The cabin door flew open, and the frustrated nanny rushed in, fretting over his wailing son. John could not be calmed, the darkness too great and the storm too fierce to dike his turgid tears. He was placed in Frederic's care, a father vaguely known to him, a father who had all but disowned him, but could not bring himself to completely renounce the only remaining part of the woman he still loved. Frederic held the lad for the first time that night, knowing that, if nothing else, his strength and size could shield the three-year-old from the tempest and perhaps soothe him. As they settled in the cot, John buried his head in Frederic's shoulder and his breathing grew steady. Frederic began to fancy the feel of Elizabeth's son cuddled in his embrace. Then he remembered Elizabeth in that spot and began to cry, hot tears trickling into his hair as he mourned the woman he had lost . . .

"Damn!" he cursed aloud, ignoring the blur of his vision. Why hadn't John just taken Pierre and fled? *Why?*

Yvette stood meekly before her father, ready to accept her come-uppance, comforted only by the fact her sister stood next to her. It had been little over a week since she had last visited the master's chambers; now she'd be pleased never to step into these rooms again.

"Two things I would have from you," Frederic began roughly, his shrewd eyes scrutinizing the child from where he sat.

He did not delight in her submissiveness. Remembering Jeannette's declaration of the preceding night, he berated himself for snuffing out the rebelliousness, the savvy, he admired. Still, she had recklessly hatched more trouble than John and Paul at that age and comprehended little of the danger she could have faced had he not intervened. Therefore, it was best to deal with her sternly.

"First," he said, "I would have your promise, your word of honor, that what happened last night will *never* happen again. Beyond that, I want it understood you will never, under any circumstance, leave this house or its grounds without permission from either myself or your governess."

"Yes, sir," she replied softly, meeting his eyes. It appeared the man's apoplectic anger had indeed dissipated, and she regained her aplomb with the pledge, "I promise."

Frederic cocked his head. "I don't want the words given casually. I expect you to hold by them, and not just when you think you may be caught. When you leave here, I want to know I can trust you, that your vow won't be broken."

"On my life, sir," she pronounced, "I give my word. I won't *ever* do anything so naughty again."

He smiled for the first time, and Yvette wondered what he found so amusing. "I believe you," he said.

"And the second?" she probed; he had mentioned two things.

"I want you to apologize to Miss Ryan. You could have caused her great alarm if she had gone to your room and found your beds empty. As it was, she was unjustly blamed for your misconduct, something she didn't deserve."

"Is that all?" Yvette asked, convinced the worst had yet to come.

"Isn't that enough?"

"Yes, but aren't you—I mean, I thought you—"

"No, I'm not," the man interrupted, his brow raised. "As angry as I was when I found you gambling at Dulcie's, I had no intention of beating you, Yvette. However, if something like this should happen again, I'll not be so lenient."

"Then—there's to be no punishment?" the girl asked hopefully.

"I didn't say that. After some consideration, I've decided my timely arrival at the tavern last evening will stand as punishment enough."

Yvette frowned. "I don't understand."

"Then let me explain." Frederic rummaged through his desk drawer, producing the reticule the girl had stuffed with an assortment of gold coins and one-dollar notes only twelve hours earlier.

Relief washed over her when the pouch jangled, and in unmasked delight, she quickly calculated the value of the purse.

"There's more than the twenty American dollars you started with," he said, as if reading her mind, "close to five times that amount by George's count."

"George?"

"He confiscated all of your winnings. If your little adventure weren't so naughty, I'd have to congratulate you. However," he continued, his voice growing hard and uncompromising, "no daughter of mine is going to gamble—let alone with dirty, low-class seamen. Is that understood?"

"Yes, sir," Yvette muttered, her moment's elation quashed with the realization of what was coming next.

"Unfortunately, lessons are often learned the hard way. And the best lesson for you, my dear, is to lose this."

"But—"

"I'm donating it to the poor."

"Just the winnings, Papa, please, I promise I won't—"

"No, Yvette, not just the winnings. You see, it was only luck that prevented you from losing last night. Do you realize what those men would have done had you continued to win? You feared a beating from me, but I guarantee they would have inflicted far worse. They would have followed you and cornered you alone."

She shuddered and meekly mumbled, "Yes, sir."

Frederic eyed his other daughter. "What of you, Jeannette? Was any of this money yours?"

"Yes, Papa. Half of it was mine. Yvette said we'd split whatever she won."

"Well, then, you've shared equally in the punishment. It had better not happen again."

"No, sir, it won't."

They watched as Frederic slid open the deepest drawer in the desk, fumbled curiously with what looked to be a false back, deposited the purse there, and replaced the wooden panel.

"It would be safer in the safe," Yvette offered.

"No, my dear, it won't remain in the house for long. I'm certain there are a few families in town who could benefit from your generosity. I shall speak to Paul about it."

He smiled at them, a self-satisfied smile that riled Yvette. She resisted uttering the recriminations that were rifling through her head, certain they would induce his wrath if they found their way to tongue.

"That will be all," he finished.

Once they were in the south-wing corridor, Yvette took to grumbling. "Just wait until I see George. He snatched all of my winnings and told Father about it instead of me! Why would he do that?"

"I don't know, Yvette," her sister attempted to console. "But if Father didn't use the money as our punishment, we could have gotten worse."

"Worse? I don't see how! All that loot and we didn't even get to count it! It's unfair, I tell you."

"Tired?"

Startled, Charmaine looked up from the lawn and squinted

against the sun that silhouetted the man looming over her. He stepped forward, blocking the rays altogether. Disappointed, Charmaine smiled halfheartedly up at Paul.

"Not tired," she answered as he sat beside her, drawing his knees up and locking his arms about them. "Just discontent, I suppose."

"Discontent? You're not blaming yourself for what happened last night?"

"Partially. I'm waiting for the girls now."

She focused on Pierre, who was pushing the swing back and forth.

"Everything will turn out for the best," he soothed, studying her with a sympathetic eye and an indefinable ache in his breast. "Charmaine, look at me."

She faced him, surprised by the raw emotion in his eyes.

"I missed you," he stated simply, his hand catching hers, squeezing it in understanding and support, instilling her with renewed strength. "How was your week?"

John left the terrace and stepped back into the house. Charmaine was already occupied. He no longer commanded her attention. His week had come to a close. Hadn't he realized that last night? He'd be wise to shut the door. He rubbed his forehead and swallowed hard.

Why was he always denied? Why did he allow himself to be denied? He grunted across the words that chastised him, the gentle petition that haunted him: *Take care of them . . . live and love again, John . . .*

Coming to an abrupt decision, he crossed the foyer hurriedly and took the stairs two at a time. He knew it was a last resort, but because he had nothing more to lose, he set his pride aside and entered his father's sanctum.

Frederic looked up from his desk.

John read the surprise in his eyes and got right to the point. "I will be returning to Virginia tomorrow. I request your permission to take Pierre and the twins with me."

Frederic was stunned by the direct petition, awed by his son's valor to take this step, especially in light of the ugly episode of the evening before. Wasn't this what he wanted, an honest give-and-take?

"For how long?" he asked.

"Forever."

"And who will see to their care when you are occupied with business?"

Is my father actually considering this request? John had expected a swift and unequivocal "no." "Miss Ryan, if she is willing. She has friends there. A move back will allow her to be closer to them."

Frederic breathed deeply and stood up. He walked to the French doors, weighing the advantages and disadvantages of such an arrangement. Here was an opening to begin setting things aright with his son, but in so doing, would he estrange his remaining offspring?

"And what of Yvette and Jeannette?" he asked.

"What of them?" John rejoined, exasperated. "What will they miss here, except a shadow of a father closeted in a room who pays them no mind, or when he does, rants and raves like a lunatic, and a stepmother who despises them? Where do *you* think they will be better off?"

Frederic smarted with the truth of the declaration, remembering his cowering daughters. Another grave mistake he needed to correct—for Colette, for himself. He turned back to John. "Why don't you stay here?" he offered. "Wouldn't it be easier if you just stayed on Charmantes?"

"Easier for you," John replied. "I refuse to participate in this—this evil charade any longer. You keep your children close not by giving them what they need, but by withholding it." He snorted in disgust when his father didn't respond. "Obviously, your answer is 'no.' I knew it would be. I come to claim what is mine—the courage you don't believe I have—and still I am denied!" Not waiting for a reply, he retreated.

But Frederic called after him, "Not all of it is yours to claim," and then to the empty doorway, "I cannot release my daughters . . . certainly not forever."

"I'm listening, John," Paul said, annoyed when his brother quietly took a seat. "Surely you didn't summon me here to watch you recline—"

"Sit down, Paul," John interrupted mildly. "I have a number of things to discuss with you. I'm not kindling a row, I would like to speak civilly."

Paul indulged him. "What is it?"

"I'd like to talk to you about Charmaine."

"What about her?" Paul queried cautiously, warily.

"Charmaine is a decent woman, good and kind."

"You don't have to tell me that, John. Remember, it was I who knew her first, I who informed you of her integrity. It took you long enough to recognize it, the noble attributes you sought to scorn and scandalize."

John concurred. "But I did recognize them. I admit I misjudged her at first. Likewise, you must agree few women can match Charmaine in worth."

"I don't discredit that observation," Paul replied, his brow a study of a mind working. "But where is all of this leading?"

"Have you considered marriage?"

"Marriage?" Paul sputtered. "Are you suggesting I marry her?"

"In a word, yes. Is it so revolting an idea?"

Severely suspicious now, Paul pressed his chin into the palm of his hand and considered the man. "What is this about, John? What is this *really* about?"

"I'm fond of Charmaine. I don't want to see her hurt."

"And you think marriage to me will prevent that?"

"Yes, I do. She loves you, you know, more deeply than I think even you realize. The night I came home, she kissed you with all the passion and love a woman can give a man. I didn't comprehend how neatly her heart was sewn into the bargain until I came to know her better, heard her speak about you. She doesn't deserve to be hurt—not by me, and not by you."

"Then why don't *you* marry her?" Paul baited, suddenly angry the man was placing them on the same level.

"Like I said, Paul, she doesn't deserve to be hurt," John returned, his voice dead serious. "I confess to my little games, but they're over now. George tells me the *Raven* pulled back into port at dawn, something about a ripped spanker and a splintered mast. When she sets sail again, probably tomorrow afternoon, I'll be going with her."

"What? Just like that?"

"Yes, Paul, just like that. I plan on telling Charmaine and the children later, but I wanted to speak with you first."

"I can't believe it," Paul muttered.

"But you must, for it's true. And it is for the best."

"Is that so? You come back here, upset the children's lives, make certain they're attached to you all over again, and then you just pull up and leave. Why? To punish Father for what happened last night? To make him look like the fiend you believe him to be?"

John's eyes narrowed, but he marshaled his anger and forced himself to answer calmly. "No, Paul, believe it or not, this has nothing to do with Father. But it has everything to do with the children. I, too, have become 'attached' as you put it, and such a relationship cannot be, can it? So, what I can't take with me, I relinquish altogether." He bowed his head momentarily, then met Paul's intense regard with one of his own. "For that reason alone, I will be aboard the *Raven* tomorrow afternoon, and I won't be back."

Disconcerted, Paul turned to safer ground, more comfortable with anger than misery. "And what does all this have to do with Charmaine and me?"

John didn't answer, but Paul puzzled over the question until all the pieces fell in place. "You're worried Father will dismiss her, aren't you? *Aren't you?*"

"No, Paulie."

"Yes, Johnny! And what better way to prevent that from happening than to see her married to me, wife to the children's brother? That would certainly insure her position in the household, wouldn't it? *Wouldn't it, goddamn you!*" When John refused to respond, Paul pressed on. "You amaze me, you really do! Banking on me to fix this atrocity!"

John's eyes hardened. "You're a fine one to sit in judgment, Paul—you, who've conquered woman after woman without a care in the world."

"Really? Well, unlike you, John, I haven't maliciously seduced a woman who didn't belong to me, just to get revenge!"

"Is that how you see it?" John muttered, the blood running cold in his veins. "All these years—and that's what you think happened? No wonder you sided with Father."

Momentarily deflated, Paul drew himself up. "Don't play me for the village idiot, John. We both know how you hate him. You've made that abundantly clear. And don't point a finger at me because I refuse to be drawn into it. You know what? You're pathetic!"

"Pathetic?" John rejoined ferociously. "You call *me* pathetic? Look at yourself, Paul. There isn't anyone in this house more pathetic than you! That's right, brother. Take a good look at yourself— sitting next to Father at the table like a loyal dog, anxiously awaiting the scraps of gristle he might throw your way. And like a loyal dog, you're blind to how he abuses you! Instead, you defend him to the end, hoping if you just show him how capable you are, how diligently you can work, maybe one day he will acknowledge you and your exceptional efforts. Work! Work! Work! Oh yes, Paul, you're good enough to get the job done. You go above and beyond! But where has it gotten you? John can shirk his responsibilities. John can shame his father with the ultimate affront, but John is still first on the will! And what about you? After all your toil, dedication, and loyalty, you're not even legitimate yet, are you? If you were *my son*, you would be! But be my guest, Paul—keep blaming me for all the evil in this house. It's all very tidy that way, isn't it? By placing everything on my shoulders, you don't have to examine the truth." John pointed at him emphatically. "*You're* the pathetic one, Paul, and damn you for not claiming Charmaine while you have the chance. You would rather chase after Father's unrequited love than return her love, freely given. Mark my words: you will rue the day you were so blind as to throw away happiness with both hands!"

Charmaine studied the pacing man apprehensively. John had said he had something important to speak to them about, and now she and the children waited for him to find the words to begin. He finally came to a standstill, as if immobility would help him overcome his impasse. He faced the twins who sat on their beds, his back to her and Pierre.

"I'll be leaving tomorrow," he said, his trembling voice belying the ease with which he delivered the simple statement.

"*Leaving?*" The single gasp fell from everyone's lips.

"Charmantes?" Yvette added, horrified. "You're leaving Charmantes?"

"That's right. I'll be aboard the *Raven* when she sets sail for the States. It's time I head home and get some work done there."

"But *this* is your home!" the girl objected. "Here, with us!"

"No, Yvette, not anymore. I have another home, you know that, one I've neglected for too long now."

"So you'll neglect us instead? Virginia is more important than us?"

"Yvette, you know that is not true," he answered softly. "But I do have other responsibilities that—"

"Responsibilities?" his sister countered. "What responsibilities?

What could be more important than your family—taking care of us?"

"Yvette, you were fine before I arrived two months ago, and you will be fine after I've departed."

"No, I won't! And you're wrong about two months ago, very wrong! I wasn't fine, none of us were, not until you came back and made everything right! We were so unhappy, but you made us laugh again! You can't leave now! You just can't! I won't let you!"

"You are making this very difficult for me, Yvette, but I must leave, and no matter how much you beg, I won't change my mind."

"But why? *Why?*"

"I've told you, I have business to attend to in Virginia *and* New York. I cannot postpone it any longer." He inhaled and drew strength from a new thought, infusing his voice with a note of excitement. "What if I promised to invite you, Jeannette, and Pierre for a visit? Perhaps next spring, when the weather warms. By then, the work I've ignored will be behind me, and I'll have plenty of time to spend with the three of you. How does that sound?"

"It sounds like a lie!" she spat back, "a lousy lie!"

"Yvette!" Charmaine scolded, her heart pounding with the climaxing scene.

"It's true!" the girl retaliated, her blue-gray eyes widened more in pain than anger, riveted first on her brother and then her governess. "He's lying, just like before. Right after we turned five, he left, promising we could visit, promising to write, promising to send passage in the springtime. But that passage never came and neither did the letters, and no one would even let me speak about it! And then, when I was finally allowed to write, I begged him to send for me, but do you think he answered? No! He just ignored that part of my letters, as if he didn't care! His letters talked about everything *but* a visit to Virginia."

She faced him again, her anguish masked by her rage. "I won't listen to your lies anymore! Father is right. All you bring to this family is pain and sorrow! You don't care about anybody but yourself! Go back to Richmond. See if I care. I swear I won't!"

"Yvette! That's enough!" Charmaine reprimanded.

John swallowed hard, the agony he experienced more for the child's woe than his own. "It's all right, Charmaine, she doesn't know what she's saying. I know she doesn't really mean it."

"I do mean it!" she protested, twisting away from him when he tried to embrace her. "Don't touch me! Just leave me alone!"

Having exhausted all avenues of reasoning, John dropped his arms to his sides, bowed his head, and left the misery-ridden room.

The evening meal, long in arriving, commenced in silence, an indication the wretched tableau had yet to come to an end. Whether gladdened or disheartened, one sweep of the room revealed that each member of the family, from adult to child, contemplated John's sudden decision to depart the island, speechless, heads bent to plates.

Best to hold quiet as well, Charmaine thought. No need to make pleasant conversation and pretend at happiness, to deal with the situation the way Yvette was. The nine-year-old was demonstrating a hearty appetite, a punishment intended for John, though he did not seem to notice. The child didn't comprehend her brother's pain, the vile situation that forced his hand. But Charmaine understood, understood enough to know the big family secret was bigger and more terrible than she had been prepared to believe.

A familiar click, followed by a retarded thud, punctured the dismal silence, awakening everyone to the realization the master of the house intended to preside over the unhappy table. Charmaine held her breath. No one said a word as Frederic approached his family. Mercifully, he didn't stop near John, but made his way toward the foot of the table and the wife who threw him a curious look before surrendering her chair and slipping into the one to his left.

Anna moved Agatha's plate and quickly laid a new place setting. As the minutes gathered, so, too, did the tension.

Pierre's candid voice shattered the uneasy calm. "Johnny?"

John looked up for the first time, his gaze locking on Frederic before traveling to the boy. "Yes, Pierre," he asked, clearing his throat, "what is it?"

"I've decided somethin'."

"Have you now?"

"Uh-huh," he stated with a resolute nod. "I've decided I'm gonna go with you tomorrow to that place . . . Vir-gin-ni-a."

John paled, but his response was chillingly unemotional. "I'm afraid you can't. You'd have to leave too many of the things you treasure behind."

"No, I don't," the lad refuted ingenuously. "I got me a trunk. I can put all my stuff in there."

John didn't know whether to laugh or cry. "The type of trunk you'd need would be entirely too big. It wouldn't fit in our cabin."

"That's silly," Pierre giggled. His older brother was just teasing him, as he'd so often done in the past. "I've seen that ship, 'member? It's tremenjus!"

"And what about the people you'd have to leave behind? Your sisters, Mainie? You love them very much, don't you? Wouldn't you miss them?"

"They can come, too! Jeannie wants to come. She tol' me so." Pierre looked toward his sister, who nodded with a weak, yet hopeful smile. "See?"

"What about Yvette? She's extremely angry with me."

"She'd come. Wouldn't you, Yvie?" he asked, his eyes imploring the girl for a similar response. But she was guarding a severe silence and refused to look his way. "Well, she would anyway . . . if you asked her."

"Even so, I still can't take you with me."

"Why not? You asked me before."

Involuntarily, John's eyes traveled to his father again, and Charmaine's regard followed. Was it sadness or turmoil on the elder's face? Perhaps both.

"That was before," John choked out, "not now."

"Why? Don't you love me anymore?"

"Yes, I love you!" John barked, belatedly leashing his strife. "It has nothing to do with that. I'd be far too busy in Virginia to take care of you properly."

"I can take care of myself. I won't get in no trouble. I promise."

"No."

"But I wanna go!"

"I said 'no'!"

With bottom lip quivering, Pierre blinked back his tears. "If you don't take me, I'll go anyway. I'll get in my boat and I'll row there all by myself!"

"You'd never last the trip," John muttered.

"I will! You'll see. And once I'm there, you can't send me back!" He turned his attention back to his plate and said one last time, "You'll see."

John propped an elbow on the arm of his chair and pressed his forehead into the palm of his hand. Frederic did the same, looking up only when his son pushed away from the table. He started to speak, but John was gone before the words were out. The moment was lost.

Charmaine quietly closed the door to the children's bedroom. They were finally settled for the night, a difficult chore in the face of all that had happened in the past twenty-four hours. Rose said "goodnight" and hobbled toward her rooms in the north wing. But Charmaine had no intention of retiring. She'd never fall asleep now; her mind was too full, the hour too early.

She descended the staircase, coming up short as John appeared on the landing. His gaze swept upward until his clouded eyes locked on her, turning keen and holding her captive. Thus they stood, neither one speaking.

"Will I see you before you leave?" she asked.

"The *Raven* doesn't set sail until late afternoon. So, yes, you'll see me."

"The *Raven* . . . It was the ship that brought me to Charmantes. Now it takes you away."

"You sound displeased, my Charm," he attempted to quip. "Could it be you, too, will miss me?"

"Yes, I shall miss you," she whispered, struggling to contain her burning emotions, disturbed by his soft chuckle. "Is that so inconceivable?"

"Somewhat, considering you've awaited this date for two months now."

She ignored the comment that held some truth not two weeks ago. "You'll write?" she asked instead.

"Yes, I'll write."

With his portion of the dialog exhausted, John turned toward the opposite staircase to place some distance between them. Despite his valiant effort, she refused to release him. "Why *are* you leaving?"

He faced her slowly. "Don't you know?"

"No," she lied, wanting only to hold him to the spot.

"Sweet, innocent Charmaine," he murmured reverently. "Better that you don't know or you would despise me as well."

"I no longer despise you . . . I could never despise you."

His eyes caressed every feature of her face. "I will carry you with me, my Charm. You've provided me with a perfect two months, a time that will have to suffice, memories to hold dear."

The scraping of wood on wood interrupted them. Pierre appeared at the crest of the stairs, struggling to push Charmaine's trunk across the floorboards.

"Pierre, whatever are you doing?"

The boy swiftly straightened, his face a mask of guilt. "I'm goin'," he admitted, expelling one exhausted breath, his determined eyes traveling from Charmaine to John.

"Going where?"

"To Johnny's other house just like I said I was."

"Oh no, you're not!" she argued, marching up the stairs with John close behind her. "Come," she said, grabbing his hand, "back to bed with you."

"No!" he objected, pulling away. "I don't wanna go to sleep! I wanna go with Johnny!"

Before the boy could sidestep her, Charmaine lifted him up, allowing John to take charge of the trunk. "Johnny is not leaving until tomorrow afternoon."

"I don't believe him," Pierre protested, struggling to get down.

"You must, because it's true," Charmaine said, holding him tightly and returning him to the nursery, where she found Yvette and Jeannette wide awake. "You are to stay in bed and go to sleep, and if you're a good boy you will see John first thing in the morning before we go to Mass."

Pierre pursed his lips. "I bet I won't! I bet he's gonna leave without sayin' goodbye, just like Yvie said."

John looked at Yvette. "No, Pierre, she's wrong," he countered angrily. "I'd never leave without saying goodbye, and you *will* see me in the morning just like Mademoiselle Charmaine promised, but only if you go to sleep."

The boy brightened. "And you'll take me with you?"

"Not this time, and no more begging."

He burst into tears. "But I wanna go with you! Please let me go. I'll be very, very, *very* good! I promise. Please, Johnny, please take me!"

"No!" John shouted. "Now, stop crying or I won't visit at all!"

The severe threat had a devastating effect. Pierre fought to stem the deluge that glistened upon his flustered face, but only succeeded in gasping for breath. Charmaine gathered him in her arms, yet could not console him. With rigid jaw, she glared at John.

It was the final blow. Disgusted, John confronted his sisters. Yvette refused to look at him, but Jeannette presented a vulnerable target, her frown of disapproval feeding his rising ire.

"Why didn't you stop him? Why didn't you call Charmaine when you saw what he was doing?"

"Pierre can do just as he likes," she answered callously, her voice unnaturally sharp, an indication that although she had remained silent, her pain was no less malignant.

"Do as he likes?" John asked incredulously.

"That's what you always do, don't you? Go ahead and run away—run away because it's easier than trying to be nice to Father. And when you're back in Virginia, you can forget about us, just like you did the last time. Yvette is right. You don't care about anybody in this family."

"Jeannette, that's not true!" he choked out. "I hate seeing you like this."

"Then why are you going?" she moaned, leaping from the bed and hugging him fiercely until he was forced to hug her back. "Please don't go! Say you'll stay! Or take us with you! We'll do anything—anything if you'd only—"

"I can't," he muttered, ripping away from her and rushing out of the room.

Charmaine lay on her back staring at the ceiling, seeing nothing of the room save her memories of John in it. It had begun that first night he'd come home.

John—when had he come to mean so much to her? When had the thought of him changed from frown to smile? Displeasure to pleasure? *He's an enigma—a one of a kind . . . You either hate him or love him, and it's usually in that order . . .* When had the Good Lord revealed the real man?

John—heir to his father's immense fortune. The thought of such wealth commanded by one individual would send some women swooning, others salivating at his feet. How sad for them; they'd be blind to the bounty beneath. John could be a beggar, and still she would count herself the richer for having known him.

John—sleeping just down the hall, or perhaps he wasn't sleeping at all.

Dismally, she wondered if she'd ever see him again. How barren the future appeared. No more picnics, excursions into town, endeavors that courted trouble and made life worth living. No more exchanging of words, matching of wits, conversations that scoffed at boredom, or plans that dismantled the most carefully laid routine. Each day, each encounter had been different, unexpected, rich and rewarding. Would the dawn steal it all from her? How was she to endure without him?

She ached for his melancholy, the decision he was forced to make, one that cut more deeply than his innocent sisters fathomed. But Charmaine understood. The pieces of the elusive puzzle pointed to one horrible, yet logical conclusion: Colette and John had been lovers; had, in fact, conceived a child together. Pierre was Frederic's grandson! It couldn't be true—but it must be true!

How could it have happened?

Colette—married to a man old enough to be her father. Was this the reason she had turned to John? It couldn't be! Surely her sacred vows had meant something. And she had claimed to love Frederic, had told Charmaine she had been attracted to him from the moment they'd met. Why, then, would she take her husband's son as a lover?

Frederic—he must have been devastated when he learned his wife had been unfaithful—that his son had betrayed him. Charmaine could just imagine John and Frederic fighting over the woman they both loved, the truth of Pierre's conception spilling out and inducing the seizure that left Frederic crippled.

John—why would he enter into an adulterous affair with his father's wife? Was this his revenge for the scorn he'd endured as a child? It had to be more than that. John loved Colette. Charmaine could feel it, knew it to be true. And he desperately loved Pierre, the precious remnant of that love.

How could Colette have allowed this to happen?

She had wreaked havoc in this house, her love for father and son tearing the entire family apart. And yet, Charmaine couldn't condemn her. What a terrible tragedy! Everyone had been affected, would suffer the repercussions for generations to come. This was the reason Colette's ghost roamed the house: her soul was not at peace!

And what of little Pierre? Would he grow up believing Frederic was his father and think of John only as an elder brother? *John had wanted to take him away,* Charmaine suddenly realized. That was the cataclysmic impasse he had reached that night she'd found him at the piano. *No one deserves to be hurt, least of all an innocent child.* So, John would sacrifice his own happiness for Pierre's welfare. But would the boy be happy without him?

Charmaine shook with the ferocity of her thoughts. Would she ever know the whole incredible story? Could this family ever bury the past? No, a situation this heinous could never be forgotten, let alone reconciled, for it lived on.

Tears sprang to her eyes, but she didn't fight them back. Grasping her pillow, she turned her face into its downy softness and cried, cried in the hope her tears would wash away her depraved conclusions.

Sunday, October 8, 1837

Pierre was ill. Though he wasn't running a fever, his face was flushed and he complained of a headache and stomachache. Obviously, he was suffering from a battered heart.

"If Pierre is not going to Mass," Yvette announced, "then neither am I!"

"Yes, you are, young lady," Charmaine remonstrated lightly. "Your little brother isn't feeling well, but you are just fine."

"Who will mind him while we are gone?" she asked peevishly.

"I'm sure John will look after him for an hour."

The declaration sent Yvette into a huff, and like the preceding night, she turned her sullen face to the wall.

Charmaine smiled to herself. Yes, John would lend a hand—his last chance to spend time alone with Pierre.

John sat on the bed beside the boy, gently stroking the tousled hair, placing each strand back in place. The house was so very quiet, the lad's heavy breathing the only sign of life in the great manor. The silence mocked the wailing of John's heart, the piercing pain so intense he could no longer fight it, and the first tears spilled on his extended hand.

Two months, he'd been granted two months. It would have to be enough, last the rest of his days. Eight weeks of laughter. Funny, he couldn't recall the heartache and frustration of having reached Charmantes too late. Only this day's anguish persecuted him now. Two months . . . If there was a God, he thanked Him.

A bloodcurdling howl rent the air, and John shot to his feet, racing out to the balcony. Across the lawns, pandemonium ruled. A stableman was doubled over in pain, the arm he cradled bent at an odd angle. Another man skirted across the paddock, shouting over his shoulder, "He's over there!" Two other men ran toward the house.

Highly agitated, Phantom snorted loudly and pranced in a circle, tossing his massive head from side to side. Abruptly, he stopped and rubbed his muzzle against a leg, then reared and pawed the air, trumpeting his unfathomable anger to the heavens. He repeated the fierce dance again and again, his hooves clattering on the cobblestone.

Three grooms approached gingerly, bridle and rope in hand.

But the stallion charged them, a surprise attack that caught one man off guard and clipped his shoulder, catapulting him backward. Before he could jump to his feet, the beast reared again and the lethal hooves came pounding down, missing him by inches.

Cursing, John dashed through the nursery. Pierre slept on. Without a thought, he reached the hallway and took the stairs three at a time.

John was leaving. Frederic paced his chamber, allowing the words to reverberate in his mind. His son was leaving—for good, this time. Damn him for going now. Damn him for going alone!

Frederic hadn't slept last night; nevertheless, he savored the burning sensation behind his eyes, the fatigue that was creeping in. He relived the scene at the dinner table over and over again. Would his family never know happiness? Would this be his legacy to his children?

Poor little Pierre—so young, so beautiful, so innocent. Frederic loved the boy in a way he'd never loved John, or even Paul at that age. He'd been given a second chance with Pierre. And what had he done with it? He'd spurned it. With bitter remorse, he remembered the months following his seizure, those wretched days when he'd languished as a mute cripple. He recalled the first time Rose had placed the tiny babe in his arms. The woman had been wise, for ironically, it had been that innocent infant who had coaxed him out of miserable nonexistence. Now, when the child had come to mean the most, when holding the three-year-old on his lap was the closest thing to happiness, he realized it was time to let go. John deserved Pierre's love far more than he did. But John wasn't about to hurt the boy by tearing him away from all the things he treasured, namely his sisters and his governess. That was why John had asked for the girls, why he'd set all pride aside and practically begged to have them. Where Fredcric had schemed, John had been honest, braving his contempt and asking for the children even though he could have stolen them the week before. And what had he, his father, done? He had denied him, again. *You keep your children close not by giving them what they need, but by withholding it.* Dear God, John was right.

Frederic raked his hand through his hair. He knew what he should do, what Colette, even Elizabeth, would want him to do. Reaching a resolution, he opened his safe and pulled three documents from his will. He sat and scrawled a last declaration on each one.

A movement at the French doors caught his eye. He blinked twice. Colette stood in the casement, an apparition so real he questioned his sanity. Perhaps he'd fallen asleep. In a rush, he stood, but for every step he took in her direction, she remained out of reach, a sad imitation of their marriage. He exited the room and pursued her along the veranda. But the wraith floated westward, slowly dissolving into the morning air. He shook his head once, twice, unsure if he tried to rid his mind of her image or recapture it.

His eyes were drawn to the edge of the pine forest. He thought he'd seen some movement at the base of the trees. Something was definitely there; something had grabbed his attention. He didn't know what precisely, and he cocked his head to better see. It did not help. Still, his eyes remained riveted to the spot—the opening that marked the path that led to the lake.

His heart quickened, and blood surged through his veins. He tried to discount the anxiety that gripped him, but could not. Unmindful of the cane that clattered to the balcony floor, he hastened back into his room, reaching the bell-pull in five large, unencumbered strides. Someone would come. Not everyone was at Mass. Again, he yanked on the rope, praying someone would respond, cursing when another minute passed and still, nothing. Enough! He was down the hallway before Felicia had reached the top of the stairs.

"Sir? You wanted something?" she asked, curious as to why his face was ashen, why he was even in the corridor.

"Get Travis."

"But he's at Mass, sir, as is the rest—"

"Get him, damn it, and get him now! Tell him to go into the forest—behind the house! Something's wrong at the lake!"

"Sir?"

"Just do it, girl!" he shouted, his fervor sending her racing down the stairs. "If Paul is there, tell him the same! Remember—they're to check at the lake!"

The churchgoers congregated in the small vestibule and spoke in hushed tones, attempting to make sense of the interruption that had halted Sunday Mass and sent Paul and Travis on a crazed mission to the lake.

"I want some answers," Agatha demanded, dismissing Benito's outrage.

"I don't have any, ma'am," Felicia replied. "Like I told you, the master, he rung while everyone was at Mass. But before I could reach his apartments, he was rantin' and ravin' in the corridor, demandin' Travis and Master Paul be sent to the lake to check on somethin'."

"To check on what?" the mistress pressed. "What was to be checked?"

"A problem of some kind. He didn't say what."

As the hour lengthened, and it became apparent the Mass would not resume, the assembly slowly dispersed.

"Come, girls," Charmaine urged, "let us check on Pierre."

The nursery was unusually quiet. Then Charmaine knew why: John and Pierre weren't there. For all the times she'd found the boy's bed empty, experienced that heart-stopping panic that left her limbs painfully weak, this time it did not, this time she smiled. Pierre was with John. John had him. One last hour together; they needed that.

A chilling scream annihilated the happy thought, then thundering footsteps.

Paul's desperate voice reached them—rapid-fire orders shot from the foyer. "Get Blackford! Now, damn it! And blankets, I'll need blankets—all you can gather! Then Rose—find her and find her fast!"

Silence—a second's silence and then: "John—my God—where were you?"

Another voice—John's. "What the hell—"

Then Paul again: "We've got to get him upstairs! Damn it, John! He's swallowed a great deal of water! We've got to—"

"What water? Where in God's name did you find him?"

"The lake! Jesus Christ, John, there's no time to explain! We've got to get Robert!"

"Give him to me, Paul. Goddamn it, give him to me!"

Wednesday, October 11, 1837

For the third consecutive morning, the sun broke free of the horizon and captured the navy blue heaven, blessing the world below with its promise of a new day. And for the third morning in succession, this was not so within the great manor, where family and servants alike awaited word from the governess's bedchamber.

Pierre lay in a state of delirium. A raging fever swept him along a maelstrom of hallucinations in which his amber eyes grew wide, perceiving monstrous images crawling on the ceiling. Charmaine called to him, but he did not respond.

Rose changed the saturated bed clothing, but no sooner were the fresh linens tucked in place than the boy was drenched in sweat again. With a click of her tongue, she returned to the task of bathing his fiery brow, laying a chilled cloth upon his forehead. He vaulted against the polar contact, but she held it in place. The compress was instantly branded. Undeterred, she removed it and tried again. Thus far, her remedies had been ineffectual, but she refused to cave in to despair. Instead, she relinquished the cloth to Charmaine, picked up her worn rosary beads, and knelt beside the bed, petitioning the Lord's Blessed Mother to intercede. Her lips mouthed the prayers while her crooked fingers counted off the smooth beads one by one, decade by decade.

As the day wore on, Pierre's condition changed. His limbs flailed against the blankets that suffocated him one moment and failed to warm him the next, his small teeth chattering in his scarlet mouth. He began to moan and call out names, incoherent phrases that slurred into "Mama" or "Mainie." Charmaine consoled him with gentle caresses and endearing whispers, cursing her inability to do more.

The shadows lengthened, and at the toll of seven, an uneasy calm descended on the infirm chamber. The tossing and turning stopped, but Pierre's lungs labored to capture what little air the selfish room offered, his wheezing amplified, though the rise and fall of the coverlet was barely perceptible. Rose tiptoed from his side and left the room. Charmaine took over her post, refusing to succumb to fatigue. She would not leave the boy until she was certain of his recovery.

Her resolve was not singular. Of all who had come to check on the boy's condition, those who remained an hour or two, or those who milled in the hallway beyond, one person had not abandoned Pierre for more than a minute at a time, departing only to see to necessaries, eating nothing. Charmaine's regard traveled across the bed to John. He had finally fallen asleep, his neck arched and head pressed into the back of the armchair. She sighed, grateful her eyes had not met his. She despised the desperation and guilt she read there. His momentary surrender to exhaustion was just as disconcerting. Yet, at least he was not pacing, a march that tore at the carpet as surely as it tore at her sanity.

For three days, he had measured the room by the length of his stride, an eternity of steps interrupted only when a knock fell on the outer door. The chamber had become a fortress he fiercely guarded, barring most, allowing entry to those few he himself selected: Paul and George, Fatima, bearing trays of food. The rest did not question his restrictions; perhaps they thought him mad. By all outward signs, the apathy apparent in his unkempt state, he was. His face had become drawn and ashen, the cheeks hollow, the chin prominent. Both carried the stubble of a beard. His sunken eyes were listless. The usually tousled, glossy hair was matted and coarse, clinging to his dampened brow. He looked like a man possessed.

Time drew on. Rose returned, though not alone. Paul was with her. Neither spoke as they stepped deeper into the room and stopped at the foot of the bed. Paul clasped a bedpost, his visage grim. He regarded Rose, nodding slightly to her. Taking the cue, she moved to John's chair.

Sensing her presence, he opened his eyes. She considered him, noting the lassitude that had taken hold, his faltering lucidity. Inhaling, she spoke. "John, I've asked Paul to call on Robert. If you'd give your consent, he'll leave immediately."

The bleary mind was instantly sharp and attentive. "No," he growled.

"But, John—"

"No!" he bellowed. "I don't want him near the boy!"

"John, I'm not a physician. I'm not schooled in the remedies employed—"

"You are," he stated vehemently, his rough voice growing earnest. "When we were young, never once did you fail us. No matter the illness, you always found the cure. Though you doubt your ability, I know you can help Pierre."

"You expect too much of me. I've done everything within my ability."

"If you can't help him, then no one can."

"You don't know that, John. We have a physician on the island who—"

"I said 'no,' damn it! I won't allow that incompetent ass to touch Pierre. My God, the man killed the boy's mother. He killed *my* mother!"

"John, you're wrong," she whispered woefully.

"Think what you like," he snarled, "but I swear, if Robert Blackford takes one step across that threshold, I'll wring his neck with my bare hands. I swear I will."

"Very well," Rose soothed in resignation. "I'll not press you on the matter. However, you will go downstairs and have something to eat. Fatima has prepared some broth, and after you've finished that, you must get some sleep."

"No."

"Charmaine and I will remain right here," she persisted. "If there is any change in his condition, we will come and get you immediately."

"No."

"John, I won't take no for an answer. You need nourishment and sleep."

"No! I said 'no'!" he barked. "I won't allow you to sneak Blackford into this room by shooing me away!"

Rose gritted her teeth, unintimidated. "I wouldn't do that, not to you or to anyone else to whom I'd given my word."

The planes of the man's face remained set, far from contrite.

Rose proceeded with care. "You're working yourself into a state of collapse, and then I'll have not one, but two patients to attend to."

"I'll be fine. Just minister to the boy and forget about me."

"Rose is right," Paul interjected, stepping forward. Though his words bordered on a command, they also rang with compassion. "John, please listen to her. You know she has Pierre's best interest at heart. I'll take up your vigil for a while."

"*You?*"

"Yes, me," Paul answered softly, impervious to the snide query. "It would benefit me to stay. If I hadn't wasted precious time arguing with Travis outside the chapel, if I had rushed to the lake right away, I might have gotten there before the boat capsized. I'd like to do something, know I've helped in some way."

"You're not at fault," John refuted tightly. "I know who's to blame."

"John, please. I'll not fail you this time. I swear I won't."

Paul awaited his brother's response, unsure if his pledge had met its mark.

John pushed out of the chair, swayed, then cast imploring eyes to Charmaine. "Promise me you will not leave Pierre—you won't permit Blackford access to this room."

"I—I promise," she stammered.

"Swear it."

"I swear it."

Satisfied, John stared down at Pierre, combed his fingers through the boy's hair, and staggered from the chamber. Charmaine watched him go, disturbed by a sudden sense of desolation. Even in his incapacitated state, John had radiated an intensity of purpose that had guarded against the enemy. She feared his abandonment and turned worried eyes to Paul.

"No need to fret, Charmaine," he said, "John will not hold you responsible."

"Responsible? What do you mean?"

But he hadn't heard her, for he'd already turned to Rose, who was speaking urgently to him. "You'd best leave immediately if you are to get Robert here before it's too late."

Charmaine reeled with the plot being hatched. "*What are you talking about?* You mean to bring Dr. Blackford to this room when you know how John feels about him?"

No answer, their muteness branding them guilty.

"I can't believe it! You gave your word!"

"Charmaine—"

"Child," Rose soothed. "There's no time for explanation. Pierre is dying."

"No!" Charmaine refuted fiercely. "You're wrong, terribly wrong!"

"I wish I were. Like John, you deny in your heart what you know to be true. The boy *is* dying and if we don't call on Dr. Blackford now, tomorrow John will blame himself for more than just this terrible accident."

"No, he can't be," she whispered, her eyes sweeping to Paul, desperately seeking some ray of hope from him, finding only defeat. "You're betraying John. You've deliberately deluded him—tricked him into leaving this room. And I won't believe Pierre is dying. God wouldn't claim the life of an innocent boy, not when there are so many praying for his recovery."

Her words echoed off the walls, then died. No one spoke, though their minds raced, searching for solutions, finding none, aware only that there was no hope to be found in hopelessness, no miracle to be wrested from the firm hand of the Almighty. Charmaine studied Paul. He quickly diverted his distraught gaze. When Rose cast her eyes to the floor, taking on the yoke of the accused, Charmaine turned away, a tear trickling down her cheek.

Silence reigned. She slumped into John's chair and took succor from the silence, reveling in its blanketing void. It was an unsullied silence, offering a peace she had not enjoyed for three long days. But suddenly, it seemed as if the room had become overwhelmingly silent, as a deeper, more intense silence enveloped her, severing itself from time and becoming an entity in and of itself. She concentrated on the silence, wondering what made it different. It was a silence that negated the gravity of the situation, a silence that lulled one into a false sense of security, a silence undisturbed. The wheezing had stopped.

Charmaine bolted to her feet and threw herself at the bed, grasping Pierre. "Rose! He can't breathe! I don't hear him breathing!" She tore away the suffocating blankets and shook him. "Pierre— breathe! Dear God—breathe!"

Her petition went unanswered, and slowly, painfully, the terrible truth took hold. Charmaine looked down at the feeble head that lolled against her arm, the long eyelashes fanning flushed cheeks. With an agonizing groan, she cradled the limp body to her chest, buried her lips in his matted hair, and sobbed.

"Charmaine . . ."

From far away, she discerned Paul's voice, felt him loosen her hold on the boy, watched Rose restore the lifeless body back to the center of the bed, was cognizant of being drawn farther from it, her vision blurred, then farther still . . .

"Let me go!" she protested savagely, reclaiming her sanity, attempting to reach Pierre again.

"Charmaine! Don't do this!" Paul commanded. "The boy is gone. You've held on long enough."

With the strength of one possessed, she wrenched free, but came up short as she stormed the bed. Pierre lay so very still.

"He's at peace now," Rose murmured.

The statement was like a knife in her heart. Refusing to accept it, she fled.

"Charmaine—wait!"

"Let her go," Rose advised, grabbing hold of Paul's arm. "She needs to be alone, and I need you here."

Charmaine reached the stairs and stumbled down them, for blinding tears distorted the shadows around her. More than once, she clutched the banister, catching herself before she fell to the landing below, still, she did not falter in her demonic pace, not even when she reached the foyer. Her legs carried her through the disused ballroom and toward the chapel doors. With muffled sobs, she closed her burning eyes, a fervent prayer racing through her mind, already on her lips: *Dear Lord, help me to accept Your will and bereave the loss of my loved one. Please . . . give me the strength to go on . . .*

She passed through the vestibule's archway before she saw him. Head bowed, John was half-sitting, half-kneeling in the pew nearest her. His elbows were propped on the bench in front of him, his forehead pressed into the white knuckles of his entwined fingers.

She rushed forward, and his head lifted. He jumped up and grabbed hold of her. "What is it?" he demanded. "Pierre—is he all right?"

She hesitated, until he shoved her aside and raced for the doorway.

"John—don't go up there! You mustn't go up there." She put a hand to her mouth as another wave of tears erupted in her throat. "Pierre is dead. Oh God, John, he's dead."

He stared, unseeing, as her words amplified—laid siege to his heart and ravaged his soul. Then silence reigned, carrying with it a cross and nails. He threw back his head and laughed pitifully. "And I came here to beg mercy from a God who has none!"

"You mustn't say that!"

"Why?" he growled. "Because I'll provoke His wrath?"

He stepped back and shouted at the crucifix suspended above the altar. "Must you punish me forever? Will I never see an end to it?"

"John! Stop it! Please stop!"

"He's taken everything from me—everyone I've ever loved."

"No, John, it wasn't the Lord's doing. He has no reason to persecute you, and you need Him now—the solace only He can offer."

"I don't want His damned solace!" he exploded. "I want my son! Can't you understand that? I want my son!"

"Merciful God," she murmured. *I was right!*

Unconsciously, she stepped back, her reaction catching his eye. "Poor Charmaine Ryan," he snarled diabolically, "subjected to evil and decadence. See, you were right about me all along! I fathered that child you loved. He was nothing more than a bastard." His voice cracked, the anger failing him, though he strove to hold it, command it. "I require no audience, my dear, so why don't you run along, back to your pristine world of morality and self-righteousness? I'm capable of dealing with this on my own, have been for quite some time now."

His cruel remarks did not affect her; no words remained to chase her away.

John damned her for holding fast to the macabre sanctuary, for gawking at him. He'd make a fool of himself soon; invading visions of Pierre assaulted him with such clarity he could feel the boy's hand in his, the brush of his pursed lips on his cheek—a swift, piercing embrace.

"Dear God," he groaned, "I loved him. Why did you take him away? *Why?*"

He drove a trembling hand through his matted locks and swallowed hard, as ineffectual at dislodging the lump in his throat as he was at barricading his grief. The tears gathered, so he tilted his head back to catch them, but they spilled over, trickling into his hairline. He was losing the battle and, with a moan, the fortress caved in.

"Oh God, Colette!" he implored, his head still thrown back as if he could see through the stone ceiling to the heavens, as if she could hear him. "Why did you abandon me? *For what?* What did you gain—but misery and death? I loved you and I needed you, but you sent me away. Why didn't you turn your back on this evil place when I begged you to? You would still be alive—*our son* would *still be alive!* Why did you think this—*this* was for the best?"

"John, don't do this! Please, don't do this to yourself!"

Someone was beseeching him, tugging on his arm. Suddenly, that someone was in his arms, and he was clinging to her for dear life, unable to let go, certain he'd be submerged in a cauldron of fire if he let go. His world was crumbling; the lofty summit upon which he was perched was quaking precariously, and the jaws of madness waited hungrily below.

Charmaine returned his fierce embrace and caressed his broad back, her yearning to be held just as desperate. His head was buried between her shoulder and cheek, and she could feel his tears on her neck, the desolate phrases he uttered, incoherent at times, painfully clear at others.

"Colette . . . Hold me! Please, hold me!"

Her arms tightened around him, pulling him closer. Then she turned her face into his chest and wept bitterly. She didn't know for whom she cried: Pierre, the tender lad, Colette, the melancholy woman, or John, the brooding man, full of life, laughter, tears, hatred, and love. A man she had yet to understand. Her heart ached for them all. And she cried for herself, the immeasurable loss she was just now beginning to experience; would have to live with the rest of her days.

"I killed him! Dear God—I killed him!"

"No!" Charmaine countered, pulling away. "No, you mustn't blame yourself! It was an accident, a terrible accident."

"Accident? No, Charmaine, it wasn't an accident. Accidents happen when people have no control over a situation. When I learned of Pierre's conception, he became my responsibility. I should never have abandoned him, but I did. I set everything on course to this end. The sins of the father were laid upon the son. He's dead because of me."

"No, John," she disputed fervently. "You are wrong. God wouldn't hurt Pierre to punish you. He was a dear little boy, whom God loved as much as you did. As for your past transgressions, they are in the past. Pierre had nothing to do with them."

"He was at the center of them!"

His voice was heavy with guilt. What was she to say to a man who had taken his father's wife and witnessed that woman bear his child?

"I should never have come back," he bit out. "He would have been spared if I had never entered his life. I should have remained a distant brother, a name occasionally mentioned, a name without a face. But Colette insisted I come, and once I'd seen him—he was such a fine boy—I couldn't turn away, I just couldn't. I knew I was making it harder on myself—on him—but I thought if I gathered enough memories, I'd be able to make the final break. I never meant to hurt him."

He turned aimlessly to the pews again, slumped onto the bench, and buried his head in his hands.

"I know you didn't, John," Charmaine soothed, joining him there.

"I didn't deserve him," he ground out. "He was too fine a boy to have a father the likes of me."

"That's not true!"

"It *is* true! If I were any kind of a father, would I have left him alone?"

"John, you had no way of knowing Pierre would leave the room!"

"Didn't I? He was determined to go to his boat only the eve before! I knew he didn't want me to leave, knew he wanted to come with me. And what did I do? I refused him, and I hurt him. I broke his heart. I saw the pain on his face—saw him choke on his tears, and then, because I couldn't stand to see him cry, I turned my own misery on him and threatened to desert him without a final fare-well. God forgive me," he sobbed, "that was the gravest sin of all! Is it any wonder when he awoke he'd assumed I'd left and ran to the lake to follow me?"

"You didn't know. How could you know?"

"No, I didn't know, but I could have prevented it! I could have told him what he wanted to hear. I could have taken him with me. Or I could have stayed. But my father was right," he sneered. "I wasn't man enough to claim what was mine. I abandoned him—not once, but twice. All these years I've hated my father for the very same thing. What a hypocrite I am, and my, how he must be laughing!"

"He's not laughing, John," she averred. "I know he's not laughing."

"Oh God, Charmaine, I did love him," he cried. "I swear I did. The only reason I didn't take him from this god-forsaken place was because I didn't want to hurt him, or his sisters. How could I tear them apart? Let the girls believe I had chosen him over them? How could I even dream of taking him away from you? I knew eventually he'd despise me if I did. But I was growing too attached to stay any longer. That's why I thought it best to leave, before it became impossible to live the lie."

Charmaine dabbed at her own tears and put a hand on his shoulder. "John, it serves no purpose to torment yourself."

He was quiet for a time, head buried on his arms. "Why couldn't God have taken me instead? He could have prevented me from hurting anyone else."

"Don't say that, John!"

"But I have. First Colette—I loved her more than I'll ever love anyone. She was never really mine, and still I took her, and I hurt her . . ."

"John, please—you're turning in circles. The past cannot be changed, but you have your entire future to look to."

"Future?" he snorted dismally. "My future will always be shadowed by the sins of the past."

"Those sins were pardoned long ago," she replied with fierce determination. "They no longer exist. If you continue to dwell on them, they will destroy you. It is far better to remember your love for Pierre and pray for him." She cleared her throat. "Pray he has joined his mother in heaven."

"Heaven," he murmured, comforted by her forgiving heart. "If only I could believe such a realm exists, that they share it. Perhaps I could find some peace then."

"It does exist, John," she promised, "and I know they are there, together, praying for you."

He was quiet again, as if weighing her sincere words. "Sweet Charmaine," he whispered, "I know you grieve, too. I shouldn't have burdened you with this, forced you to become my confessor. You should be appalled, and yet, you are compassionate. You haven't condemned me. Why?"

"Because I know you loved Pierre. I do not think you are wicked."

"Then what?"

"Lonely."

"Aye," he nodded, "lonely and alone."

"Again, you are wrong," she argued softly. "You have your sisters. You have Rose and George, even Paul. And you have me. If you ever need a friend, I will always be here for you."

"Aren't you afraid I might tarnish that friendship?"

She chuckled plaintively. "If you didn't succeed in tarnishing it in the beginning, then it certainly won't happen now."

Her response brought a doleful smile to his face, but it swiftly took wing.

"If you'd prefer to be alone, I'll retire."

"No, stay with me," he said, taking her hand in his and clasping it lightly.

They remained that way for a long time, contemplating the consuming sorrow, drawing solace from the peaceful sanctuary and each other.

Charmaine sighed deeply. *The greater the wealth, the deeper the pain . . .* Sadly, her mother had been right. For all their fortune, the Duvoisin family had suffered greatly, would continue to suffer. Marie's presence was strong now, and Charmaine took succor from the aura of commiserate love.

When they eventually left the chapel, they found Fatima waiting for them outside the doors, dabbing at her eyes with her apron. She coaxed them to the kitchen, though they ate little of the soup she set before them.

Charmaine faltered first, bowing her head as she succumbed to weariness. Visions of a dimpled-faced Pierre besieged her. She closed her eyes, and they grew stronger, distorted by her exhaustion. "Dear God," she whispered.

"Charmaine," John called, his hand tightening over hers.

Her head came up at the sound of his voice.

"Come, we must get you to bed."

She felt his arms enfold her, leading her through the dining room to the staircase. She was at the top step without remembering how she got there, and suddenly, she was facing that room again—her room, John's room—knowing what lay inside. Her mind snapped into focus.

The chamber door opened, and Father Benito stepped out. He assessed them, his dark eyes condemning John. "I've blessed the body," he said curtly. Charmaine was certain he wanted to say more, but he turned away.

"I'd like to look at him one last time," John whispered once the priest had left them. "Then I will take you to a guest chamber. Will you come with me?"

She nodded, allowing him to lead her into the chamber that had been their prison for so many days. Rose was still there, preparing the small body for burial. She looked up from her labor, her worried eyes waxing thankful when John moved forward. Paul pushed away from the wall where he had been leaning, exhaling once he noted his brother's lucidity. George was there, too. He'd spent the past few days with the twins, and suddenly Charmaine fretted over them, wondering if they knew, and if not, how she would tell them.

John stepped up to the bed. Charmaine stayed close behind, fearful of leaving his side, knowing the last time she had allowed him to depart, the gravest disaster had befallen her.

He looked down at Pierre for untold minutes. The boy was no longer drenched in perspiration, his face no longer twisted in pain.

The desperate struggle had ceased, the battle relinquished, and now a desolate solitude settled upon the room. Pierre was at peace. John studied him still. Had he come to grips with his death? In that moment, it became Charmaine's sincerest prayer.

Then he was speaking, not to his son, or to those gathered in the stark room, nor to God, but to Colette. "I entrust him to you, my love. Take him and keep him safe until the day when we are all together."

The supplication sent shivers down Charmaine's spine. A stillness greater than death came to life in the room, and she was infused with the power of its resurrection. Her eyes swept across the chamber, yet no one seemed affected by the tangible presence vibrating through every fiber of her being. Just as quickly as it coursed through her veins, the invader retreated, draining her of every sensation save the thud of her hammering heart. When she looked down at Pierre, a smile kissed his lips, one that had not been present before. Colette had claimed her son.

Chapter 8

Thursday, October 12, 1837
Midnight

*P*AUL raked his hand through his tousled hair, breathed deeply, and entered his father's chambers. The man was as he had left him hours ago, despondent and disheveled. He hadn't moved from the chair near the French doors. He wore the same clothes as the day of the accident, his eyes were red and distant, and three days' growth of beard marked his drawn face. His visage mirrored John's.

Paul walked over to him, and slowly, his gaze lifted. "He's gone," Paul rasped, swallowing hard against the blistering pain in his throat.

Frederic's head bobbed forward.

Realizing his sire was crying, Paul turned to leave.

"And John?" came the deep voice, cracking.

"He's managing."

Again Paul attempted to leave. After the last three days, he couldn't take on the burden of his father's agony as well. But this time, a piece of paper lying on the floor halted his step. He picked it up, his eyes skimming over the document as he returned it to the desk. He found two replicas there. "What is this?" he asked incredulously.

His father looked up, then averted his face. "My legacy to John—too little too late."

"You were signing custody of the girls and Pierre over to him?"

"It doesn't matter now, does it?" Frederic whispered.

"But Yvette and Jeannette as well as Pierre?"

"John asked me for custody of all three children on Saturday. But because I refused to take a good look at myself, I denied him again. By the time I thought better of it, it was too late."

Frederic breathed deeply, his face masked in sorrow. "My grandson is dead because of me. Colette, forgive me . . . he's dead because of me."

Moonlight spilled into the chamber, cascading across the carpet, illuminating the foot of the bed and the man who could not sleep. In a daze of fragmented slumber, John contemplated the room, his wretched life, the dust motes suspended on moonbeams above him, moving neither this way nor that, silently mocking him.

This time he had floated with the tide. The outcome was worse than when he attempted to twist circumstance in his favor. Stupid fool! When would he learn his actions always led to disaster? Never! He had continued to challenge God, his father. And because of that, Pierre was dead, Pierre and . . .

The night air blew into the room carrying with it the scent of lily. She had come, a presence as alive as the past. It was not the first time she had haunted him in the hours before dawn, so he knew he was dreaming.

Colette . . . on the threshold of his chamber, her limitless charms unbridled for the hour's love, her flaxen hair unbound, suspended on the buffeting breeze, her eyes, pools of blue, her full lips slightly parted, inviting his impassioned kiss. The moonlight silhouetted her naked body beneath a sheer gown of cerulean silk.

With a groan, he closed his eyes. Undaunted, she floated to the bed as if certain he could not resist. "John," she whispered, "my dearest John."

Never before had she spoken, and thunderstruck, he jumped to his feet. With hand outstretched, he tentatively touched her arm, expecting the apparition to evaporate. It did not, and he was over come by rage, his fingers closing over her shoulders and digging into her flesh. "Leave me alone! You've tormented me enough!"

She placed her cheek against his chest and encircled his waist with her arms. "Don't send me away," she implored. "Not yet."

"Send *you* away? It's you who've abandoned *me* time and again!" He shook her until her head jerked back and tears spilled from her eyes. Still, he persisted. "Go away! You're dead, goddamn it, you're dead!"

"Not while you suffer. I longed for you to come back to Charmantes, John, but not for this. You know what you have to do, what I've begged you to do."

Death . . . So simple a solution.

John pulled her to him, and his lips snuffed out her petition. He lifted her into his arms and laid her on the bed, tearing away the transparent veil. He pressed himself upon her, making love to her more fiercely than ever before, entwining her dark hair through his fingers, kissing the hollow of her neck, that delectable spot he'd tasted only once before. Her soft panting and timid endearments heightened his desire. She was so unlike the woman he remembered, and he reveled in this unfamiliar innocence, her virginal touch.

The clean redolence of morning dew invaded his senses, an airy breeze liberated of the heavy essence of lily. His mouth traced her jaw, coming to rest on her parted lips. Her inexperience reignited his ardor, and he took her again, his breathing ragged when finally he lifted his head to behold her.

"Charmaine . . ." he whispered hoarsely in confusion. Her arms were slipping from him, and though his embrace tightened, she melted into the bedclothes, and he awoke.

"Damn!" He sat up and buried his throbbing head in his hands, his eyes burning like white-hot coals. "Damn," John murmured again. Of whom had he been dreaming—Colette or Charmaine?

Paul loitered indecisively in the empty hallway. More than once, his fist lifted to the guest chamber door before dropping again to his side. Ten steps forward and another ten back. *She is likely asleep. I shouldn't disturb her. Yet, perhaps she isn't. Perhaps she needs a shoulder to cry on.*

He wanted to be there for her, had wanted to comfort her and hold her last night. But Rose had detained him.

Now, hours later, with the body prepared, he remembered Charmaine, how she had returned to Pierre's deathbed, dry-eyed and standing stalwart beside his brother. Her pretense at inner strength was as heart wrenching as her initial bout of hysteria. He knew her fortitude was a drama enacted for John's benefit. She'd been there for John, enabling him to return to the death chamber and behold his son's corpse. But who had been there for her? With new resolve, Paul quietly stepped into the room.

Agatha sat before the looking glass and studied her reflection. For all her years, she was still quite fair. She smiled prettily at her flawless ivory neck framed by the stark black collar of her unadorned gown. A touch too drab, she decided. She flipped open the jewelry case and selected one of the few pieces that remained. She'd been using Elizabeth and Colette's jewels to pay the blackmailer, occasionally dipping into her monthly allowance, but never touching the estate she'd inherited from her deceased husband. What a sage decision, that! Her crafty eyes narrowed. She'd have to accept the loss of some of her hard-earned wealth. It was an investment, and today that investment would pay off. *All of this will soon be behind you, my dear.* She pinned a diamond-encrusted brooch to her widow's weeds, and patted back the wisps of hair at her temples. Peering into the mirror again, she subdued her enthusiasm and twisted her face into a mask of remorse. Satisfied, she stepped gracefully into her next, most promising, role.

Charmaine stirred, rolling from her cramped side onto her stiff back. It hurt to breathe deeply, a pain that comes from crying for too long, and she had a throbbing headache. Still, she smiled as she awoke. She'd been dreaming! Thank God it had only been a terrible nightmare.

She stared at the white ceiling, then turned her head. *This is not my room.* She shifted uneasily and clutched the coverlet. Not a dream. *Dear God—not a dream!* She closed her eyes to the searing pain, but they flew open, taking in the man slumped in the armchair across the room. *Paul.*

She turned her face aside and whimpered into her pillow. Horrific, indelible images assaulted her: the death room, Pierre, the chapel, John—each one impossible to suppress. And yet, to get through this day, she must.

Slowly, she mastered her anguish and forced herself to sit up, then stand. She crossed the short distance to the sleeping man. Kneeling beside the chair, she laid a gentle hand on his brow, furrowed in exhausted slumber, and chased the lines away, placing that one stray lock back into place. He did not stir, his breathing even and deep. She studied his handsome face in the first rays of dawn, so youthful in sleep, dark lashes fanning his cheeks. Her hand dropped to his arm and patted it once. "Thank you," she whispered, heartened by his protective presence. Then she withdrew to dress.

"Did you hear me?"

"Yes, Agatha, I heard," Frederic grumbled from the French doors, gracing his wife with a slight turn of the head, his grim profile silhouetted in the early light of dawn. He'd just finished bathing, making himself presentable for the agonizing day ahead, and already his wife was pestering him. "Charmantes is lacking in social graces," he reiterated as if by rote, "and I should consider sending the girls to a female academy in London."

His thoughts were far away, his senses reeling from lack of sleep. *I must visit my daughters first. This time they won't suffer alone . . .*

". . . and you, my dearest, will rest easier knowing they are in safe hands."

"Agatha, please, I don't want to discuss this—"

"I know," she interrupted compassionately. "You are troubled by more pressing concerns. But this will be the last time John hurts you."

Frederic faced her with a scowl. "What are you talking about?"

"John is unfit to be called your son," she pronounced rigidly. "Surely you can see that now."

"I see no such thing," he countered, his voice deadly.

"Then you are blind!" she rejoined, steeling herself to meet his ire. "The boy was placed in his care, and John abandoned him for that beast of his. He knew the child was desperate, but did he care? No. In fact, he reveled in Pierre's heartache."

Frederic stood stunned at his wife's incredible assertion. "Are you mad, woman? John loved the boy—is grieving this terrible tragedy."

"A tragedy that could have been averted. Perhaps John didn't foresee Pierre reaching the lake, but you can be sure he hung his hat on the hopes the child would wake up, become hysterical, and throw this family into turmoil again. He's deviously exploited all three of your children, Pierre in particular."

"That's preposterous. I'm to blame for what happened, no one else."

"Really?" she asked wryly. "Then you've been duped, duped into believing everything is your fault. Granted, you may have been roused to anger, Frederic, but that does not make you culpable—naïve, perhaps, but not culpable. I, on the other hand, have sat back and watched, and what I've witnessed over the years has been difficult to stomach. The first night you joined us for dinner is a perfect example. John spoiled our meal that evening. He was hostile from the start, cleverly bringing his mother into the conversation, ridiculing your love for her, ridiculing me." She paused momentarily in disgust. "How dare he behave like that in front of family and servants?"

"He has every right to hate me," Frederic replied sadly.

"No, he does not," Agatha refuted. "You've been far too clement with him. How long will you allow your love for Elizabeth to be the reason for excusing him? She's been dead for thirty years, and she doesn't live on—not in her son!"

His eyes turned black, but she was not shaken. "You yourself admitted he was not a reflection of Elizabeth. What is left then—the seed of a brigand?"

"My seed," came the deadly response, "*mine*. Anything he is comes directly from me. I am his father."

"But—"

"Don't," he snarled contemptuously, "don't resort to your ugly premise concerning John's paternity. I ceased to believe it long ago. He is *my* flesh and blood."

"That is impossible!"

"I thought so once, but not anymore."

"But you cannot be certain!" she objected vehemently.

"I am certain. One has only to look at him to know he is mine. You said I was blind. Well, in fact, I was, and it has cost me dearly. I believed your brother when he delivered John, worrying over his small size, determined to convince me John was born a month early. I believed him when he blamed the babe for his mother's death. And, God forgive me, I believed him when he calculated the date of conception and—even though he knew Elizabeth and I had been lovers before her abduction—concluded he was no son of mine, rather the spawn of some heinous crime against her. But I believe him no more, Agatha. I'm through listening to this nonsense."

"But, Frederic," she implored, "Robert would never deceive you. You do him a great injustice."

"There is only one person in this house who has suffered an injustice, and that is my son. For the first ten years of his life, I scorned him. By the time I realized what I was doing, it was too late. I know that now, know it will always be too late for John and me. I wasn't fit to be called a father, and he has every reason to hate me. But I won't ever do anything to hurt him again."

"But you'll allow *him* to hurt *you*," she bit out, marshaling her rage in order to make the most of this opportunity. "Is that how Colette conceived his child? You were so determined not to hurt him you overlooked the most reprehensible of behaviors—the seduction of your wife! What's next?"

Frederic's eyes turned blacker. "How do you know that?" he growled.

Agatha grimaced in disgust. "Then Robert *was* right."

"Robert—always Robert!"

"What else would he think? Yes, he told me all about the twins' birth, how Colette cried out for John during their delivery. Tell me, are they his, too?"

"No, Agatha," he ground out, "they are mine."

"Then how can you be certain of Pierre?"

"Let us just say, I'm certain." He smiled bleakly at her. "So you see, John wasn't exploiting anybody. He loved Pierre and only wanted to be a father to him."

"I'll never believe that. He puts on an admirable performance, but the truth is he despises you and you'll *never* gain his love. He's determined to destroy this family."

"And how is he going to do that?"

"By alienating you from your other children," she declared.

"You've allowed him to feast on his jealousy—jealousy over his own siblings, jealousy over Colette. He won't be satisfied until you're in the grave. Just look at the way he treats Paul! He envies the bond you share. And now that Paul has the other island, his envy has soared. But has he ever tried to be the son Paul is? *Never!*" she exclaimed with an emphatic slash of her hand. "He has, however, fostered discord and acrimony whenever possible. You want to believe he came back here to be a father to Pierre. But I say he came back only to make you suffer. Why can't you see this? You're too good, Frederic! He's had two months to ingratiate himself back into the twins' lives—Pierre's life. And for the whole of those two months he's been able to endure your presence in the house. Then, quite suddenly, he can't tolerate you anymore? How gullible can you be?

"He plotted the events that have branded you the villain, starting with his little excursion to Dulcie's. Why, in heaven's name, would he take the children *there*? I'll tell you why, he set Yvette up. He set *you* up! And you took the bait! All he needed was the remark you made in the foyer that night to hang his head and flee. My, what an actor he is! And it all worked out just as he planned. By the next day, everyone was pining over his banishment from Charmantes, believing his tyrannical father had made his life so miserable, so unbearable, he was forced to desert his sisters, forced to desert his own son! I can just imagine what he said to them: 'I wish I could stay, but I'm no longer welcome here. Father hates me. No, you can't come with me, Pierre. He won't let you.'

"But you *were* willing to relinquish the boy, weren't you? That was the reason for our visit to Espoir, wasn't it? You gave John five days—five days to claim Pierre as his son. There was a ship available. If he wanted to be a father to the boy, why didn't he just take him? Answer me that! And don't tell me it was because he couldn't bring himself to break Pierre's little heart. He certainly didn't have trouble breaking it four nights ago at the dinner table, did he?"

She shook her head in revulsion when Frederic didn't answer.

"Pierre might have been too young to understand what was happening, but John saw to it your daughters understood only too well. It's sad they've been manipulated into blaming you. What did you say months ago? You were tired of being viewed as the sinister patriarch? Well, my dear husband, you'd better grow accustomed to it. You'll end up being blamed for Pierre's death, too. And why not? You've welcomed everything else John has dished out." She feigned a vile taste in her mouth. "Not me, I've had enough of it! You think I hate him? Well, I do. I hate him for all the misery he's put you through. But that's fine; he despises me as well. Why? Because I see him for what he is.

"Believe what you will, Frederic. Believe he's your son. But the next time he stabs you in the back, don't get angry with me. Just remember Colette and how he wormed his way into her bed. He will stop at nothing, *nothing* I tell you. Continue to protect him if you must, coddle him, use his inheritance to keep him close, but don't lament when he succeeds in destroying your family. You'll be left with naught. And John? He will have it all—that smug smile painted across his face, your fortune—everything. Just remember, Frederic, I warned you."

Frederic cleared his throat, attempting to dislodge the lump that had tightened there, and faced the French windows once again. "Send Miss Ryan in to see me when she awakens," he said as Agatha turned to leave.

He knew she was astonished, intrigued. Maybe he could do something right today, something that would please everyone in his family, even his wife. First he'd find out if the young governess would consider visiting Richmond with his daughters.

Agatha leaned against the door and breathed a sigh of relief. It hadn't gone quite the way she had planned, but a window of opportunity definitely remained open. Her husband wanted to speak to the governess. Yes, opportunity knocked.

Think, don't rush into this! Think!

She crossed the narrow corridor and entered her own apartments. It was still early and she had plenty of time, time to plot and plan. *And while I work out all the details, Frederic will be dwelling on what I said.*

She smiled wickedly. Though Frederic longed to make peace with his estranged son, the bad blood remained, and if John provoked him, Frederic's volatile temper would rule.

Robert's suspicions had turned out to be true: Colette was a tramp. Agatha's delight increased. She had attempted to verify her brother's hunch the morning John arrived home, surreptitiously slipping into her nephew's room, snooping through his desk drawers, and locating the letter everyone had been whispering about. Unfortunately, the meddlesome governess had charged into the room, forcing her out onto the balcony, a narrow escape. When she returned to the bedchamber a few days later, the letter was gone. Nevertheless, she had pieced the story together over the weeks that followed. Today, everything made sense, all her speculation confirmed.

Yes, John had good reason to loathe Frederic. She would stir that cauldron of hostility until it boiled over into the final showdown. *Oh yes, dear nephew, this morning, I will provide the rope and you will hang yourself!* Moments ago, she'd set the stage. Now, she had to arrange the players. She would even help them with their lines. Then, she'd sit back and enjoy the theatrical.

Frederic slumped into his chair. *Oh God, Elizabeth, what have I done?*

The years fell away and she was trembling before him, fearful he'd send her packing. That had been his intent. He'd spent days convincing himself England was the proper place for her. But here she stood, offering herself to him as long as he'd let her stay. His pitiful assumption that she was too young for him was laid to waste that night. She gave him everything, even her heart, asking nothing in return, save the safety of his arms and a home on Charmantes.

Even the next day, she remained innocent to how she had affected him, her eyes welling with tears when he insisted she forget the sensual experience they had shared. He should have been grateful she believed the worst, that she meant nothing to him. After all, he was taking her back to her family. He had other plans that did not include her, a promise to keep.

But fate intervened. His infatuation only intensified during their crossing, and instead of avoiding her, he found himself seeking her out. By the time they reached Britain, she held his heart in the palm of her hands. He loved her.

Had he known what awaited them in Europe, he would have turned back to Charmantes, coveting their sanctuary there. But hiding from Elizabeth's family was not a solution. Beyond that, he wanted to wed her and needed a priest. And so, they forged ahead for the sake of respectability. But before the final banns were posted, their future was irrevocably tainted.

In late January, she was abducted and savagely raped by a band of highwaymen. For the better part of a week, he had nearly gone insane combing the countryside, ultimately praying when there was nothing else to do, thanking the very angels when, by the mercy of God, she was miraculously returned to him. Her fate at the hands of the ruffians did not matter to him, as long as she was alive.

For weeks she was despondent, and the wedding postponed, but he refused to leave her side. Slowly, he coaxed her recovery. It was then her disapproving parents had a change of heart. If Frederic married their daughter and whisked her away, the shame of her abduction would be forgotten. So, they wed in late March and returned to Charmantes, putting aside thoughts of her brutal violation.

In early April, Elizabeth announced the wondrous news. She was with child. Frederic should have been elated, but the worry in her eyes confirmed his fears: the child might not be his. Thus, an innocent babe was on his way into the world, a world that would not receive him well.

Just after midnight on September 29, 1808, eight months after her abduction, John was born. His parents had been married for all of six months, and yet, he was, according to the mores of society, their legitimate son.

The delivery had been long and hard, the bleeding effusive, and though the infant was small, his position had been breech, stealing his mother's life-blood. Frederic cried into her dampened bedclothes, felt her feeble hand caress his tousled hair, heard her rasp some final endearment with a plea he name their son after her deceased brother, John. Then she departed him forever, leaving him desolate in the wake of so miraculous an event as the birth of a son.

He turned his blind rage on Robert, blaming him for Elizabeth's death. The man quaked in fear, but Rose interceded, stepping between them, the newborn in her arms, petitioning Robert to assess the baby's health. In a matter of minutes, Robert was clicking his tongue and muttering, "Certainly not a full nine months in the womb. To think they killed her in the end."

"Who? Who killed her?"

"The brigands. I'm sorry, Frederic, he's far too small to be yours . . ."

More than a week passed before Frederic even looked at the baby, quickly turning away in disgust. *If you were not half Elizabeth, I'd cast you to the dogs and be damned.* Revolted by his insane hatred, yet unable to shake it off, he held fast to his disdain and spurned John.

Paul's presence only made matters worse. Frederic knew he was this baby's father. In fact, he often thought of *Paul* as Elizabeth's son, cherishing the fond memory of her mothering him in those weeks before her death. Here was a happy child, who grew into a genial lad. John, on the other hand, was an obstinate fellow, who took pleasure in vexing everyone. True, there had been moments when Frederic felt a certain closeness to him, an ember of contrition, but bitter memories always intruded, snuffing out the fragile flame. If not for John, Elizabeth would still be alive.

The years fell in upon themselves, and suddenly, John was a young man. "He's such a handsome boy," Frederic's eldest sister, Eleanor, had admired. She resided in the States, but, on one rare occasion, had ventured home. "The picture of you at that age, Frederic . . . the very picture . . ."

Yes, he had been blind, but the damage had already been done: John bitterly resented him.

Joseph faced John and prayed Yvette's remarks concerning her elder brother were true: "It's just a charade to make everyone tremble. He's really a coward. He told me so."

Charade or no, the man was giving one fine performance, for John scowled down at him, seemingly oblivious of the water he had drawn for his bath.

"That will be all, Joseph," he muttered as he settled into the brimming tub. "Oh and Joseph, Miss Ryan is sleeping in the guest chamber next door. She shouldn't be disturbed until she rings for someone."

"But she's already up and about, sir."

John turned a bleary eye upon the lad. "Yes, I suppose she would be."

"Sir?" Joseph queried.

"Nothing, it was nothing."

"Sir?" the lad began, courageous in the face of John's debilitated state. "I just wanted to say I'm sorry about your younger brother, sir. I know—"

John closed his eyes.

"—you loved him, sir. We all knew that. And, well, I just wanted to tell you how sorry we are about what happened."

John could not answer. He wondered how he would survive the day's condolences, the unbidden reminders that would trespass upon his guarded heart and prey on his vulnerability.

"Joseph?" he rasped as the boy reached the door.

"Yes, sir?"

"Thank you."

"Yes, sir," the boy nodded. He exited the somber room, allowing John to take up soap and brush and scrub his body clean.

"That's right, Jeannette, cry," came the soothing voice, "cry until you can't cry anymore, and then, you'll feel better."

"I'll never, *never* feel better," the child sputtered.

"You don't think so now," Charmaine comforted, "but you will. Someday, when you remember Pierre, it will be of the happy times we spent together . . ."

John leaned his forehead against the closed door and shut his eyes to the piercing pain. He should go in, attempt to console the girls as Charmaine was doing, but he couldn't. He had neither the strength, nor the desire to embrace his sisters' loss. His own was too great, too fresh.

"But why did he die?" Jeannette sobbed.

"God was probably punishing him for pretending to be ill on Sunday."

"Yvette!" Charmaine remonstrated sharply. "You know that's not true!"

The girl burst into tears. There was a moment's pause, and then Charmaine's voice again, her words indiscernible, though John strained to hear them.

"Why did God do this to us?" Jeannette implored. "Wasn't Mama enough?"

"Oh, Jeannette, I don't have those answers. But you still have each other, and you have me. You know I love you very much, don't you?"

"Yes," came the two trembling voices.

"And you have John. He needs your love more than ever."

"Why?"

"Because he loved Pierre, and he is sad, too. If we comfort each other, one day the wound will heal and this terrible time will fade. Then you'll smile when you think of Pierre, and you'll laugh when you say: 'Remember when we went picnicking at the beach and Pierre dumped sand on Johnny's head?' or . . ." Charmaine's voice broke off.

"It's all right, Mademoiselle," John heard Jeannette say. "You loved Pierre as much as we did, so you don't have to be strong for us."

"She's right," Yvette added, "you should cry, too."

"No, Yvette, I've cried too much already."

With head bowed, John walked away.

"You are dismissed, Miss Ryan. Your services are no longer required."

Jaw slackened, speech stymied, Charmaine stared aghast at Agatha Duvoisin.

"My dear," the mistress reprimanded with head canted, "don't look so surprised. And please, close your mouth. It is quite unbecoming."

"But—why?"

"Surely you're not serious. The reason is quite obvious. Pierre is dead."

Charmaine flinched. It was one thing to speak of the boy's accident herself, quite another to hear his death uttered heartlessly. "And I'm just to leave?"

"You have until week's end."

"But that's—"

"Tomorrow," Agatha supplied, her lips curled in a ruthless smile.

"And if I refuse to go?" Charmaine demanded, no longer impeded by confusion and pain, but quite fired up by the mistress's edict.

"Refuse? My dear, you have no say in the matter."

"And who does have a say, Mrs. Duvoisin? You? Does anyone else know of this decision? Your husband? Paul? Should I take this matter up with them?"

"Miss Ryan, do you really think Paul would question his father's authority for a little trollop who has caught his fancy? Surely he's tired of you by now."

"You are a vile woman!" Charmaine accused.

"And you are an impudent little fool," Agatha hissed. "But this shall be the last time you address me in such a manner! You are responsible for the death of an innocent three-year-old. My husband, blind to your neglect up until now, has finally seen the light. The twins are to be sent to a boarding school, a fine English academy, and a governess is no longer required."

"You cannot be serious!" Charmaine objected.

"Oh, but I am, Miss Ryan. The past three days have forced my husband to take stock of his posterity. He's contemplated all his options concerning the welfare of his remaining offspring, and when I spoke with him earlier this morning, he asked to see you."

Charmaine's eyes widened.

"Yes, Miss Ryan," she acknowledged, eyebrow arched, "this is his decision, not mine, and I warn you now, he is not happy with you, not happy at all!"

Charmaine paled, fear clashing with her anger.

The chamber door slammed shut, and Agatha was once again alone. She smiled in self-satisfaction. She'd played it just right, had struck the most promising chords, and now, Charmaine Ryan, incensed by the injustice of it all, would stand before Frederic, her temper ablaze. With any luck, she'd overstep her bounds and seal her own fate. More important, she'd initiate the final confrontation between father and son.

Agatha hesitated as a wave of apprehension swept over her. *What if Frederic suffers another seizure? Worse still—what if this battle proves fatal?* She brushed aside such a possibility. It was a risk she was forced to take.

Her eyes hardened. She mustn't waste time. The governess's audience with her husband would be brief; therefore, every second counted. It was time to speak to the twins, Yvette in particular. She'd be quite upset to learn her father had summoned her precious "Mademoiselle" to his apartments and was, at this moment, dismissing her. She'd run to John, inform and infuriate him, spur him into mindless action. Agatha had made certain he was in the house before setting her stratagem in motion. When John stormed into Frederic's chambers, there would be no rational truth seeking, only that vicious hatred they doggedly shared. And her husband would, for all his righteous resolve, deliver the final blow.

Charmaine's palms were sweating, and her stomach churned violently. Where was her valor now? Even her zealous rage had simmered down. As she stepped into the master's quarters it evaporated completely, like a drop of dew before the gates of hell. Damn her impulsive temper! Agatha had baited her.

The man she faced was no demon; he sported no fangs, sprouted no horns. His staff was a crutch that supported his crooked frame, a body that appeared to have further withered. This could not be the man who had bred contempt in his own home, abandoned one son and embraced another. Reason insisted both sides were guilty, that John had wronged as well. But John had also loved. Where was Frederic's love?

Instantly, Charmaine repented her rush to judgment. Frederic *had* loved Pierre! She had only to look at him to know that. He couldn't run and play with the boy, but he had loved him and had feared John might whisk him away. Suddenly, it all made sense. Frederic hadn't flaunted that love to enrage his estranged son; he was merely gathering his own memories. Charmaine wondered if John could ever understand this. Sadly, Frederic seemed prone to injuring those who should have been closest to him. But she realized now, the older man had been backed into a corner with no escape.

Frederic assessed her much as she did him, his eyes sweeping upward, searching her face and measuring her pain. It was a moment before Charmaine realized he had addressed her. "How are you faring?"

The concerned query took her by surprise. He blamed himself; it was etched across his face.

"As well as can be expected, sir," she murmured, fighting back tears, grateful he didn't know she had been privy to the truth about Pierre's conception and birth. "I'm sorry about Pierre."

"Charmaine, you don't have to apologize to me. It was an ugly accident and no one, least of all you, is to blame. But I do accept your condolences."

She nodded, cleared her throat, and changed the subject. "Is there a reason you wanted to see me this morning, sir?"

"Yes, but let us sit down." He motioned to a chair opposite his desk, and as he moved behind the secretary, she cautiously crossed the room.

Fatima told George she had sent breakfast into the study for John. George found him there, gathering up the papers on the desk. George didn't say anything, but put a comforting hand to his friend's shoulder, then poured him a cup of tea from the untouched tray.

"I haven't seen Paul this morning," John said. "Has he left?"

"He's upstairs."

"I've lost track of the days, George—don't even know when the next ship is due in port."

"Why?"

"I'm going back to Richmond, after the funeral."

George bowed his head to his tightening chest and stinging eyes. The study fell silent, but for the rustling of papers John mindlessly shoved into a valise.

The door burst open, and Yvette charged in, followed closely by a sobbing Jeannette and a concerned Paul.

"Johnny," she blurted out, "Father is sending us to a boarding school, and he's called Mademoiselle Charmaine to his chambers. He's going to dismiss her!"

"*What?*" John's face twisted in feral disgust. He abandoned the papers and headed toward the door.

"John!" Paul called after him, but George grabbed Paul's arm. "Let him go."

"But they'll kill each other—"

"Leave them be," George advised sharply, holding fast Paul's arm. "They need to have it out, once and for all. You can't keep protecting them from each other. You'll only end up being blamed for interfering."

Frederic waited for Charmaine to be seated. "How are my daughters?" he asked. "I assume they know about Pierre?"

"Yes, sir, they know." She looked down at her hands, reliving the girls' grief, witnessing the horrific disbelief that contorted their faces when they learned their younger brother would no longer be a part of their lives. "They were asleep last night," she whispered hoarsely, "but I was there when they awoke. They're extremely upset and have been in tears all morning. I should be getting back to them soon."

Frederic nodded. Charmaine Ryan was the only ray of hope on this dismal day. God had sent his family a blessing when she had come to live in his house. "They are not going to face their loss alone," he vowed. "This time I will console them. I want you to know that."

Charmaine silently thanked God. "They would welcome seeing you, sir."

"Would you like to bring them here or would you prefer I visit the nursery?"

Charmaine relaxed with the query, choosing to answer it with one of her own. "Sir, you're not going to dismiss me, are you?"

His brow lifted. "Why would you ask that?"

"Mrs. Duvoisin said you were sending the girls to a school in Europe."

Frederic mastered his instant ire. "Her idea, not mine," he ground out. "That's the last place my daughters need to be right now. They need their family, and you, Charmaine. They've suffered two terrible tragedies this year. I want to see them emerge from the second as successfully as they did from the first. I want to see them whole and happy again."

"So do I, sir."

"That brings me back to the reason I wanted to speak to you this morning. John came to my quarters on Saturday morning and asked if—"

The unfinished statement hung in the air. Charmaine grimaced, and Frederic read the torment in her eyes. "What is it, Miss Ryan?"

"Nothing, sir," she lied, suppressing another urge to weep, the sudden chill that left her trembling.

Her shallow denial left Frederic unconvinced. "Have you seen John this morning?" he asked, dreading some unfathomable answer.

"No, sir, not this morning."

Apprehension gripped her. She did not want to discuss John with his father.

"Last night?"

"Yes, sir." She was back in the chapel, back in John's arms, reliving his piercing pain, powerless to her tears.

Frederic was moved by her compassion. "Would you like to talk about it?"

"He blames himself!" she blurted out. "He lays all blame on himself."

Frederic's eyes grew turbulent, but before he could comfort her, there was a wild commotion from beyond. The outer door banged open, and John charged in, slamming the door shut behind him.

"You lousy bastard!" he shouted, taking in Charmaine's tear-stained face. "You've reduced her to tears already? How despicable can you be?"

Frederic's eyes narrowed. "What's going on, John?"

"You tell me, Father! Why don't you tell me?"

Charmaine jumped up. "John! Listen to me!"

Her petition fell on deaf ears. For all his apparent outrage, he wasn't seeing her at all. "You enjoy watching the women in this house cry, don't you?" he sneered, stepping deeper into the room. "It makes you feel powerful, doesn't it?"

Frederic shot to his feet, fists clenched, Agatha's allegations ringing in his ears. "I don't know what you think is happening here, John, but—"

"But what, Father? What don't I understand? I'll tell you what I don't understand—how you can rob your children of love and affection! Are you out to hurt the girls now, or just me? Maybe that's it: hurt Yvette and Jeannette, hurt John. After all, it worked with Pierre, didn't it? Didn't it, goddamn you?"

Frederic paled, the calumnious words a minor attack when set against the torment in his son's face. "John, I'm sorry about Pierre. I never—"

"Don't! Don't even say it, because I'll never believe it. Pierre was only a pawn in your cunning game of subterfuge and power."

"Please, John, you misunderstand," Charmaine interrupted, stepping directly between the two men.

He looked at her for the first time. "No, Charmaine, you're the one who doesn't understand. I told you once: my father is the master of manipulation. Pierre was a valuable piece in his scheme, valuable because he was my—"

"Watch what you say in front of the governess!" Frederic warned.

"Why, Father? Are you afraid she'll find out she works for a fiend?"

"John!" Charmaine gasped. "Please, don't—"

"She knows everything, anyway," John announced, ignoring her protests.

"So," his father snarled in derision, "you've shared your intimate relationships with the hired help?"

John chuckled ruefully. "When the 'hired help' offers more compassion than my own family—yes. Charmaine knows Colette had a husband and a lover. What she doesn't know is the lover should have been the husband!"

"That's enough! I want you to leave—now!"

"No," John growled with a fierce shake of the head, "I'm not going anywhere. I want to know why Charmaine is being dismissed? Why, damn it?"

"But, John, I'm not!" Charmaine countered in surprise.

He wasn't listening. "You wouldn't give the girls to me when I asked for them, but a boarding school will suit them just fine! Is that how you shower them with love and affection? Or is this just another way to hurt Colette? Even though she's in the grave, you still want to hurt her! Damn you! Damn you to hell!"

"John, stop it! Please stop it!"

"No! I want some answers! You manacled Colette to you by withholding her daughters. You attempted to do the same to me. And now they're to be sent away? Cast aside? Why, because they're no longer of use to you?"

"John, I have no intention of sending them away. I was—"

"Liar! Always deceit and lies with you! God, how I loathe them! How I loathe you! How can you stand there and lie again and again to me—to Colette?"

"I don't know what you're talking about!"

"Don't you? She loved me! Me! We were to be married! But somehow you manipulated her into breaking the banns!"

Charmaine gasped.

"That's right, Charmaine, I knew Colette first, but my father convinced her I'd never amount to anything—that I didn't have a penny to my name, save what I would inherit from him one day. The great Frederic Duvoisin, on the other hand, could take care of her family here and now, rescue them from poverty. So, Colette sacrificed herself for her poor crippled brother. And what did it gain her but a miserable cripple of a husband instead?"

"It wasn't all about money, John," his father murmured dolefully.

"What then? Love? Don't tell me she loved you! She was so sad when I came back into her life she had forgotten how to smile. It didn't look like love to me!"

"What would you know of love?" Frederic lashed out.

"Nothing that came from you!" John fired back, a volley that met its mark. "You say you loved my mother, but I don't believe that, either. If you did, you would never have done what you did to me. But unlike you, I loved my son. And now he's dead—dead because of your hatred for me!"

Frederic inhaled, wounded. *Agatha is right: John loathes me, and that will never change.*

Still John persisted. "You've taken everything from me, haven't you? Anything—anyone I've ever loved, you've managed to wrench them away."

"John," his father attempted again, "I'm sorry."

"Don't! Don't you dare grovel with an apology now, for I will *never* forgive you! And I'm glad Colette came back to me, that she finally followed her heart. When she looked upon you, it was with pity—pathetic pity, nothing more. If only you had died first, that fair lady would now be *my* wife!"

Charmaine recoiled, the agony on Frederic's face piercing. "John!"

But Frederic was armed for his own battle. "That *lady*, as you call her, was far below such a title. You blame me for her death, but you don't even know how she died. She miscarried a child that was not mine. Yes, John," he sneered smugly, savoring the befuddled expression on his son's face, "she loved you so much she took another lover."

John laughed scathingly, the consternation gone. "Who fed you that shit?"

"Blackford—" Frederic faltered "—ask Blackford."

"No, I won't ask Blackford. He's a filthy liar who'd say anything to cover up his incompetence—if he told you that at all!"

The logic of John's assertion took hold, making it difficult to breathe.

When Frederic didn't respond, John continued, his words low and tight. "I loved her, Father. I loved her because I knew her, knew her to be decent and good. Maybe you can't comprehend that, and I pity you for it, but I loved her. And unlike you, I doubted her only once. So your newest lie falls upon deaf ears." He shook his head. "You always believed the worst about her, didn't you? Even when I first brought her here, you were disdainful of her. She could feel it, she fretted about it. But I told her not to worry, you'd come around. Little did I know. I suppose after she accepted your proposal, it confirmed your opinion of her—that she was out for the Duvoisin money. But she cared about her family—her brother—and that is why she married you. What a fool I was to desert her, not once, but twice, to honor her perverted sense of duty! I should have known you'd destroy her! I should have protected her from that."

"John, I never meant—"

"If only I could do it over again," John ranted on, "I would never be so stupid as to leave her here with you. I wouldn't care if you disowned me. I never gave a damn about your fortune. I'd forfeit every penny of it for just one more second of her time!"

Frederic bowed his head to remorse, the poignant sincerity of his son's declaration. He was swept back to those last two nights, holding Colette in his arms again, and tears sprang to his eyes. "I know you'll never believe this, John, but I, too, would forfeit it all."

"You're right, I don't believe you. It sounds good, but it's just another lie."

Suddenly, everything made sense to Frederic: that one deception, conceived nearly ten years ago, had led to this. "You've only been lied to once, John," he whispered. "I thought you knew the truth. These last few years, I thought Colette must have told you the truth."

"Told me what?" John prompted, confused.

Frederic glanced uncomfortably at Charmaine, then pressed on. "I was attracted to Colette when she first came to Charmantes." John snorted, but Frederic ignored him. "I mistook her coquetry for something else, and late one night, I seduced her."

"I don't believe it!" John railed, bombarded by a fleeting glimpse of Colette flirting with his father. The nocuous image sent his innards plummeting. "Seduced or raped?" he demanded venomously.

The chamber fell deadly silent, and in those mounting seconds when no denial came, John's face drained of color. The memory was gone, replaced by an uglier scenario: the painful truth. "You forced her! Goddamn you to hell, she was pure and innocent, and you forced her!"

He dove at his father, but Charmaine threw herself in his path, grappling for his arms. "No, John! Stop it! You're not going to change anything this way! Stop!"

The sanity of her petition penetrated, and John faltered. He glanced down at the hands that held him, took in Charmaine's desperate face. He looked back at his father, but Frederic had collapsed into his armchair, head bowed, by all outward signs a man condemned.

John stepped back, but when Charmaine's hands dropped away,

he clasped one of them, turned, and pulled her from the iniquitous room. Together they snaked through the crowd loitering in the corridor. There was Agatha, aquiver with anticipation, the worried twins, a concerned Paul, George, even the servants.

The next thing Charmaine knew, they were in her room. Pierre's body had been removed, the bed made, the furniture dusted, and the French doors thrown wide to catch the soft morning breezes. The tenebrous reminders of those four terrible days were gone. Everything was immaculate, mocking the turmoil that tainted their hearts.

John leaned heavily on the doorframe, head resting against a raised forearm, eyes staring down at the emerald lawns. When it seemed he'd never speak, Charmaine said, "Your father has no intention of sending the girls away. I wasn't called to his quarters to be dismissed."

He glanced over his shoulder. "You shouldn't have been exposed to that."

"I should have left," she concurred.

But he wasn't listening. "Rape," he muttered in revulsion. "But why? Did he hate me that much? Or is he really that evil? Never once, in all those years, did it occur to me that was the reason she deserted me. My God! I wronged her so many times in my mind, chastised her, and still she loved me. She knew I was consumed with jealousy, yet she never told me the truth. Why did she allow me to believe the worst—that she had chosen my father's fortune over me—that *she* was to blame?"

When the quiet room yielded no answers, he looked back at Charmaine.

"I had no idea you knew Colette first," she said. "Were you truly betrothed?"

He stared outdoors once again, transfixed. Charmaine held silent. When he spoke again, the story unfolded.

The year had been 1827 and George, Paul, and he were attending university in France. "We were hell-raisers then, at least I was," he said, with a sad chuckle, "spending less time at the books and more time carousing. The spring semester was half-spent before I first glimpsed the young lady whom Paul had been squiring from one Paris soirée to another. She was beautiful," he whispered reverently, "and the moment she wrinkled her fine aristocratic nose at me, I was determined to have her. Such an objective proved more difficult than I had initially imagined, and once I had lured her away from my brother, I found that, although she pretended at being a woman of the world, she was quite proper and innocent. But it was too late for me. I had fallen in love with her, and she, with me, or so I thought. Torture became my reward, and since I'd been unable to seduce her, I realized the only alternative was marriage. True, I was young, but if seventeen was not too young for a woman to marry, then nineteen was not unreasonable for a young man.

"Her mother objected fiercely. The woman did not fancy the likes of me for a son-in-law. But thanks to the gossip of a family friend, she was assured of my family's wealth and the inheritance that would eventually fall to me, and not Paul, as she had originally believed.

"That same friend suggested the wedding take place on Charmantes so Colette's mother could meet my father and ascertain my standing as heir to the family's holdings. I was reluctant to involve him, but Colette persuaded me to return home for the wedding. Her childhood friend would accompany us, along with Paul and George. It would be romantic, she reasoned, and although I didn't want to wait, I loved her and wanted to please her.

"So, we laughed over the workings of the adult mind and surmised Colette's mother hoped to snare my widower father. Her husband had lost most of his fortune to the revolution, and after his death, she had to rely on any device, including Colette, to see that she and her son, Pierre, were cared for.

"Such assumptions were close to the truth. As soon as we arrived on Charmantes, Adèle Delacroix set her sights on my father. He was not interested . . . not in Colette's mother, at least." John snorted in contempt as he contemplated his sire's true motives.

"Over the years that followed, I wondered if Adèle had taken my father's snub in stride, then manipulated Colette into his arms in her stead. Had she used her son's infirmity to convince Colette to forfeit me for the immediate security of his fortune? I had walked in on several conversations that supported that possibility. The woman was intuitive, alert to every word my father and I exchanged. It didn't take her long to size up our strained relationship. When we argued, it only served to heighten her anxiety. He didn't think I was prepared to step into marriage and work for a living, an assertion I was determined to prove wrong. I started by lending a hand in the fields . . ." John's words dropped off, and Charmaine watched him work through the details, his scowl darkening. "Suffice it to say, Adèle fretted over the inheritance that might be withdrawn if I didn't behave myself. If nothing else, she burdened Colette with talk of responsibility and family loyalty, exploiting Colette's love and concern for her younger brother.

"All I knew was, one day we were planning our wedding, and the next, Colette was breaking the banns. She wanted nothing more to do with me. At first, she was diplomatic, telling me she had grown fond of me, that she didn't want to hurt me, that the charade had gone on for too long. She had been out to catch a rich husband, and when Paul didn't fit the bill, she had turned to me. She had to think of her family, her crippled brother, in particular. His medical bills were mounting, and she had planned to send her mother home with an allowance to pay them. But when it became clear my father controlled the purse strings, she had turned her sights on him. I begged her not to sacrifice our love. I told her I would work harder; I could provide for all of them. She shook her head and told me it wasn't enough. She needed the money now. When I asked her how she could throw our love away, she broke down and cried. When I tried to embrace her, to reason with her, she turned away. She swore she'd never loved me. I became furious, though I knew her words were ludicrous. I threatened to tell my father she was a tramp—a sly, conniving whore. But she only laughed, saying, 'He knows what I am, and he doesn't care. He wants me anyway!'

"I ran from the house, and I didn't stop. I stumbled over my own two feet with that last vision of Colette, her eyes swollen from crying, swearing she didn't love me, had never loved me. I boarded the ship that was in port and awaited its departure. Even then, a part of me wanted to go back, to hold her and shake the lies from her, certain she wouldn't have cried if the lies were true! But another part of me was crushed, so I didn't go back, and I swore I'd never return to Charmantes. I'd forget her as easily as she could me.

"I went to Virginia and took to running my father's business there, determined to gain independence from the damned fortune that had always kept me under his thumb and had now ruined my life. But in the months I was there, I was consumed with anger and hatred. I hated her mother, even her brother. I hated my father for interfering, even though I concluded he'd married her to save me from the mistake he had maintained I was making—saddling myself with a money-grubbing wife. But mostly, I hated myself for still wanting her, loving her, my self-loathing paramount only to my hatred for her. I was not very different from my father at that time. Many nights, I raped her in my dreams, driven by one single desire: to inflict pain on those who had hurt me, pain upon Colette, and pain upon my father. So, I broke my vow and returned.

"He and Colette had been married less than a year, and she was heavy with child, close to delivering. She greeted me cordially, as if I were a long-lost brother, as if nothing had ever happened, as if we were one big, happy family—my father included. I wanted to vomit. But they dropped that charade once they realized I wasn't about to accept the cozy life they were now living. For a week, not one word passed between us, but my hatred continued to fester. Then, one night, I cornered her in the drawing room, and we had it out. I enjoyed making her cry, was even more satisfied when my father barged in. We would have come to blows, but Colette collapsed onto the sofa, and he ran to her. She was in labor.

"I left for Virginia right away, unaware she had delivered twins, and didn't go back for four years. When I did, it was obvious something had changed between them. My father's foul moods were worse, and Colette rarely smiled. At first I gloated over her sadness; she was getting what she deserved. I decided to spend time with the twins. They were sweet and innocent, and winning them over was easy. More important, here was an opportunity to be cruel to their mother. I'd ignore her completely, exclude her from excursions I planned with the girls, and when my father put a stop to that, I convinced Yvette and Jeannette their mother was responsible. Colette knew what I was doing, but she never turned them against me. It made me angrier. I wanted her to regret she had chosen my father's fortune. I invited women to the house and openly flirted with them. She disapproved, but never said a word. After a time, I grew disgusted with the game. Then, one morning—" he inhaled deeply, held the breath for a moment, released it "—I left. A little distance and time, and I'd get on with my life. I was wrong. When I got back to the States, I couldn't stop thinking about her. I realized she was more miserable than I was. I remembered our happy times in France, her radiant smile that could light up a room. My father had robbed her of that, and it wasn't fair. And so, I went back again.

"My father had begun developing Espoir. He was seldom on Charmantes that summer. The girls' enthusiasm threw us together, and it was easy to pretend he didn't exist. I fell in love again, this time with a very different woman. As the weeks went by, instinct told me she loved me still. Her misplaced sense of responsibility had gotten us into this mess, and although she tried time and again to shift any blame away from my father, how I hated him for it. I knew he could have helped her family *without* demanding payment in return. If he loved me, that's what he would have done. But no, he didn't want *me* to benefit from his charity. Instead, *he* greedily enjoyed the pleasures his money could buy, making Colette his whore as easily as he set me aside. Their marriage was a sham.

"When Colette told me she was carrying my child, I pleaded with her to leave him. I'd acquired my own fortune. We could go to New York, where nobody would know about the past. But my father denied her custody of the girls, and she refused to desert them. That led to a vicious row. My father and I said things to each other that can never be forgiven. I vaguely remember him collapsing, and still, I shouted at him. Then Colette was screaming at me, demanding I leave, and Paul was there, pulling me out of the room . . .

"I loved her, Charmaine, will always love her. Now, after all these years, I know the truth: Colette wasn't a mercenary, and she wasn't a saint. She married my father because she was humiliated, and she stayed with him because of the girls and her guilt. He exploited those emotions, but she never loved him."

John faced her, his eyes fierce. "You know the rest," he murmured, his voice suddenly raspy. "She refused to leave him—to *ever* leave him. When I realized he wasn't going to die, I went back to Virginia, alone." He turned back to the French doors. "No longer will I be haunted by the image of her kneeling before him begging his forgiveness. I finally know the truth. She loved me."

Frederic gave Jeannette one last squeeze, and the girls left him. His gaze lifted to Paul. "See they get back to the nursery," he directed. "Perhaps Rose could look in on them if Miss Ryan is not there."

Paul nodded. "I'm sorry about this, Father. I tried to calm

Yvette before she went running in search of John. You're certain you're all right?"

"Yes, I'm fine. You can send Agatha in now."

Agatha drew a chair even with her husband. "I'm sorry," she whispered. "I know I caused all of that."

Surprised, Frederic scrutinized her expression, looking for a flaw in the genuine contrition he heard in her voice. "Why did you tell Miss Ryan I was sending the girls to a boarding school?"

"We did discuss it," she replied evenly. She studied the hands in her lap, her long fingers rotating her wedding band thoughtfully. "I know. Nothing was decided, and I should have held my tongue. But Miss Ryan can be quite insolent, and I lashed out imprudently. I'm sorry."

"And John—you made certain he heard the same tale."

Agatha squared her shoulders. "When has he believed anything I've said?"

Frederic was given pause. Agatha was right. Sadly, he realized his son had been looking for an excuse to lambaste him; doing so in front of the children's governess was vindictive, at best.

Before he could think about it, Agatha was speaking again. "I've been fretting over what I said to you this morning, Frederic. I was wrong, terribly wrong, to say what I did. You've been hurt by so many of your loved ones, and I ache with the knowledge I have gathered with them."

"Agatha—please," he beseeched, warding off the sympathy she seemed wont to bestow. "The funeral will be in less than an hour's time, and I need a moment's peace before that ordeal begins."

"As you wish, my dearest, as you wish." She departed his company, uncertain as to the outcome of the morning's row.

Chapter 9

CHARMAINE woke with a start and sat upright in Pierre's bed. Someone was crying. She stood and crossed the room, settling next to Jeannette who was moaning in her sleep. "Wake up, sweetheart. You're having a bad dream."

Slowly, the girl surfaced from the dregs of a disturbing slumber. "Oh, Mademoiselle Charmaine," she whimpered. "We were in the fishing boat with Johnny. It started to rock and—and Pierre fell out! But then he started to swim. I think he was all right." She groaned woefully. "Oh, why couldn't that have really happened? I miss him so much!"

"I know, sweetheart, I know," Charmaine consoled. "But he's with your mama now. She's watching over him, and she's no longer alone."

Charmaine cuddled the distraught child, stroking back her hair until her breathing grew regular. When she was certain Jeannette slept, she eased her head back onto the pillow, drew the thin coverlet over her, and kissed her cheek.

Standing, she stepped out onto the balcony, happy to find it had stopped raining. She breathed deeply, drinking in the night air that carried the wisps of hair off her neck and eased the pain in her breast. Her moment's reprieve was swiftly stolen; she hung her head and choked on the tears she fought to subdue.

Just one week ago, they were living in paradise. One week ago today, she and John, the twins and Pierre had traveled to the lake nestled in a hidden forest and passed a wondrous day together. One week ago tonight, that flawless week came to a jarring end when cries from the front lawn ruptured her sleep, and Yvette tore into the house. Now, one week later, Charmaine could almost laugh with the insanity of it. This tragedy over a silly game of cards!

At least it was behind her. Pierre had been buried yesterday, a brilliant day that mocked all that had transpired earlier that morning: the confrontations and revelations, the lies and the truths. The breeze had been mild, the sun's rays strong, the day clear and bright, full of mendacious promise. John's eyes had been as dry as the day had been splendid, and that had been a lie as well.

So many lies . . .

Frederic had also made the journey from chapel to burial ground, one arm around Jeannette's delicate shoulders, the other hand clasping his cane as the entourage escorted the small coffin to its final resting place next to Colette's grave.

Yvette had attempted to console John, but he remained aloof, and after a while, she moved to Charmaine instead, head bowed, sniffing back her tears.

Everyone from the manor had been there, even Rose and George this time. The latter clasped John's shoulder supportively, remaining with him to the end, watching as the overturned earth was shoveled onto the small pine box, his arm quickening when Jeannette stepped forward and placed Pierre's stuffed lamb on top of the mound.

Not once did father or son look each other's way, and no sooner had the company arrived home, the clouds rolled in and the skies opened up, shedding the tears the two men refused to weep. The remainder of the day had passed in solemn misery. Today had been no better.

Charmaine wiped her tears away. She should retire to her own room, but she had no desire to sleep in the bed in which Pierre had died. Sooner or later she must, but not tonight.

A sound from the end of the balcony drew her round. She was surprised to find Paul there. He strolled closer, standing before her now. She had not had a moment alone with him since finding him asleep in the armchair just yesterday morning. But that was an eternity ago.

She read the sorrow in his eyes, just now realizing the depth of his grief.

"It is very late," he whispered. "Are you having trouble sleeping?"

"Any sleep I've had has been fragmented and disturbing," she replied. "I keep hoping I'll become too tired to think and . . ."

Her words dropped off as Paul gathered her in his arms. She grabbed hold of him, buried her face in his chest and willed herself not to cry. He stroked her hair and caressed her back. When the tears did not come, he squeezed her tightly. "Go ahead and cry, Charmaine," he encouraged. "You've been strong for so many others. Let me be strong for you."

They came in a deluge.

Paul battled his own anguish, taking solace from the feel of her in his arms. "I wanted to be there for you yesterday," he rasped.

"I know you did," she whimpered weakly, her tears still effusive, face pressed firmly to his shirtfront, unwilling to pull away.

"We're going to get through this. There will be happy days again."

"I pray God you're right, Paul, because I don't know how I'm going to go on without him. I miss him so much already."

"You will, Charmaine, I promise you will."

They remained entwined for some time. When her pain subsided, she stepped slightly away, but Paul leaned back into the balustrade and drew her next to him, his arm resting possessively around her shoulders.

"Perhaps we can do something with the girls tomorrow," he offered. "Perhaps a ride into town together."

Charmaine hugged him closer, her cheek resting upon his chest, conveying how much she appreciated his concern.

Much later, he retreated to his rooms. It had begun to rain again. Brushing his lips across hers, he bade her goodnight. Charmaine watched him go.

Entering her own chamber, she strode to the bed, tore back the blanket, and climbed in. It was a long while before she slept, but as she hugged her pillow, she conjured the security of Paul's embrace, and her eyes grew heavy.

Saturday, October 14, 1837

If you want to believe the worst about me, you continue to do so, Frederic . . . Frederic awoke with a start. He'd been arguing with Colette, her eyes flashing fire at him, so much like those first few weeks of their marriage. And yet, her words were not of long ago. They had been spoken to him recently, only a month before her death.

He closed his eyes again, hoping to recapture his dream. But as the minutes ticked by and sleep eluded him, he rose from the bed.

Dawn was upon the island, and although the French doors faced north, the early morning sun shone through the rain-spattered panes, spraying a spectrum of colorful dots across the morbid room. Frederic slumped into the armchair and stared at the pinpoints, their intense brightness blinding. Still he contemplated them; if he stared long enough, everything became black and white.

He was bored of this room, weary of his prolonged internment. He thought of John, his son, and a feeling welled up inside him, a feeling he had only begun to acknowledge. His eyes blurred with the realization he loved his estranged son, loved him intensely. More than that, Frederic admired him. For Frederic, it had been so much easier to be angry than sad, cruel than kind. And so, he had allowed jealousy and pain to keep him away from the one precious thing that could heal him: his own flesh and blood. But unlike him, John had borne life's wounds, accepted the suffering. He hadn't passed his cross onto an easy victim. And, for all his anger and hurt, even his mistakes, John could live with his decisions, live with himself.

Frederic bowed his head. When had he become such a pathetic fool? There would be no forgiveness, hadn't John said so? But then, why should there be?

Pierre was dead, and the cold truth pierced like a knife. *Pierre is dead because of your hatred for me.* Frederic had never considered the far-reaching consequences of his obstinate bitterness, never imagined it could bring such ruin down about him. Had he become so depraved he would allow the destruction of his own family, or worse yet, the death of an innocent three-year-old? Now he had to face it. He'd betrayed Elizabeth, John, and Colette.

Colette . . . He had misjudged her from the outset. When she arrived on the island at the age of seventeen, her delicate beauty took his breath away. More disturbing was her demeanor—something in her manner of speech and behavior that constantly reminded him of Elizabeth, an attraction that grew stronger and more difficult to suppress each day.

Colette's motives were equally disconcerting. Although John was obviously smitten, Frederic grew wary. First, there was her mother. He read the woman quickly, the worry of looming poverty in her eyes. Then there was Paul, who'd been dropped as a suitor when Colette learned John was the legitimate heir to the Duvoisin fortune. And lastly, there was Colette herself, born and bred in decadent France. Frederic had experienced its depravity firsthand, was certain this young lady could teach his son a thing or two, a supposition reinforced by a few saucy conversations he'd overheard. She'd even gone so far as to flirt with *him*. So, he had serious doubts about her innocence, concluding her purported virtue was merely a hook to reel John into marriage. She wasn't about to give up her body without a ring on her finger and money in the bank. Clearly, this was a near-destitute family capitalizing on an unprecedented opportunity to mitigate their woe.

As for John, he didn't object to his son sewing his wild oats with her, but Frederic felt he was far too young and undisciplined for marriage. Unlike his industrious brother, John was hardly the model student at university. With the exception of his music studies, John just did not have the patience to sit through long lectures, nor the interest in doing the work to make his grades. Frederic had received numerous letters from the university complaining of John's lackadaisical attitude and disruptive presence in class. Few instructors were willing to have him in their lectures, as John was always bent on challenging their assertions or, once he had homed in on their flaws, humiliating them in front of the other students, who would laugh uproariously at his jokes. When it became clear the Sorbonne was not about to spurn the Duvoisin money, the professors resorted to giving John passing marks just to avoid another semester of his grating presence. Since university had not settled him down, Frederic felt John needed hard work and worldly experience before he married.

When Frederic overheard Colette telling her friend the game she played with John was far more elaborate than kissing stable-hands in the hayloft, he had had enough. He wasn't about to allow her to perform favors for some commoner and then play the virgin for his naïve son. No, Frederic concluded, the time had come for Colette to be confronted by a man who had the experience to see through her façade and handle her appropriately. If money was what she was after, he would spare his son the mistake of marrying a mercenary, young and beautiful though she was. Oh yes, John would be furious with him, but he was used to that. There would be plenty of other young ladies to conquer. In time, the dispute would be smoothed over, and Frederic's intervention applauded.

Unbidden, came vivid images of the sultry night that sealed Colette's fate . . .

He had arrived home late, tired and aching from a grueling day in the sugarcane fields. The house was dark, save for the lamps flickering in the corridor. He'd assumed everyone was abed and headed toward the kitchen to get a drink. He had reached the dining room when he heard the giggling and whispers of young women carrying from the garden beyond. He moved into the archway, which afforded him a view of the courtyard. Colette and her friend emerged, bubbling over in animated conversation, and although they conversed in French, he remembered enough of the language to understand their banter.

"I still say Paul is far more handsome," her friend said, "but alas, he won't be the rich one."

Frederic strained to hear Colette's response, but her voice was hushed.

"Their father is just as handsome," her friend continued. "Such a waste to leave him to your mother! Maybe I can have him!"

"Ssh!" Colette admonished, moving closer. "Someone might hear you!"

"You know, *you* could have him!" the friend pressed on. "I think he's attracted to you!"

"Stop it, Pascale!" Colette warned, but with a wicked chuckle added, "Then again, I could practice kissing with him!"

"Yes," the shameless girl giggled, "I'm certain he knows just how it's done, and if he tutored you, then you would have nothing to worry about on your wedding night." Their laughter increased.

"Pascale, you are terrible!" Colette reprimanded with a click of her tongue.

They laughed again. "We should be seeking our beds," Pascale said. "Are you coming?"

"I need something to drink first. It is so hot here, I'll never get used to it. You go ahead, Pascale, I'll see you in the morning. Goodnight."

Colette passed through the swinging kitchen door, but drew herself up when she found him standing at the table, pouring himself a glass of water.

"So, Mademoiselle Delacroix, I understand you are thirsty?"

She nodded, but blushed under his piercing gaze, her poise shaken. He poured a glass, his hand brushing hers as he handed it to her. She finished it quickly. "More?" he asked.

"No, thank you," she murmured with a tremulous smile.

"Then if you are retiring, let me escort you to your room."

They walked down the hallway, Colette leading the way. Frederic considered her feminine figure, the delicate arch of her neck, the graceful undulating of her hips as she climbed the stairs.

When they arrived at her chamber door, she swung around, and he stepped in close. He turned the doorknob behind her, pushing the door open. She stepped into the room, and he followed. She seemed surprised by his impropriety, but not alarmed.

"I also understand you wish to practice the art of kissing to prepare for your wedding night," he stated, closing the door behind him.

She inhaled. "You overheard my conversation with Pascale."

"Yes."

He stepped close to her again and cupped her chin, gently nudging her face upward toward his.

"We were only being silly," she replied nervously, pulling slightly away. "We are both giddy from this adventure and the excitement of being here."

"Are you?"

"Yes," she giggled tensely, though her blue eyes sparkled, as if titillated by the unfolding encounter.

She can't wait to tell Pascale about this.

He abruptly grabbed the hair at her nape, and pressed his lips to hers. Whether dumbfounded or excited, she did not step back, and he took hold of her shoulders, pulling her against him. As the kiss deepened, his tongue parted her lips, probing and caressing.

"Monsieur!" she exclaimed breathlessly when he drew away.

"What else would you like to practice, Mademoiselle?" he asked, similarly shaken, his voice husky in his ears. He boldly caressed the length of her back, his hand coming to rest on her buttocks. "That is, if you need any practice."

"Monsieur, really, I think you misunderstood."

"Oh, I understand very well," he replied, as he began to work at the buttons of her bodice. The fresh smell of her was as intoxicating as her lips, fanning the passion he thought he was capable of controlling. "Come now, we both know French girls can be coy—skilled at the art of acting virginal when, in fact, they are not. Especially society girls such as yourself."

"Really, you do misunderstand!" she insisted shakily.

She backed away, but came up against the bed, stumbling onto it. There she lay, the bodice of her gown open, revealing the lovely swell of her breasts above her corset.

He followed her, stooping to pull off his boots, ripping open his shirt, and undoing the buttons of his trousers. When she attempted to scramble away, he chuckled and lunged across the bed, pulling her back into the center of it. She struggled for only the moment it took to pin her beneath him, her protests snuffed out as his mouth captured hers. He worked at her corset until the stays were released and the beauty of her firm, round breasts revealed. He squeezed them, taking delight in how they molded to the shape of his hands, his senses inflamed by the guttural groan that rumbled in her throat.

"*Mon Dieu,*" she whimpered when his mouth left her lips to sample a nipple, trembling fiercely, though the room was quite warm.

Even when he knelt above her to pull off the last of her clothing, and stood to quickly remove his own, she did not move, did not scream, apparently realizing the futility of resisting, and the embarrassment it would cause her. Her only protest was a modest, *"Non, s'il vous plaît!"*

But his ardor was piqued. "Too late, demoiselle," he said, lust heavy in his voice. "Of all the instructions your mother gave you about cornering a rich husband, did she not teach you if you play with fire, you will get burned?"

She frowned up at him, and he read defeat in her eyes, submitting as he parted her legs. He kissed her passionately and penetrated her with one hungry thrust, surprised when she vaulted against the rending intrusion, a muffled cry of pain erupting from her throat. It was then he realized her innocence, but his own need was great and could not be quelled.

She struggled anew, attempting to push him away, but he grabbed her buttocks and pressed deep inside, all the more eager to have her. When she had accepted the full length of him, he lay still, enjoying the feel of her breasts against his chest. He devoured her lips, drinking in her agony, cupped her face between his hands and rained kisses along her jaw to her cheek, wet with tears. She refused to look at him, so he tenderly tasted each moist eyelid, waiting for her to relax beneath him. When she sighed, he began to move against her, gently at first, and then, when he could no longer contain himself, harder. She grasped him tightly, her nails digging into his shoulders, her eyes still closed to what was happening. Her arms fell away once his passion was spent and, as he released her, a sob escaped her bruised lips.

When he rose from the bed, he took in the bloodstained linen and the second onslaught of tears. They confirmed what he already knew: she had been a virgin, exactly what everyone else had believed her to be, and he experienced a sharp stab of shame. He had made a grave error, his assumptions concerning her virtue unfounded, and he was overcome with regret, comprehending the implications of his vile behavior. He had soiled this young woman, spoiling her prospects as a future bride to his son, or anyone else for that matter.

He stared down at her for a moment longer, but when he tried to speak to her, to sit on the edge of the bed and wipe the tears from her eyes, to apologize, she only moaned, pulled the covers up, and turned away, refusing to even look at him. At a loss, he quickly dressed and abandoned the room.

The next day she remained closeted in her chambers, claiming illness, refusing to see John, her mother, even her friend. Late that evening, when all were abed, Frederic breached her chamber again, this time to propose marriage. She had no choice but to accept.

Over the next few days, Colette's heartache became his pain. She insisted on speaking to John alone, and although Frederic was of a mind to tell his son the truth, she vehemently objected. He never knew precisely what she said to John, but surmised she accepted the unjust title of "mercenary" and "harlot" in order to prevent greater repercussions. John was devastated, nonetheless.

Today, Frederic grieved with the weight of it. Because he'd been uncomfortable with his son's bitterness, he chose to brush it off. John would recover from his broken heart. He was young, he'd find another, he'd forget Colette. As for himself, Frederic worked at making Colette forget as well. She was in his blood and he couldn't concentrate for thinking about her. For all her feeble protests, she hadn't truly fought him, hadn't attempted to push him away until it was too late. Why? Was she frightened of him, or did she fear her own intense attraction? He grew to believe their encounter hadn't been rape, but seduction.

The first few weeks of their marriage had been tumultuous, and his pulse quickened with the memory. He recalled her fiery mettle, the times she fought his conjugal forays, the many nights she succumbed to passion and moaned in his arms. She never cowered before him, though he felt she worked hard at the poise she displayed.

Thrown into the mix was her unconscionable opposition to human bondage. Here was a mere slip of a girl who avoided speaking to him, yet had the effrontery to question his morality over holding slaves. He remembered their many altercations and thought specifically of the slave, Nicholas. She had been unconventionally vocal arguing the Negro's plight. Determined to rule his domain with an iron hand, Frederic turned tyrannical. It became a contest of wills. And only when he took her to his bed did she momentarily retreat. A familiar warmth spread through his loins as he thought about it. No other woman had satisfied him like Colette, save Elizabeth. But then, he often thought of them as one and the same.

Weeks turned into months, and their stormy relationship turned tender. The consuming fire remained, but Colette no longer sidestepped his passion behind a pretense of injured pride. She welcomed his lovemaking and slept contentedly in his arms night after night. Then she was with child, and his heart nearly burst with joy. During that year, he felt blessed; he'd been given a second chance.

He often thought about John, wrestled with the letters he could write, what he might say to make amends. But somehow, he knew he'd only make matters worse. In the end, he could only hope that time would heal all.

And then that time came: John returned. Colette was heavy with child, and though she greeted him congenially, John could scarcely look her way, his eyes simmering with unmasked repugnance when she and Frederic occupied the same room. As the days wore on, Frederic bristled with the intended slights and silent insults. Why had his son come back? He obviously still loathed them both. John's motives became painfully apparent toward the close of the week—that wretched night when his voice rang out from the drawing room, his wrath so intense Frederic could hear him from the second floor. Frederic flew down the stairs, horrified when he came upon the scene. The only thing that prevented them from coming to blows was Colette, prone on the sofa in the early throes of labor.

The twins' delivery was difficult, lasting over twenty-four hours, but Frederic remained by her bedside, refusing to leave even when Blackford demanded he do so. He was paralyzed by fear, reliving Elizabeth's labor some twenty years earlier. It was then he prayed, bargaining with the Almighty to spare Colette. "Give her something for the pain, damn you!" he blazed as she writhed in agony.

Blackford complied, and he calmed down when the laudanum took effect. Even so, her breathing remained ragged, and from time to time, her head twitched on the pillow. He soothed her, smoothing the hair from her sweaty brow and murmuring words of encouragement close to her ear. She became delirious and called for John over and over again. When she couldn't be comforted, he turned away in misery.

Hours later, it was over, and two healthy girls were presented to him. But the love he was wont to bestow upon them only the day before was gone.

He never touched Colette again. Sadly, he accepted the fact her heart would always belong to his son. He had robbed them both. That she eventually took John as a lover shouldn't have come as a surprise, or hurt as it did. He'd acknowledged the inevitable years earlier when she had openly flirted with his business associates at dinner one night. Her desires were quite clear, and they did not include him. When she admitted to her affair with John, begging him to understand, denouncing their marriage as a mistake, he assumed she had told John the truth. But she hadn't.

Looking back on those years, he realized Colette had continued to protect him. Even in her suffering, she had placed the precious tie between father and son above her own yearnings, in the beginning as an unwilling bride, and later as his wife. She'd only stopped trying when he had succeeded in breaking her spirit, not by taking her to his bed, but by setting her from it, by denying her that fragile bond of love that had just begun to blossom between them. He gulped back a wave of blistering emotion. To prevent an irreversible rupture, Colette had concealed the truth from John to the end. She had cared about them both so very much she had protected them from each other.

Frederic bowed his head to the saddest fact of all: after everything he had done to her, the havoc he'd wrought, his continual condemnation, Colette had never once condemned him. Instead, she had believed the best about him, cherished him more than he ever knew. She must have known his innermost insecurities, understood the ferocious front that was his shield, and comprehended what would be most important to him in the end. Now she was dead, and he had allowed that to happen as well. Even in the grave, he had not relieved her of her terrible crucible, though he owed her a great debt. *If you want to believe the worst about me, you continue to do so, Frederic . . . You don't trust me . . . even now, you don't trust me . . .*

No, ma fuyarde, he vowed, *I do trust you. I will never believe the worst again.* Blackford had lied. *Why?*

Frederic rose from his well-worn seat. This would be the last time he languished here all day.

Robert received Frederic's one-line message before he opened his small clinic for the day. As he closed the office door behind Joseph Thornfield, he wondered about the urgency of the dispatch. Was the man ill? He dismissed the thought quickly, certain his sister would have informed him first. Perhaps *she* was ill. This, too, he ruled out. Surely the note would have contained words to that effect. Why, then, was he needed immediately at the manor? Maybe the truth was out.

He counseled himself calm as he donned a waistcoat and jacket. Now was not the time to lose his composure. This probably had very little to do with him and quite a lot to do with his errant nephew, who refused to seek a physician's care for Pierre. Now that the initial shock had passed and the funeral was over, these unresolved issues could be properly addressed. Certainly Agatha would be pleased with the outcome. Hadn't this been what she was pressing for all along? John had definitely dug a hole for himself this time.

Robert grabbed his hat and physician's bag and stepped out of his small abode. Best to be punctual.

Charmaine hugged herself against the chill in the house and shivered. The foul weather of yesterday had not broken. The rainy season of late August and September had come at last, a constant drizzle, tenacious in the wake of the brilliant sunshine that had mocked Pierre's funeral barely two days ago.

Lies. That one word continued to plague her, scream at her.

"You should have accompanied Paul and the girls into town."

Rose shook off the brooding silence, and slowly, Charmaine turned away from the tear-splattered panes. "Not in this weather," she said.

"It will be clear by afternoon," Rose predicted as she looked up from her knitting, her dexterous fingers blindly feeding the wool to the clicking needles.

Charmaine agreed absentmindedly. "No doubt Paul is annoyed with me. He didn't have just his sisters in mind when he offered the outing at breakfast."

"I'm surprised Yvette decided to go," Rose conferred.

"I'm not," Charmaine replied, leaving the drawing room casement and sitting beside the woman. "John left the house early, and since she hasn't been able to engage his attention here, she's hoping to catch him in town."

Rose shook her head. "She's a wonder. So much like her mother."

Charmaine heard the woman's tears and fought to control her own misery. "Dear Lord, Nana," she breathed. "What a mess!"

Rose set her knitting aside. "Would you like to talk about it?"

Charmaine hesitated, uncertain of what Rose knew. But the elder's melancholy eyes told Charmaine she knew everything. "Oh,

Nana, that day in the master's chambers . . . it was terrible. And John, he said things I should never have heard."

"There, now," Rose soothed with a pat of the hand, "I thought as much. But you must use this revelation to cultivate understanding for all those involved."

"Understanding?" Charmaine queried incredulously. "How can I possibly understand a hatred that has existed for twenty-nine years—a hatred that has bred so much evil here?"

"Evil? Charmaine, you're speaking about people, people whom you've grown to love, who are fallible and have made mistakes, grave mistakes, but mistakes, nonetheless." Rose paused a moment, and then with a half-smile said, "All is not so lost. You're reaction is only natural. But time will be the greatest healer, time and companionship. The girls need you more than ever now."

Charmaine contemplated the wise statements. "But what if I'm dismissed? Mr. Duvoisin did not want me to hear the ugly things of which John accused him. Now I'll stand as a constant reminder of his humiliation."

"Frederic will not send you away," Rose declared resolutely.

Charmaine was not so certain. She thought of Agatha and the confrontation she had generated. "Why did Mrs. Duvoisin lie to me? To what end?"

"To set John and his father at each other's throats again, to have John expelled from Charmantes once and for all."

"But why? Why does she hate him so? He's her nephew."

"Come, Charmaine," Rose reasoned, "you remember what it felt like to be the target of John's sharp tongue. Agatha has never bowed meekly to his ridicule, though she's endured it for years. Now that she is Frederic's wife, she's set her teeth in. John has dug his own grave where his aunt is concerned."

Charmaine snorted. "I should have seen through her little game."

"Not a little game," Rose whispered ominously. "Suffice it to say, Agatha bears her own scars, and though they should have healed long ago, she nurses them often, lamenting the cross she was given to carry. In the future, take heed."

"I intend to," Charmaine bit out, "with both the master and the mistress."

Rose's brow gathered. "Charmaine, don't be so quick to judge Frederic. Remember, he has been wronged as well."

"That is a result of his own doing."

"Perhaps, but perhaps not. He is, for all his faults, a good man. I came to Charmantes when I was your age, Charmaine. Frederic was *my* little Pierre. I helped to raise him, and it does not please me to witness his pain. I know he feels a grave responsibility for all that has happened between John and himself. I believe he would like to make amends. This is, however, a difficult thing for a man who lost the woman he loved and allowed his grief to turn into a knot of resentment. John's mother had a dauntless, spirited character. It's a trait she passed on to her son, a trait that served John well in withstanding Frederic's bitterness in those early years, but ironically, one that constantly reminded Frederic of his dead wife." She sighed, her eyes deepening in sadness. "The rumors are true. Frederic *did* blame John for Elizabeth's death. But Frederic's animosity was not without foundation; it was erected on the belief that John was not his son."

Charmaine's eyes widened in shock, and she listened intently as Rose retold the story of Elizabeth's abduction and rape. "Frederic and Elizabeth had been married only six months when John was born," she finished.

"But surely John is Frederic's son! One has only to look at them."

"Yes, Charmaine," Rose said, "they are most definitely father and son. But when John was only a boy, there was no way to tell. That doubt added to Frederic's torment and nurtured a subtle hostility. By the time Frederic accepted John as his own flesh and blood, it was too late. John had grown to despise his father as much as he believed his father despised him. It seemed no matter what Frederic said or did, he could not rectify the situation. In fact, when he attempted to, he made matters worse. John delighted in testing Frederic's patience, his antics and caustic barbs limitless, always determined to have the last laugh. In time, the need to inflict injury became an ugly habit we grew accustomed to living with."

"Does John know what happened to his mother?" Charmaine asked.

"No," Rose whispered. "It's something Frederic never talked about, and it wasn't my place to speak to John on his behalf. Either way, it wouldn't have made one whit of difference."

Charmaine pondered this newest revelation. It did not exonerate Frederic, far from it. How could he have blamed an innocent babe for something over which he had no control? How could he have been so malicious? Charmaine bit her tongue against the accusations and said instead, "That explains John's childhood, but what of Colette?"

"Frederic thought of her as his salvation, his second chance. You met Colette when her health and spirit were already failing her, but she was quite mettlesome when she first arrived on Charmantes, much more like Yvette than Jeannette. For all her fairness of feature, her personality mirrored Elizabeth's. She held her own with John much the same way Elizabeth did with Frederic. I noticed it, and so did Frederic. She turned that spunkiness on him, and though he tried to ignore the disturbing similarities, they also charmed him. He resorted to avoiding her, dismissing her with barely any decorum. Colette, in turn, wondered how she had offended him. In an attempt to win him over, she unwisely initiated conversations that bordered on flirting." Rose breathed deeply and let out a soft sigh. "Then there were those times when . . ."

"When what?" Charmaine probed.

Rose rubbed her brow, seemingly disturbed with the memory. "Colette knew things—it was strange really, as if . . ."

"As if what?"

"As if she'd been here before." Rose chuckled, a false, uncomfortable chuckle. "But listen to me, an old woman rambling on, losing her sanity. It was just fate, sad, twisted fate that pushed Frederic and Colette together until . . ."

Her words trailed off, and Charmaine wondered if Rose had any idea of what had really happened. *Rape* . . . She grimaced with the word. Then, swift and sure came Colette's declaration of long ago: *I love him still,* leaving Charmaine extremely confused.

"Just give me the truth. All I want is the truth."

Robert Blackford was dumbstruck in the face of Frederic's wrath, having all but written the man off. But here he stood—imposing—the clothing freshly laundered and pressed, the cane more a scepter than a crutch. His cheeks and chin were clean-shaven, the hair well groomed, and the eyes denoted the workings of a keen mind.

"The truth?" Blackford hesitated. "What are you talking about?"

"My wife—my deceased wife, Colette. I have, on good authority, reason to believe the condition that led to her death was not the one you purported it to be. Now, as I've said, man, I want the truth."

"Frederic," Agatha gasped in dismay, "are you suggesting Robert has lied to you?" She, too, had been summoned to her husband's quarters and was visibly surprised to find her brother there.

"Isn't that obvious, woman?" Frederic sneered, his steely gaze settling on her for the moment.

Blackford applauded the interruption, her stupid comment clearly designed to give him time to think his way out of this unexpected attack.

"And you," the man was saying to her, "will do well to hold your tongue. You had very much to gain from the unhappy outcome of Colette's infirmity."

Agatha's eyes welled with tears, severely wounded.

"Who maligned my diagnosis, Frederic?" Blackford interjected. "I was the only physician who treated your wife. Who told you—"

"Never mind who told me! I found out!"

Robert faltered. *Who is the informant?*

"I'm waiting, man. Your muteness is branding you guilty."

His mind spinning unprepared, Blackford acknowledged only two avenues open to him: the lie or the truth. There was no choice but to gamble and stay the original course. "If you have reason to doubt me, then I have every right to know what information has contradicted my diagnosis."

"You have no rights!" Frederic seethed. "Your practice on this island is a product of my goodwill. I am your benefactor, but that can change in the blink of an eye. Now, I know my wife was not unfaithful to me; therefore, she could not have miscarried a child. Why did you lie to me?"

The tableau held until Agatha stepped forward. "Robert is not to blame, Frederic," she said softly. "This is all my doing. I'm at fault."

She bowed her head to Frederic's piercing gaze, his eyes narrowed in disbelief over her sudden confession. She breathed deeply before braving his regard once again, tears trickling down her cheeks. "Robert never wanted to mislead you, but I implored him to intercede. He did it for me."

She seemed at a loss for words and groped fruitlessly for a handkerchief. Coming up empty, she used the palms of her hands to wipe away the deluge.

"What are you saying?" Frederic pressed.

"I love you, Frederic!" she choked out. "You know I've always loved you! After Colette's death, your mourning turned to madness, and my heart ached for you. When I realized you were hell-bent upon destroying yourself, I couldn't stand by and watch you slip away from me. I convinced Robert to cast Colette in a bad light so she wouldn't be worth the grief you were expending on her. I thought it would bring you to your senses, back into the world of the living.

Then there were your children to consider. They were struggling to overcome the loss of their mother, and you weren't there for them. Instead, they heard the rumors about you and began starving themselves, too."

When Frederic's brow arched in dismay, Agatha paused, allowing that bit of information to seep in, certain he would question Rose or the governess about it. She pressed on, the contrition in her voice heavy and convincing. "I was wrong to do what I did, I know, but I was beside myself with worry, frightened if drastic measures weren't taken, your children would lose you. You had so much to live for: your sons and daughters, and, yes—*me*. I prayed to God you'd live for me!"

Frederic took the story in, his gaze shifting from the silently sobbing Agatha to the solemnly resigned Blackford. *So . . . John had been right.* Disgust welled up in the pit of his stomach, disgust for himself and his pathetic conduct after Colette's death, which had led to this vicious lie about her. He couldn't blame these two, not when he'd set the stage for their tactics. Nevertheless, he couldn't bear to look at them. "Get out of my sight!"

They departed quickly, leaving Frederic to his disgust and a surge of pity that congealed in his breast, pity for Agatha and her continued degradation.

By early afternoon, the relentless drizzle had ceased, and the sky cleared. The only evidence of the two-day downpour were teardrops that sparkled on the tip of each blade of grass. Charmaine marveled at the wonder, her pain ebbing in light of the beauty around her. Paul had not yet returned with the girls, and now that the day had turned fair, she didn't expect them for another hour. She cherished her time alone, meandering down the long, cobblestone drive, remembering Pierre.

With no destination in mind, she walked into the stable, located the stall of the dapple-gray mare she'd ridden just two weeks ago, and stroked the horse's soft muzzle. "She's a beauty," came a voice from the shadows.

"Yes, she is," Charmaine agreed, allowing the speckled head to nuzzle her as she faced the groom who approached. She had seen the man often enough, though surprisingly, she didn't know his name.

"One of the few in this paddock that can be called gentle," he continued, massaging the arm that was cradled in a sling. "Hand-picked her myself when Master John was determined to find you a suitable mount. He sent me all the way to Virginia, he did."

"Really?" Charmaine asked in astonishment.

The middle-aged man nodded. "Mr. Richards made all of the arrangements and covered the cost of the livery fees once the horses arrived on Charmantes, but I do take credit for the choice of mare and ponies."

She sighed, her heart momentarily light. "And I thank you, Mr. . . . ?"

"Bud," he supplied, "just call me Bud."

"Bud," she smiled. "Have you seen Master John?"

"No, ma'am, not since early this morning when he rode off."

"Into town?"

"No, ma'am, into the west fields. I think he needed to be alone. He's nursin' a bit of guilt, what with Phantom distracting him the way he did. Here he comes to my aid and leaves the child alone. But he didn't know what was gonna happen."

Astounded, Charmaine listened to the scenario. Up until now, she'd only heard bits and pieces of the events that had drawn John away from Pierre's bedside. "Phantom? He'd gotten loose?"

"Yes, ma'am, as was a regular occurrence. Sometimes he can act downright demonic. On Sunday morning, the look in those black eyes was near lunacy, and when he cornered me, well, I confess, I thought I'd seen my last day on God's green earth! Thank the Lord above that Gerald diverted his attention and saved me from those hooves, else I'm sure I'd have been trampled to death."

"And John?" she asked.

"He must have heard the commotion from the house, 'cause the next thing I know, he was circlin' the horse and tamin' him a bit. But Phantom didn't calm as quickly as he normally does when he catches sight of his master, and it took some time to get him corralled. Then Master John tended to me. Now I wish he hadn't. I hold myself responsible and wish it were me instead of that little boy . . ."

"Don't," Charmaine countered, "there's no point in blaming yourself. We all feel responsible for what happened. But then, nothing we did or didn't do would change what God intended all along, would it?"

"Thank you, ma'am," Bud muttered emotionally, "thank you."

Charmaine smiled up at him, experiencing for the first time in many days a sense of reward. She eyed the mare. "Would you saddle her for me?" she asked.

"What—to ride?"

"Yes," she answered quickly, lest she lose her daring.

He obliged, and not ten minutes later, she rode off, slowly at first, taking the trail that led to the back of the house and the west fields. Her initial nervousness yielded to determination, and she repeatedly told herself: *If I encounter any trouble, John will soon be along to help me.*

It would be good if she met up with him. She needed to see him, talk to him, reassure herself all would be well with him. At the house, he had all but ignored her these past days, and she worried over his continued isolation. True, he eschewed everyone's company, but she was different. She knew his pain better than anyone else. He had confided in her, a baring of his soul that must have meant something. And yet, perhaps he regretted his confession and avoided her now because of his shame.

Robert Blackford stared at his sister in disbelief as they made their way down the hall. She held silent, her expression warning he should do the same. It wasn't until they had climbed into his buggy and it rolled through the front gates that she let out a cheer of unmitigated delight.

"Oh, what a stroke of wonderful, extraordinary, marvelous luck!"

"Woman, are you mad?" he enjoined angrily, searching her face for a sign her senses had returned. "I nearly lost my head to the executioner in there!"

"Robert, Robert, Robert," she cajoled, taking his hand into her lap and patting it reassuringly. "Do you think I would have allowed that to happen? Quite the contrary. Things could not be better. You fail to see the benefits we stand to reap. You must learn how to find good fortune in a setback! Fortune, Robert," she chortled again, "fortune! The truth is out. I'm certain our extortionist will be extremely disappointed. Poor man, he thought he had everything arranged so comfortably." She pouted prettily for emphasis. When his laugh blended with relief, she went on. "What did you think of my acting? Was I convincing?"

"You practically had me crying, dear sister!" he laughed again, suddenly in awe of her ability to think under pressure, her stately beauty. "You should consider the theatre. It's not too late, you know. Think of it—New York!"

"No, no, Robert. This production is far more profitable."

"How do you suppose Frederic knew about Colette?"

"It doesn't matter. If he had any more information, he would have challenged my story. Personally, I think he was bluffing."

"Nevertheless, he's suspicious of us."

"And we admitted he had reason to be suspicious," Agatha replied. "But now he views any unscrupulous tactics on our part as concern for his welfare. How can he fault us for that? No, Robert, we needn't worry about Colette anymore. We have other matters to address."

"John?"

"Yes, John."

"Agatha, he is leaving Charmantes. Paul said as much when I spoke with him after the funeral."

Agatha eyed Robert speculatively. She did not doubt his assertion, but leaving was quite different from expulsion, her good humor suddenly tainted.

"You are Frederic's wife now," he continued, "mistress of the manor—of Charmantes. What more do you want?"

"I want it all, Robert. I want the rightful heir named sole beneficiary to the Duvoisin holdings. Don't tell me you won't sleep more soundly knowing Frederic's fortune will pass to Paul and Paul alone. As it stands now, John will cast us to the dogs the moment Frederic dies."

Robert cringed, silently agreeing with his sister's prediction, and whipped the mare into a brisk trot.

Charmaine didn't cross paths with John, and found upon her return she hadn't left the paddock but five minutes when he arrived home by way of the main road. She handed the reins to Gerald and headed toward the house.

John was not in the study, nor in the drawing room. As she returned to the foyer, she noticed the correspondence sitting on the table there. The letter crowning the odd assortment was addressed to her. It was from Loretta Harrington, and she quickly broke the seal and devoured its contents.

Dear Charmaine,

Your last letter upset me. You know I am not one to judge others before I have actually met and come to know them, but I cannot help but be deeply troubled over your description of John Duvoisin. I pray the man is not quite so intolerable as he seems, but still, you have me worried. Perhaps there are other reasons behind his dark moods . . .

Dear Lord, Charmaine groaned. She would have to answer Loretta tonight, scripting a letter that would erase the scurrilous image she had painted of John. She did not know how she would bring herself to write about Pierre's death.

The hour was late. Charmaine had just finished her prayers and was getting into bed when a knock fell on her door. She pulled on her robe and opened it. John was standing there. "Were you asleep?" he asked.

"No, not yet," she replied.

"I must speak with you for a moment, Charmaine," he said, gesturing for her to come into the hallway.

She felt uneasy, knowing she wasn't going to be happy with what he had to tell her. She followed him to his dressing room and stepped inside. He closed the door and leaned back against it. She turned to him, waiting for him to speak.

"I am leaving for Virginia before daybreak tomorrow."

She drew a deep breath and closed her eyes. Didn't she already know this was coming? *The girls will be devastated.*

"I have imposed upon your kindness already, Charmaine," he continued, "but I hope you will do me another favor, and give Yvette and Jeannette my goodbye. I didn't tell them myself because I cannot endure their pleading for me to stay. I do not want to refuse them."

"Must you leave?" she whispered.

"Aside from my sisters, there is nothing left for me here. If I could, I would take all three of you with me, far away from this hell. But my father rejected that request a week ago, and he will be less inclined to allow it now."

She was stunned and could see the bitterness smoldering in his eyes, aware of his thoughts. If he had been allowed to take them, Pierre would still be alive.

"Don't tell them that," he enjoined, reading her expression, his voice dead serious. "They will hate him for it. I do not hold my father responsible for what happened, only myself. None of us would be suffering this misery if it weren't for my terrible judgment four years ago." The room fell silent until he spoke again. "So, will you tell the twins goodbye for me?"

"Yes, of course I will," she ceded. "Will you come back?"

"I don't know," he replied. Then, seeing the despair in her eyes, he added, "In the spring, perhaps my father will change his mind and allow the girls to visit Virginia, once the turmoil has settled here."

"They are going to be very upset with this," she said. "They will miss you. And what of you? You will be all alone. You should not be alone right now."

"I cannot stay. In Virginia and New York, I have work to occupy me, and I have friends there. I neglected much while I was here." He sighed. "So, I will take a page from my brother's book and keep busy."

She nodded in resignation. Though she wanted to press him to change his mind, she knew he wanted to avoid an emotional scene. It would be cruel to attempt to sway him. She said instead, "I will miss you."

He smiled for the first time, a hint of warmth reaching his eyes. "Well, then, at least one good thing came from my visit." He opened the door. "I will miss you, too, my Charm."

As she reached the doorway, she hesitated and looked up at him.

"Thank you," he murmured.

She knew what he was doing could not be easy. She was compelled to comfort him, to convey some small measure of mercy and kindness before he set out to bear his crucible alone. She breached the short distance between them and encircled his waist with her arms. Closing her eyes, she pressed her cheek against his chest and listened to the steady beat of his heart. She took comfort from his arms closing around her shoulders, his chin atop her head.

"Goodbye, John," she whispered, pulling him tighter to her, emotion now rising painfully high in her throat, "goodbye." Then she pulled away and fled the room.

Sunday, October 15, 1837

The next morning, George greeted her and the twins at the chapel doorway. They were early for Mass and stood in the empty ballroom, smiling sadly as he walked toward them. He'd come to convey the news Charmaine already knew and had told the girls when they awoke: the *Falcon* had set sail at dawn, and John was aboard, heading back to Virginia.

"He left notes for you," George said. "They're on the table in the foyer."

As the girls ran to retrieve them, Charmaine looked back at George. "I'm worried about him, George. He'll be alone."

"He wants to be alone, Charmaine," George replied softly. He never thought he'd hear such concern for John from her. "He will be all right."

The girls returned with their letters; one was for her. She ushered them through the vestibule and sank into the nearest pew as she opened and read the brief words penned in masculine scrawl.

Charmaine,

I am grateful for your kindness these past days. Mostly, I thank you for the love you gave Pierre. You are a fine person, and the twins are fortunate to have you. I know you will give them the comfort they will need in the days to come, and I hope they will do the same for you. If you are ever in need of anything, do not hesitate to call on me. George knows where I can be reached.

John

Charmaine folded the letter and slipped it into her pocket. She looked up at the crucifix above the altar. The words in the note left her empty: very kind, friendly, detached. *And who will comfort you, John?* her mind screamed.

But she understood John's departure in the same way she now understood why he had come home. The things that had drawn him to Charmantes no longer existed. Colette and Pierre were gone, and he was estranged from his father. And though she knew he cared deeply for the twins, they belonged to Frederic, not him. He no longer had a reason to stay.

She looked to the girls and read the disappointment in their blue eyes. They turned away in misery and slowly walked to their usual seats at the front of the chapel. Charmaine marveled over their fortitude; neither of them pressed the matter with the lamentations they had used before. Perhaps they knew they could never recapture those happy, carefree days before Pierre's tragedy.

Charmaine resigned herself to that reality as well and began to pray she'd be able to accept it. There was nothing she could do. John's decision had been made, and there was no turning the *Falcon* back now. It was time to move forward, to find comfort in the mundane and routine. They had done so before, they would have to do so again, difficult though it might be. But as she willed herself to look to the future, a terrible loneliness stole over her. It was as if she were losing Colette all over again, and for the first time, she realized John had swept that feeling of loneliness away the moment he had stepped into her life.

She was just about to rise when Frederic entered the chapel. She didn't breathe as he limped past her and joined his daughters. She watched in wonder as Jeannette swiftly stood, hugged him, and coaxed him to sit first.

Agatha was equally surprised when she entered the sanctuary moments later. Charmaine heard the woman whisper, "Why didn't you tell me you were attending Mass? I would have come down with you," but she couldn't discern Frederic's response. To Yvette's displeasure, her stepmother sat next to her.

Charmaine remained exactly where she was, leaving without a word as soon as the Mass was over. She had no desire to converse with the master of the manor and knew the twins could find her in the nursery. She even avoided breakfast. But at lunch, Travis informed her Frederic wanted to see her privately in the study at one o'clock sharp.

She was stunned by the message. Why the study? Why the meeting in the first place? He'd had days to mull over what she knew. Had she become a liability, a shameful reminder of his terrible secret, just as she'd suggested to Rose? Would he dismiss her after all? Rose had assured her this would not happen. Still, she was upset.

At five minutes to one she left the girls in their room and made her way to the library. She was trembling as she knocked on the door.

"Come in."

The room was unusually bright with both sets of French doors thrown open, sunbeams splashing onto the large desk and across the carpet. Frederic was seated at the secretary, papers strewn over it, stacks of ledgers piled on the floor nearby.

"How are you, Miss Ryan?" he asked, motioning for her to sit down.

"I am well, sir," she lied, unable to read his intent from the polite opening. "You wished to speak to me?"

"Yes. I won't detain you for long. I wanted to let you know I am making some changes in my daughters' schedule."

Charmaine gulped back her dread. *Here it comes.*

"From now on, they will spend their Saturdays with me. They are to be dressed and in the dining room at nine o'clock this coming Saturday morning. They will be in my company for the whole of the day, so from nine in the morning until seven in the evening, you are released of your duties."

"Released of my duties?" she repeated, confused, noting only the word "released." *Is he dismissing me?*

"You are free to spend your Saturdays as you wish. I will only infringe upon that freedom on those days I am indisposed or otherwise occupied. Is this satisfactory to you?"

Charmaine paused, unsteady. "It is not a matter of what is satisfactory to me, sir, but to respect your wishes regarding your daughters."

"Miss Ryan," Frederic smiled, "I am giving you a day off each week. Your wages will not be affected, as I will expect you to be able to change your Saturday plans if you are needed. Is this not satisfactory?"

"It is quite satisfactory, sir."

"Good. Then you will have my daughters ready at nine o'clock six days hence. That is all, Miss Ryan. You may return to the twins."

Charmaine let out a great sigh of relief as she closed the study door behind her. Not dismissed! More important, Frederic had acted as if nothing had happened between them. She was immensely grateful.

Yvette was not happy with the news, decrying this latest turn of events. "He's just trying to copy Johnny! He'll never be like Johnny! Now our Saturdays are ruined!"

Charmaine looked at Jeannette, who remained ever so quiet, then back to Yvette. "Perhaps your father wants to make time for you both while he's still able. Even if he is imitating John, is that such a bad thing?"

Yvette pondered Charmaine's reasoning, then flung herself into a chair. "But what are we going to do with him all day?"

"Why don't you start thinking of some ideas? I'm certain your father will appreciate the help."

The girls took up her suggestion, leaving Charmaine to wonder just how Frederic would execute the grand plans they had already conjured: picnics, excursions into town, ship rides, and lawn games. He had barely left his chambers in four years. Would he really be out and about with two nine-year-olds? Charmaine shook her head and laughed in spite of herself. What other changes would they face in the coming days?

There was a knock on the door. Yvette jumped up, but her hopeful face dropped when Paul stepped into the room. "Good afternoon," he smiled.

She grumbled a greeting and trudged back to her desk.

"Good day, Paul," Jeannette greeted cheerfully.

"I've brought you a surprise," he offered pleasantly.

Yvette looked up in renewed interest.

"A cargo came in from England yesterday with a whole cask of sweets made from the sugar grown on Charmantes. I thought you'd like some." He produced a paper bag from behind his back and offered it to Jeannette.

She snatched it from him quickly, exclaiming an enthusiastic "thank-you." Yvette joined her sister to inspect the booty and pick out the choice pieces.

Paul looked to Charmaine. "There were fresh kegs of tea as well. Fatima is brewing some now. Would you like to join me for some on the porch?"

"That would be nice," she answered, leaving the girls to their plans.

"You were working today?" Charmaine asked once they were sitting outdoors.

"It couldn't wait. But the cargo was inventoried by early afternoon."

"The cargo was from the *Falcon*?"

"Yes," he replied, his eyes never leaving hers.

"Did you see John this morning?" Charmaine asked softly.

"We rode into town together."

"Did he say anything to you?"

"Not much." He sighed. "John wanted to go back to Virginia, Charmaine. I don't blame him. It's been unbearable here the past few days. He's neglected a lot the last two months, and at least in Virginia he'll have the distraction of work." His voice was sympathetic. "I knew the girls needed some cheering up. They couldn't have been happy with the news."

"They did, and the candy helped. It was kind of you to think of them."

Fatima arrived with the tea and poured two cups.

"How are you faring?" Paul asked. "Any better since Friday night?"

"I'm doing what I need to do to get through the days," she replied honestly. "I try not to think about it. And still, I curse myself for leaving Pierre that morning." Tears sprang to her eyes.

"It wasn't your fault, Charmaine," he comforted, taking her hand. "It wasn't John's fault, either. How many times had you left him to nap or come downstairs at night when you were certain he was asleep in his bed? You only did so knowing he was safe and sound. It wasn't a lapse of responsibility to do that, Charmaine. Every parent does the same."

"I know you are right," she replied, dabbing her eyes. "Still it's difficult not to think 'if only I'd done this, or if only I'd done that.' And it doesn't help because I miss him terribly."

"I know you do," he replied, his warm hand stroking hers. "I do, too."

They fell silent, sipping the piping hot tea, until Charmaine broached the subject of John again. "John told me everything that morning," she mused tentatively, a little nervous Paul might grow weary or angry with the topic.

He looked at her, but did not seem annoyed. "But you're still curious."

"I'm curious to know how you feel about it. I never imagined you met Colette first."

He leaned back in his chair and drew another long sip from his tea. "I was not in love with Colette, if that's what you would like to know. I cared for her as a friend, a friendship that grew deeper with time. When we first met, I was attracted to her. She was beautiful. She knew her way around Paris society and introduced me to her circle of friends. So when John caught her fancy, I wasn't jealous, not after a while anyway. There were plenty of women to pick and choose from, most of them willing . . ."

She could feel a blush rising to her cheeks. "But you were so angry at John those first few days after he came home."

He shook his head. "He was bent upon provoking me. So, in my anger, perhaps I overreacted. Still, I never understood why John took the relationship as far as he did, and I blame him for that. Granted, he was engaged to Colette, and yes, my father should never have interfered. But once Father did, and Colette made her choice, John should have left it alone. Instead, he chose to torment her. He hated our father so much, he drew her into an impossible situation."

"And Colette had no free will in the matter? John controlled everything?"

Paul massaged his forehead. "Charmaine, neither Colette nor John ever provided me with the details on how their affair started, or how long it lasted. What I do know is John was not lacking for other prospects. There were many women who, at the drop of a coin, would have fallen at his feet, ready and willing if he'd only given them the time of day. So why a love affair with a married woman—no, worse—his father's wife, when the alternative is so easy and clear? John hurt my father deeply, and not just physically. Imagine how it felt to be cuckolded in his home, by his son, and afterward, wonder how many others in the house knew about the scandal."

Live by the sword; die by the sword, Charmaine thought, though she didn't say so. "But John loved her," she insisted instead. Fleetingly, she read surprise in Paul's eyes, as if that possibility hadn't occurred to him before.

"Then I don't understand love," he replied, exasperated now. "Perhaps I haven't experienced it yet to judge whether one loses his rational mind over it."

Enormously disheartened, she couldn't respond, and again they fell silent. But as her distress dissipated, she measured his remark and, for the first time, understood his disdain for John's actions. Even so, his view of the matter was highly impersonal—that one woman could so easily be replaced by another.

She poured him a second cup of tea, not wanting the conversation to end on this contentious note. "Your father called me to the study earlier this afternoon."

"The study?" Paul asked quizzically.

"Yes. It looked like he was working there. He'll be taking charge of the girls on Saturdays from now on. I'll have that day off," she finished on a laugh.

Paul was astonished and smiled. "Well, then, I'll have to work harder during the week so my Saturdays are also free."

Frederic was present at the dinner table that night, and although he worked at being cordial, his efforts fell short. The girls spoke to him, but only to answer his questions, their responses stilted. With a resigned smile, he dropped the artificial repartee, allowing his daughters their melancholy.

Before the meal was over, Yvette asked to be excused, complaining of fatigue and a stomachache. She promised to go straight to her room. But when Charmaine reached the nursery, the girl was nowhere to be found. The week, culminating with John's unannounced departure that morning, had taken its toll on the headstrong nine-year-old.

After a quick search of the house, Charmaine found her in the stables, sitting on a pile of hay in the corner of Phantom's stall, clutching her kitten and crying. Her stoic façade had crumbled.

"Johnny took Phantom with him this time, Mademoiselle Charmaine," she sobbed, rocking back and forth. "That means he's *never* coming back! Oh God! I want my brother. I just want my brother!"

Charmaine did not offer encouraging words to the contrary. The last time she'd insisted on miracles, disaster had stepped in to laugh at her. She'd stopped believing in miracles, anyway. Thus, she knelt down beside Yvette and hugged her close, allowing the child to embrace her misery and shed her bitter tears.

A⁺
AUTHOR
INSIGHTS,
EXTRAS, &
MORE...

FROM
DeVa
GANTT
AND
AVON A

QUESTION AND ANSWER READER'S GUIDE
FOR *DECISION AND DESTINY*

1. What is the significance of the title *Decision and Destiny*?

The impact of a decision upon one's destiny is a recurring theme throughout Book 2 of the Colette Trilogy. It is both John's and Frederic's foremost dilemma. In the novel's climax, John is tormented by his decision *not* to act: *This time he had floated with the tide. The outcome was worse than his attempts to twist circumstance in his favor. Stupid fool! When would he learn his actions always led to disaster?* Frederic suffers comparable remorse, but unlike John, his torment is born of a decision *to* act, to manipulate destiny. *Last night, he had debated his choices and struggled with a decision, frustrated to conclude it lacked direction. The* Raven *pointed the way, provided the rudder. Frederic rubbed his brow, detesting this course of action, his thoughts sinking like a deadweight on his chest. If only John and he could speak civilly. But that option was closed to them; John would only accuse him of scheming—exactly what he was forced to do.*

One might ask: Do our decisions govern our destiny or is our destiny just preordained fate? Readers should ponder the book's subtitle, *Colette's Legacy.* Is Colette's legacy a product of her decisions or her destiny? And what exactly is her legacy? Is it a family splintered or a family reunited?

2. Isn't Colette's legacy a direct result of Frederic's actions?

Colette's and Frederic's lives are intertwined, as are their fates, thus Frederic's actions most definitely affect Colette's legacy. But Colette's legacy cannot be fully appreciated until the trilogy comes to a close and all components of the story revealed. Only then can the reader contemplate how Colette scripted her own legacy and determine whose actions had the greater influence.

3. What are Frederic's motives? He appears contrite; if so, why does he deliberately provoke John the night he presides over the dinner table for the first time?

Upon John's return home in *A Silent Ocean Away*, Frederic is eager to make good his promise to Colette—to make peace with his son. But John, in his hatred, resurrects all the old animosity, cementing in Frederic's mind the hopelessness of the situation. Even so, Frederic *is* contrite, and his regret intensifies as he witnesses the bond of love developing between John and Pierre. Acknowledging his family's unhappiness, yet unable to find a fruitful solution, Frederic devises a devious one. He deliberately provokes John in an attempt to stir John to action—to force him to make a choice. He even goes so far as to visit Espoir, leaving John free to claim Pierre. But John recognizes the ploy and, misreading it as a trap, refuses to take the bait.

4. How was the idea of a father/son love triangle conceived?

Early plotlines consisted of a love triangle between brothers—Paul and John—vying for Charmaine. In order to develop an attraction between Paul and Charmaine, while convincing the reader that Paul was the sole hero and John, the scoundrel, it was important that John remain stateside. To accomplish this, a plausible explanation for his prolonged absence had to be established, and the story of John and Frederic's stormy relationship grew, culminating in Frederic's stroke, John's departure, and their mutual exiles: Frederic to his room and John to Virginia. In addition, John's reason for seeking out the children and spending time with them had to be logical; Pierre became *his* son.

5. *Decision and Destiny* seems to parallel *A Silent Ocean Away* in structure. Was this intentional?

Definitely. First, there are nine chapters in each book, something that will recur in Book 3. In addition, pivotal events occur within certain parallel chapters, such as Colette's and Pierre's deaths in Chapters 7, respectively. There are also parallel scenes: Charmaine finds John at the piano in *Decision and Destiny*, much as Colette finds Charmaine at the piano in *A Silent Ocean Away*, and a third piano scene will occur in *Forever Waiting*. There are three parallel boyhood recollections: George recalls the Gummy Hoffstreicher story in *A Silent Ocean Away*; John recounts the rescue of Father Benito in *Decision and Destiny*; Paul will also reminisce in *Forever Waiting*.

The reader should identify the other sets of three that do not necessarily depend upon the three-book structure, but rather on the trilogy itself. For example: Colette's letter surfaces three times: once in *A Silent Ocean Away*, twice in *Forever Waiting*. In addition, the reader should not overlook the three love triangles that foment the conflict: Charmaine/Paul/John; Colette/John/Frederic; and Frederic/Agatha/Elizabeth.

6. As you read *Decision and Destiny*, it is clear a great deal of groundwork went into character and plot development. How do you "map out" a complex story?

We have found that "mapping out" a story does not always work, whereas writing does. The writing process taps into a creative vein that enables an author to surmount obstacles created by too much contemplation or worse still, writer's block. Through the writing, the story unfolds, character traits solidify, and subplots emerge. These combine, allowing the author to explore other possibilities: how to weave the tapestry together, tweak the nuances, and employ the literary devices necessary to make it a deep and thought-provoking work. The first book, *A Silent Ocean Away*, lays the important groundwork for what is revealed in the second book, *Decision and Destiny*, and in the third book, *Forever Waiting*.

7. *Decision and Destiny* is not only intense, but enjoyable and sometimes lighthearted as well. How was this accomplished?

We wanted the Colette Trilogy to be entertaining, but even seemingly innocent discussions and carefree encounters contain clues as to where the story is headed, and at times, they become the foundation for pivotal events. The twins' birthday picnic, though lighthearted, is teeming with these clues. When rereading that day, pay attention to: the symbolism behind the story of Colette's two horses, Charity and Chastity; the conversation between John and Charmaine concerning Paul's womanizing and possible marriage proposal; John teaching his sisters to swim; Yvette's eavesdropping; and Charmaine's premonitions.

John's recounting of Father Benito's rescue, in combination with his approval of Yvette's mischievous antics, bolsters Yvette's pursuit to mimic him. This fuels her excursion to Dulcie's, which leads to Frederic's rage and his confrontation with John. Together, these set in motion a domino of events that result in Pierre's death.

Pierre's death also stems from his desire to accompany John to Virginia. His only means to do so is to sail there in the boat John has purchased for him. The boat was procured because Pierre wanted to go fishing. And he wanted to go fishing because he sat in awe of George's hilarious fishing story involving Gummy Hoffstreicher and John. That seemingly innocent recollection, which was no more than a boyhood escapade intended to lighten the mood at the dinner table in *A Silent Ocean Away*, drives the novel to its climax—the turning point for the entire trilogy.

8. Humor is effectively employed throughout the novel. Is its primary purpose to lessen the turmoil?

Humor is a powerful tool that, when properly employed, can take a reader on a roller coaster of emotions: from a summit of laughter into a valley of tears. And though levity can be a device to alleviate tension and sorrow, it can also heighten these feelings. Certainly melancholy is much more bitter when compared to happy times. Charmaine's very thoughts following Pierre's death: *Just one week ago, they were living in a paradise. One week ago today, she and John, the twins and Pierre had traveled to the lake nestled in a hidden forest and passed a wondrous day together.* And again, when

John leaves Charmantes after Pierre's death: *She looked to the girls and read the disappointment in their blue eyes . . . Perhaps they knew they could never recapture those happy, carefree days before Pierre's tragedy.* Humor's primary purpose, therefore, is not to lessen the turmoil, but rather to take the reader by surprise and prime him or her for it.

9. There are elements of the supernatural and indications of a ghost wandering the house. Is this plausible?

Throughout life, we are confronted with the unexplainable. Readers should ask: *Is* Colette's ghost roaming the house or is there other mischief at work? As the Colette trilogy took shape, everything had a credible explanation; we exploited the incredible—the possibility of a ghost—to camouflage nefarious motives. As the writing neared an end, however, our imaginary ghost demanded the possibility of life. Thus, we leave it to the reader to decide. We also leave you with this quote; while contemplating it, recall how this event changed John's perception of Charmaine. *"Oh no," Pierre replied resolutely. "Mama wakes me up and sometimes she visits me when I take my nap. She took me to her big room that day when that auntie spanked me."*

10. There are also hints of reincarnation throughout *Decision and Destiny*. What is the connection between Colette and Elizabeth?

Again, that is for the reader to decide. But allow us to quote our characters' views on the matter:

Why wouldn't {Elizabeth} come to him in his greatest need? He knew the answer. Even now, Elizabeth remained with Colette. (Frederic, *A Silent Ocean* Away)

No other woman had satisfied him like Colette, save Elizabeth. But then, he often thought of them as one and the same. (Frederic, *Decision and Destiny*)

"Then there were those times when . . . Colette knew things—it was

strange really, as if . . . she'd been here before." (Rose, *Decision and Destiny*)

"Colette . . . was not Elizabeth. Yes, I know what you saw in her, the many similarities. I saw them, too." (Agatha, *A Silent Ocean Away*)

Read on!

Following is a preview of the third book in the saga of the
Duvoisin family . . . their friends, their lovers,
and their foes . . .

Forever Waiting

COLETTE'S APPEAL

Coming in 2009 from Avon Books

Chapter 1

Friday, October 20, 1837
Freedom . . . 56 miles west of Richmond

BRIAN Duvoisin was black. Born on the Duvoisin plantation thirty-five years ago, he had been a slave for most of his life, that is, until the day John Duvoisin signed the document that freed him. Having no surname to place on the legal paper, John suggested he use Duvoisin. Brian agreed. Grinning, John shook his hand and called him "brother."

At first, Brian was wary of John's motives, but he remained on the plantation. He really had no choice. Where else in the South could a penniless, unskilled colored man go?

John emancipated many other men, women, and children that week, and his indignant neighbors swiftly dubbed the Duvoisin estate "Freedom." Within the month, John erected an elaborately carved sign above the plantation's main gates. Freedom it was.

John grew to respect Brian and, with each passing season, placed greater responsibility upon his shoulders. The field workers respected him as well. If John wanted the plantation to remain productive, especially when he was away, Brian was the man to have there.

Brian's wife was also free, for John had purchased Wisteria Hill, the adjacent estate where she lived, releasing those slaves as well. At first, Brian puzzled over his wife's emancipation; leaving Virginia was possible now. He'd gained some skills beyond the backbreaking field labor. He could travel north, take Nettie with him, earn a living, and keep a roof over their heads. Why he didn't go, he couldn't say, other than John relied on him.

Today, he was the only black overseer in the entire county. It did not sit well with John's neighbors, who opposed paid Negro help. But John never caved in to the pressure; rather, he seemed to revel in the controversy, holding firm to his decision. His staunch resolve garnered Brian's steadfast loyalty and trust. Now, four years later, the two men were close friends.

Stuart Simons was white. Though born and raised in the South, he was a Northern sympathizer, a posture embraced by his Quaker parents, who had instilled in him a deep sense of right and wrong. Because he rebuked a number of Southern viewpoints, finding employment had been difficult until he met John. Eventually, he became Freedom's production manager.

John knew Brian needed the protection of a white man, especially when he was abroad in Richmond or New York. Therefore, John situated Stuart on the plantation to discourage his neighbors from harassing the black overseer when he was away. It proved a wise move. The first time John had left Freedom on an extended trip, there had been an incident, one easily quelled when Stuart appeared to greet the men who just happened to stop by for a "visit."

Because Stuart had an easy manner, and because he also respected Brian, they became friends. Stuart quickly learned the workings of a tobacco plantation. He already knew the ins and outs of the shipping business, overseeing the loading and unloading of Duvoisin vessels in Richmond after the fall harvest. This year, John had relied heavily on both men, for he had been away the entire summer and fall. But the plantations rested in capable hands, so Freedom and Wisteria Hill's harvests were the least of John's worries.

Tonight, the two men sat at the kitchen table, discussing the year's production. Cotton prices were down fifty percent, and although cotton was not grown at Freedom, John wasn't going to like it. The brokers in New York were not buying. If the newspaper reports were correct, Congress had authorized the issue of ten million dollars in short-term government notes to stem the panic that was sweeping across the country.

It was thus John found them—deep in worried conversation.

Though John's comings and goings were always unpredictable, they looked up in surprise. He'd notified them some months ago that he had traveled to Charmantes. They knew him well, having spent many a night with him after an onerous day in the fields, drinking and talking into the wee hours of morning. For John to go home, something had to be wrong. One look at his face and they knew they were right.

"Good God, man," Stuart breathed, "you look awful."

John grunted and slumped into a chair.

"What's the matter?" Brian asked.

"Everything," John chuckled wryly, "as always."

Stuart leaned forward. "Did you see them?"

"Just my son," John said softly, tenderly. "Colette was dead before I reached Charmantes." Propping his elbows on the table, he drove his fingers through his tousled hair before whispering, "Pierre died a week ago."

"John," Stuart murmured, "I'm sorry."

"Me, too, John, me, too," Brian consoled. When the silence became uncomfortable, he asked, "What are you going to do now?"

"Try to forget . . . try to forget."

"Maybe this will help," Stuart offered, extending the paper with the rankling financial figures.

For the next few hours, they examined plantation documents, discussed the tobacco yield and production costs, shipping, the New

York brokers, and the economy. John seemed unconcerned with the rumors of the dissolution of the conservative Bank of the United States and the failure of three banks in England. Stuart shook his head; the man obviously knew what he was doing.

When all topics had been exhausted, John stood up and stretched. "I've had enough for one night."

As Brian and Stuart rose, he broached another subject. "You'll be going into Richmond tomorrow?"

Stuart nodded. "I'll be leaving at the crack of dawn."

"Do me a favor then, would you?"

"What's that, John?"

"Visit Sheriff Briggs and find out if a John Ryan was ever apprehended."

"John Ryan?" Stuart puzzled. "He used to work for you."

John's brow lifted in interest. "Really?"

"I believe he was being sought in connection with his wife's death."

"That's the one."

"I remember Briggs coming to the wharf and questioning the men. I don't think he was found. Why in heaven's name are you interested in him?"

"Locating him is important to a friend of mine and its important to me."

"I'll see what I can find out. If the authorities aren't a help, I'll make a few inquiries of my own around town."

John nodded a thank you and turned to leave.

"How long are you planning to stay in Virginia?" Stuart asked.

"Aside from a trip north, you'll be seeing more of me from now on."

Both Brian and Stuart smiled, happy to be in the man's company again, but reading John's face, they knew the sentiment was not reciprocated.

The next afternoon, Stuart went directly to the sheriff's office. Briggs seemed annoyed, grumbling something about "white trash" and that wife beating wasn't a crime. Disgusted, Stuart realized he was getting nowhere fast. He might uncover something at the wharf. With the Duvoisin clout, the authorities might be persuaded to re-open the case. He was not disappointed. A few longshoremen had seen Ryan scrounging around for odd jobs, but his appearances were sporadic, and no one remembered exactly when they'd seen him last.

John was displeased. "Could you ask the men to keep an eye out for him?"

"Sure, John," Stuart agreed, "next time I'm in Richmond."

Saturday, October 21, 1837
Charmantes

Charmaine and the girls arrived in the dining room well before nine o'clock. Today was the first Saturday they would spend with their father. True to his word, Frederic was waiting for them. After breakfast, the threesome departed the manor, leaving Charmaine alone.

Yvette dragged her feet, her father's steps quick and sure by comparison.

"What is the matter, Yvette?" he asked as they arrived at the paddock.

"Nothing," she grumbled sullenly.

Frederic only smiled.

Gerald appeared with Spook and Angel, and Yvette perked up. "We're going to go riding today?"

"That and other things."

Paul emerged from the barn with a meticulously groomed stallion.

"Papa," Jeannette breathed in alarm, "you're riding Champion today?"

"I'm going to try, Jeannette."

Paul had his doubts, but he'd been unable to talk Frederic out of this folly and knew it would be futile to try again now. "I ran him hard yesterday," Paul said, "so he shouldn't be straining at the bit today."

"That's fine, Paul. I might need some help getting in the saddle, though."

Frederic swallowed his pride and endured the humiliation of mounting the horse he'd ridden countless times. He stumbled only once, his lame arm buckling under him as he pulled up and into the saddle, his chin hitting Champion's neck hard. His eyes shot to Paul, who'd swiftly averted his gaze, pretending he hadn't seen. The awkward moment passed as Frederic situated himself atop the steed. Paul secured the cane to the saddle, nodding in approbation. They were all set. Frederic breathed deeply. "Come, girls," he encouraged, "we've Duvoisin business to attend to."

His smiling daughters were already on their ponies. Together, they trotted down the cobblestone drive and out the gates.

"Where are we headed, Papa?" Jeannette asked enthusiastically.

"The mill."

"The lumber mill?"

"I have a great deal of catching up to do," he answered, "and I'd like to start by meeting the newest men working for me. Wade Remmen is first on the list."

Jeannette was beaming. This was going to be a wonderful Saturday! As for Yvette, it was going to take more than a visit to the mill to please her; however, the ride was pleasant.

Paul watched them go, then headed toward the house. Charmaine was all his today. He found her in the gardens reading a book. A melancholy smile greeted him, causing his heart to hammer in his chest. He remembered the feel of her in his arms just one week ago, and he longed to hold her again, to comfort her. He sat next to her on the bench they had shared an eternity ago.

"So, Miss Ryan, what are we going to do today?"

She regarded him quizzically. "You're not working?"

"I said we'd spend time together."

Her smile turned sweet.

"A visit into town?" he suggested. "Or perhaps a walk along the beach?"

The mill was abuzz. Yvette and Jeannette's eyes widened as they approached, for they had never imagined the sweaty toil here. A score of men labored with teams of draft horses, pulling long, thick logs to a central building where they would be milled. A huge water-wheel rotated briskly at the far end of the structure, plunging into a deep ravine. Planks were emerging on the other side, where they were swiftly hoisted onto a buckboard for transport to town. The screech of saws, the shouts of men, and the whinny of horses punctuated the air.

"Yvette, Jeannette?"

They tore their eyes from the engrossing commotion and looked down to find their father had already dismounted.

"Are you coming?"

As Frederic and his daughters approached, one man looked up, then another, until all work was suspended. Jeannette searched for Wade, spotting him near the tree line, speaking to a young woman. Her smile vanished. "Now where is this Mr. Remmen?" her father asked, puzzled by her glum face.

"Over there," she pointed.

Frederic eyed the couple. The young woman was quite lovely, with straight black hair. She didn't belong at the mill, and apparently Wade Remmen was telling her so, his voice raised in agitation.

"I don't care if it *is* Saturday, nor that you're bored, I've work to do!"

Dismissing her, he turned back to the mill, immediately spotting Frederic and the girls. His momentary shock gave way to a frown. He strode toward them with a determined gait. "Mr. Duvoisin," he pronounced, extending a hand. "Yvette," he continued with a nod, "Jeannette. What can I do for you, sir?"

"My daughters and I are abroad for the day, and having heard a great deal about you, Mr. Remmen, I thought it was time we met." Frederic glanced over Wade's shoulder to the edge of the forest, but the woman was gone. "We didn't mean to interrupt—"

"No," Wade replied, "that was my sister. She wanted to spend the day with me, but Paul asked me to work. She's young, and I don't like her going into town on her own. So what does she do?" He threw up his hands in exasperation. "She walks here instead." He exhaled loudly, then shook it off. "Would you like to see the mill in operation?"

An hour later, they set off again, this time toward town and the warehouse, where they would reconcile invoices against lumber deliveries and finish up the day's business at the bank. Frederic had something he wanted to show Yvette.

Stephen Westphal was astounded when Frederic stepped up to his desk. He scrambled to his feet, sputtering, "Well—isn't this a surprise?"

"Yes, Stephen, the first of many."

"What can I do for you today, Frederic?"

"The mill account—I'm going to place Yvette in charge of it."

"Pardon?" the banker exclaimed loudly, his astonished query overpowering Yvette's similar response. "But she is a mere child—a female!"

"She is also a Duvoisin and my daughter," Frederic replied. "Like her mother, she has an acuity for figures. Now that Paul is preoccupied with Espoir, I'm going to make use of other resources." He draped his arm affectionately across her shoulders and drew her close. "I'm willing to *gamble* on Yvette's ciphering abilities and see if she is capable of handling the books. If her sister shows some interest, I'll find something for her to accomplish as well. Now, if you'd be so good as to provide a ledger of this month's transactions, I'll go over everything with her this evening."

They lunched at Dulcie's, a place Yvette thought never to see again, let alone in her father's company. The townsfolk stared openly at them, which made her feel important. *So this is what it means to be a Duvoisin.*

"Did you ever give that money to the poor?" she courageously asked.

"What money, Yvette?"

"You know what money."

"Actually, no."

When her father didn't elaborate, she dropped the subject. Still, their banter was easy, and she truly enjoyed being with him.

"Papa?" Yvette asked as they rode home. "Will I really be in charge?"

"Of the lumber mill books? Yes." She smiled exultantly. "But I warn you now, Yvette, it is not going to be easy."

"Don't worry, Papa," she assured, "I'm capable. I won't disappoint you."

Frederic chuckled, unable to remain serious. For the first time in years, his heart swelled with pride.

"What about you, Jeannette? Would you like to take charge of something?"

"Well, I'm not as good with figures as Yvette is, Papa, but I'll help if I can."

"Only if you want to, princess, only if you want to."

They arrived home by three o'clock. At the girls' insistence, Frederic allowed them to groom their ponies in the paddock. He retreated to the house.

They had just finished currying Spook and Angel when their stepmother swept past them without so much as a word of greeting. Yvette eyed her suspiciously as Gerald rushed over. They exchanged a few words and the stablemaster nodded toward the carriage house, where a chaise stood ready. Agatha climbed in, flicked the reins, and steered the buggy through the manor gates.

"That's strange," Yvette murmured.

"What is?" her sister asked.

"Auntie going out for a buggy ride."

"Why is that strange?"

"When have you ever seen her riding out alone—without a driver?"

"Never?" Jeannette supplied thoughtfully.

"That's what I thought."

Authors' photo by Deborah Michaels

DeVa Gantt

The workday is over, the dishes put away, and the children are tucked into bed. That's when **DeVa GANTT** settles down for an evening with the family. The other family, that is: the Duvoisins.

DeVa Gantt is a pseudonym for Debra and Valerie Gantt: sisters, career women, mothers, homemakers, and now, authors. The Colette Trilogy, commencing with *A Silent Ocean Away* and continuing with *Decision and Destiny,* is the product of years of unwavering dedication to a dream.

The women began writing nearly thirty years ago. Deb was in college, Val a new teacher. Avid readers of historical fiction, the idea of authoring their own story blossomed from a conversation driving home one night. "We could write our own book. I can envision the main character." Within a day, an early plot had been hatched and the first scenes committed to paper. Three years later, the would-be authors had half of an elaborate novel written, numerous hand-drafted scenes, five hundred typed pages, and no idea how to tie up the complicated story threads. The book languished, life intervened, and the work was put on the back burner for two decades.

Both women assert the rejuvenating spark was peculiarly coincidental. Though Val and Deb live thirty miles apart, on Thanksgiving weekend 2002, unbeknownst to each other, they spontaneously picked up the unfinished manuscript and began to read. The following week, Deb e-mailed Val to tell her she'd been reading "the book." It was a wonderful work begging to be finished, and Deb had some fresh ideas. By January, the women's creative energies were flowing again.

Unlike twenty years earlier, Deb and Val had computer technology on their side, but there were different challenges. Their literary pursuit had to be worked into real life responsibilities: children, marriages, households, and jobs. The women stole every spare moment, working late at night, in the wee hours of morning, and on weekends. The dictionary, thesaurus, and grammar books became their close companions. Snow days were a gift. No school, no work. Deb could pack up overnight bags, and head to Val's house with her two children. The cousins played while the writers collaborated.

Wherever the women went, they brought the Duvoisins along. From sports and dance practices to doctors' offices, from business trips to vacations, an opportunity to work on their "masterpiece" was rarely wasted. One Fourth of July, Val and Deb edited away on their laptops on blankets in the middle of a New Hampshire baseball field while their families waited for night to fall and the fireworks to begin.

Both women agree the experience has been rewarding and unexpectedly broad in scope. Writing a story was only the beginning of a long endeavor that included extensive research, arduous editing, and painstaking proofreading. Next came the query letters sent to agents and publishers, each meeting a dead end. Self-publishing was the only option—a stepping-stone that would enable them to compile a portfolio of reviews and positive feedback. Thus they became adept at marketing their work, all in the pursuit of reaching a traditional publisher. Within two years an agent had stepped in and HarperCollins agreed to publish the work as a trilogy.

Today, the women look back at their accomplishment. The benefits have been immeasurable. Perhaps the dearest is the bond of sisterhood that deepened: they have shared a unique journey unknown to most sisters. Their greatest satisfaction, however, has been seeing their unfinished work come to fruition: the Duvoisin story has finally been told.